The Welsh Traitor's Daughter

First volume in The Welsh Warrior series

By

Arianwen Nunn

Dedication

To my incredibly supportive family, who believe all things are possible but particularly for my very patient husband, who has spent so long making sure this story could be told.

Acknowledgments

Many thanks to Darrell Wolcott for his sage advice.

About the Author

Arianwen Nunn was born in Wales in 1958. After spending her early life between Wales and England, she studied English Literature at Swansea University, and post-graduate studies at Bristol University led her to take up teaching. Moving to Papua New Guinea with her husband, she discovered a very different world. Four years later, Australia became home to Arianwen, her husband, two children and now, two grandchildren. Arianwen is pass[...]te about history and all things Welsh.

Understanding a little about Welsh Pronunciation

The Welsh alphabet has 28 letters, including seven vowels: A, E, I, U, O, W and Y and twenty-one consonants: B, C, Ch, D, Dd, F, Ff, G, Ng, H, L, Ll, M, N, P, Ph, R, Rh, S, T and Th.

Ch is pronounced as in Ba**ch**: **Uchdryd** is pronounced **Uch-drid**

Dd is pronounced as the 'th' in Pa**th: Grufydd** is pronounced **Griffith; Robert of Rhuddlan** is pronounced **Robert of Rith-lhun**

F is pronounced as the 'v' in **V**inegar: **Angharad ferch Owain** is pronounced **Ang-har-ad verch O-wain**

Ff is pronounced as the 'f' in **F**inger.

Ll doesn't have an English equivalent, but it sounds a bit like **Thl: Llewelyn** sounds like **Thl-well-in**.

W, as a vowel, is pronounced like in **Soo**n or **Bu**ll. W is also used as a consonant as it is in English: To**w**n

Rh is pronounced as in **Rh**ino

Y at the end of a word is pronounced as the 'ee' in **Flee: Gronwy** is pronounced **Gron-wee; Rhys** is pronounced **Reece.**

Y in the middle of a word is pronounced as the 'u' in **Fl**u**tter** or as the 'i' in **D**i**n: Rhydir** is pronounced **Rud-deer; Meilyr** is pronounced **My-Ler.**

U is pronounced as the 'ee' in **Deep**: The Welsh word for Wales is **Cymru** and is pronounced **Cum-ree.**

A few of the other names in the book:

- **Einion: Ay-knee-on**
- **Hywel: Howell**
- **Cadwgan-ap-Bleddyn: Cad-oo-gan ap Ble-thin**

The Family Line of Angharad ferch Owain

Gronwy ap Einon m Ethelfreda ferch Eadwine of Mercia;
their children:

- Edwin ap Gronwy <u>m</u> Iwerydd ferch Cynfyn (sister of Bleddyn ap Cynfyn); their children:
    - o Owain ap Edwin <u>m</u> Morfudd ferch Ednowain Bendew; their children:
        - Gronwy ap Owain
        - Rhydir ap Owain
        - Meilyr ap Owain
        - Llywarch ap Owain
        - ***Angharad ferch Owain***
    - o Uchdryd ap Edwin m Nest ferch Llewelyn Fychan; their children:
        - Madog Penllyn ap Uchdryd
        - Idnerth Benfras ap Uchdryd
        - Iorwerth ap Uchdryd
        - Owain ap Uchdryd
        - Uchdryd Cyfeiliog ap Uchdryd
        - Maredudd ap Uchdryd

The Family Line of Gruffydd ap Cynan

Idwal Foel ap Anarawd m̲ Raggnildr; their children:

- Iago ap Idwal m Afandreg ferch Gwair; their children:
  - Cynan ap Iago had children with unknown woman/women:
    - Gruffydd ap Cynan
    - NN ferch Cynan
    - Tanwysti ferch Iago
    - Crisli ferch Iago
- Cynan ap Idwal m Rhanillt (daughter of King Olaf Sigtryggsson of Norway); their child:
  - Gruffydd ap Cynan (cousin of Gruffydd above) m NN ferch Llychwy; their child:
    - Gwenllian ferch Gruffydd

The Family Line of Cadwgan ap Bleddyn

Cynfyn ap Gwerstan (House of Mathafral) m Angharad ferch Maredudd (House of Dinefar); their children:

- Rhiwallon ap Cynfyn
- Iwerrydd ferch Cynfyn m Edwin ap Gronwy (see Family line of Angharad)
- Bleddyn ap Cynfyn (King of Powys and Gwynedd) m Haer ferch Cillyn of Powys (1st wife); their children:
    - ○ Cadwgan ap Bleddyn m Gwenllian ferch Gruffydd; their children:
        - ▪ Owain ap Cadwgan
        - ▪ Madog ap Cadgwan
    - ○ Cadwgan ap Bleddyn married a second wife; their children:
        - ▪ Henry ap Cadwgan
        - ▪ Gruffydd ap Cadwgan
    - ○ Cadwgan ap Bleddyn had other children by other mistresses:
        - ▪ Maredudd ap Cadgwan
        - ▪ Einion ap Cadgwan
        - ▪ Morgan ap Cadgwan
        - ▪ Other siblings
- Bleddyn ap Cynfyn had seven other children: Iorwedd, Maredudd, Madog, Rhyrid, Gwenllian, Denis and Llywarch.

Contents

Chapter 1: The Stranger (January 1093)

The stranger leaned forward and glowered at his host.

"Forty pounds, Lord Owain, forty pounds a year is what Robert of Rhuddlan pays the King of England for the pleasure of ruling the Welsh Kingdom of Gwynedd. For forty pounds, they can enslave whomever they choose, despoil our land, strip the kingdom of its riches and give nothing back. Does it not seem to you, as Norman appointed Welsh guardian of Gwynedd, that is an appalling travesty of justice?"

An uneasy hush came over the room. The flaxen-haired stranger's fingernails dug into his palms. Owain looked at his four sons, young men sheltered from so much of life's harsh reality. Gronwy, the eldest, strong but hasty; Rhydir, intelligent, older than his years, always supporting his two younger brothers; Meilyr, the tall, well-built philosopher; and Llywarch, smaller, feisty, opportunistic and with such a joy for life. How Owain responded here had the potential to change everything. He shrugged his shoulders and lifted his eyebrows in a gesture of resignation, yet his steely grey eyes were alert.

"Lord Gruffydd, we are not able to argue with the might of the Normans. They would swat us like flies."

Gruffydd slapped a strong hand down on his long, outstretched leg in frustration and spat out his words, "Damn it, man, would you betray your country for the petty approval of your Norman lords?"

A finely dressed girl glided into the room with a silver pitcher and stopped in her tracks. Owain's four sons leaped up; the fury in their eyes showed they were ready to pounce upon the man who had insulted their father, while at the other side of the fire, the stranger's three henchmen, battle-hardened, powerful, but young and eager, sprang into action, fingering their knife pouches.

Owain quickly held up a warning hand to his sons, reminding them that these men were guests in their house. Just as his brother Uchdryd stepped out from the fireplace, impressively built and used to command, he also made a calming gesture, ensured it had been registered by all the men and then spoke to Lord Gruffydd.

The girl slipped back into the shadows watching and listening as her uncle's deep voice resonated throughout the room.

"Gruffydd," he growled, "you go too far. As my brother says, you are a guest in his house. I brought you here to seek partnerships, not to create enemies."

Gruffydd opened his mouth to retaliate, thought better of it and nodded to the older man. He breathed deeply and his heavily muscled body relaxed slightly. He focussed on the arm of his tunic and, though immaculate, brushed something away with a ringed hand, lifted his head and spoke again, this time more measured and with less ire.

"I apologise, my lord, I can wield a sword or axe in battle as well as any man but I am not yet the master of my own tongue when I feel so deeply for a cause." He looked around the room defiantly. "And this is a cause for which I would gladly give my life."

The host acknowledged his apology with a nod, and while Gruffydd signalled for his men to resume their seats, Owain made clear that his sons were to do the same. The girl felt uneasy. These were strong, fighting men who could cut their family to pieces in a moment, but Uncle Uchdryd had brought them there and she trusted him completely.

"Sire, my whole life has been forged with the hope of uniting our Welsh princes together against the Norman foe. We have such an opportunity right here, right now. The English king, William Rufus, is distracted overseas trying to wage war on his brother Robert Curthose, Duke of Normandy. Now is the time to be part of something bigger than ourselves and strike our oppressors before everything we have: our culture; our brave people; and our rich lands are nothing more than a distant memory."

Owain sat back in his chair and stretched out his legs. His bearing was that of a younger man but grey at his temples and flecked through his thick, wiry hair betrayed his years. He patted the neck of his wolf hound, which stared briefly, gazed around and returned to his slumber. The only noises now were the crackling of the fire as pine logs were repositioned and the muffled sounds of the servants in the kitchen talking and eating their supper.

The girl moved silently around the room, refilling the drinks, and then took a chair close enough to observe the conversation but far enough to avoid attention.

Owain coughed and, sermon-like, spoke to an attentive audience, his carefully cultivated voice emotionless.

"When the Conqueror arrived in 1066, he demolished the English resistance with speed and precision. He had a strategy before he ever set foot on this island, with his army reinforced by Norman might. These are men who have been drilled in warfare since they were babes in arms. We would be mad to contemplate overcoming such might. They are unstoppable. Even the best of the Saxons was unable to contain their onslaught, and parts of Gwynedd have been in Saxon hands often enough."

Owain saw Gruffydd wanted to say something but continued even so. "The Normans relish the fight; it is all or nothing. They enslave, they build, they secure their military bases, and they import foreigners to infiltrate the conquered land. Their stone castles are impossible to capture. What resistance do we have here in Wales to compare? We have not moved on from wooden. One fire-blazed arrow is all it takes. No, Gruffydd, we are not strong enough to suppress the Norman military might, their mail-clad soldiers, their towering castles dominating the landscape, watching who travels where, by road or by river, who buys what at the markets beneath their turrets…"

"We can be strong enough, Lord Owain," Gruffydd insisted, cutting off the older man in full flow. "Together, we can outnumber them, especially while so many of their fighting men are engaged in

Normandy. After all, we are masters of this land. The hills and mountains provide sanctuary for us but are hateful to them! We should not be afraid of their stone castles: we can destroy them with cunning and fortitude, and again, I say it, now when they are vulnerable, when so many of their leaders are overseas, their eyes are not on us!"

"Bold words," said Gronwy slouching in his chair, sharp eyes narrowing out of a fat, suspicious face, "but what advantage is it to us? You think of being King of Wales, no doubt, leading the brave Welsh to victory, but others have as strong a right." He slurped noisily and glared across at Gruffydd.

The girl drew a deep breath. Her brother, Gronwy, had been drinking heavily most of the afternoon and through the evening, and she knew the signs of his temper. With his tone and deliberately inflammatory words, she could tell he had little time for their guests. Owain glared at his son, but Gronwy had gone past the point of being diplomatic.

Gruffydd retorted quietly but with vehemence. "My right to be King of Gwynedd is stronger than any man's, but that is not at issue here. Somebody needs to unite the Welsh kingdoms against the Normans; whoever can do that might well be considered the King of Wales. I will submit to any such man. So far, I don't see many challengers lead that charge.'

Owain caught his brother's eye and then glanced quizzically at this confident young man while his sons looked at each other with surprise at this astounding announcement.

Meilyr, shoulder-length brown hair taking on copper tones from the fire, now made his case softly but with conviction.

"With respect, Lord Gruffydd, many have claims to Gwynedd. How many kings of Gwynedd have there been since our grandfathers were born, and how many of their heirs might say they have a right? To my brother's point, our family also has a claim."

4

Owain leaned forward, put a gentle but firm hand on his son's arm and turned back to his visitor, who was bristling but caught a warning glance from Uchdryd and composed himself.

"And as I said," Gruffydd replied, more loudly than before and with emphasis, "I will ride beside anyone whose claim is stronger than my own and is qualified to quell Norman ambition. To be clear though, my line descends from King Rhoddri Mawr and King Hywel the Good. In Gwynedd, there is no truer claim. My family was betrayed, and I seek retribution. Your family might also claim contention for the throne though it is not as strong. So far, you have chosen to manage Gwynedd for the Normans rather than to assert that right by the sword. What I ask of you now is to restore Hywel's laws and unite Welshman with Welshman."

Owain was taken aback by the straight-speaking young man and was unused to being put on the spot. He looked at his sons and then at Uchdryd before he spoke, folding his hands in his lap and rubbing his top thumb against his bottom thumb as if sharpening a blade.

"When Gruffydd ap Llewelyn united Wales under his kingship, he did it with the help of the Mercians. My ancestors supported Gruffydd but in the end, he would have done better to have negotiated more and battled less. He antagonised Harold Godwinson. If, however, both Harold and Gruffydd had conducted peaceful negotiations, Harold and a combined force of Welshmen would have been too strong for William of Normandy, and 1066 would have been a Norman defeat. It wasn't and I have done the best I can to maintain a harmonious relationship to keep the peoples in the parts of Gwynedd I administer protected from the impositions of the Normans.."

"For now, Lord Owain," came the retort from Gruffydd, his deep blue eyes flashing, "but the stone castles are appearing like mushrooms, and soon we will be like South Wales, where the true Welsh have been forced off their land and Flemish settlers till the best landholdings for their Norman lords. Time moves on and, as each day passes, an opportunity to take advantage slips through our fingers. We see things differently, you and I, but I will not die without having tried to protect our Welsh culture, laws and ways: that cause is what I live for."

***

Later, when Gruffydd and his men had retired, Owain beckoned his slender, fine-featured daughter and called her to sit with them near the still-blazing fire. He watched her move with the grace of a deer, nubile, noiseless and doe-eyed. She reminded him greatly of her mother, who would have been so proud of her.

Rhydir lifted the chair Gruffydd had vacated and pulled it close to the fire for her.

"So, my sons, what do you make of our visitor?" asked Owain carefully.

Uchdryd leaned against the fireplace and watched the theatre in action. He had many times seen Owain persuade his audience that they were voicing their own opinions while, really, he carefully manoeuvred them into thinking what he wanted them to think. '*Sly old fox,*' he thought to himself, '*isn't that the way he had seduced the Normans into believing him their greatest ally? Lord Owain, every man's champion without raising a sword: fair, reasonable, pious Lord Owain, beloved by all, including me, damn it*!'

Earnest Meilyr, with his dark brown watchful eyes, spoke first.

"Uncle Uchdryd believes the Lord Gruffydd to be a good fighter, and you must think he has a chance, uncle, or you would not have brought him here. I would like to think that was so."

"The best warrior I have seen, to be honest," said Uchdryd. "He fights with a lot of heart but plenty of this." He tapped his head. "He reads his opposition well and inspires his men to give more than they thought they had to give. To see him fight, one on one, his strength, speed and skill, the sheer energy and lack of fear; it is something special."

This was praise indeed, for Uchdryd was known as a formidable foe. His brute strength was still evident in his broad shoulders and thick arms. He had trained some of the most impressive warriors of the time.

"He works at it like a man possessed, up before the rest, methodical in everything he does, perfecting each thrust of the sword every chance he gets."

"But can he command men, Uncle?" interrupted Gronwy, too loudly, emboldened by the drink.

Uchdryd exploded with his rich, rough laugh, enjoying Gronwy's impertinence, and then, crossing his arms, winked at his brother, hazel eyes twinkling.

"Are you the authority on leading men now, Gronwy?" Uchdryd teased. Gronwy flushed deeply as colour flooded his face and throat. Uchdryd put a palm up in acknowledgement, "Yet you ask a good question. You are as astute as your father, if not as diplomatic! Will men follow him to unite Wales? He trusts few men in truth. His experience and that of his family have been that few men, even men close to him, can be trusted. Those whom he trusts would follow him to the ends of the Earth."

Rhydir spoke quietly so that the party had to lean in to hear him. Ever courteous with his sensitive face, he always seemed thoughtful or even sad. A thick lock of hair fell across his dark, rather wistful eyes and he directed them to a place far beyond the fire's flames.

"I think Gronwy is right, Uncle, you can be a magnificent fighter and inspire those who fight under you, but the Welsh princes are wild horses, all ambitious, all unpredictable. Much as I would like to see the Normans gone, it will be an extraordinary man who can convince our Welsh princes to follow any other man's lead."

'He's growing up,' thought Uchdryd running a hand over his balding pate and breathing in deeply so that the nostrils flared above his bushy grey moustache.

Now, he spoke with real admiration as he tried to articulate his thoughts to his nephews. "Inside him is that passion for uniting Wales. Genuinely. It is not about him; it is about what it means to be Welsh. If he can communicate that passion, those men will join him because the time is right and they want an end to the constant unrest. We have not had it too bad here but, as Gruffydd says, we need to see what has happened and is happening in the south. We would be fools not to realise Norman ambitions here in the North as well."

'If someone dangles something which you cannot achieve by yourself and you want it badly enough, then you may well take a risk, and maybe Gruffydd's ideas will tempt those wild Welsh princes,' Owain mused as he surveyed his sons before resting his eye on his daughter.

"Well, Angharad?" he asked as he gazed proudly at the bright-eyed creature who had followed the conversation so intently. "What do you say?"

Gronwy shifted impatiently in his seat and belched.

"What would she know?" he asked, scowling contemptuously and lifting his beaker to his full mouth, swigging noisily before wiping his lips with the back of his hand.

Angharad was unflustered and looked at her father with clear-eyed sincerity.

"Father, you have created a peaceful place for your family, for the people of the lands you have in your care. You have seen princes come and go; princedoms fight each other. Perhaps the question should not be whether this man can unite Wales but whether this man can keep the Normans at bay. The Normans are thriving on resistance and stamping it out. While they sit like wolves in England, ready to move at any time, what chance do the Welsh have except to earn petty victories? Could the Welsh princes stay united long enough to keep the Marcher Lords on their side of the border? The troubles in Normandy will not last forever, and then they will turn their attention to matters on home soil. So, what would our family gain, the people you administer gain, by turning our peace into war?"

Llywarch, stocky, cheerful with his shock of ebony curls, smiled widely at Angharad and then hit the table laughing out loud!

"A woman's answer, Father," he grinned conspiratorially, winking at his brothers but including Angharad in his friendly difference of opinion. "I like what Gruffydd had to say. We have one language even though we have separate princedoms, our culture is unique, there is much to unite us, and we know our land and our mountains better than they do, so why not use that advantage? Why should we accept these Frenchmen trying to take what is ours?"

Uchdryd nodded his approval. "Fighting words, Llywarch. You have the passion of a Welsh warrior."

Llywarch smiled now, though sheepishly.

Owain turned to Angharad.

"Your brothers like the idea of a united Wales but are not sure that our friend here has the wherewithal to pull off such a grand enterprise. What do you say?"

Gronwy muttered under his breath at the attention being paid to his sister and glowered at her with contempt.

"I think we should wait and see how his visits with the princes go before we commit ourselves," she proposed. "If Powys and Deheubarth rally behind our visitor, then we should reassess."

Owain smiled at his daughter appreciatively.

"Lady, you speak well," he acknowledged, "and there is much of your mother in you, God rest her soul." Then, looking at Uchdryd, he continued, "My children would be surprised to learn that once I could wield a sword as well as you!"

Uchdryd nodded, "Better, in fact!"

"I am not without ambition, but I know my talents lie with my brain and tongue and not with my sword. As I am always reminding you, our family is from the hierarchy of the mighty Mercians and the warring Welsh. I have used the skills I have been given to honour both sides of our heritage and yet, I believe, keep the Normans from interfering too much in our business." He got up from the chair and, though he seemed a smaller man when they were separate, as he stood next to his brother at the fireplace, they were of a height. He put his hand on Uchdryd's shoulder.

"You ride with Lord Gruffydd to Powys in the morning and let us see what appetite there is for his proposal from the princes of Powys. Cadwgan ap Bleddyn and his brothers, Iorwedd and Maredudd, are always ready to stir things up!"

"Careful, Owain, you know my allegiance to Cadwgan. As the leader of Cadwgan's warband, it pays well when they stir things up," responded Uchdryd half-jokingly. "And what of the boys, Owain? We have not yet resolved that. All of them are past fourteen, and other boys younger than them have already been sent out to squire with noble families and learn the arts of war. You have not encouraged it, and I believe it is a skill they still need to have."

Owain turned back to his boys, "It is true, what I have taught them of managing land, looking after those who work the land, will stand them in good stead, and I had hoped that their path would be a peaceful one, such as mine has been, but I would not hold them back if that is their wish."

Llywarch jumped up immediately, "Uncle, I would ride with you and learn from you." Turning to his brothers, he asked eagerly, "What of you?"

"Wait a moment," said Owain sternly, "not all of you."

"I will stay with you, Father," said Meilyr, not out of lack of courage but because, of all the boys, he and his father had the best relationship, and he valued learning from him.

"But I would go if you will allow it," said Rhydir with much less fervour than his younger brother.

Owain nodded. "Then Gronwy and Meilyr stay. Gronwy, you and your brothers have been fighting each other for years, and your swordsmanship is good enough. Meilyr, you can practise with your brother."

Uchdryd beamed. He liked his nephews and would enjoy the time with them. "Then you two will need to rise early and prepare yourself, for we are up with the crow."

"Thank you, Uncle," cried Llywarch, feverishly excited and, taking his leave, almost ran out of the hall. Rhydir, the taller and most well-built of the siblings, followed him with less enthusiasm.

'Rhydir is going because he and Llywarch are so close,' Angharad reflected.

As Angharad slipped between her blankets that night, she thought about the visitor, Lord Gruffydd. He had hardly acknowledged her. She had observed him as he delivered his case: confident, undoubtedly intelligent but less than respectful, and certainly quick-tempered. He would be considered handsome, taller than her father, with a warrior's physique, thick blonde hair, and large piercing pools of eyes. Yes, intelligent eyes, she thought, and he spoke well even though he was too brash, almost uncivil in his manner. God-fearing? She doubted it.

The young noblewoman mused how such a stranger had the power to tip the careful political balance her father had worked so hard to achieve. If her father sided with Gruffydd, what if he was not successful? It was so easy to be left with nothing at the hands of the Normans. Their home and lands could be confiscated, they could be enslaved or killed. She could be married off to some brutal, bloodthirsty Norman. Did Gruffydd understand what was at stake when he was asking for their support? But then why should he care? Ambitious men didn't really concern themselves too much with others and what others would sacrifice for that ambition.

"Dear God," she prayed, "protect our family in these uncertain times. Let peace reign in our lands." Uneasiness was stirring within her that

11

she had not felt since her mother had fallen ill. Storms were brewing, she knew, and as she closed her eyes, all she could see was the flaxen-haired Lord Gruffydd with the light from the fire dancing across his face.

Chapter 2: Rhys ap Tewdwr (April 1093)

An icy black night was turning into a pewter grey dawn as Angharad hurried around in the kitchen to ensure that her brothers and their guests were well provided for on their journey into Powys. The kitchen hands had been up late talking to some of Gruffydd's party and now they were not as sharp about their duties as they should be. This was their opportunity to get news from the rest of Wales and sometimes even of family members who had taken work in other parts. She hurried them along, giving them clear instructions about what had to be done before the visitors left, and although she was younger than any of them, they accepted her requests willingly.

On the other side of the courtyard, the rhythmic song of fresh milk hitting the pails and the lowing of cows waiting for their turn with full udders gave the morning a sense of normality, yet with Angharad's brothers leaving for who knew how long, it was hardly usual.

She crossed the frosty courtyard to check on Iori, the stable hand. She was surprised to see Meilyr and Gruffydd deep in conversation. Gruffydd, dressed in thick leather and long leather boots which were shining from polish, was admiring a hawk that Meilyr had on his gloved hand. A sword hung from a belt at his waist and she noted a crystal pommel decorated the hilt. The scabbard, in contrast, was plain other than some fine gold decoration near the top. He wore a cloak of sealskin held in place with a gold brooch.

The horses' breath came out in puffs like smoke as they ravenously chewed their barley straw and oats. Iori, square-faced and having almost no forehead, was a burly cheerful lad who was delighted to have had so many animals in his charge overnight.

Iori nodded to the horses, "These are fine beasts, my lady," he whispered. "It would be good to have some of our mares in with them if they were here again. Think of the power coming from those hocks. Look at the strong hindquarters, and they are fast, I wager."

Angharad asked Iori to bring the saddlebags for her to fill, and, leaving the kitchen door open for him, she busied herself, enjoying the cold draft of morning air tinged with a hint of salt from the breeze blowing in from the sea.

"My father is expecting a gyrfalcon from Norway in the next weeks," explained Meilyr as he and Lord Gruffydd stood outside the kitchen door. "This one may not like that!"

"They get used to each other if you handle them carefully," said Gruffydd. "Your father will enjoy the challenge of hunting with the bigger bird. They have so much power, and they can bring down prey three times their weight. They are different from the falcons and hawks you have but worth the effort all the same."

"You have one yourself?"

"I had one when I was in Ireland. It broke my heart to leave her behind but my life has not been settled. No one home or one place to rest my head. Have you thought of building a mews?"

"We have kept them inside the house, but we were thinking of building some sort of proper housing once the gyrfalcon arrives."

"Then, when we come back this way next, we will help you. It can be done in a couple of days. I still have the plans in my head for the one I built in Ireland."

Meilyr smiled a wide smile, "I think my father would be delighted. He would love to take you hawking, I am sure. This little beauty caught two pheasants on the wing yesterday and there is plenty of game hereabouts."

Gruffydd slapped Meilyr on the back. "I look forward to it and we will have the mews up in no time. A south-facing window so the birds can bask when there is sun, a sturdy bathing pan, look out for a good sandstone rock for the birds to perch or freak, and you will need plenty of space between perch and wall so that they don't damage their feathers. You should keep the corners dark so that they can hide and watch, and it is important to have solid foundations so that no foxes can dig underneath to get in. Even a cat can hurt a hawk enough to kill her."

Iori had brought all the horses across the yard and suddenly, there were people everywhere adjusting bulging saddlebags and a smell of newly polished leather. Iori beamed as he busied himself with saddles, blankets and bridles, running a rag over stirrups and attending to the various needs of the assembled men. Gruffydd gently patted his horse and nuzzling up to his ear, Angharad heard him half whispering,

"A long journey today, Cadell. I hope you had plenty of oats."

She noticed the silver on the horse's harness; the quality of the craftsmanship did not escape her.

Angharad, heavy-hearted, and the rosy-cheeked, affable maid, Susannah, moved around the group with drinks, bread and cheese.

A cold drizzle started, and as Angharad reached Gruffydd, she asked, "Will you come inside, my lord, until this has passed?"

"Thank you, lady," he replied, looking up at the sky, "this is only the start of a day of it, and I am keen to make progress into Powys before nightfall." His horse, a stunning glossy black cob, the tail high set, moved his hooves as if urging action, his ears pricked forward.

She turned quietly and embraced her departing brothers, wishing them a safe journey and trying to dispel her fear that she may not see them again.

"I'll look after him," said Rhydir quietly, nodding towards the irrepressible Llywarch, noticing the tears welling up in her eyes.

"I know," she said resignedly, "but you take care as well. Stay close to Uncle. I hope you don't have to use those swords of yours."

Uchdryd appeared by his brother's side, embraced Meilyr and turned to his niece.

"We didn't hear you play the harp, Angharad. Gruffydd has a fine ear for music and would have enjoyed your playing and sweet voice."

Angharad blushed as Gruffydd considered her for the first time with any real regard.

"You are very generous about my abilities, Uncle."

"Too modest, my girl!"

Final goodbyes were said, and then her uncle bellowed, "Shall I lead ahead?" With a clatter of hooves, they were gone.

***

In the days and weeks that followed, the manor was much quieter. Gronwy and Meilyr had fewer outside tasks because of the time of year but, as if inspired by their visitors, spent time improving their skills with sword, spear and bow. Meilyr would read and spend time with the hawks while Gronwy would ride, even in the rain, vanishing for hours at a time.

When Lord Owain was not instructing Gronwy and Meilyr, he often spent time with Angharad explaining the differences in the Welsh laws of Hywel Dda and the legal system the Normans adhered to or discussing the history of their family and the lands around. She loved these times and bathed in the joy of being with the father she loved and respected so much. Her thirst for knowledge had come from his, and she soaked up everything she could learn from him.

Thankfully that year, there had been few frosts to destroy the seeds on sowing, so the local farmers hoped for a good crop. There had been little rain, which pleased those who worked the land and had allowed Angharad to ride frequently with Iori in the surrounding countryside. There was little danger from thieves where they lived away from the main roadways, and should any strangers try to camp in the vicinity, they were quickly spotted and encouraged to move on. Owain preferred that Angharad did not ride alone, although he was more than confident about her skills as a horsewoman.

Owain's llys or manor was securely situated on a plateau between two heavily wooded ravines. Angharad would often ride through the glades, sometimes stopping at the well of St Michael, where a little stream rose to join the River Wheeler. Equally lovely to her was the ride to the Seven Springs, bubbling to form a tributary to the River Wys. Occasionally her journey would take her onto the moor of the White Stone, where another ravine extended into a steep chasm. She could see right across to Rhuddlan from there, where Norman Robert had his castle and the administrative centre at Bryn, half a mile from that fortress. From Bryn, Robert's men managed the fertile agricultural lands which supported the castle garrison. The mills, fisheries, iron mines and land worked by slaves, which had once been income for the King of Gwynedd, now fed into Robert's coffers.

As Angharad gazed across the valley nestled in the protective hills, she often thought of times long ago when the Romans had had a small camp here. She imagined soldiers marching along the straight Roman road to the Roman fort at Chester. Local people said that on a moonless night, you could often hear the Romans marching over the moor. Reminders of Roman times were still all over Britain: the roads, of course, mainly still used and straight as the flight of an arrow; the forts, often taken over by the Welsh or, more recently, the Normans; and the scarred landscape where they had mined, such as in the Halkyan Mountains nearby, where they had unearthed lead and silver.

***

Angharad never failed in her weekly visit to the tenant families of the district, always bringing something for the children or nourishing food or herbs if someone in the family had been sick. Most days, she would ride to the church of St Michael at Caerwys and pray with the priest for continued peace. Now, more than ever, her mind was on the unsettling discussions when Gruffydd ap Cynan had been brought to their home by Uncle Uchdryd, and she thought of her father's words, 'Peace is a prize, but it is hard won and easily lost.' Could their peace be easily lost? She reassured herself that her father's relationship with Earl Hugh of Chester was a good one and that the Earl had little to gain by removing their family while everything ran so smoothly under her father's guardianship.

17

The priest said that everything was in God's hands and that they should continue with prayer and good works, yet sometimes she was confused about whose side God was on. Was he on the side of Earl Hugh?

Earl Hugh, known out of his earshot as Hugh the Fat, was the Norman Marcher Lord who had appointed her father as the high-born Welsh official for parts of Gwynedd he and his vassals had claimed as theirs. Hugh thought of himself as a godly man supporting the churches and paying a tithe of a fine horse every year to the Abbey at Chester, but Angharad knew that he was also brutal, gluttonous, and constantly humiliating his wife with his open infidelities. She thought of Robert of Rhuddlan, Earl Hugh's nephew, regarded so highly among the Normans for his valour and yet his cruelty was well known, especially to the Welsh, whom he had no hesitation enslaving, maiming or killing.

In recent times, Angharad's mind often returned to Lord Gruffydd. She tried to understand someone whose passion for warfare and defeating the enemy did not seem to marry with the man who had advised Meilyr on building a mews for their hawks, who loved music, and whose affection for animals suggested a gentler soul.

Spring started showing her face and the manor hummed along in a gentle rhythm. It was a cause of celebration to get through the winter and to see the new lambs and calves being born. The woodlands and stream banks were now covered with celandine, and bursts of violets, primroses, and daffodils added colour to a previously dowdy world. It was a time of hope. The previous year's harvest had been a good one, but Angharad remembered other years where hunger had taken the lives of the young and infirm. All seemed to be peaceful, but it was soon after Easter that news arrived that shocked their family to the core.

Late one evening, one of Uchdryd's men arrived, his horse a lather of sweat from hard riding and he, mud-splattered and tired. His story was incredibly distressing. Uchdryd had sent him to inform them that Rhys ap Tewdwr, ruler of Deheubarth, had been killed by Normans in Brycheiniog. The news that came was confusing. It was not clear whether Rhys had been betrayed or whether the fight that led to his death at the hands of Normans had been instigated by them or by him. Angharad felt desperately sorry for the family but was also concerned about the wider implications of this death.

A few days later, Uchdryd arrived along with Llywarch and Rhydir and the house was full once more but the joy of having her brothers home was diminished by an overarching uneasiness. Owain quizzed Uchdryd on what he knew as they all sat for supper.

"Ah, it was well planned, Owain. No sooner than Rhys was killed in Brycheiniog than Bernard of Neufmarcher took over three cantrefi in the district."

"You really think it was planned?" asked Owain gloomily.

"No doubt. Rhys was paying his forty pounds to the Normans for ruling his own land. Everything was sailing along nicely, and then he got word that a castle was being erected, a stone castle, mind you, at Aberhonddw at Brycheiniog."

"On his brother-in-law, Bleddyn ap Maenyrch's land?" asked Owain.

"Yes, you are right. Well, you know Rhys, he wasn't happy about that, so he took a few of his men, teamed up with Bleddyn and rode into Brycheiniog. He had been celebrating Easter with the family; they were all at his llys and, the next thing, one of his teulu, the most senior in his war council, rides in saying that Rhys and Bleddyn had both been killed and there were a fully armed Norman party heading their way. He and a couple of his supporters insisted that Griffith, Rhys' heir, go with them to safety. The younger brother Howel felt it was best to stay with the Princess Nest, so Griffith fled to Ireland, knowing there would be a price upon his head but not imagining that they would harm his young brother and sister."

Angharad blinked back the tears that gathered as she listened, appalled, and took a deep breath. Everyone knew of the beautiful

Princess Nest, who was loved and respected for her gentleness. How must she be feeling with her father killed?

"Tell them what happened, Uncle," Llywarch urged.

Uchdryd took a deep breath, "Arnulf de Montgomery took Prince Howel, and he is captive. Princess Nest was sent to the court of William Rufus, probably to work for one of the noble families there. Bernard de Neufmarche is keeping Bleddyn's son, Gwrgan, captive, although he is allowed to ride anywhere if accompanied by Bernard's knights. There is talk Gwrgan will receive some land at Cathedine, which is a small area between the Brecon Beacons and the Black Mountains but that is just a show to keep the peace. Now Bernard is calling the ancient kingdom of Brycheiniog, the Lordship of Brecknock. Can you believe the audacity of these men?"

"Arnulf de Montgomery has Howel, you say?"

"He does. And Arnulf, who is wet behind the ears, is encouraged by his father, Roger, Earl of Shrewsbury, who has 'given' Dyfed to young Arnulf and is setting up his base in Ceredigion at a place they are calling Pembroke."

"They are already building a castle there, father," added Rhydir with concern.

"A stone castle?" asked Gronwy.

"No," elaborated Rhydir, "not yet. So far, it is more like a stockade but the stone castle is bound to come. It is set up high and has water on three sides, so we hear."

"So Arnulf has the whole of Dyfed?" asked Gronwy.

"Not quite," explained Uchdryd, "the east of Dyfed has been 'given' to William Fitzbaldwin, who is the Sheriff of Devon and Rufus has commissioned him to establish another castle…"

"On the River Towy, I wager," guessed Owain.

"On the Towy just south of where the old Roman fort was at Carmarthen."

"So, you have Earl Roger from his base in Arystli sending in his host from that side into the fertile river valleys of mid-Wales and then his son, Arnulf, who occupies Ceredigion and starts building a castle at the mouth of the Teifi while his hosts pour into Dyfed and Bernard De Neufmarche has dispensed with Rhys, so he is clear now to take land as he wishes."

"They didn't waste any time," commented Owain bleakly.

"Only a week or so before Gruffydd and I met with Rhys ap Tewdwr. Gruffydd laid it on the line that the Normans were not to be trusted. They were just bringing in their friends and encouraging them to take whatever they wanted: lining them up on the borders and then securing their legitimacy. Gruffydd reminded Rhys how only a few years back, Iestyn, Prince of Morgannwg, had been so comfortable with the Normans that he sought assistance from Robert Fitz Hamon to defeat Rhys himself and then, within a year, Iestyn's lands were gone and Robert Fitz Hamon was building a castle in prime position in Cardiff on Iestyn's lands! All the lands between the River Taff and the River Tawe filled with Normans!"

"Yes," offered Owain, "but Iestyn was a fool! What did he expect would happen? Rhys, in fairness, was always much shrewder."

"Not shrewd enough to ignore what was happening on his doorstep. Think of how the Normans are taking steps to feather their nests and push us all aside, Owain! Osborn Fitz Richard married the daughter of our Welsh king, Gruffydd ap Llewelyn. Why would he do that if he had no intentions in Wales? Then what happens? Bernard of Neufmarche marries Osborn's daughter and has his eye on the lands at Brychan. He smells the rich pickings of the Llyfni Valley and the Vale of Usk. Next, he occupies Talgarth. But that's not the half of it. Ralph Mortimer takes manor after manor between the Wye and the Severn. William Fitz Baderon sits in Monmouth, extending his territories every day."

"I know, I know," said Owain. "The Valley of the Clunis is now held by Picot di Say. Richard de Lacy swept up Weobley and the commote of Ewais has gone to Alfred of Marlborough. Most of Archenfield and the Dore Valley is Norman along with the honey renders. I know what is happening. I am not a fool, Uchdryd."

Uchdryd raised his eyebrows a fraction and Owain looked glum.

"Think well, Brother. Gruffydd and I urged Rhys to be careful. He had been useful in keeping the Welsh kings in Powys at bay, but the Normans were getting hungrier for more land and might have dispensed with him unless we united against them. Gruffydd pleaded with him to think seriously about joining forces."

"He decided against it?"

"Rhys wouldn't hear a word of it, even though he knew that Cadwgan in Powys was committed to the Welsh cause. Or maybe because he knew Cadwgan was committed. No, Rhys was satisfied with things as they were. He was short-sighted, Owain. See what is happening only weeks after they put him to death. At the eastern end of Dyfed, Fitz Baldwin is building a castle in Carmarthen on the Towy River. The whole of Deheubarth, Rhys's kingdom, Brother, is already Norman and no respect is paid to Rhys' sons. These Normans are commanding one waterway and land route after another with their castles."

"I know you are worried about what will happen here, Uchdryd, but Earl Hugh and Robert of Rhuddlan gain no advantage by changing things with us."

Irritated by his brother's refusal to respond adequately to the gravity of the situation, Uchdryd exploded, "Owain, I am telling you that unless we make a stand, there will be no lands for any of us soon. How could you respect a man like Hugh the Fat? Everywhere he goes, he is surrounded by an army of knights. He has hunted his lands to devastation. He has no time for his husbandmen or his priests. He can scarcely move, he is so fat, and he has an army of children by concubines. Robert of Rhuddlan has had half the Welsh around here

22

slaughtered, or they are in fetters or enslaved and you are casting a blind eye to it all!"

"Uchdryd, I am not the hare who is going to put my head up for the bowman to shoot me?"

"No, Owain, you are the hare who will keep his head down and be taken by the dogs!"

There was an uneasy silence.

"So, Powys has definitely committed to rise against the Normans?" asked Owain, sidestepping the turn of conversation.

"Cadwgan ap Bleddyn is with Gruffydd. If any move is to be made, they will be the ones to make it."

"Cadwgan will make a stand with Gruffydd soon, you think?"

"I do, and I will be with him. There are men from Deheubarth who are sickened by what has happened to Rhys ap Tewdwr's family. They will be with us."

"When will you strike?"

"Cadwgan and Gruffydd will choose the timing, but, as I say, it won't be long, Owain, and then you will need to declare your hand."

Angharad found it hard to rest that night and when she did, it was a fitful sleep. Over and over in her mind she was trying to imagine how this could all be resolved but they seemed to be stuck with impending doom on either side.

Chapter 3: An Unexpected Conversation (May 1093)

With the house full again, Angharad was up early to oversee the daily chores and to organise the provisions. She dressed by the first light of rose-pink dawn and the last light of the waning moon, treasuring the stillness broken only by nature's song in the trees and the bushes around the manor.

Angharad had been deep in thought sometime later when her father found her and asked her to walk a little with him. She recognised the look on his face and knew that something was on his mind. It was likely about the same matters that were keeping her awake at night, and she was looking forward to the opportunity to understand the issue on a deeper level.

The day was fresh, so she wrapped her red woollen shawl over her dress against the cold. Her father smiled at the beautiful young woman in front of him, large eyes eagerly attentive. '*Such wisdom and dignity for her years*,' he thought. They walked underneath the blossoming trees, now showering them both in petals dislodged by the breeze. A cuckoo called in the distance and swallows darted and dived around them.

"Angharad, you are a young lady now and you have been mistress of this property for some years, managing the household with the maturity of a woman far older."

"Thank you, Father!'

"As you know, when I die............"

She blanched and opened her mouth to say something, but her father held up a quietening finger and continued.

"When I die, this property will be divided amongst your brothers, and though you will be provided for, it is time now for you to find a match and a home of your own."

Angharad was no fool and this was often something that had been light-heartedly discussed with her maid, Susannah, as they talked of the young men from local families. Since she was quite small, she would often dream of someone whom she could not see clearly but knew to be there, someone who had an energy she was drawn towards, and, on waking, she would think this was what it would feel like to be in love. She had assumed that she would one day meet that person. She almost wanted to tell her father, but he would think her fanciful.

"You know, of course, that your marriage is important to cement relationships and bring honour to the family and I have been giving thought to whom would be of best advantage."

Angharad was shocked. She still felt very young and had not seriously thought such a prospect was imminent. Her heart sank at the thought of leaving the only home she had known.

"Angharad, I don't need to tell you that you are descended from the earls of Mercia on one side and the Kings of Gwynedd on the other. You speak many languages: Welsh, French, English, and your Latin and Greek is as good as mine and indeed as good as most clerics. You play the harp and sing with the sweetest voice I have heard, and everyone applauds your beauty and disposition. Don't forget, I am well respected and, as my daughter, you would be an asset to any Norman lord."

"Norman lord, Father?" cried Angharad too hastily and then looked down so that her feelings of horror would not betray her further.

"Of course, a highborn lady of your strong Welsh heritage would be a jewel to any Norman."

How could she communicate her utter dread of marrying a Norman husband? Norman knights did not respect women, and the difference between the Norman laws and the Welsh laws made that abundantly clear. Marrying a Norman would not only give her no voice but she would have none of the freedoms she was used to as mistress of their manor. The Normans she knew of were beasts who hurt, raped, pillaged and destroyed. They gorged themselves on excess and satisfied their lusts with any woman whenever they chose. Was her father truly contemplating such a life for her? She shuddered as she thought of Hugh the Fat, with his eyes undressing her as she played the harp, a man whose stench disgusted her. Then Robert of Rhuddlan, whose animal behaviours even included maiming and blinding women and priests. Yet such thoughts were not worthy of her. How many times had her mother drilled into her the test by which Socrates decided what thought was worthy to pass on and what was not? The three sieves: are you certain it is true; is it something good or positive, and finally, is it necessary to disclose it? She had schooled herself to measure her words thus.

She steeled herself. "Have you someone in mind, Father?"

"You know Earl Hugh of Chester well."

Her heart sank further. Was he thinking of Earl Hugh's illegitimate son, Richard, who lived in Normandy? Was she to find herself so far from Gwynedd and her family? Or was it the other illegitimate son Oteuo, an educated man but one whose penchants followed his father's and who lived at the English court?

Her father went on. "As you know, Earl Hugh's wife died in childbirth. He is a generous man and one who would position you to protect your family."

Angharad stopped, her face ashen as the reality of what was being asked of her sank in. Surely her father could not think so little of her that he would send her as wife to such an unholy, disgusting man?

"Do not be shy, Angharad. You are indeed worthy of such a man, and I know he is very fond of you. It would be a wonderful match."

Her mouth was dry, and she was trembling as she replied, desperately searching for the right words.

"Father, the earl has but lost his wife, and I think it is too early to approach him with such a suggestion."

She wanted to cry out, '*No, no, how could you even think that I would want to marry such a man? Do you have so little feeling for me that you would sacrifice me to protect the family? You, whom I have honoured, adored and respected. You, who has been at pains to educate me and teach me to think for myself.'*

"As usual, you may be right, my dear," her father replied, "but we should not take too long as the opportunity may be missed."

She felt sick. He saw her as an opportunity; something that could be given away. She needed to get away, to think.

"Father, the clouds look so heavy now, and you do not want to get caught in the rain. We should turn back."

Her father looked up at the bulging clouds, heavy over the mountains.

"Always clouds looming, Angharad. Always clouds looming when you turn your back."

For a moment, her natural empathy rose, and she felt ashamed of her powerful reaction to his suggestion. She reflected on how hard her father had worked to protect his family, to keep their lands and a good living. Others had been evicted from their lands, and some had ended up in captivity or worse. Then out of the corner of her eye, she saw a red-faced maid scurrying from out of the dairy. Gronwy lurched out behind her, hoisting his pants over his oversized belly, smacking his lips, and following the girl with his eyes as she ran into the kitchen. Angharad felt betrayed. Gronwy, who had little respect for anyone and was far from a model son, was not being lined up with a Norman wife. He would inherit his father's title and choose whom he would marry while she, the dutiful daughter, was sent away to 'protect' the family.

So many conflicting emotions coursed through the young woman. She felt an overwhelming sense of powerlessness and disappointment that her father saw her potential marriage to Earl Hugh only as a vehicle for the security of his family and did not understand the life of purgatory to which he would be subjecting her. Could her father not see that wealth and status were not even compensating considerations for being married to such a man? She would be trapped. The Laws of Hywel the Good, which allowed women to

27

divorce their husbands, were not Norman laws, and she would lose so many rights afforded to Welsh women that Norman women did not enjoy.

Despite the shock she had suffered, her gentle nature would not allow her to belie the fact that she loved and respected her father so deeply. She must steel herself; had she not prayed for a solution to the dangers her family might face? The day seemed an interminably long one and when Angharad felt everything was in order, she asked Iori to saddle up her horse, Seren, and with him behind her on his own pony, she ambled down through the woods, trying to relive some of the pleasure she always took in this time of the year.

The sweet smells of the rain-washed leaves and blossoms filled the air. Vibrant bluebells filled these ancient woods with their sweet scent, and she mused that it was strange how a flower poisonous to humans and most animals was a herbalist's answer to nightmares. Bluebells were believed to be beloved by fairies, yet the sap of which was used to attach flight feathers to arrows. Life was full of contradictions. She heard a horse behind them and turned to see Meilyr following her down the path.

"Father said you may be here," he called. Coming up to Iori, he said he would ride with Angharad from here so that the stablehand could return to the manor.

She smiled as she waited for her brother to catch up. "It is so beautiful."

A jay, pink plumage and a flash of blue, flew screeching across the woodland glade.

"A master of mimicry," commented Meilyr watching the bird fly into some tangled branches. "I heard one barking like a dog once."

She looked surprised and pulled Seren to one side so that they could walk together.

"You don't seem yourself, Angharad. Is it what happened in Deheubarth that is troubling you?"

"Yes, that and…" she stopped herself. Of all people in the world, she could trust Meilyr, and it would be good to seek his counsel.

"And?"

"And Father is considering putting me forward as a wife to Earl Hugh."

Meilyr reined in his horse and looked at her.

"Earl Hugh?"

"Yes."

His look of horror told her that she had not been overreacting. He took a moment and then spoke carefully.

"From what I hear, he is off to Normandy to fight with King Henry. He may not return, of course."

Angharad saw a tiny glimmer of hope but immediately felt guilty about where her mind was going.

"He's not in the best of health. He isn't what you might call a fit man," he continued.

Angharad closed her eyes, but all she could see were Earl Hugh's leers.

"Did you tell Father how you felt?"

"It is not a matter of my feelings; it is a matter of how to protect our family. Father believes that such a marriage would tighten bonds and give me some influence."

"Father has been unsettled since Gruffydd ap Cynan came here. You only have to listen to Uncle Uchdryd to know that there is unrest all over Wales and that what happened to Rhys ap Tewdwr has inflamed tensions. Gruffydd will start harrying the Normans and when that happens, we are vulnerable. Don't forget that Lord Gruffydd wants the whole of Gwynedd back with his family and where does that leave us? We are lords of the lands in eastern Gwynedd."

"But these lands were given us fifty years ago by King Llewelyn ap Gruffydd. Why would Gruffydd ap Cynan change anything as far as we are concerned?"

"Because he sees his rightful dues are going to the Normans, and Father is instrumental in that."

"So, what you are saying is that Gruffydd ap Cynan is asking for Father's support, and if he doesn't give it and Gruffydd is victorious, we lose our lands. If Father does give it and Gruffydd is victorious, what then?"

"This, Father has to negotiate; there has to be a price for support, but, in doing that, he risks Gruffydd losing and the Normans wiping us out."

"So, if I were Earl Hugh's wife, Father thinks there is a chance I would be able to stop him from obliterating our family if, indeed, the Normans defeat the Welsh in their uprising?"

"I suppose Father thinks he may be able to do nothing, stay neutral. If his daughter is close to the Norman camp, they will not take vengeance on us if Gruffydd gains any successes and equally, no matter what happens, will not follow the lead of the southern Marcher Lords who have destroyed the families of Deheubarth."

He looked at his sister, whose eyes were filling with tears.

"Angharad, it may not even happen. None of it may happen. Earl Hugh may perish on the battlefields of Normandy, he may have given a promise to some other Norman lady, he may decide not to come back from Normandy at all, and despite the mutterings, Gruffydd's plans may come to nothing."

"You are right, Meilyr," she said, hoping that what he said was true, yet he had not said that if it came to it, she should refuse to marry Earl Hugh. Even Meilyr knew that she could not do that. That was clearly not an option.

"Hear the woodpecker?" asked Meilyr changing the subject as they came out of the wood into a meadow of spring blooms. The tap, tap, tap of the little beak boring into the wood reminded her that life presented challenges and that they could be overcome. They kicked their horses on to gallop across the meadow, and the breeze flew into her face.

The ride was good for her and she loved being with Meilyr, who was always so kind. They turned for home and galloped along the edge of the meadow before returning gently through the woodland, staying on a well-used path and avoiding old moss-covered fallen trees and tangled undergrowth. As they walked their horses to the stable, Meilyr stopped for a moment, turning to his sister.

"Don't worry about Earl Hugh, Angharad. As I said, anything could happen while he is in Normandy; you might find that he marries someone else. That would not solve our problem with the repercussions of conflict, but it would mean you would be saved from that, at least."

Inside the stable, Gronwy listened to their conversation as he pushed the dairy maid further into the straw, putting a fat finger over her lips so that she kept her silence. '*Interesting,*' he thought.

Chapter 4: An Evening with the Bards (June 1093)

A few weeks passed, and one morning, very early, the sound of hooves in the courtyard alerted Angharad to activity outside. She dressed quickly, hastily washed her face and headed for the hall, wondering who could be visiting at such a time. Her father and Meilyr were already up speaking to a slight but fit-looking young man whom she immediately recognised as a being from one of the prestigious Welsh families who had joined Gruffydd ap Cynan's household. When they were old enough, many young men would do this to gain the necessary skills that would enable them to take their place in the Welsh hierarchy upon their father's death. *'Unless the Normans wipe out the Welsh hierarchy,'* she thought, all too aware of what had happened in England. She joined them in welcoming the young man, Bryn, and had a maid come in with bread, cheese and ale. The fire was already lit and although the morning was not cold, they gravitated towards it.

"What news?" asked Meilyr once Bryn had had something to eat and drink. Bryn combed a hand through his thick tangle of dark brown hair. He turned and addressed himself to Owain.

"My lord, if it pleases you, Lord Gruffydd is on his way back to Anglesey and asks if he might rest his horses and men here for a few nights."

Owain immediately offered them all a welcome.

Bryn smiled widely and added to Owain and Meilyr that his master had made a promise for him and his men to assist in the building of a mews for their falcons if they still required it.

Meilyr beamed, and Owain confirmed that they would be delighted to learn from his lord's expertise and that since they had heard that their gyrfalcon was on its way, their return was very timely.

"We are expecting a group of bards today or tomorrow," Owain continued, "so the timing is perfect for that also. We have not had such entertainment for a while. It will be good to hear their news and yours also."

"Then I had better hasten back to them to let them know," said Bryn, finishing off the ale he had been given. "They are camped about an hour away."

"Before you leave, have you heard any more news of Rhys ap Tewdwr's family?" asked Meilyr with a look at Angharad, as he knew she was very concerned about them.

"Rhys's eldest, Griffith, is in Ireland safely and will stay there until it is safe for him to return. The Princess Nest is at the English court and being taken care of by Prince Henry and his household, it seems. Of the other brothers, the news is not clear, but I am sorry, there are rumours that they have been killed."

Owain and Meilyr gasped, shaking their heads at such an inconceivable crime. Angharad steadied herself on the back of a chair, a cold chill running down her spine. This was unthinkable. These were royal children. She looked at her brother and took a deep breath. Although she berated herself for her selfishness, her immediate thought was whether Hugh the Fat would allow the same to happen to her family and whether, if she really became his wife, she could protect them. She shuddered.

As the squire departed, Gronwy entered the hall, red-eyed and clearly the worst for his evening drinking. He gestured with his head towards the departing squire and raised his eyebrows at his brother.

"What does that one want with us now?"

Owain caught his son by the arm. "The courtesy that we should extend to all guests, Gronwy," he spat through gritted teeth. "Go and make yourself presentable and remember you are representing a noble house."

Gronwy looked as if he had been punched in the face and was about to retaliate when he thought better of it and lumbered away.

Owain watched Gronwy with a look of disgust and then turned to immediate action "Meilyr, fetch Rhydir and Llywarch. We have work to do. Let us show our visitors the best hospitality in these parts. Angharad, make sure that we have a feast worth remembering."

Angharad set about organising the food and bedding required for what would be a very busy few days. She sent servants to the fishermen on the River Clywd for fresh fish and, from the fishermen nearer the sea, white crabs and cockles. While Welsh sheep were small and known for their delicious flavour, she knew she would still need to ask the shepherds for them to choose well from the flocks which had grazed along the seashore eating seaweed. She was well aware that the sweet, buttery texture and rich flavour of those sheep were always commented on. It was arranged for a pig to be killed and seasoned with wild thyme; it would be roasted on a spit over the next days. Their fowler was out getting birds. She checked on their honey stores, had fresh bread baking in the oven outside and there was hare and venison as well as pease porridge.

In a huge pot in the courtyard was a cawl with plenty of bacon, leeks and cabbage to flavour the thick soup. She arranged to remove a couple of cheeses from the brine in which they were soaking and, as she did, she mused how in the Welsh laws of Hywel Dda, while the cheese was in brine, it belonged to the wife, but when it was taken out to eat it belonged to the husband. She had not yet worked out why that was so and had always intended to ask her father, whose knowledge of the Welsh laws was second to no man.

Feeling satisfied that things were under control and the servants were able to prepare everything in good time, Angharad washed herself in rosewater and put on a finely embroidered woollen tunic with a brooch that had belonged to her mother pinned at her shoulder. Susannah brushed her hair and styled it attentively with braids pinned carefully around her head.

"You will be the fairest they have seen, lady," she remarked proudly, but Angharad shivered suddenly, thinking that this was what they had always said about the Princess Nest.

Her irrepressible uncle's resounding voice in the courtyard announcing his presence interrupted such thought.

Both Uchdryd and his family and Gruffydd and his small party had arrived together. Uncle Uchdryd was booming, "Where are you all? Are you sleeping on such a beautiful day?"

He winked at his strapping two sons, Young Uchdryd and Madog, while his wife, Nest, gave him her warning look, which was intended to contain him somewhat but did the opposite.

People appeared from everywhere, the servants taking care of horses and bags and the family welcoming their various guests. Gruffydd dismounted easily from his black stallion, and Angharad dropped into a deep curtsey.

"Lady Angharad," he addressed her smiling, "Thank you for allowing us to impose upon you once again. Your uncle has not stopped telling us about your beautiful singing voice. I do hope that with the entertainment planned, we will have the opportunity to hear it! He also tells me that you play the harp beyond compare."

"My uncle flatters me," said Angharad, blushing prettily.

"We will see about that," chuckled Uchdryd, "My Lord Gruffydd has a rare appreciation of music and, I would add, a fine singing voice himself, so we are in for a rare treat, wouldn't you say, Owain?"

"Of course," laughed Owain, "we make all our guests perform for their supper! Come on in, everyone."

Angharad arranged refreshments for all the guests and was delighted that she could spend some time with her Aunt Nest, with whom she had always had a close relationship. Nest was a tiny bird of a lady, in whose neat face a small, upturned nose and large observant cornflower blue eyes dominated. She was a perfect wife for the impulsive and larger-than-life, Uchdryd as she steadily ran the household and raised the family seamlessly, allowing him just to be Uchdryd. When Angharad's mother Morfudd had died, Nest had stepped in to help and, therefore, knew her niece and nephews well.

Angharad showed her aunt some of the embroidery she had been working on; they spoke of cloth Nest had bought to make into a fine tunic and indulged in general chit-chat before Angharad needed to return to her hosting duties.

"There are some fine young men who have come along with Gruffydd ap Cynan, Angharad, did you notice?"

"Aunty, you are wicked. I haven't time to be noticing young men."

"Well, you are getting to an age, you know. Gruffydd ap Cynan himself is quite a catch for someone."

"He is a warrior, Aunty."

"Your uncle is also a warrior, Angharad! There is more to that young man than meets the eye. He comes from good stock, is well-educated and gentlemanly, and you cannot deny he is handsome. Uchdryd speaks very highly of him." Angharad blushed.

'He is handsome, Aunt.'

"Did you notice his boots?"

"His boots, Aunty?"

"Riding in from who knows where and not a speck of dirt on them."

That Nest noticed someone's boots in all the commotion made Angharad laugh out loud, but then she saw her aunt looking at her very seriously.

"You look very pale, Angharad. Are you worrying about Gronwy?"

Angharad looked alarmed, "Gronwy?"

"Oh, I should not have said anything."

"Gronwy?" asked Angharad again, confused as to what her aunt might be alluding to.

"Uchdryd is concerned about him."

"Why?" asked Angharad. She knew that Gronwy was drinking a lot and had a terrible temper, but that was nothing new, so why would Uchdryd be particularly worried now?

Her aunt spoke in a quiet, sing-song voice hardly above a whisper. "You must say nothing now, please, but he has been spending a lot of time drinking and gambling in the local inns, and there is talk that he has, well," she hesitated, "been involved with the daughter of one of your tenants. She has fallen pregnant."

Angharad let out an involuntary gasp and covered her face with her hands.

"Does my father know?"

"Uchdryd has not told him."

"Why not?"

"Uchdryd and your father have had their differences over Uchdryd's support of Gruffydd ap Cynan and Cadwgan ap Bleddyn. Since Uchdryd agreed to be the leader of Cadwgan's warband, there have been tensions between him and your father. Cadwgan and Uchdryd are cousins, after all, and Uchdryd went into service with Cadwgan's father, Cynfyn, when he was just fourteen. There are deep ties there, but Owain feels Uchdryd is putting Gwynedd at risk, particularly because Gruffydd ap Cynan does not come of age to claim his kingship for another few years. If he were of age to claim his

37

inheritance, the men of Gwynedd would surely all rally behind him, but he needs to be at least twenty-eight years old. Anyway, with things difficult just now, politically, I mean, it would not be good to stir up trouble between father and son."

Angharad tried to take everything in. Gronwy's behaviour was a stain on their family's name, and surely her father needed to be told. Then there was the ever-present concern of the political issues which might divide their family. She sighed.

"Are you alright?"

"Aunt Nest, I remember such wonderful days as a little girl, when all we cousins would play together, and there was nothing in the world to trouble us. Suddenly, I have grown up so quickly. Now, everything is difficult, and people are conspiring against each other. Making the right choices about what to do is difficult."

"The innocence of youth! I remember you so well, tottering around after your brothers and cousins and trying to do everything they did. No matter what they did, you would never complain. Your mother would have been very proud to see how you have grown up. Life is full of difficult choices, my dear, and sometimes, what your head tells you and what your heart tells you is in conflict. I can see now that you are wondering whether you should tell your father about Gronwy. Just keep an eye on him but say nothing. What is done is done."

"How could he have done such a thing?"

"Gronwy was always the most difficult of all the children, always angry about something, fighting for the sake of fighting. I can remember him tying Madog up and throwing him into the pig pen one time and we were looking for him everywhere. He needed to go into another household and learn the discipline of being part of a warband, get rid of some of his rage, but your father has always been so reluctant to let him go."

Further voices from the courtyard heralded another group of arrivals; this time, their cousins, the Bendews, had arrived.

"Don't worry so much, Angharad. Things always work out in the end. Come, you need to welcome your guests and I am keeping you talking here!"

Soon after the arrival of the Bendews, the bards were greeted with great enthusiasm. They were a group of six who had arrived on foot but had two ponies carrying their belongings. They would travel from lord to lord, entertaining their guests in exchange for food, shelter and a small payment. As well as singing or reciting stories of battle glory, love and family history, they provided all the latest gossip on what was happening in different courts around the country and other news from abroad.

The bards brought in their instruments carefully and with much reverence. These were the tools of their trade. The tallest bard, a young bewhiskered redhead, held in one hand a crwth, which was a gut-stringed instrument carved from one block of sycamore wood with a soundboard made of deal and a bridge of cherry. In his other hand, he held the bow made of wood and horsehair. Behind him came an older bard, gaunt with a grey beard, striking brown eyes and long sensitive hands, who carried a pibcorn. The pibcorn was a pipe horn made of elder and had six finger holes and, at the end of the pipe, a bell shaped from a cow horn. Next came a short, squat brown-haired fellow with an open mobile face carrying drums and cymbals and behind him, a tall old man with a round face and eyes like an owl carrying his harp. Then came a weedy blonde-haired youth carrying a bundle of clothes and tripping up over them as they dangled on the floor. Finally came the most senior with a dignified, long grave face and silver-grey hair partly hidden beneath a wide-brimmed hat. They were all made to feel welcome and ushered inside.

The house was a merry one with much laughter and music. Long trestle tables had been laid out, and benches pulled out from the sides of the hall. Trencher after trencher of food was brought in, and many fine stews were served on plates of freshly baked bread. Compliments were flying on the delicious food, and the guests enjoyed gossip, jokes and news. After all had had their fill, the tables were cleared, and it was time for the evening's entertainment to commence.

The main bard introduced his company. The first poem of the night was in praise of King Gruffydd ap Llewelyn, a tale which had been first spun by Gruffydd ap Llewelyn's court poet, Berddig, and made popular thereafter. It related to the Welsh king's famous meeting with King Edward of England on the River Severn. Great store was set on this meeting between two mighty kings. The bards told how neither Gruffydd nor Edward wished to cross the river as this might have been construed as their being the weaker. Finally, the impatient Edward decided to cross and got into a ferryboat, whereupon Gruffydd, ever magnanimous, strode into the water and carried the king to the bank on his shoulders.

The much-loved tale was enthusiastically received. It spoke of wonderful times when Wales was united under Gruffydd ap Llewelyn, famous for his great vigour and daring!

"He cleared the place of English settlers right through from Rhuddlan to the Vale of Maelor." Ednowain Bendew reminded his fellows. Ednowain's beautiful sister Morfudd had married Owain, and the two men had become even closer when she died, as they shared the sorrow of her loss. Ednowain was born only a few months before Owain but had lived a comfortable life and looked older. Where Owain's hair was thick, Ednowain had lost most of his and what was left was iron grey. Where Owain was lean and muscled, Ednowain was portly. The two men, though physically different, were matched in their knowledge of what was going on in the world and by their generosity. They enjoyed each other's company immensely.

"He was a great king," said Uchdryd shaking his head dolefully, "but betrayed in the end."

"Yes, he was," Ednowain agreed, "but he got too big for his boots and forgot that a king needs to look after all his subjects. If he had visited all his Welsh subjects and made himself known to them, he would have won their support, but he thought he could rule everyone from afar."

"I remember my father saying to me just before he died that, in the previous one hundred and twenty years, thirty-five Welsh princes had been killed by Saxons, Vikings and Welshmen," intervened Owain, who had been listening to the conversation with interest. "That is a lot of princes!"

"And now we could add those killed by Normans to the tally!" said Ednowain gloomily.

"Let's not dampen our spirits," said Owain chidingly, "why waste a good mead?" He gestured to the bards to continue.

The next poem of the night was the famous tale of Culhwch and Olwen. This was the best of folk law and legend, such descriptive poetry that it transformed even the most disinterested listeners into enthralled participants on the journey. All sat transfixed as the bard recited the story of a fantastic world of giants, beasts and men who swear oaths and fulfil their destiny through trial, fight and hunt. There for a while, all the passionate huntsmen in the audience felt they were on the hunt: they experienced the rush of excitement, the risk, the suspense. How they were all stirred by the noble character of Culhwch, a mighty hero on his worthy steed winning the giant's daughter, the beautiful Olwen.

All the women listened, imagining themselves as the yellow-haired Olwen with her rosy cheeks, bright red dress, golden torc and many rings. Olwen was so gentle that white spring flowers would appear where she trod.

How silent the room was as Culhwch was placed at the court of his cousin, King Arthur, with his mighty warriors all named and described. Arthur, the mighty hero king and protector of Roman Britain against all invaders, loomed large for the listeners. Pride of place in Arthur's court was given to warlock warrior Cai, whose hard-drinking and incredible fighting skills were astonishing.

Then, the audience imagined themselves with Culhwch at the court of Ysbaddaden, father of Olwen, the Chief Giant, savagely grotesque and whose forty demands seemed impossible. Finally, though they knew the story well, Owain's guests relished in the satisfaction of winning Olwen, who was to be Culhwch's wife for the rest of their lives together. Happily ever after!

Not one of the groups failed to be aroused by the telling of such a stirring Welsh folktale emphasising the best qualities of the Welsh folk heroes: bravery, tenacity, beauty and ingenuity among them. The talk of the men immediately turned to restoring Welsh pride in fighting the Norman foe. Men gathered around Uchdryd and Gruffydd, who both earnestly elaborated on why the timing was right for action against the Normans.

"There is so much discontent. William Rufus is a very different king from his father, William the Conqueror. The Conqueror was willing to honour the relationship between the Welsh kingdoms and England, but Rufus is greedy. He wants everything but gives nothing," said Uchdryd savagely.

"He would not do well as a Welsh prince," Gruffydd asserted shrewdly. "Here, our soldiers are warriors because it is an honour and a privilege to fight for your lord, but, in the Norman way, most of the soldiers are forced to fight."

Ednowain Bendew listened solemnly and then added, "That is very true. Welshmen fight from the heart for their loyalties, but the Normans, mighty as they are, are driven by greed or fear. From everything I hear, Rufus is obsessed with every kind of vice, including," he looked around and hushed his voice, "I am told, he is a sodomist."

Uchdryd nodded vehemently and then, in hushed tones, added, "Everyone says that he is not a dignified man, nothing that would set him apart from the common man. No piety or morality at all."

"He has scant respect for the clergy!" added Gruffydd.

"Not a good-looking man, either," added Ednowain, "pot-bellied, though not as fat as his father."

"Is it true that the Conqueror was so fat that when he died, they had to squeeze him into a sarcophagus, and his body burst?" asked Llywarch, wide-eyed, who had been delighting in being part of the conversation.

They all grimaced.

"It is true," said Owain seriously and, looking disgusted, added briskly, "but we won't speak of that when we have all eaten well!"

"Do they call him Rufus because of his red hair?" continued Llywarch irrepressibly.

"He did have red hair when he was young, but it is yellowy now, they say. His face is red and florid, and he has different coloured eyes. Now there's a sign of no good," carried on Ednowain.

"Apparently, the fashion in his court is for long hair, like women, curled with curling irons, no caps, long filthy beards like goats and shoes, long and pointed, like a ram's horn so that they can barely walk in them. Even their long robes and mantles trail filthy on the ground, restricting movement, and they have long gloves so that they can't even use their hands," said Uchdryd, drawing whoops and applause as he minced and hobbled around imitating Norman courtiers.

"Very true," laughed Gruffydd, "the fashions are ridiculous, but, in fairness, apparently, Rufus is fearless in battle with incredible strength."

43

"Good for him," said Uchdryd. "Let him go and fight with his brother in Normandy and leave us to do our worst back home!"

"And so, we will, by the Face at Lucca!" laughed Gruffydd using the oath for which William Rufus was famous.

"Tell me, lord," said Llywarch curiously, "do you think it is true that in North Wales, here, we have the best spearmen, and in the South, they have the best men with the longbow?"

"Hah," said Gruffydd, "they are good with their bows in the South, but we are their equals with any weapon: bow, spear, mace, axe, javelin."

"Do they make their bows of elm as we do?" enquired Rhydir.

"Yes, elm is the best," replied Gruffydd.

"And do they use them at short range and long range as we do?" asked Rhydir.

"They do. At short range, our Welsh bowmen can shoot through mail and saddles; nothing stops them, and they are sure in their shots."

"I'll tell you another difference," added Uchdryd with a wide grin, "up here in the North, we wear one shoe when we are fighting so that we can balance on rough terrain, but in the South, they wear two shoes."

Llywarch lifted his eyebrow in question.

"It is true!" laughed Uchdryd, "Some still prefer to wear only one shoe in battle!"

"And you, Uncle?"

"I start with two but have often ended with none!"

Everyone laughed.

"Come, you men," Owain called across the room, "do not let the women outdo us at dancing. We have music to make every foot tap!"

Soon, the hall was whirling with energetic youth and those who wished to recapture some of those heady times of years long gone. Angharad spun, her red robes flowing out behind her, as she enjoyed the company of her cousins.

"A fine niece I have there," said Uchdryd to Gruffydd cordially.

Gruffydd watched her as she laughed and twirled, colour in her cheeks and her fine eyes sparkling. "She is indeed a most fetching young lady, Lord Uchdryd," said Gruffydd formally and then, indicating Uchdryd's sons who were dancing with great vigour, added, "and your sons do your family credit."

Uchdryd beamed good-naturedly, "I cannot complain, Gruffydd. They have loving hearts and are as brave in combat as I could wish."

"When our battles are won," said Gruffydd wistfully, "I wish for a large family, sons as fine and handsome as yours, skilful with sword and bow, and daughters as noble and beautiful as your niece. A huge llys with a welcome for everyone: bards and musicians to keep our culture thriving, whitewashed churches dotting the countryside and land where nobody is starving. Do you think we can accomplish such a dream, Uchdryd?"

"Part we can do by the sword, part we can do by honestly managing Gwynedd, but, by God Gruffydd, part of that can only be done when you have a wife!"

At that moment, a group of dancers careered past them and as Angharad brushed into Gruffydd, she looked up apologising before being pulled once again into the centre of the hall. Gruffydd watched her appreciatively. She was indeed an exquisite young woman.

Chapter 5: Falcons (June 1093)

There were many sore heads the following morning after the entertainment had gone on late into the night. Long mattresses filled with reeds had been pulled against the far wall of the hall, and for those who did not have beds of their own, this provided enough comfort to get some welcome sleep. Some were still deep in their slumbers when Angharad came into the hall. Others were sitting with a brychan, a stiff, coarse blanket, around their shoulders. After taking in what needed to be done there, she went back to the kitchen to give instructions to the servants. The door was opened wide to let in the beautiful morning sun, and when she glimpsed out, she was surprised to see the Lord Gruffydd already up and in deep discussion with Meilyr, just as they had been a few months before.

She smiled. She realised they would be discussing the mews, where to put it and what materials would be needed. The gyrfalcon was on its way, she knew; Meilyr and her father could think of little else. After his previous discussions with Gruffydd, Meilyr had already amassed the materials he thought they would need.

The local families started to say their goodbyes, and it was with a heavy heart that Angharad farewelled Nest and her lively red-haired cousins. The Bendews, living as close as they did, she often saw at church or would call in on when out riding but her Aunt Nest was a little too far for such social calls. The bards also moved on but thanked everyone profusely for their welcome: thanks which was wholeheartedly reciprocated. Owain asked them to stay a little longer next time, which they promised they would. Ever the generous host, he insisted they left with plenty of nourishment for their journey.

Having the house so full had made for a wonderful distraction. Angharad had put her concerns about Earl Hugh and the unsettled political situation to the back of her mind, yet, like a niggling pain, they were still there.

The young woman concentrated on making sure everything ran smoothly for their remaining guests and, by noon, was intrigued by the speed at which the mews was progressing from the time of gathering the necessary materials to seeing her brothers, the male servants, Gruffydd and his men all getting involved in erecting the new building. She was fascinated by the way Lord Gruffydd was as capable with a saw or hammering nails as he was directing the activity. Everyone, even Gronwy, seemed willing to take his advice and by the end of the afternoon, the mews was built and the falcons and hawks transferred to their new home.

The talk was about training new birds and how, at first, the hawks' eyelids were sewn shut until they were used to the sound of their new surroundings. Hawks were carried around on their owner's arm for several days to get used to the falconer before unsewing the eyes and allowing them to fly between perch and falconer. They discussed the merits of keeping the floor clean to avoid mould; which meat to use on a lure before allowing them loose on live prey; how chicken wings were good tirings for falcons and hawks to pick at; how kestrels would love chasing down live grasshoppers; and how falcons preferred open fields whereas hawks preferred marshland and woodland. Everyone had something to say. Angharad fetched her own pet falcon from the house and carried the hooded bird, jesses tied to the bird's feet and to her gloved hand, across the courtyard to join the others.

Gruffydd was standing back admiring the new construction when she came up behind him. Hearing her steps, he turned and was surprised to see her with the bird.

"She's a beauty," he said, admiring the peregrine falcon on her gloved hand.

"Thank you, my lord. She doesn't get as much exercise from me as I would wish," said Angharad, "she is a recent gift, and I am very new to hawking."

"She seems very comfortable with you, lady," he remarked, putting his arm in front of hers. He asked, "May I?"

She allowed him to take the bird onto his arm. He crooned to it softly, holding it high to better observe it.

"She has a nice temperament," he commented and then equally gently handed her back. He led Angharad into the mews and to the compartment they had allocated for her hawk. Everything was clean and neat. The birds were tethered but with long enough leashes to fly a little to the preening stone in the centre or to move about on their perch.

"This is wonderful," she exclaimed joyfully. "We will be the only ones in this part of Gwynedd with such a mews but I think soon everyone will want the same. The birds will be much safer here and less disturbed by what is going on in the house."

He smiled at her enthusiasm.

"Lady Angharad, I would be more than happy to take you hawking if you have the time and want to gain confidence with your bird. It is important to fly them regularly because; otherwise, they become stale."

"My lord," blushed Angharad. She was going to tell him that she would not want to put him to such trouble but then she found herself saying. "If you have plenty of patience, then I would enjoy that. I will ask Iori to accompany us, I am not yet able to ride with the hawk by myself, and I am sure Meilyr would be delighted to let you fly his hawk."

"I would be pleased to see as much of the country around here as possible. I am not familiar with it, having spent most of my time in Gwynedd in Anglesey or roundabout so that you would be doing me a favour."

Within the hour, Angharad, on her white palfrey Seren; Iori, on a sturdy grey gelding; and Gruffydd, elegant on the fleece-lined saddle of his black stallion; were up on the White Moor. She had been surprised at how easily she and Gruffydd could talk together of the bards, bardic tradition, Welsh culture and its similarities and differences to Irish and a myriad of other topics of interest to them both. They spoke of Angharad's desire to one day visit Bardsley Island off the Llyn Peninsula, where Saint Cadfan and the Kings of Llyn founded a monastery centuries before. It was also claimed that Merlin, the druid of legend, was buried there and they discussed beliefs in Wales about Merlin and Arthur.

Angharad pointed out different areas they could see from their vantage point: the mighty Snowdonia Ranges, the birthplace of the Conway, Dovey, as well as the Clwyd River, which they could see below them flowing past Rhuddlan Castle. In the distance, the River Dee was visible as it met the sea after its long journey from Bala Lakes down through Chester to the estuary, where quicksand was a trap for the unknowing. She pointed out Holywell, famed for the healing waters which sprang out of a rock hidden in a deep, narrow wooded valley.

"Many centuries ago," Angharad explained, "Wenefrede lived there. She was the daughter of noble parents. Her mother was Wenlo, who was the sister of St Beuno."

"St Beuno is dear to me as he built the little church at our family home."

"Did he really? I think he is the saint I admire the most. His memory is revered in these parts. The story goes that St. Beuno visited his relations in Holywell and liked it so much that he built a little church there, too, at the foot of the hill and took in his niece Wenefrede. When she decided to become a nun, it is said that her suitor Caradog became so furious that he decapitated her, but a healing spring emerged where her head fell. St. Beuno restored her to life, and Caradog mysteriously fell dead with the ground opening and swallowing him. St. Beuno returned to Caernarfon and, before leaving Holywell, promised that if anyone came to the stone he sat on before he left and asked three times for grace in St. Wenefrede's name, it would be granted them."

"And what do they believe happened to Wenefrede?" asked Gruffydd.

"She became the abbess at Gwytherin at the source of the River Elwy eight years later."

"So her head must have been firmly on her neck by then!" replied Gruffydd, lifting one eyebrow somewhat irreverently. He caught her look of surprise threw his head back and laughed.

Angharad couldn't help smiling her wide smile though she felt she probably should not have. She thought Gruffydd looked magnificent when he laughed. She turned her horse slightly and then pointed out somewhere else in the distance.

"Down there is Maen Achwyfan, where there is a huge ancient stone cross called the Stone of Saint Cwyfan. It is decorated with carvings: of animals, men and lots of knotwork. They say that there is no taller cross in Wales or England."

Not once did the Normans come into the conversation. Her respect for Lord Gruffydd only grew as she realised he was both highly educated and sensitive. Was this the same man whose prowess with the sword and axe was legend? She thought of her Uncle Uchdryd, whose prowess in battle had defined him all his adult life and yet a gentler, good-natured soul she had never met. She found it hard to comprehend these two conflicting sides of the man who was both lauded and respected.

Now they stood under a blissfully cloudless sky with only the breeze blowing the grasses, poppies, foxgloves and cowslips. It was peaceful and the only other sign of human life was a shepherd in a far-off meadow taking a flock of sheep to be sheared. The heavy Welsh wool was much prized and their fleeces would bring good money.

Angharad's bird, still hooded, moved on her arm a little uncertainly and she stroked the plumage on its chest to settle it.

"Lady, you need to hold your arm a little higher, like this." Gruffydd demonstrated with his own hooded hawk, which mewed softly as he felt the change to his perch. Then, removing the hood and jesses, he freed the bird, letting it soar into the sky, the small bells on its feet tinkling. The hawk circled at first and then almost stopped in the air, quivering before plummeting to the ground.

"Shall I fetch him, lord?" said Iori. "He has taken down a pheasant."

Gruffydd smiled and nodded. Iori rode ahead a few minutes to where the hawk was sitting atop its quarry.

"Let me show you," Gruffydd said and then came around behind her so that she felt his chest against her back, almost nestling her. He lifted her arm so that her own bird fluttered its feathers in response. She felt a flush course upwards from her neck into her face and was surprised at her response to Gruffydd's proximity. The feeling of solidity but comfort from his body and exhilaration almost overwhelmed her.

Gruffydd seemed to hold her arm a few seconds longer than he needed to, and at that moment, she involuntarily turned to meet his eyes. Her look was returned and he searched deep into her eyes as if he was seeing her for the first time. The silence between them was a comfortable one and as she moved away and they focussed on the falcon, she knew that this man, this stranger, embodied the feeling she had dreamt of all these years. Was he the one she was meant to be with? The unexpectedness of this had thrown her completely. Her heart pounded so loudly that she was sure he could hear it. She longed to reach out to him, to touch him but was fearful of ruining the warmth that had developed between them. What would he think? Then her own bird was loose and soaring into the heavens. She followed it, and as it swooped, she turned her face excitedly back to his and found he was watching her, not the falcon.

51

They flew the bird, again and again, watching it soar into the cloudless sky, hovering effortlessly with such grace, floating, almost motionless on long stretched wings, then plummeting, faster than an arrow, faultless in detecting its prey. Her eyes were drawn to his again and again, and each time she averted her gaze to the distant mountains and valley as she caught him looking at her. This was not Gronwy lustfully eyeing the dairymaid nor the salacious undressing of her by Hugh the Fat's leering. This was something quite different. Did he feel something for her, or was this a mere friendship between two lovers of music, nature and history?

"You are tiring, my lady," he said at last somewhat reluctantly, "and this beauty has flown so well. Shall we head back?"

"I am not tired at all, but you are right. We probably should make our way back."

He smiled gently.

"Allow me to help you up onto Seren."

That beautiful moment in time, that escape from reality, where, like the hawk she had floated, abandoning herself to the sensation of sheer joy, was now over.

As he lifted her, his hands encircling her tiny waist, she felt sensations she had not experienced before. Her whole body seemed to be pulsing at his touch. Angharad's fingers fumbled with the reins. She thought he must surely see the effect he was having on her and she felt a flush cover her face and neck again. She longed to be alone to collect her thoughts but, at the same time, could not wait until he helped her down from her horse so that he would touch her again. The return journey passed too quickly.

Gruffydd swung easily off his horse as they reached the courtyard and came to her side to help her dismount. Lifting her easily, he put her gently on the ground, and she felt a shiver of pleasure. She dropped into a deep curtsey, giving her time to compose herself. She thanked him, and then, as they walked across the courtyard together, a young woman she did not recognise approached them. Her clothes were poor but her face was comely, although she looked somewhat distraught. As soon as she saw that the woman was well advanced in pregnancy, Angharad's focus shifted abruptly. She wrenched herself from the pleasure that had absorbed her all afternoon, quickly excused herself, leaving Gruffydd somewhat puzzled by her haste and walked swiftly towards the young woman.

"Can I help you?"

"I would speak with the mistress of the house."

"I am the mistress."

The woman looked surprised, as Angharad was probably a few years younger than she was. She looked around as if searching for someone.

"Mistress, I need work."

"I am sorry, I see your condition but we have no need of any other helpers."

"My family have disowned me, mistress. I have nowhere to go," she clawed at Angharad's arm desperately, her lips trembling and her eyes pleading.

Angharad was about to say something, but the woman began to weep great heaving sobs, so she led her quickly to a small wooden bench behind the stables.

"This was your brother Gronwy's doing, mistress. He promised he would marry me. He promised me." She threw a frantic glance around, "Now he will not even see me."

Angharad threw her arms around the girl, feeling the violence of her sobbing and her desperation. She racked her brain as to what to do. If she confronted Gronwy, she knew it would be worse for the girl, and she would bear the brunt of his temper. To tell her father was not an option. They could not have her here. What could she do?

"What is your name?" she asked, patting and rocking her as she would do a child in distress.

"Bethan."

"Are you Heulwen and Rhidian's daughter?" she asked, placing her now as one of the daughters of hill farmers who were their tenants.

The girl nodded and then started to cry inconsolably again.

Angharad was not so familiar with this family, being a little further away than she would ride, and she tried to think how she could best approach the question she needed to ask gently.

"You have been pregnant for some time, your parents must have noticed."

The girl nodded again.

"But they have only now asked you to leave your home. Why is that?"

"When they first found out, they were angry, but I told them that Gronwy would marry me. We waited and waited for Gronwy to come to the farm again but he didn't. I went to look for him at the inn. I saw his horse and waited there but when he came out, he was angry with me and told me that the child was not his and he did not want to see me again. When I told my parents, they were furious with me."

Now, the sobbing was almost convulsive, but it sounded as if Gronwy had not forced himself upon the girl, at least, although he had clearly made promises that he had no intention of keeping.

"I will need to speak with your parents," she said at last, "but I cannot do that today. We have guests here I must attend to, and it is getting late."

"No, please do not, my lady, my father will be angry."

"Let me try at least. Wait here for a moment."

Angharad looked around and then headed into the stables, where Iori was singing as he groomed the horses.

"Iori, I am going to ask you to keep a confidence and to help me."

"Of course," he beamed.

"You cannot ask me why, but I would like you to hide a young woman in here tonight and tomorrow. My father is going to hunt in the morning, so people will likely be coming in and out, but you must keep her hidden. Do you understand?"

Iori nodded but seemed confused.

"Then, when everyone is gone to hunt, I would have you come with me up into the hill pastures. She will need to ride a pony as will you. We will need to be gone and back before the hunt returns."

Iori's eyes widened, but he agreed. Angharad fetched the girl and told her to hide herself, explaining that she would bring food and drink for her shortly, which she did without anyone noticing.

She made her way hurriedly back to her chamber and took her mother's silver brooch out of the little cloth bag she kept it in. She kissed it, eyes closed, and thought of her mother. Then, deciding to wear it one last time in her mother's honour, she changed into a clean linen shift with a fetching red tunic, pinning the brooch carefully at her shoulder.

It was a much quieter evening, with everyone still exhausted from the festivities of the previous day and the men with their physical efforts creating the mews. They ate, spoke of the bards and the people at the hall the evening before and Angharad made sure everyone was well provided for.

"Angharad," said Owain, "we must let our guests hear your voice and your playing. Come, Meilyr, bring your crwth and Rhydir your pibcorn."

Angharad blushed but took her place at the harp, discussing with her brothers which folk tune they would play.

"Every master should give his chief musician a harp, a crwth and a pibcorn, Hywel the Good wrote in his laws. Well, I haven't a chief musician, but I have the instruments and the players!" chuckled Owain.

Gruffydd and his men, Hywel, Aeddan and Meirion, laughed with him and congratulated him on his good sense. Then Gruffydd leaned forward to listen.

The three had decided on a folk tune where Angharad would play and sing the verse, and they would all join in the chorus. The room filled with the sound of the notes of the harp, and she began to sing in a sweet lilting voice. She was aware of Gruffydd gazing at her with a speculative look and hoped she was performing her best. She sang of King Arthur's journeys to the Underworld, the feats he achieved and of his noble warriors. Her voice was mesmerising, and everyone sat still, but when Rhydir played his horn, and Meilyr bowed his strings for the chorus, everyone joined in, knowing the song so well. Gruffydd was moved as he watched Angharad's long fingers skipping over the strings with such dexterity and was entranced by the haunting sweet voice recalling the ancient legend. The song ended to much applause and laughter.

"Wonderful, wonderful!" enthused Gruffydd. "Music feeds the soul!"

"When you have your own court, we can have music every night," called out Aeddan, his blue eyes sparkling with pride at his envisioned future.

"A while to go before that happens," said Gruffydd wistfully. "Many battles to fight."

"Well, Tangwysti, the prophetess, predicted that you would become a king," offered the usually solemn and silent Meirion. Turning to the others, he said, "She met with Lord Gruffydd and, in front of us all, presented him with a fine shirt and tunic made from the cloth once worn by King Gruffydd ap Llywelyn before she dropped to her knees and predicted our lord would also be a king."

"As I said," said Gruffydd, feeling uncomfortable with the attention, "we have a journey to go on to get to that point. Let us not talk of fighting tonight but have another tune, enjoy a day of hunting tomorrow and then set out on our mission."

"Another song," shouted Owain, and they were soon all lost in the music apart from Gronwy, who watched Gruffydd with a sour expression.

Chapter 6: The Hill Farm (June 1093)

There was great excitement the following morning as the men got ready for the hunt. Angharad observed Gronwy carefully and prayed that Bethan would not show herself. Deceit was not condoned in their household, and she felt sick that she was covering up Gronwy's bad behaviour, but she didn't know what else to do. Iori, at her instruction, had brought all the horses out into the courtyard very early so that there was no need for anyone to enter the stables. She gave him a look, which he returned with a tiny nod indicating all was well. The hounds on their leashes were yapping and jostling, excited as the horses sidled and snorted, impatient to be gone.

Gruffydd was already on his great horse, which tossed his head, ready for what he knew would come. He bowed his head to Angharad and gave her a warm smile.

"You are not joining us on the hunt, my lady?" Gruffydd looked disappointed.

"I do hunt, although I prefer the chase to the kill. Today, though, there are things I must attend to."

"Your company will be missed, but, hopefully, we will not return to you empty-handed."

There was some milling around, calls for servants to assist with various tasks, and men choosing their boar spears from a pile near the door. Then, with great clamour, the party vanished out through the gates and was heading towards the woods.

Angharad watched them all go with great relief before getting her cloak. Putting her little cloth bag containing her brooch into a leather pouch, she ran down to the stables.

Iori was waiting for her with the three mounts.

"Bethan!" she called, and the girl came out from the back of the stable, her eyes puffy and red with crying.

"We must leave quickly," she urged. "Twilight is very quiet, and you should be able to ride her. Iori will lead you."

Looking around her to check that nobody was observing them, they set off through the gate. They had got no further than the first corner when, to Angharad's abject horror, Owain returned, leading his dun-coloured courser, which was limping.

He stopped in his tracks, as did they, and Angharad scrambled for what she could say. Her heart thudded.

"Father," she said as she saw him quickly assessing the situation, "what has happened to your horse?"

"He stepped awkwardly and I am feared he has bruised his left forehoof. I need to change my mount."

"Take mine, Father", she said immediately

"But you are going somewhere and who is this?" he demanded, looking from Angharad to Bethan severely.

"This is Bethan, Father, she is the daughter of one of our tenant farmers. I am helping her to get back to her home."

Bethan looked terrified and colour flooded into Angharad's blanched face, her eyes scarcely able to hold her father's, who was not slow in noting that the young lady on Twilight was heavily pregnant.

"Iori, I will take your horse, if I may, so I can get back to our guests." He handed the reins of his horse to Iori and mounted Iori's steed. "Angharad, we will talk later," he informed her icily, immediately reading Angharad's discomfort. Then he spurred his horse on and cantered back towards the woods.

"Iori, I think I will manage to bring back the pony on the lead rope and Seren is very easy. I hope I haven't put you in a difficult position with Father."

"Please do not worry, my lady, I am more concerned about you travelling alone," said Iori sympathetically. "Your father will not be pleased."

That is true, Angharad thought bleakly but was more worried that if her father grilled Iori, as he surely would, then he would be expected to tell the truth about Bethan, such truth as he knew at least.

Iori continued to protest about her travelling alone but she allayed his discomfort about letting ladies travel alone by reminding him that there would be little to fear in the hill country and that they would take things slowly. Both mounts were gentle-natured.

The two women set out, Bethan clearly uncomfortable because of her pregnancy but not complaining and Angharad wondering what she could say to her father. She had rarely experienced the reproachful, almost threatening, tone of his voice, and she dreaded the confrontation that she knew would come later. He would be furious about her travelling so far unaccompanied. How had she become caught up in this tangled mess?

As they passed the woods, where bluebells and violets grew thick away from the sun, she could hear the calls of the huntsmen and the barking of the hounds. At one time, Gronwy's voice called out clearly from close by that he had spotted a boar and Angharad imagined how upsetting hearing his voice would have been for Bethan. She glanced across at the sorrowful girl who was also fearful of the cold disapproval of her parents. Two women who would suffer unreasonably because of the selfishness of her brother Gronwy. Up and up, they wound, past the edge of the wood and onwards into the summer pasture, stopping only once at a spring.

"I was to have married someone else," said Bethan as they plodded on up through the meadows where tall sun-ripened grasses brushed against their legs and slowed their progress, "but when Gronwy came, I let him go even though I loved him and he me. We had known each other since we were small children, but I did not love him as I did Lord Gronwy."

Angharad's stomach turned as she thought of how Gronwy had spoilt this young girl's life.

On and on they went, sometimes startling a buck hare or a pheasant from their hiding places. Finally, they forded a trickle of a stream and, shortly after, arrived at the farm below the towering mountains shimmering silver framed by a cloudless blue sky. Skylarks rose with their piping song into the heavens; blue butterflies flitted from plant to plant, the tranquil scene belying the angst of the two women riding the mountain path.

The farmhouse was a small, humble dwelling constructed of turf and surrounded by a stone wall. Four pregnant black cows ruminated under a tree, and chickens and ducks walked around looking for snails. Everything looked neat and well-tended.

"Stay here," instructed Angharad as she dismounted, tethering Seren to an apple tree branch, causing a shower of blossom. Her heart was pounding as she went forward and knocked at the door, not really knowing what to expect. She looked back at Bethan, who sat white-faced, gripping the reins of the pony, enjoying a feed from the lush grass.

Bethan's father opened the door and, seeing Angharad, he immediately bowed his head. He was a stocky man with rugged features, sunken eyes and cheeks reddened by years of fighting the elements, but he did not look unkind.

"Please, may I come in?"

He looked beyond her to where Bethan was sitting on the pony; his face became rigid.

He moved aside to let Angharad into the small dark dwelling, still staring at his daughter, who shot him a pleading look. Inside, Bethan's mother was at the loom and, when she saw Angharad, jumped up and dropped into a curtsey. They ushered her to a chair and offered her what little refreshment they had, which Angharad declined, although she was glad to be able to discuss the matter at hand with them while seated. Bethan's mother looked worn out, with dark circles under her eyes, and her fingers trembled as she fidgeted with her tunic.

Angharad took a deep breath and, desperately trying to control her own fear and emotions, began with simple honesty,

"This is not easy for me and I do not wish to intrude, but I am afraid that my brother has been intimate with your daughter," she said, hoping the best approach was to deal with matters directly.

The pair looked down, and Angharad noticed that Bethan's mother was shaking. She had the same heart-shaped face and dark hair as her daughter and had obviously been just as beautiful in her youth. Now hard work had left her skin wrinkled and coarse and tiny red lines coursed her cheeks.

"And I understand that you have asked Bethan to leave your home."

Her father now looked up and spoke passionately, "She has shamed us. She was to marry a young farmer from a neighbouring property, a fine young man. She has been headstrong and foolish. Whenever Lord Gronwy had reason to visit us, she allowed her head to be turned and, although we warned her that she was not for the likes of him, she did not heed us."

"What is done is done and cannot be changed. Mistakes are made. I understand that times are hard and that an extra mouth to feed will be difficult, but I thought perhaps if you were willing to take her back," she pulled out the little leather pouch and unfolded the material revealing the silver brooch, "this may help."

The mother gasped, but Angharad held it out to her. She knew the brooch's value and could see from the exchange of glances that the pair were already calculating how this would help them. The father looked away.

"She is so sorry for what she has done," she pressed, "and I am so sorry that my brother took advantage of her good nature. She has nowhere to go, and she is desperately unhappy."

"Is she here?" asked the mother.

"She's outside," said the father gruffly with a backward gesture of his head.

The mother's face brightened. She lifted her skirts and, hastily excusing herself, vanished through the door to her daughter.

"Are you willing to take her back?" persisted Angharad.

The man did not look up but thought for a while and then nodded silently.

"Thank you," said Angharad, pressing the brooch into his hand. She got up swiftly but not before noticing the colour that had flooded his face and how uncomfortable he looked.

"I would not take this if I had a choice," said the father quietly, "but we have the other boys to consider, and times are hard."

Angharad nodded and felt incredible relief as she walked out of the door into the sunshine. Having said her goodbyes to the two women clutching each other at the farm entrance, she started her way back, trotting then cantering as she led the pony Bethan had ridden as if she could escape the reality she had left behind. One obstacle over, now it was time to start considering what she would say to her father.

Could she have acted differently? She was unsure what she could have done. She thought about Gronwy's drinking and gambling. His obsession with dice she knew her father would strongly disapprove of, and he seemed to be becoming more and more objectionable, but what would her father say if he knew how his son had misled the daughter of one of their tenants? He was different from her other brothers somehow and, as the eldest, far from being someone her brothers could look up to as he was frequently aggressive and sour.

She thought of poor Bethan and how smitten she had been by her brother. *Had he shown her any kindness? Had he ever loved her?* Her thoughts meandered and soon she was thinking once again about Hugh the Fat and praying that his stay in Normandy would be a long one. She cringed at the thought of a marriage with such a man. She knew that her father would not have suggested such a thing unless he was almost certain that such a proposal would be taken favourably by Earl Hugh. She shuddered.

As Angharad rode, her thoughts returned to Lord Gruffydd, and she relived the moments of the previous day over and over. She could not tell why she felt guilty about such thoughts: she had done nothing unseemly but there was something about the way that he made her feel that unnerved her. It was a long ride but as she came back towards the valley nearest to her home, she heard the hunt still in progress and was grateful for it. She had time to check on the preparations for the meal and to attend to various household matters before they returned.

Later, the clattering of hooves in the courtyard signalled that Owain would be speaking to Angharad at any moment. She took a deep breath. They had returned with a boar and announced their return with great whoops of joy and calls for the servants to assist them. In anticipation of something being caught, a great fire had been burning ferociously in the courtyard and a spit at the ready. She could hear her father promising that it would be for their supper that night. Then excusing himself and asking his sons to look after their visitors, he came to find her.

"Angharad," he said sternly, "walk with me, please."

A chill wind had come up, and clouds now covered the sky, so Angharad threw her cloak around her, and they walked into the copse away from the visitors in the courtyard. Her father stopped abruptly and turned to face her. They regarded each other in silence. She could see that he was trying to control his fury. She felt the heat rise in her cheeks.

"Are you going to tell me what is going on?" Owain asked frostily.

"Father?" she tried to suppress her anxiety, forcing herself to respond calmly.

"Why were you riding away from the manor with Iori and that young woman?"

"I was taking her home, Father."

"Why?"

Angharad hesitated. "She is pregnant, Father."

"I could see that."

"And unmarried, Father."

"I supposed as much."

"Her parents had asked her to leave their home."

"Quite right. What had it to do with you?"

"She asked me for help?"

"Why you, Angharad?"

"She is one of our tenants?"

She saw a faint spark of realisation in his expression.

"Who is the father of her child, Angharad?"

Angharad looked at him blankly, her eyes wide and appalled.

"Well," he persisted

"Gronwy."

"Gronwy!" Owain exploded. "Gronwy!"

"Father, please…."

"You have betrayed my trust, Angharad. You have gone behind my back, colluding with Gronwy."

"No, Father, he does not know anything."

"What?"

"I kept it to myself, Father."

"Except for Iori. By now, all the servants will be tittle-tattling."

"No, Father, he would never say a word."

"So, you have made him a party to your deception. And I suppose you have paid off the family with money from our household coffers."

"No, Father, I did not. I gave them my brooch."

At first, he looked confused, then his eyes flashed with contempt and his lips thinned. "Your mother's silver brooch? The brooch I gave her on the day we were married?"

Angharad could hold in her tears no longer.

"I have given you everything, Angharad. I have given you an education, treated you as an equal with your brothers and made you mistress of this household, but you have bitten the hand that feeds you, girl. You are devoid of principle! Get out of my sight."

Angharad's mind was a turmoil of shock. She felt as if her father had disowned her. She felt empty, worthless and dirty. She ran back to the house and into her chamber to compose herself, washing her face and trying to calm down. Her father had never spoken to anyone like that before. She knelt below the little cross on her wall and started to pray for forgiveness when the door burst open. She turned around and rose unsteadily to her feet as Gronwy strode into the room, furious and wild-eyed.

"You bitch!" he shouted, "You vicious bitch. You will be sorry for this, I grant you!"

He glared at her with loathing; then he turned on his heel to leave when he suddenly leapt back at her, hitting her across the head with the flat of his hand so that she flew across the room, landing against her wooden garment chest. She looked up in shock, but Gronwy had vanished. She had never been struck before, had never thought that someone would want to harm her physically, let alone her brother, in the sanctuary of her chamber. Gingerly she got to her feet and looked into the shined bronze mirror. She would have bruises on her head and hip. She was dishevelled but nothing marked her as the victim of an assault. She did not want to draw attention to herself in front of the guests she must shortly face.

She started and swung around as she heard a sound at the door but it was Meilyr looking at his sister, whose face was painfully white as she clung to the doorframe.

"Are you alright?"

She nodded, her throat tight and hardly trusting herself to speak.

"You know?" she said finally in an almost inaudible whisper.

"I overheard Father and Gronwy. Father is furious."

"I know, Father is angry with me for deceiving him." She explained the situation to him in a shaking voice, omitting to mention Gronwy's attack, and Meilyr listened attentively.

"This will blow over, Angharad. You should have come to me. I would have dealt with it."

Angharad shook her head.

He put his arm around her shoulders to console her. "We have guests, and Father will need you to put on a good face. Come, pay no attention. It is not your fault. You know Father will be angrier with the shame of what Gronwy has done more than anything else. Reputation is hard won and easily lost. We cannot do anything about it now. Let things settle down, and I will speak to Father."

By the time Angharad reached the hall, the servants were already putting out the trestles and boards in readiness for the evening's feast. As they waited for the main meats to cook, small delicacies and Welsh ale were being served. Seeing the preparations, she slipped into her familiar role as hostess. She felt as if she was part of two different worlds: in one, she was a deceitful disobedient daughter, traitorous hated sister and victim, and in the other world, she was capable, well thought of by the household staff and frequently complimented by guests.

Angharad had begun to recover from her father's wrath and the incident with Gronwy, and although her father was frosty with her, it was less so than earlier on. Gronwy glowered at her from across the room, but she just attended to the various needs of their guests and her family, and within an hour or so, the atmosphere in the room was congenial, other than Gronwy drinking more heavily than ever.

Gruffydd's men, Hywel and Aeddan, were animated as they chatted to Rhydir and Meilyr about a huge white stag they had seen when they were travelling in Powys one early morning. These tall, strong men had seemed so hostile when she had first met them some months ago but now she realised that they were friendly, down to earth and no shirkers from hard work or hard living. Aeddan was the livelier of the two, with an engaging grin and easy laugh, and Hywel was almost shy but the first to offer help.

Llywarch and Meirion were playing a board game together with pieces made of antlers that Llywarch had carved himself. Meirion had the serious expression of a man further on in years than himself. His face was long and sallow, his eyes large and doleful, but when he did smile, which was not often, it would light up his whole face.

"Have you ever played Hazzard?" asked Gronwy sullenly as he loomed over them.

"I am no good with dice," confessed Meirion. "I would rather save my luck for when I really need it!"

"Gronwy thinks of nothing else, well almost nothing else," said Llywarch, his dark eyes flashing with cheek but receiving a ferocious scowl from his brother.

Huge platters of freshly cooked boar were brought into the hall along with newly baked bread, mounds of vegetables, as well as cheeses, pies and pottage. The young men were ravenous after their exertions, but Angharad noticed that her father ate and drank little. She, too, had little appetite, something which Gruffydd noticed.

"Lady Angharad, can I pass you some meat? The acorns in your woods have made this boar one of the sweetest I have tasted."

"Thank you, Lord Gruffydd, I will take a little. After all the efforts of your hunting men, it would be a shame not to enjoy it!'

The meal ended, and everyone retired to the fire, which was small only because it was summer.

"Play for us, Angharad," called Meilyr. Angharad made her way to her harp and played a sad lilting melody befitting her mood. Gruffydd smiled across the room at her and, despite her feelings, she could not help but smile back.

"My Lord Gruffydd, you sing as well as any man," said Meirion, "we should repay our hosts with the sound of your fine voice."

Gruffydd's brow flew up, and he looked embarrassed. "Ah, there are much finer voices around the hall than mine."

"Please," said Owain, "and Angharad will play for you. It is a welcome gift to hear the hall resound to a new voice."

"Then I cannot refuse," said Gruffydd, his expansive smile lighting his face as he strode across the room to take his place next to the beautiful harpist.

"What will you sing, Lord Gruffydd?" asked Angharad.

"The song of Pwyll's love for Rhiannon," said Gruffydd.

Angharad smiled in agreement, and her fingers easily plucked the melody as Gruffydd's deep baritone filled the room. She could not help looking up at this fine man who stood at her side and tried to put everything else out of her mind. He would leave the following day, and she wanted to savour this last evening. She would deal with what lay ahead later. Meanwhile, Gronwy watched the two pensively like a rat smelling something more between them than singer and harpist. He watched his sister's smiling face, clearly besotted with this man, and he stroked his chin.

When Gruffydd finished singing, there was hearty appreciation and a call to sing again, which he did. By the end of the evening, Owain himself was tapping his feet to the rhythm as everyone joined in different well-known songs.

The night ended well but Angharad slept fitfully and was up when she heard a clatter of hooves in the courtyard as Iori readied the horses for Gruffydd and his men. She looked out and saw that he had been up early. The visitors' horses looked well brushed with bridles, saddles, bits, straps and all leather gear shining like new. She had hastily chosen a simple blue tunic which, although she didn't realise it, set off her eyes and showed the curves of her increasingly womanly figure. She bustled around to ensure they all had something to eat and drink before they left and packed food to take with them for the journey.

Gruffydd came over to speak with her, and she blushed at the attention.

"I thank you for the kind hospitality, Lady Angharad," he said tranquilly, his large eyes sparkling with genuine pleasure.

"It was very little compared to you helping us with the mews and teaching me to fly my hawk better."

"A pleasure. I enjoyed it very much. I do hope we will have the opportunity to go hawking again soon."

She felt a rush of sadness, and before she could stop herself, she blurted out, "Stay safe, Lord Gruffydd. You and your men."

Angharad felt someone standing too close behind her and half turned to see her eldest brother. She quickly sidestepped, almost expecting another blow.

"I would like to add my thanks to you, Lord Gruffydd," he said with forced charm. "We will expect our gyrfalcon any day now, and the mews will be a fine home for her."

"I hope so," said Gruffydd pleased, "and perhaps I might see her flying before too long."

"Of course," said Gronwy. "We will all be here unless Angharad has deserted us for Earl Hugh by then."

Gruffydd flinched as if he had been struck. Angharad stepped back and looked appalled that Gronwy should raise such a matter before Gruffydd.

Gronwy feigned surprise and gave a short, mirthless laugh, "Oh, I am sorry, sister; I thought it was common knowledge Father had been discussing your future with Earl Hugh."

Angharad's cheeks were burning with shame that she should not have felt. She looked at Gruffydd, but he gave a curt nod and thin smile. Then, seeing Owain, he strode across the courtyard to express his thanks before vaulting into his saddle in great haste.

"You thought that was your way out, did you, Angharad?" whispered Gronwy viciously in her ear, "Well, not anymore, I think! Besides, Earl Hugh was my idea, one of my better ones. I told Father how important 'position' was to you. He thought it was very clever!"

An involuntary sob caught in Angharad's throat. Gruffydd reached the gate and, with a stiff bow from the saddle, spurred his horse on, his men close in behind him, leaving a cloud of dust that slowly settled as they vanished out of sight.

"Stay safe, Lord Gruffydd. You and your men." mimicked Gronwy in a high whining voice in Angharad's ear.

Angharad found herself unable to speak. Forcing back angry tears, the young woman turned on her heel and, trembling with hurt, headed for her chamber, where she flung herself on her bed, trying to come to terms with what she was feeling. It was not only humiliation. What she had felt when she was with Gruffydd had been so deep, so intense, but she had not allowed herself to continue down the path of imagining that they could be together. There were so many obstacles to such a course: her father's position and relationship with the Normans; her father's intentions to secure their family position by an alliance with Earl Hugh, Gruffydd's sworn enemy, but now, even if the other objections could be overcome and even if Gruffydd had a fondness for her, Gronwy's comments would have cast her as someone who was already spoken for.

Angharad felt immeasurably sad, though her common sense told her she needed to put aside things she could do nothing about. Her response to Gronwy's comments was irrational, she told herself, even though he had shown a lack of any social grace in discussing what would be private family affairs. The extent of his anger towards her was utterly unfair since she had been trying to help him and protect their family's reputation from the thoughtlessness of his actions. Fostering such indignation was fruitless, she decided finally, and she resolved to try to repair the relationships she had with her family, to accept that above all, she must honour her father and, hard as it was to try to forget about Lord Gruffydd, who had made her so happy for those brief few days.

Chapter 7: Robert of Rhuddlan (July 1093)

July had arrived hot and dry. All the farmers were busy with haymaking, sheep-shearing and ploughing the fallow fields. The days were long, and everyone was active, making the most of the dry spell. Things had thawed between Angharad and her father. He was in perfect humour as his gyrfalcon had arrived to great excitement and was even more spectacular than he had imagined. The great white bird dominated everyone's thoughts. Owain and her brothers spent long hours training and flying her. One day, however, Owain called her aside and handed her a small package. She looked up at him with confusion.

"Open it," he said, watching her intently.

She opened the package carefully and gasped as she revealed her mother's brooch. He had sought out the hill farmer and exchanged it for an acceptable sum of money before it changed hands elsewhere.

She was delighted and moved. Even Owain smiled when he saw her face light up.

"I was very harsh with you, Angharad. I know how much that brooch meant to you, and I see that you sacrificed it rather than coming to me for money. I also recognise that your act was one of common humanity. I am still disappointed, however, with the deceitfulness, even though I do understand the motivation. I would hope there will not be any error in judgment in the future."

This was as near to an apology for his harsh treatment of her as she might ever expect from her father, and she felt an incredible lifting of the burden she had carried in the last weeks. From then on, things improved between them, although he seemed less inclined to spend time with her alone as he had done previously. She missed those times but had so much to do to run the household, especially as harvest approached, and she was well occupied.

Gronwy refused to speak with his sister, but she kept trying, always remaining polite and considerate. She often wondered about Bethan on the hillside and whether her little niece or nephew had yet been born. Gronwy, of course, never mentioned them, but from what she could tell, he was less obvious in pursuing his lusts, at least leaving the servants alone at the manor, no matter how his eyes roamed. She had noticed that the women, while still wary of him, now moved around the manor more freely and were not, as before, quite so nervy when they were completing tasks alone.

Over the weeks that followed Gruffydd's departure, she had schooled herself to think of him less often. It was not easy. She would often revisit their time flying her falcon or the time they spent enjoying music in the evening, but then she would try to focus on whatever she was doing and pray that she might lessen her longing for that time together.

One morning, Angharad had meandered down to visit the little church in the valley below, where she felt immense solace. She had a close relationship with the priest, Father Luke, whom she had known since childhood. He was a grey-haired man with a flat nose, wide forehead, and generous mouth, and he was equally quick to laugh or show compassion. His hazel eyes were intelligent and thoughtful. The church was so close that nobody needed to accompany her. She enjoyed the freedom of riding alone on the dusty baked track, the scent of Seren's sun-warm maned mingling with the aroma of newly cut hay.

"How are you, Father Luke?" she asked after she had spent a little time in prayer in the little church and noticed the priest was not looking his usual cheerful self.

"I shouldn't complain as there are many who have greater troubles, but it is difficult times for the Welsh church, my lady."

"Is it all the pressure to conform to the Norman way of doing things?"

"That and to submit to the authority of the English Archbishop of Canterbury. It is no secret that our congregation and we as priests have huge disagreements with the Bishop of Bangor."

"Hervey le Breton," said Angharad.

"Indeed. You will understand when I say, confidentially, that his appointment was put in place last year by the Earl of Chester to gain further control of Gwynedd. It has not gone down well, and you know he is forced to carry a sword around with him, which he uses on those he should not have. Everywhere he goes, he has a group of Norman knights protecting him. A fine way for a man of God to behave."

Angharad lifted her eyebrows in surprise.

"Still, he keeps excommunicating anyone who challenges his authority. They are determined to bring the independent Welsh church under Roman influence. It has been worse since the Life of St David was written and distributed throughout the church. They want us to stop writing about the Welsh saints and those who influenced our religion. They even insist on stopping us from passing on our Welsh history and learning. Everything that makes the church in Wales special and meaningful to our people they want to replace with Roman ideas and Norman rules."

He shook his head and then added bitterly. "They are insisting that priests should not marry or that the children of priests should not inherit their clerical posts."

"I hear that in the south, they are already expecting the congregation to pay a tenth of their income to support the priests."

"They will also force it here and draw boundaries to show which church someone must belong to. I can't see any harm in the way we run things now. Think of all the learning that will be lost along with our art and culture that the church supports."

Angharad knew how vital the church had been in her education and how she turned to the stories of the Welsh saints for inspiration in trying times. It also did not seem natural to her that priests should be forced to be celibate, especially when their family lives were an example for the families of their congregation. Indeed, having family yourself would mean that you could better understand the problems that families might encounter.

As they were deep in conversation, a distraught-looking young man burst into the chapel, shouting hysterically that Robert of Rhuddlan had been killed. "He's dead! He's dead!" the man wailed, terrified.

The priest ran to him, holding him by the shoulder as the man almost collapsed, trying to catch his breath.

"Slow down, slow down, sit here. What are you saying?"

Trembling as he stuttered out his news, the messenger began his horrific tale. "There has been an attack. Three ships have sailed under Great Orme and have pillaged all the land in the area. They set the buildings at the castle alight and ravaged it."

The priest crossed himself. "And Lord Robert?"

"Lord Robert was having a noonday sleep at Deganwy when the news was brought to him. He immediately galloped there with a few of his men, thinking to stop what was happening."

"Go on," encouraged the priest while Angharad felt the grip of fear in her stomach.

"When they got to the cliffs, they saw that the attackers, the Welsh, had taken captives and were binding them ready to become slaves and driving cattle ahead of them to the ships as well."

"Welsh, you say?"

"The attackers were Welsh. Lord Robert was in a dark fury. He demanded that his followers rush the Welsh on the dry sand below before the tide came in, and they could sail away, but…" he stopped for breath.

"But?"

"But they wouldn't follow him. They said the mountain was too dangerous to go down, so only Robert and Osbern d'Orgeres, his shield bearer, went down, not afeared of the steepness. The Welsh hurled their spears, and Robert was protected only by his shield. Osbern was killed immediately. Dropped like a stone. Robert kept fighting, but eventually he too was killed, and they cut off his head and fixed it to their masthead."

Angharad gasped, horrified by what she heard, and the priest crossed himself again.

"Then some of Lord Robert's men did give chase in boats, and finally, the attackers threw Robert of Rhuddlan's head into the sea."

Angharad sat down heavily. Her first instinct was one of abhorrence. Could this have been Gruffydd? Could that be the same man, so gentle with her, so kind to everyone, the same man who had sung of love, commit the barbaric act of beheading someone? Surely, it was enough to kill someone, but deliberately beheading them was against all human nature. She felt sick, her stomach churning. The shock made her feel weak, so she struggled to breathe. She prayed silently that it was not Gruffydd who had done this.

"Who was leading the Welsh?" asked Father Luke. Angharad's heart froze at the question, terrified of the answer.

"I do not know, Father, but I know they had three ships, is all."

"And they took some of Lord Robert's people captive and took his cattle, too?"

"Yes, they did indeed."

The priest shook his head, closed his eyes, and deeply breathed. How often had he taught against looting, stealing cattle, burning buildings and capturing men and women who would end up as slaves? Were the Welsh any better than the Normans? And there would be repercussions!

"Where are they taking Lord Robert's body?"

"To Chester, Father."

"There will be a price to pay for this!" the grey-faced priest warned. "The fury of the Normans will be upon us all no matter if we were no part of it."

"I must go back to the manor and warn my family," gasped Angharad, standing unsteadily as the gravity of what had occurred sunk in.

"Everyone must be aware of what has happened and be prepared for retaliation," the priest warned gravely. "Your father will know what is best to do."

Angharad made her way outside to where Seren chomped the grass surrounding the little church. Birds swooped to catch insects, and, in the fields, she heard children's laughter. It seemed impossible that the scene was so peaceful as if nothing had changed, yet everything had been turned upside down in her world. She left the two men without further delay and galloped Seren back along the fastest route.

Her father had already heard the news and was deep in discussion with his sons about what to do. He looked pale and concerned, but a look of relief crossed his face as he saw his daughter safe at home.

"This is the start of it, Father!" said Llywarch excitedly. "This is the beginning of the fightback they have all been talking about. We should go to Uncle Uchdryd and see what the plans are."

"You are not going anywhere," said Owain sternly, grabbing his youngest son painfully by the ear. "First, you are too young, and secondly, we do not want to show our hand yet either way."

"Father, this is how we will learn to fight," Llywarch began to protest, but he stopped abruptly when his father glowered at him.

"It is not all about fighting, Llywarch; avoiding the fight is harder. Do not be so anxious to give up your life, Llywarch. Death comes soon enough." Owain chastised him sharply. "Never take these things lightly. Do not forget that you might throw yourself into a fight, but others would then feel duty-bound to fight alongside you. Think of the consequences."

"So, what are we going to do?" sneered Gronwy, still at odds with his father, "Nothing, I suppose!"

"Gronwy," returned his father savagely, "if you want to stay part of this family, you respect me and do as I see fit as long as I am the head. Do you understand? Do you?"

Gronwy's face was like thunder, but he nodded his assent and looked away. Owain then beckoned everyone to draw near. He spoke quickly with firm decision.

"Angharad, did you hear anything about where they will take the body?"

"They are taking the body to Chester, Father."

"Then I will go to Chester, but I had better look in at Rhuddlan first and try to settle any commotion there!" decided Owain. "Meanwhile, you talk of fighting. I want to barricade every weakness this manor has with whatever carts or ploughs you can find. I want every able man with bows and swords ready. We don't know how this will turn out. With Earl Hugh still in Normandy, it is unlikely there will be an immediate attack, but I am not taking any chances. Can you make sure we have good supplies of arrows, Rhydir? Bury the valuables until we are sure what is happening."

"Of course, Father."

"Meilyr, you arrange for Iori to get men and take our livestock and spare horses up to the high pastures. Every one of you, you understand, every one of you must stay here and be prepared, night and day until I return."

Owain's children agreed, and he continued. "Angharad, send for extra provisions to cover us if we cannot go out. We have our well here inside the courtyard, but I want every container filled with water in case we have fires to deal with."

The young woman nodded and started mentally calculating what to do.

"Llywarch, some of the men are handy with slings, so you are responsible for ensuring we have stones for shots. I want large stones piled in case we need to hurl them. Most of the valley will know by now, but I will let each farm I pass know there may be trouble and ask them to spread the word. Gronwy, you are in charge here until I return, and everyone follows your instruction in my absence."

Gronwy looked at his father in surprise, and the other siblings exchanged glances. Owain was aware of their interaction and ignored it.

Angharad endeavoured not to show her despair as the reality of their situation sank in.

"So, we are truly fighting the Normans?" asked Llywarch, puzzled as his father's instructions seemed contrary to what he had initially said.

"No, we are not, Llywarch. We are doing nothing, but if it comes to it and we are attacked, we will defend ourselves. Is that clear? I want no heroics or aggression. Just stay calm and do nothing other than what I have instructed you. Gronwy will make the decisions, and you will take his lead. You do not leave here until I return, do you understand?"

They all nodded, even Gronwy, who seemed pleased about his father's acknowledgement.

Meilyr had been thoughtful for a while but said, "The timing of the attack is clever because now is the hay-making season. That would have been wealth in Robert of Rhuddlan's coffers, which now stays with the farmers. Robert doesn't have heirs, Father, so who will take over his land?"

"Not legitimate heirs, no, and I suspect Earl Hugh will see this as an opportunity for himself when word gets to him. Anyway, I must see how it all falls out. Meanwhile, do not contact Uchdryd under any circumstance. Do you understand?"

"But Father," protested Rhydir, "we have been side by side with Uncle Uchdryd. What if he contacts us?"

"Gronwy will know what to do. Be polite but non-committal. Are you clear?"

"Yes, Father."

"And if I do not return or send a message to you, then Gronwy, you need to protect the family and what is ours as best you can. At that point, you need to enlist Uchdryd's help."

A cold chill ran down her back, and Angharad felt her heart pounding as she watched her father ride under the gateway, which held their family coat of arms, with three men's legs conjoined at the thigh in a triangle argent. How easily it could be ripped down and destroyed with the rest of their home.

Her brothers started to put everything in motion. Gronwy took charge and rose to the occasion, with the servants and his brothers responding well. This was a side of him she had rarely seen. He walked around the manor's stone wall, looking for signs of weakness. Ammunition for bows and slings was collected and put at points around the manor wall. Ladders were brought to the entrance, and some extra ladders were made so that all walls were protected and could be scaled if necessary. A pile of ash wood shafts was assembled, ready to take the iron spearheads that the smith was already turning out in his forge. Piles of extra logs were brought and lined the main wall. Horses were saddled and ready for a quick escape if need be. Servants were instructed on how to assist the bowmen and those using slings. They were also told to run for the woods and to split up if they were overcome.

Angharad took her mother's silver brooch and some household valuables and asked Rhydir to add them to the collection he would bury.

"What will happen, Rhydir?" she asked, her voice taut and brittle.

"Hopefully, Father will be able to smooth things over, but right now, if I were a Norman, I would want heads to roll for what happened. If Earl Hugh were here, he would already be marching into Wales before other people get the same ideas about rebellion, but praise the Lord, he is in Normandy. Robert was his cousin and would want revenge, but he may see an opportunity here. There is a fair chance he will take Robert's land for himself."

"But what if the Welsh join forces and try to regain the land?" she persisted.

"Then it becomes interesting:" he replied calmly, watching Gronwy directing a group of men to reinforce the palisade.

"Would the Welsh see us as traitors if we side with the Normans? Do we have to fear aggression from our neighbours?"

Rhydir thought momentarily and concluded, "I can't imagine that our family are seen in that light. If it weren't for Father, things would be much more difficult for the farmers around here. That is known; you only must look at other parts of Wales and what happens under Norman rule. Anyway, we are wise to protect ourselves just now."

"Would Lord Gruffydd hurt us?"

"No, I do not believe he would. Not unless we were the ones to threaten him."

Angharad felt real fear, not of Lord Gruffydd but of Norman reprisals. She knew how brutal the Normans could be and shook her head to think that only this morning she was riding around the countryside alone. Now, they were erecting barricades. Adding to her misery was the barbarity of the beheading, and the horror only grew in her imagination. Wherever she went within the manor, this was the focal point of the talk, that and how vengeful the Normans were likely to be.

***

Gronwy had the servants fill every container with water as instructed in case of fire from burning arrows, and the women looked terrified. Angharad worked alongside them and reassured them that these were only precautionary measures, yet she felt empty inside. When all was as prepared as possible, Angharad called them together in prayer and afterwards suggested that they get to rest. Who knows what would be happening over the following days?

Rhydir and Llywarch, then Gronwy and Meilyr, took turns resting and then staying on vigil through the night, but all was quiet. Iori returned early the following day and reported that he had heard nothing more other than that Rhuddlan castle was empty and that the guards from there who remained had accompanied Robert of Rhuddlan's body to Chester. Angharad felt ill and uneasy, concerned at what was before them and shocked and still distressed at the possibility that Gruffydd may well be responsible for beheading Lord Robert and of taking captives. The idea of people being bound and sent into slavery disgusted her, and while she knew that many of the workers in Gwynedd were slaves, she had not before come face to face with the reality of their capture.

They all endured three long days of anguished suspense until their father returned, grim-faced and tired, but they all felt a sense of relief. He sat the family down to discuss what he had done over the previous days.

"Rhuddlan castle is a mess," he said gravely. "The raiders burned, destroyed and left it a shell. There was nobody there by the time I arrived. They had captured Robert's servants, apart from a few slaves who had run off and returned only when the raiders had gone. I sent them to the priest at Rhuddlan, and he will try to find new homes for them. The guards had accompanied the body to Chester."

"Is Robert of Rhuddlan already buried?" asked Meilyr.

"Yes, I helped to arrange the service for him at the new abbey of St Werburgh the Virgin. The Earl of Chester has only recently finished building the monastery. He appointed Richard, a monk of Bec, to establish a band of devotees there, and so it seemed the most appropriate place for a Norman knight and cousin of the Earl of Chester. I arranged for the bards to create fitting music and poetry to send Robert of Rhuddlan on his journey, and it looked well that I was there giving tribute. After fifteen years of sheer brutality, he will not be missed in these parts, but I glossed over that and spoke of his prowess as a warrior."

"Is it true, Father, that Lord Robert was beheaded?" asked Angharad, still haunted by that thought.

"It is," her father replied.

"Father, was this Gruffydd ap Cynan's doing?" asked Angharad, hoping against all hope for an answer she knew in her heart would not be forthcoming.

85

"Yes, he and his cousin of the same name."

Angharad's heart sank. Confirmation of what she had dreaded to hear. "I can hardly believe such a man as stayed with us here could do such a barbaric thing."

Owain looked thoughtful. "He is a man who is not afraid of conflict but is no animal. His cousin will have done the beheading. The cousin was imprisoned for many years in Chester. He has an old grudge against Robert of Rhuddlan and the Marcher lords from years ago; this will be just the start of it."

"I have heard that story from Uncle Uchdryd," said Llywarch. "The older Gruffydd ap Cynan was tricked into capture by Hugh the Fat. He was in the shackles at Chester when a blacksmith from Edeirion, Cynwrig Hir, came with some companions to buy necessities. They say he saw Gruffydd in the city square while all the burgesses were eating, and as he was unguarded, they carried him away and managed to knock off his shackles. They hid him in their own homes for a few nights and then took him to Anglesey, where he hid with supporters."

"It is true," said Owain. "He has been in Deheubarth hiding in caves apparently and getting much support to oust the Normans. I understand that he has also been over in Ireland and gained more support there. Meanwhile, he and the younger Gruffydd have been seeking help from Godred, King of Dublin and the Isles of Man and the Hebrides."

"Why would Godred be interested in helping Gruffydd?" asked Rhydir, puzzled.

"Family links in part; their families are descended from Olaf Sihtricson, and he owes Gruffydd for assisting him in battle, but more than that, there's trade. There has been solid trade between Wales, the Islands and the Irish Norsemen. The Normans threaten those trade routes, and so it is for their benefit to assist Wales to remain Welsh," explained Owain.

"So where does that leave us?" asked Gronwy bluntly.

"I do not consider myself a warrior, and I do not see my place at the head of a fighting band, though I would if I were pushed to it. What I have tried to do, and I want you to learn from this, is to forge a middle way. There is a vacuum in this part of Gwynedd now, and the Normans want order more than anything else in Wales. I have been to Chester in person, seen by all, and offered that I continue, as before, to oversee the orderly functioning of the lands that were Robert's. When Earl Hugh returns, he doubtless expects to take over those lands, with Robert being his cousin and indebted to his uncle for assisting in his expansion. I am sure those lands are already his in the earl's mind. If, however, Gruffydd's campaign is successful, we will not oppose him but bend with the winds."

"So, we are safe, Father?" asked Angharad, considering the information doubtfully.

"What is safe, Angharad? None of us is 'safe'. Yesterday is yesterday; today is today, and tomorrow is tomorrow. We do not know what will happen; all we can do is watch, glean information and stay out of sight as much as possible. What we have now is a comfortable life. I am one of the fifteen chief lords of North Wales. I would like to hand that honour to my heirs intact, but I have to be very, very careful, or we could lose everything. At this moment, are we likely to be stormed by Normans or Gruffydd and his men? No. The Normans are invested in troubles in Normandy and are distracted. Gruffydd needs time to galvanise his forces and concentrate on that, but we must be careful what we say and to whom we say it and keep our eyes down. Do you understand?"

They all nodded their agreement, and soon, the barricade was dismantled. Everyone was cautious, but life slowly fell back into familiar patterns. Angharad had much to occupy herself with running the household, but when she found herself in quiet moments, her thoughts would plague her. She found it impossible to focus on even the simplest embroidery or reading. She tried vainly to quell her restlessness. Each day Earl Hugh remained in Normandy, Angharad said a prayer of relief.

Angharad could not help but think of Gruffydd and was unsettled by that feeling that she had had, an intimacy almost, and her certainty that they should have been together. How could she have been so mistaken? How could she have been deceived into believing him such a good man when he had behaved no better than a barbarian? Had she thought that, somehow, he would save her from what now seemed a certain destiny with a Norman tyrant? What reality existed beneath the polished exterior he presented to the world? Try as she might, her thoughts kept returning to him; his looks and small kindnesses had imprinted themselves on her memory. She consoled herself that, whatever her future, those few days they had spent together could never be taken away from her.

Within a short time, as Owain had hoped, news had arrived from the Earl of Chester asking Owain to take governorship of Robert of Rhuddlan's lands and to do what he could to maintain the status quo. The earl also confirmed his intention to absorb Robert's lands into his own, and until he was back, he did not want headaches to deal with. Owain was now Earl Hugh's most senior representative in Gwynedd. Owain would not be expected to fight against his own people but to ensure Earl Hugh got his dues and kept his lands intact.

"If I had not acted quickly," Owain explained to his family, "we might have lost everything. Overseeing the funeral and settling things down worked to my advantage. I had to be visible at those crucial times and be seen as separate from Gruffydd's attack. I also had to water down any concern over ongoing danger and relay the message that this was just an opportunist event and retaliation from the elder Gruffydd for his imprisonment."

"But if Gruffydd mounts further attacks, what then?" asked Meilyr reasonably.

"Then we deal with that when it happens. Enough for now that we are not impacted, and while Earl Hugh is in Normandy, we have time to work out a suitable response."

Things did seem, once again, to settle down. Summer passed, and autumn flooded their world with colour as squirrels ran from tree to tree, burying their nuts for the challenging months ahead, and glossy blackberries were abundant on bushes. Elderberries hung heavy with rich purple juice. The pungent smell of cut grass wafted from the barn, and the granary was bulging with sacks holding wheat, oats and barley. Apples and pears were ladening branches, and hips and haws were redolent. This was a plentiful time in the agricultural lands surrounding them, and spirits were high.

Something had been on Angharad's mind for some time, and she waited for a suitable moment when she might catch her father alone and in good humour. One morning, her chance came when she found him alone in the mews, feeding small titbits of chicken to his gyrfalcon. The bird was stunning, snow white with black spotting on its wings and body and immediately turned to look at her with sharp eyes.

"She is beautiful," she whispered as she went inside, gently avoiding disturbing the birds.

"Beautiful but, like most beautiful things, dangerous," mused her father. "To be handled with great care."

Angharad waited a moment, then she said cautiously, "Father, at the time of the haymaking, I know I disappointed you by deceiving you. I have learnt from that, and I would now ask your permission for something I would like to do but of which you may not approve."

Owain looked at her carefully.

"Father, by this time, Gronwy must have a son or a daughter, and I would like to visit the mother and child with some small gifts."

Owain turned fully to face her and asked in a chilly tone, "Why would you open old wounds, Angharad? Money has been given to them, and you going there can only inflame a situation which is hitherto under control."

"Because the little child is my little niece or nephew because Gronwy made promises he did not keep and because I feel it is the right thing to do."

Owain stroked the breast feathers of his gyrfalcon and then turned to her, his eyes frosty so that she almost regretted her request.

"I strongly advise you against it, but I will not stop you. If you insist on going, take one of your brothers with you, not Gronwy, obviously and stay cautious."

As she walked away across the courtyard, she reminded Owain of his wife. He sighed. Angharad was a woman now, there was no doubt. She was well educated with astute intelligence and an agile mind. Maybe her mind was too agile, and he resolved to move ahead to secure an arrangement with Earl Hugh. The right time had not yet presented itself. Still, perhaps with the unrest, a suitable Welsh bride boasting descent from both Welsh and Mercian royalty, a woman of exquisite beauty, capable and god-fearing, would be regarded all the more advantageously. He looked down, stroked his gyrfalcon gently, and thought about what a coup it would be to bring respect and security to the family. In his mind's eye, he could already see himself visiting his daughter in Chester castle, his grandchildren learning from the most educated tutors, developing their equestrian prowess and martial skills from the Master of Horse and the Master of Arms. Yes, what a coup that would be.

A few days later, Angharad woke early, marvelling at the dazzle of icy stars in the cloudless firmament. Frost had carpeted their world, and as the sun lifted itself into the sky, the world shone as if diamond strewn. Angharad and Meilyr mounted their horses and journeyed from the frosted valley floor through woods where icicles sparkled and moss covered the rocks and trees. They rode into the high pastures with the grace of the mountains looming ahead. The air was clear and pure, and the stillness of the crisp, magical morning touched their souls.

Meilyr led the way, armed now with his sword and a knife, but he was not expecting to need to use them. The Normans rarely ventured into the hills or mountains, and this was not a place where thieves were common. They journeyed upwards, only stopping for water at a crystal spring where the water was refreshing and sweet. There were few people to meet up here, and though wisps of smoke scattered beyond the pastures indicated that there were dwellings, it felt as if this world was theirs alone. A small, heavily laden boy was ambling along the path leading a placid bull. He stopped to gaze at them as they greeted him, smiled shyly and plodded silently on.

As they ascended, there were patches of snow in places left over from the last snowfall. When they finally got to the small holding up beyond the meadows, they slipped off their horses and went to knock at the door. They could hear someone chopping wood nearby and had time to notice the neat stone-enclosed farmyard with a pig pen, several plump chickens and a fine cock strutting around.

Bethan came to the door, and as she saw Angharad, her face broke into a charming smile. Angharad introduced her brother, and the girl led them inside. In a wooden cradle next to a loom which Bethan had just vacated was the tiniest baby wrapped in a woollen blanket.

The mother lifted the baby and held the sleeping angel out to Angharad, "His name is Rhys," she whispered, kissing his little downy head.

Angharad held the almost weightless little mite in her arms, looking down at his tiny face and smelling his milky sweetness. He looked healthy and strong. She could see Gronwy's firm jawline but his mother's attractive heart-shaped face.

Bethan's mother came in from milking their half dozen cows and was delighted to see Angharad and her brother. She had the same wide-eyed beauty as her daughter, but her face was lined by work and weather.

"I saw the horses. We don't get many visitors up here, so I was worried, but I am so happy to see you," she gabbled to cover her nervousness.

Everything in the household was simple but neat and clean. Fresh straw was on the earthen floor, and the fire roared and cracked brightly. Beside the fire, logs and kindling were stacked neatly in baskets woven from reeds. She noticed how clean both mother and daughter's clothes were, even though they were made of rough, heavy wool against the cold, and there were many repairs. A big pot boiled on the fire, and the stew inside smelt delicious, flavoured with mountain herbs.

The mother and daughter were enormously grateful for the pack of gifts the pair had brought, including some cloth, blankets and foodstuffs. They touched everything with reverence and thanked the pair again and again.

When her mother went to get some refreshments for them, Bethan quietly asked, "How is Gronwy?"

Angharad replied guardedly that he was well.

"I am glad," said Bethan generously, and her voice had no longing. She seemed pretty content with her life on the farm with her tiny child. "Without your help, I am unsure what would have happened to us. I am a hard worker, but not many will take on a servant with a baby."

They did not stay long as they did not want to impose on the family, but as they returned down the mountain, the siblings reflected on the simplicity of the farming family's lives.

"Hard work but honest work," said Meilyr.

"It is hard work. Backbreaking work for much of the year. They don't seem to mind it. Bethan is so beautiful," mused Angharad, "it is such a shame that Gronwy did not think to marry her."

"Angharad, you are such a dreamer and want the best for everyone, but you know better than that," retorted Meilyr. "Our spouses are not whom we may wish to marry. Our spouses are chosen for us to do honour to our family, to protect our families. Gronwy is the eldest son, so he must make a cautious alliance that will be useful. It would have been unthinkable for him to have married someone who brought nothing in return. She is beautiful, I grant you, sweet-natured, and you can see that she has pride in herself and her child, but, Angharad, such a marriage would not further our family."

"I know," admitted Angharad sadly. "I do know that, really. I was just thinking out loud that I wished things were different."

Meilyr thought for a while and then said, "You were thinking about yourself as well, weren't you and wishing Father was not so committed to suggesting an alliance with Earl Hugh when he returns?"

"In part, I thought maybe….," she began and then checked herself abruptly.

"You thought that maybe Lord Gruffydd would take you away to Anglesey, and Father would consider it a good match?"

Angharad's eyes shot up to Meilyr's, and she blushed deeply.

"We could all see that you liked him, and he certainly seemed to like you. There will be many such encounters, and you can enjoy them, but in the end, your marriage will be made by Father."

Angharad closed her eyes and, not denying it, blurted out, "Gronwy told Lord Gruffydd about Father's intentions, you know."

"With Earl Hugh?"

"Yes."

"That was to pay you back for telling Father about Bethan, I warrant."

"Yes, I know."

"But despite what he did or what you felt, Angharad, a match with Gruffydd would be flouting our family's allegiances in front of the Normans. Father would not have allowed it. Besides, Lord Gruffydd is embarking on the fight of his life from what I can understand and in no position to be marrying anyone."

"I know," agreed Angharad sadly. "It was just a few happy days when I didn't even dare to hope, yet there was something so comfortable about him. Almost as if I had known him before. Then, when I heard about Robert of Rhuddlan, about what they did to his body after he was killed, I realised I had been deluded, stupid."

"To do what Gruffydd intends is no small thing, Angharad. War is bloody, gory and men like me, who would rather spend time reading than wielding a sword, do things which seem impossible, unthinkable."

Angharad looked sharply at her gentle brother and was shocked to think that he might ever kill anyone. Yes, he was a skilled swordsman and bowman, but such skills were expected of a nobleman; indeed, all Welshmen took pride in practising their weaponry. The thought of him ever needing to use those skills in earnest was not something she had dwelled on.

"The ransacking of Rhuddlan and Robert of Rhuddlan's death was the first blow against the Normans, and it was successful. Beheading Lord Robert, whoever did it, was a symbolic gesture, and it is not something anyone likes to do, but remember, Lord Robert would not have thought twice about doing that to any Welshman that crossed him."

She shuddered. "Do you think Gruffydd can defeat the Normans?"

"You should ask if I think he can win back Wales for the Welsh. I don't know; it is too early to tell, but I do know there is a groundswell of support for him, and Cadwgan ap Bleddyn and the men of Powys stand with him."

"What will he do next?"

"He will be building up his teulu, the men who would gladly give their lives for the cause, the men who will form his court and the chief positions there. He will be getting mercenaries from abroad, Ireland, the Isle of Man, Norway and wherever else he can. Then he will attack every Norman castle in Wales to weaken the Norman grip."

"The Normans will try to hunt him down, won't they?" said Angharad in a small voice.

Chapter 8: The Fall of the Castles (1094)

"Gruffydd hasn't wasted any time," said Uchdryd, slapping his knee and beaming at his brother, whose face remained impassive as he stretched his legs out to the fire around which the family sat.

"He has built up his teulu nicely; he has men from the leading nobles who have come with horses and squires, are well-armed, some older bringing wisdom to the band, and some younger with vigour for the fight. Then, quite a few families have sent their sons for training, and these will work their way through to form a solid group in a few years. He even has his own bard! A few too many Viking mercenaries from Dublin are earning his silver for my liking: they are a wild, undisciplined bunch, but they know how to fight! Godred has given him sixty ships, mainly manned by Islesmen."

"And how many can he count on to go into battle with him outside his teulu?" asked Owain, thoughtfully stroking his chin.

"A couple of hundred from Gwynedd and probably double that in foreign mercenaries. He even has some support from the church."

Owain turned to his sons. "Gronwy, do you and your brothers understand the importance of the teulu?"

"Of course," scoffed Gronwy, "it is a group of the most important men who owe allegiance to the lord. They will give him their lives in battle; in return, he looks after them, feeds them, clothes them, shares anything they take in battle, gives them land, arranges good marriages for them."

"You are right, Gronwy, but never forget, boys, that a strong teulu is a sign of power to those in your own lands and those in other lands. It allows the lord to build firm bonds and keep close to those who may usurp his power. Remember how many times in Wales a ruler has been brought down by those close to him when he loses their trust? When they feast, hunt, and live together, the lord gets to know his teulu, and they get to know him. When discussing the strategy to move forward openly, everyone working together is powerful."

"And personality is everything," added Uchdryd. "You must be honest, strong, generous and intelligent to keep those allegiances. You can make mistakes, but you must admit them and be seen as a man who learns from those mistakes but is supportive of everything which works for the betterment of all. And your father is right; if you get too proud and too concerned about self-interest, you lose that trust. A man can be the strongest warrior on the battlefield, but he needs to have compassion and vision to be a leader of a teulu."

"So," asked Owain shrewdly, "has the Lord Gruffydd the money to back him?"

"He has done well, but I think there will be a debt around his neck for years! Even if he takes Anglesey back from Norman control, the Normans have bled it dry."

"Why did Godred give him the ships, Uncle?" asked Llywarch.

Before Uchdryd answered, Owain interjected impatiently, "You know this, Llywarch, think boy, your mind is your greatest weapon. Where have the Normans built their mottes?"

"On the river estuaries and along the coast, Father."

"Why, Llywarch?"

"Because they want to command the waterways, Father."

"Why, Llywarch?"

"To control any attacks on them."

"And?"

"To control trade, Father!"

Owain put out his hand and tousled his son's head.

"You do listen sometimes, then! So, what have I told you about why Godred would want to send ships to help the Welsh to stay Welsh?"

"To protect his trading routes, Father."

"Exactly!"

"Tell us about what happened at Aberlleiniog, Uncle," continued Llywarch enthusiastically. All the brothers leant forward to hear the tale, and although Angharad feigned disinterest as she embroidered a length of fine cloth, she was listening as intently as the others.

"The castle at Aberlleiniog is one of Earl Hugh's. It stands overlooking the Afon-y-Brenhin valley on a very steep-sided hill, a real symbol of dominance. Across the Menai Straights, it faces another of Earl Hugh's castles at Abergwyngregyn. You can imagine the signalling that went on between the two, but I am getting ahead of myself."

"How many Normans defended the castle, Uncle?" asked Rhydir, the most practical of the brothers, for whom facts, not fancy, were the building blocks of life.

"Normans, there were a hundred and twenty-five and then others who were supporting the Normans, men of Anglesey who did not yet know Gruffydd's strength and his battle skill. They were protecting themselves and their lands, expecting the Welsh would fail." He cast a sideways glance at his brother, who chose to ignore it.

"And on Gruffydd's side?"

"Well, Rhydir, around the same. Anyway, let me tell my tale. In the early morning, Gruffydd arrived. You can imagine what they were thinking as those vessels, like ghost ships, sailed out of the mist across the water into view. The sun was rising, and Gruffydd stood on the prow of the lead ship, the sun shining on his golden shield, his golden hair like a halo around his head. He pulled his grandfather's sword from the scabbard and held it high as the ships drew onto the beach. Then the long trumpets sounded, and he jumped off into the water at the head of the throng. Behind him, his banners lifted high."

"Were the Normans surprised?" asked Llywarch, eyes shining as he imagined the scene.

"Surprised? Shocked! You should have heard the commotion as they called to each other: it was utterly unexpected. Then the clamour started, the shrieks and shouts of Gruffydd's men as they hurled abuse at the enemy, the pounding of sword and spear on shield. They started to advance up the side of the hill, bloodcurdling screaming as they came through the woods, the noise echoing, and then the thick smoke and leaping flames as they set fire to the wooden buildings, one after another."

"They were all on foot?" asked Meilyr

"They were all on foot. No place for horses there."

"Carry on, Uncle," said Llywarch, enjoying the story immensely.

"You can imagine the Normans looking down from their bailey, and there was Gruffydd now with his two-edged axe leading the men. The Normans came out. Not all, no, they left some defending the castle. Now they met their match! Gruffydd was upon them wielding his axe, slicing through the Norman armour and behind him, his men, the teulu in their red tunics, javelins at their sides seemingly everywhere, the rest a sea of green, white or red capes, no fear, just the joy of battle. The battle raged all day, men falling on both sides; swords, knives, axes, javelins and bows, everything thrown into the fight. Never once did the Welsh falter. They stormed and took the outer bailey. The Normans sent more men out, and arrows showered down on the Welsh from the inner bailey. On and on, they fought until nightfall. Imagine the Normans looking down on the fires along the coast as men prepared to battle on. The castle was besieged, with no way out and the land around razed and destroyed."

"But there were many dead?" said Meilyr solemnly.

"Yes, yes. Many from both sides and among them Gruffydd's harpist Gellan who would have sung the praises of Gruffydd and his teulu. Gruffydd was more determined than ever to overcome them. He inspected the dead and gave them honour, prayed for their souls and took note of who they were and what families they had come from. The armour and weapons were stripped from the enemy dead and distributed through the camp. Then there was an alarm cry as men started moving towards the woods and shore from all directions."

"The Normans?" asked Rhydir.

"Ha! No. They realised the calls were friendly messages in Welsh. It was the men of the five cantrefi: Llyn, Eifionydd, Ardudwy, Rhos and Dyffryn Clwyd. These are the men of rich lands, incensed by the Norman presence, angered by the attacks on their lands and church. The feeling in the camp was overwhelming; there were whoops of joy, and men who should have been exhausted from battle rose, refreshed and eager to go to battle again. Aberlleiniog fell and was burnt, nobody left inside and on they went to Nefyn on the Llyn and took the castle there. It has given us back our pride.'

And those men saw Gruffydd as their leader?' asked Owain.

'Without question. Loyalty is won through action, and he has proved that he can defeat the foe. The plunder was substantial, and it was divided fairly among all. As I have said before, this is just the start. He intends to keep harrying the Normans, putting pressure on the castles and building up the resistance behind them. He has plans in place, a firm strategy, and is wise beyond his years. The word has spread throughout Wales, and now men are ambushing Normans as they move from place to place, attacking, looting and taking back some of what is theirs. Meanwhile, castle by castle is falling."

"There will be some castles that will not fall," said Owain. "Some will hold tight and hope that they will be relieved or that Rufus will invade if they can hang on."

"Maybe those closest to England, but the way things are going, there is much Welsh anger. Take Cadwgan ap Bleddyn, he was seething as he watched while Roger of Montgomery led a force up the Severn Valley from Montgomery and across the Cambrian Mountains into Ceredigion. Montgomery wanted Deheubarth for himself and quickly erected castles in Cardigan and Pembroke. He was ready to make Deheubarth completely his own, but he fell ill at Christmas and died in Shrewsbury in July, so he didn't achieve his mission. His son, Arnulf, is too green to take on experienced campaigners. Cadwgan knows and will exploit that by joining his forces with Gruffydd. They are targeting every castle methodically in Gwynedd, Ceredigion and Dyfed."

"Meanwhile," interrupted Owain, "Earl Hugh is still in Normandy and has asked me to keep order in Robert of Rhuddlan's lands, which he will have for himself upon his return. Where does that put us?"

"For now, Owain, Gruffydd is set on those parts of Gwynedd that have physical Norman presence, the same in Ceredigion and Dyfed. How long that will take is anybody's guess, but they will move swiftly. Meanwhile, he is looking to repair Anglesey to its former glory and take the leadership of the cantrefi who have joined and supported him. Even with the booty they are taking, the debt will hang like a millstone around his neck. As for the east of Gwynedd, if you do nothing, he will do nothing: that he has agreed, for my sake."

"While Earl Hugh is in Normandy, that is not an issue, Uchdryd. I don't need to interfere as long as I have my lands safe here. Earl Hugh is calling me Governor of Gwynedd, which, as you know, means nothing except that he will leave us be. When he returns, you know he will be on the offensive. I have some ideas about safeguarding ourselves from the Normans but I want you to clarify to Gruffydd that I am sitting on my hands where he is concerned."

The allusion to Hugh the Fat and her father's ideas of preserving their position and lands made Angharad's stomach turn, but she told herself that she had been given a reprieve and was grateful for that.

As the weeks went on, news trickled in of castle after castle falling at the hands of the Welsh. The Welsh would appear unannounced, take the castles by storm, burn the buildings, kill the Norman soldiers, take whatever they felt valuable, including livestock and then retreat into the woods and mountains. Within a very short time, not only had Anglesey been restored to Gruffydd and the line of Aberffraw, but the Norman nobles in Gwynedd had retreated, and Ceredigion and the whole of Dyfed, except for the castle of Pembroke, were back in Welsh hands.

***

Angharad and her father had been visiting her Uncle Ednowain Bendew and Aunt Gwerful, who had been unwell.

"Don't fuss, my dear," Gwerful protested as Angharad emptied her small bag of herbal medicines, small pots of honey and some honey oatcakes. "When the blossoms come out, I am always like this, and it goes straight to my chest but you should not worry about me so. Nevertheless, thank you so much for bringing these. You are a most thoughtful girl!"

Gwerful squeezed her niece's hand in her old wrinkled one.

"Did you hear about Pembroke Castle?" said Ednowain, eyes twinkling.

"The Welsh took it?" asked Owain, surprised.

"No, indeed. Not that one! That wily Gerald of Windsor was doomed. Fifteen of his knights had left by darkness across the sea the night the castle was first besieged. So, what does he do? He could have been a Welshman!" laughed Ednowain. "He was so angry that he gave the deserters' lands and dignities to their squires, then he dressed up his

102

common soldiers in the knights' clothing and had them parade back and forth on the ramparts. Crafty! Next, he sent a message to Neufmarche to say not to bother sending reinforcements for four months as he was coping and well-stocked with food. Of course, he arranged this to be 'lost' and delivered straight into the hands of the Welsh through Bishop Wilfrey. For his final trickery, he threw down his last four flitches of bacon and cut them into pieces, saying he had plenty and maybe they needed some."

"I can't believe it!" said Owain, shaking his head.

"There's cunning for you! Anyway, your brother it was, and Hywel were leading the troops, and they fell for it. They decided not to waste their time and, after plundering the surrounds and amassing a great quantity of booty, mind you, went off, later finding out how they had been tricked but giving credit to the craftiness of Gerald all the same."

"We should all stock up on bacon then!" Owain jested. "Humiliating for Uchdryd."

"Apparently, Cadwgan and he had significant words. You know what a hothead Cadwgan is!"

"I do." Owain grimaced and shook his head but added more seriously, "I have news that Rufus is to send a force in to wipe them out."

"Good luck with that!" Ednowain gave a curt laugh.

Owain looked at his cousin askew and asked with a distinct trace of disapproval. "You are backing the Welsh then?"

"Look at it this way: the Welsh will never be drawn into a pitched battle in Norman style, with steeds, armour, and all their war machinery. That would be madness. They will fight in the mountains or by ambush or come out of nowhere and attack when least expected."

"Meanwhile, I must ensure that the Normans do not despoil the lands. It is hard to feed an army; when men are hungry, they go on the rampage."

"Not Gruffydd and Cadwgan's men. They have instructed them that not one ear of wheat, not one beast, should be taken from the Welsh unless fairly paid for, and they know that the penalty for so doing would be harsh." Ednowain countered with a hint of triumph in his voice.

Owain raised his eyebrows. "That will take some iron control. There's not much food in the mountains."

Ednowain shrugged, "They are getting food gifts from everywhere, and it has been a good harvest this year. Who will lead the Norman troops with Earl Hugh in Normandy?"

"Earl Hugh, the new Earl of Shrewsbury, along with five of Earl Hugh's prominent barons: Robert Fitz Hugh of Malpas, William Malbanc of Nantwich, William Fitz Nigel of Halton, Constable of Earl Hugh, and Hugh Fitz Norman of Mold, brother of Radulph Fitz Norman, the Steward of Chester."

"Ha!" scoffed Ednowain. "Hugh Fitz Norman comes to fight for his land, but he has hardly been in Mold and has let his lands go almost entirely to waste. He spends all his time in Suffolk. Earl Hugh has taken some of the best forests and scrublands for hunting. The rest, all land above the flood plains along the River Alun, there are just a few small struggling farmsteads. Good woodland around there up to the hills. Shame! Same with Malpas. When Earl Edwin of Mercia held the lands Malpas took over, they were profitable and healthy, but now look at them. The Normans have no idea about working the land just how to divide it up, make calculations, take, take, take and then bring in their friends to plunder and take a share of what is not theirs by right." He shook his head regretfully.

"Cousin, you have to be careful," Owain commented warningly. "That kind of voiced resentment leads to people losing their land and position."

"I am saying to you only, Owain, and by God, I hope I can trust you, but I wouldn't mind seeing the Welsh back in control here."

"Be careful, Ednowain," Owain half whispered reprovingly with a sidelong look at the servants. Angharad recognised the danger signal of the twitch of her father's mouth and was relieved when he changed the subject abruptly.

"Gwerful, did the merchant bring the new cloths?"

"He did, Owain."

"Then, Angharad, go with your aunt and choose what you wish. Don't hold back; the coffers can cover whatever takes your fancy. It is time you had some new garments befitting of your beauty."

Angharad flushed with pleasure. This was a rare surprise, and she looked forward to choosing with her aunt, who got up now and took her niece's arm to guide her through to another room where the merchant awaited them. Her flush of pleasure turned to foreboding, however, when she heard her uncle say, "You old fox, Owain. You expect Earl Hugh to come back to sort out the mess and are still thinking of the match."

She didn't hear her father's response, but suddenly, a familiar sinking feeling grasped her stomach, and the new fabrics lost their allure.

Chapter 9: Coed Yspwys (1095)

As Owain had foretold, it was not long before William Rufus sent a force of Normans into North Wales to subdue the Welsh. In late October, Owain had been asked to direct them to where the Welsh armies were based. He agreed but insisted that he would have no part in any battle against his countrymen and that if Earl Hugh expected him to manage his lands, he needed to be neutral in that regard.

"Just take us to where we need to be and leave the rest to us," William Fitz Nigel dismissed Owain summarily. When the Welshman raised the question of feeding the army and how best to do this, he was again put in his place and given scant respect.

"Three days is all it will take, and we have our supply carts at the ready," Owain was assured. "Worried we will impose on your resources, are you?"

Owain fumed inwardly but remained impassive.

'*Arrogant bastards,*' he thought, watching the preening, prancing knights outdoing each other as they showed off their finery and barked sharp orders to their troops.

"Half of these are Hugh the Fat's barely literate ill-gotten issue," he thought scornfully as he watched the Norman nobility turn Chester into a festival city. The king arrived bejewelled and dressed in the finest array, surrounded by a fawning retinue but there was no doubt he was there for business.

As senior Welsh lord in those parts, Owain presented himself to have an audience with Rufus but was told that the king was too busy with his plans for the campaign. Owain slighted, took himself back to his lodgings and felt his age. It seemed such a short time ago that he, Lord Owain of Tegeingl, was one of the most respected men in the north of Wales. When his father died over twenty years before, what hopes he had had for the future. Now, who was he? He knew some Welsh called him 'traitor', and the Normans treated him with disdain. It sickened him.

The next day, men and horses milled around Chester from early dawn, chattering and bantering while they waited for their superiors. Wearing a finely woven red tunic embroidered with gold thread and a red gold-clasped cloak lined with ermine, Rufus finally emerged from the castle and led his men out of the town. His jewel-hilted sword glinted at his side, but he wore no mail coat or armour. They were confident, and as the knights led their foot soldiers through the Welsh countryside, they were a gleaming, impressive and threatening foe. They laughed and sang as they marched along as if they did not have a care in the world.

Knowing the Norman tendencies to rape, pillage and destroy, word travelled quickly, and those who could, hid themselves and their livestock, removing what harvest they could, and headed for the woods and mountains or even over to Anglesey. On marched the Normans in cheery knowledge that this would be a swift victory, and they would celebrate back in Chester within a few days. The force was divided into detachments, which took the roads converging on Snowdonia with its dazzling sweep of snow covering the summit. It also brought woodmen to cut through the thickets and woodland, which hid the enemy and impeded their progress.

On the first day of November, the force pitched their tents at Mur Castell, once an old Roman fortress, not knowing that this was said to be where Lleu, hero of Welsh legend, was said to have held his court or llys. Almost immediately, they realised the futility of their intention to cut down trees and groves to force the Welsh out of hiding to fight in the open. Where forests met the bleak, barren wastes, trees whose roots had reached deep into the ground for hundreds of years were entwined together in deep, dark, impenetrable thickets. The cloud-wrapped dark majesty of the mountains of Snowdonia towered above them with foreboding, and the weather threw its worst at them. Icy winds brought driving hail and rain, and they felt the grey, raw cold knifing through to their bones. Heavy mud clung to hooves and boots, making progress slow. Sparkling streams became raging rivers of fury. Precipitous ravines, where massive boulders that had plunged from the mountainside were strewn haphazardly amongst violently foaming torrents, impeded onward movement. Damp, dismal soldiers crowded on ledges uncertainly, easy to pick off for steady Welsh bowmen hidden behind shadowy, ragged rocks. The soldiers could hear the shouts of the Welsh ringing eerily clear in the thin air, but wherever their eyes searched, there was nothing.

The Welsh were in their element: no rain, mud or cold concerned them. While the Norman soldiers complained of the conditions and lack of food, the Welsh were untroubled and untiring. The heavy Norman armour and horses had no advantage on the mountainside, in the marshes and heavy woods, and the Welsh took every opportunity to block their way, ambush them and attack them from all sides when their weapons were ineffective. The Normans struggled to mount and dismount in their armour, the horses slipped and fell, and the troops were exhausted as they clambered up the rocky inclines and slithered down the muddy slopes where the foe waited with ready steel.

Finally, the Normans accepted they were beaten and clawed their way back to Chester, a disheartened, decimated shadow of the impeccable war machine that had left that city. The mountains resounded to the celebrations of the Welsh, victorious in what became known as the battle of Coed Yspwys. They were now rich from Norman booty, weapons, horses, provisions and armour. Men who had never had their own swords now brandished weapons and scabbards engraved with emblems from foreign soil.

The valiant Welsh sang songs praising Gruffydd and Cadwgan, lifting their horns of mead in celebration and feasting on the Norman supply wagons they had raided early on. Having come of age to take his rightful place at the head of Gwynedd, Gruffydd ap Cynan was crowned with a simple ceremony and no disputes.

***

Spring was coming upon them again in Tegeingl; the days were getting longer, and life was quiet at the manor until a commotion the like of which they had never heard before led the whole household outside the manor to look down across the valley. Shouts of joy reverberated around the hills as men left their work on the land, women left their looms, and children left their play to run and shout praise to those who had vanquished the foe.

There in triumphant glory were Gruffydd and Cadwgan, their horses a head above the others, leading their war chiefs, Uchdryd among them, beaming from ear to ear. All were stopping and talking to the people of the land, tousling the hair of scruffy youngsters who already knew the story of Coed Yspwys and wanted to touch the feet of the victors.

Angharad's heart leapt involuntarily as she saw Lord Gruffydd, his carriage unmistakable, his blonde hair shining golden.

"Angharad, get the house ready to welcome your uncle," shouted Owain, who hustled all the servants back into the house. Angharad quickly changed into a beautiful blue robe embroidered with cornflowers.

As the hooves and shouts of welcome echoed across the courtyard announcing the party's arrival, Angharad glanced through the open kitchen door to see Gruffydd swing gracefully off his horse: tall, muscled, pristine, authoritative. Beside him, Cadwgan, powerfully built, rougher, swarthier, older but commanding huge respect.

"Lord Owain," said Gruffydd, looking his host straight in the eye, "we impose upon you once again."

"Lord, you are most welcome. Congratulations both on your victories and on your coronation."

Gruffydd bowed fully, thanking his host, and stood back to allow Cadwgan to be introduced. Cadwgan's shrewd brown eyes had been swiftly assessing the manor's security but now flicked back to give full attention to his grey-haired host. Where his hands were roughened with physical endeavour, his face flushed and lined with purple veins from exposure to the elements and hard-drinking, Owain's hands were those of a scholar; his face showed years of frowning over manuscripts in dim light. Cadwgan had no resentment for Owain's life choice; after all, what Cadwgan achieved by valour on the battlefield was what Owain had achieved by negotiation and intellectual strategy.

"Lord Owain and I have not had the pleasure of meeting in many years but Uchdryd has kept me up to date with your family. You have fine sons, Owain," said Cadwgan as he nodded to the four brothers standing beside their father. "You young men would have learnt much by your uncle's side these last months."

The four young men coloured somewhat and looked uneasy, but Cadwgan ignored that and continued, "My eldest shares your name, Lord Owain, but already, as you are known for your wisdom, he is known for his wildness!" He indicated his son, as tall and russet-haired as he was, but slimmer in physique and with sparkling brown eyes and full red lips. The son bowed low and, as he raised himself, spotted Angharad hovering at the kitchen door. He gave her a mischievous grin, which in turn was noted by Gruffydd, who caught sight of her before she stepped hastily backwards against the wall out of sight. She covered her face and took a deep breath, humiliated at how stupid her retreat must have seemed. She wondered what on earth was the matter with her.

"My sons would have preferred to have been at their uncle's side, Lord Cadwgan," Owain said carefully, "but my position here is no secret. I make it clear to Normans and to Welsh both that I govern these lands but will not take sides."

"Understood, but we do thank you for guiding your Norman friends to where we had an advantage, though there were many other places you might have chosen for them to track us down."

110

"Lord Cadwgan, I will not take credit away from your men's fighting skills because even I, who have forgotten much of what I learnt as a youth, know that the better fighters won and would have won on any Welsh hillside. It was a worthy victory. Enough, come inside and take cheer."

As the men moved inside and into the hall, Angharad busied herself, directing the servants to prepare suitable refreshments when a shadow crossed the open kitchen door, and she looked up to see Owain ap Cadwgan framed in the doorway.

"So, this is where you are hiding your beauty, Angharad ferch Owain?" said the young man, looking her up and down. "You are as lovely as they say, even….." he paused and cocked his head on one side and then slowly enunciating, he looked her in the eyes and said, "Yes, even lovelier."

"Sir," said Angharad, as his eyes lingered on her shapely body, "I am at a disadvantage and need to make haste to ensure you are all well welcomed."

"Ah, Angharad ferch Owain," he replied, "I wager you could make a man very welcome. Perhaps later, you might show me the manor and a taste of Tegeingl's hospitality."

Angharad paled, then blushed, confused about what to say, when suddenly Owain found himself yanked back out into the sunlight by the scruff of his neck.

"I think you have lost your way, Owain," said Gruffydd, positioning himself firmly between Owain and the doorway. After briefly turning, he gave Angharad a curt bow and whisked Owain away.

Angharad tried to compose herself and berated herself for not being dignified enough to go into the courtyard and greet the guests as the lady of the manor rather than cowering and peeping behind the door. Now, she looked ridiculous.

Finally, having rerun the situation many times over in her head and getting crosser with herself each time, she summoned the courage to walk into the hall, directing the servants with refreshments.

Gruffydd was in a chair near the fire. Their eyes locked for a second, and then he looked sharply away. Younger Owain, on the other hand, stared at her, smiling confidently. As she drew near, he said, "We have heard much of your skill on the harp, Lady Angharad. Is your music as beautiful as you?"

"My daughter's playing outshines the bards themselves," said Owain, pleased, 'and while we eat, she will play for you.'

"A pleasure I eagerly await," smiled the younger Owain, who drew what seemed to be a frown of warning from Gruffydd.

The conversation continued around the recent victories, including a daring attack on Montgomery Castle, where the garrison was slaughtered entirely and the castle left a shell. Angharad shuddered. They spoke of death and killing as easily as they might have discussed a successful crop or a herd of cattle.

"We mustn't be complacent," said Gruffydd, leaning forward and speaking earnestly. "We have done incredibly well and have a force of men that fight beyond their strength, working to one common aim and each one protecting the other. It is awe-inspiring to be a part of something like this, but the Normans must never be underestimated." All the men nodded thoughtfully. "They are holding Glamorgan and Brecknock, and from there, they are attacking Gower, Kidwelly, and Ystrad Tywi, though they are facing stiff opposition from our allies."

"Hmm," chuckled Uchdryd, "Old Rufus has had a hell of a year. Trouble in Normandy, trouble in Wales and then in his own camp with the Earl of Northumbria."

"What happened there exactly?" asked Rhydir. "It is confusing to me."

"And confusing to Rufus, too!" laughed Uchdryd, winking.

Cadwgan took up the story. "As it seems, Mowbray and William of Eu supported Stephen of Aumale instead of Rufus for the English Crown and garnered the support of other barons who, when it came to it, got windy and left him and William of Eu to face the music. Anyway, in addition to that, Mowbray seized some Norwegian vessels on the Tyne. The merchants complained to Rufus, who commanded Mowbray to attend the 'Curia Regis' to explain their actions. Well, he ignored Rufus, who sent an army against him, besieged his castles, and finally, he was wounded and captured. His wife was holding Bambrough Castle but gave in when they threatened to blind her husband. He's imprisoned now, which was a better end than the other troublesome lord, William of Eu, experienced. He was blinded and castrated on the order of his own brother-in-law, Hugh of Chester."

Angharad felt sick. *Had Hugh the Fat such little regard for his own family members?*

"Meanwhile," Cadwgan continued, "Roger de Lacy has been exiled, and his lands at Weobley given to his brother, Hugh."

"Poor Rufus has a handful there with those barons!" commented Uchdryd cheekily, drawing a laugh.

"So, what is next for you?" Owain asked, turning to his guests, "What do you plan from here?"

Cadwgan answered first. "With the castle of Montgomery taken, I think we should continue the raids across the border into the hearts of Shropshire, Herefordshire and Cheshire."

Owain's eye twitched. *Too close to home*, he thought.

"Let them have a taste of what it is like to always have to be vigilant. When our people had taken their animals up to the high pastures in the summers, the Normans sneaked in, took their fertile land and built

113

their castles. Well, we are not about building castles, but, by God, we know how to use fire and how to take booty!"

"Only two castles are still garrisoned in Gwynedd, Deheubarth and Ceredigion," said Gruffydd.

Uchdryd winced, "Don't anybody mention bacon! I don't eat it now! Too many bad memories! That was the worst mistake I have made in my life, leaving Pembroke Castle without finishing them off. Now it guards the Cleddau River and the waterways from the sea and is positioned to make attacks."

Cadwgan looked sour and glowered at Uchdryd.

"It would indeed have been nice to have finished them off, but you lost no lives, which is important too. We lost too many at Aberlleiniog, which was my mistake," said Gruffydd. Angharad's head shot up in surprise.

"Rubbish, man, that was the start of it all. Aberlleiniog is the tale that fires the pride of every Welshman!" shouted Cadwgan.

"Even so," said Gruffydd, "there are many fatherless children, wives without husbands. The best way is to fight as we did at Coed Yspwys, where we hardly lost a man!"

"Now, don't start getting sentimental," said Uchdryd, changing the subject. "Lord Cadwgan, tell them about your personal plans."

"Oh that," laughed Cadwgan, "well, with all this warring, I thought it was time to get some land from our friends across the border an easier way. In Clun, in fact!"

"Clun," said Owain, surprised, "that is Picot di Say."

"Who is shitting himself as he sees the Welsh getting stronger every day. So, Picot and I have come to an arrangement over his daughter."

Owain's eyebrows shot up.

"Come, man," Cadwgan responded affably to Owain's surprise, "you, of all people, know the value of having a foot in both camps and after Wales is back with the Welsh, there should be no hard feelings. They stay on their own side of Offa's Dyke, and we stay on ours. Besides, it was when I heard about your plans for your family that I decided what an excellent idea that was."

Angharad looked up sharply, red-faced, and pleadingly at her father.

Cadwgan blustered on, "Gruffydd, I should arrange a nice Norman wife for you. That would cheer you up, seeing as you are now one of the most eligible bachelors in Wales with songs and poetry written about you!"

Gruffydd smiled wanly and said nothing, his eyes lowered. He took a deep swallow of his mead. Angharad tried to fight the sinking feeling in her stomach and the tears that threatened to spill from her eyes.

"Come Niece, let's have some entertainment," called Uchdryd from the fireplace.

Angharad smiled modestly, keeping her eyes down to compose herself and moved across the room to her harp as the servants cleared the tables and trestles, rearranging the benches and chairs so that all would have the advantage of the fire and the performer. The young men stood, and young Owain came up behind her so that she was aware of his physical presence close to her, too close to her. Across the room, she saw Gruffydd observing her speculatively.

In honour of the battle of Coed Yspwys, she chose a song from a Welsh legend about Lleu, his llys, and his beautiful wife. As she looked up, she caught Gruffydd's eye, saw his wistful expression, and wondered if he was still thinking about the losses at Aberlleiniog. Surely, this man was no monster. Her playing and voice filled the hall with such sweetness that no heart was unmoved as she lost herself in the music, long fingers easily flying across the strings.

As the music ended, young Owain bent over her to offer her mead, muttering, "Beautiful, so beautiful!" and running his fingers down the back of her dress.

Angharad looked up, startled, and pulled away.

"You are wasting your time, there," said Gronwy caustically, "she is keeping herself for an old Norman goat!"

For a dreadful dragging moment, she noted Owain's surprise, the leer on Gronwy's face when suddenly Meilyr pushed Gronwy out of the way.

"You are drunk, Gronwy," he growled under his breath, "Get out and leave your sister alone."

"Or what? Will I have you to answer to?" sneered Gronwy indignantly. "Oh, I am afraid!"

Meilyr drew himself to his full height and powerfully ushered Gronwy across the hall.

"Come, Owain," slurred Gronwy with a look over his shoulder, "I will take you to where your attention will be appreciated."

Young Owain grinned from ear to ear, swilled back the last dregs from his cup, wiped his mouth on his sleeve, turned to give an elaborate bow to his audience, and the two departed the hall with some muttering from those present.

"Two peas in a pod, our firstborns," commented Cadwgan. "They have had it too easy in life!"

"You may well be right," Owain said, shaking his head. "Gronwy needs to learn to show respect. He has shamed me in front of my guests, and I can only apologise."

"Nonsense," said Cadwgan, "we are all men of the world here. And your mead really is excellent! Who can blame him for enjoying it?"

Angharad sat shaken at her harp, trembling with humiliation. When she looked up, Gruffydd was at her side.

"Are you alright, lady?" he asked gently.

"Thank you, my lord," she replied quietly. "My brother has a foolish tongue sometimes."

Gruffydd looked towards the hall entrance where the two men had vanished.

"You have arranged a wonderful feast for us all at short notice, and no man could ask for finer music than you and your harp have provided," he said sincerely. "Thank you!"

"You are always welcome," said Angharad, genuinely looking at his face. "Whenever we go to the mews, we think of you and your kindness."

Now, Gruffydd was starting to look uncomfortable. He shrugged his shoulders and smiled, "That was nothing. I do hope you have been enjoying your hawking, lady."

"Thank you, I have," she said. She was about to tell him about her bird when he bowed abruptly and turned to his men.

"We leave at dawn and have only hours before the cock crows," he said. "We shall no longer take advantage of our host's wonderful hospitality. Lord Owain, I thank you once again for your kindness and generosity."

The young woman felt her heart and spirit sinking. She organised for the servants to put out the bedding and blankets around the hall but then excused herself. As she walked through to the kitchen, she looked out of the open door to see Gruffydd and Meilyr deep in conversation. She thought it was nice that they had formed a strong friendship in such a short time.

Angharad returned to her chamber and took off her robes, carefully laying them beside the pile of delicate new garments fashioned to impress Earl Hugh. She sighed, sitting heavily on the bed and then Lord Gruffydd once again filled her thoughts, his gentleness to her, how he had looked at her, and how he had pulled Owain from the kitchen door. "Stop,'" she berated herself under her breath! "Stop torturing yourself! He is polite, is all, and I am young and inexperienced and feel flattered! Soon, he will be married to a Norman wife! Stop thinking and dreaming like a child and accept that unless Earl Hugh turns your father down, you will soon be a Norman's wife yourself." A Norman who had blinded and mutilated his own brother-in-law when he revolted against Rufus. She felt sickened and went to bed but tossed and turned, listening to the noise outside of the porter stamping his feet to keep warm, the low sounds of animals in the stables and the bark of a dog, as a fox, no doubt, came too close. She measured her sleeplessness as patterns from moonlight through the trees travelled slowly across her room. At some point, there were low voices and the sound of her father's footsteps making his way to his chambers and then unmistakeably Gruffydd talking to the porter, making a joke, and walking across the courtyard to the stables. Up so late, she thought and must have drifted into sleep as she woke to her maid, Susannah, shaking her gently.

"Mistress, your father requires your attendance. The guests will be leaving soon. I have everything ready for them."

Angharad jumped up quickly and washed herself before dressing in one of the new gowns which Susannah had laid out on the bed. She had hardly any time to brush through her thick hair before plaiting it and making her way to the hall. All of Gruffydd's entourage was already outside attending to their horses, except for Gruffydd himself, who was inside the hall with her father. Both men seemed very serious, standing in the rushlights' half-light.

"Angharad," said Owain, beckoning her into the hall. "Lord Gruffydd would speak to you." She hesitated momentarily, then stood tall, straightening her shoulders and moving towards the pair with as much dignity as she could muster.

She noticed how handsome Gruffydd looked, his leather garments and fine wool tunic showing off his muscled frame. He looked at her tentatively from under his brows, his eyes glistening with fervour. He held his thick woollen travelling cloak lined with squirrel fur over one arm, and the gold clasp twinkled by the light of the new fire.

"Lady Angharad," he started, his voice soft but serious, as Owain walked away to leave them together. She noticed him fingering the clasp of his cloak almost nervously. "Forgive my bluntness. I am not a man with soft, flowery words. You scarcely know me, and I have little to my name and debt I must repay, but I will most certainly build up Gwynedd and rule it well. I understand you have another choice that would see you living a life with great wealth. I can offer you title only and an opportunity to restore our Welsh culture, see our Welsh church flourish, and the lands of Gwynedd once again enriched."

Angharad stared at him incredulously, hardly comprehending and hardly daring to comprehend in case she was mistaken.

"My lord," she stammered breathlessly, "I am unsure if I understand."

He took a deep breath and said, "Lady Angharad, I am asking you if you would consider becoming my wife, my queen."

Angharad gasped and let out a small cry, "My lord, my father would never agree….."

"We have agreed. It is your choice to make. If you prefer not, then I will not trouble you further and will understand your decision."

Angharad was so stunned she could barely speak. She took a step backwards, gazing at Gruffydd wide-eyed. His eyes registered her shock and showed hurt; he stiffened, and his face fell, but he controlled himself with dignity to field the rejection he thought was coming. Angharad immediately read his reaction, and she recovered herself quickly.

"Yes," she said fiercely as if his words and their meaning might escape her grasp. "Yes, lord, I will."

She saw him breathe a sigh of relief and then, he placed his hand gently under her chin and lifted her face to his so that their eyes met. He drew her closer, and then he was kissing her so gently on the lips that she threw her arms around him, holding him close, wishing that this moment would go on forever. His arms were wrapped around her, his hair falling across her cheek, and she could not believe that this was really happening. Finally, he drew away but, still holding her, said, "I must go, my lady. I am not sure for how long, but I will send word, and, all being well, we will be married in the great church in Bangor."

"I will wait for you, no matter how long," she promised breathlessly.

He smiled his wide smile at her and held her hand gently. Even through her elation, she noticed how exhausted he looked. How many battles are ahead of him yet? How many evenings giving his all to encourage his men? How many days riding across the length and breadth of Wales, no matter the weather and the uncertainty they were riding into? They walked back into the courtyard together, where her father looked at her quizzically. There was no fanfare, announcement, or impassioned parting as her future husband vaulted onto his horse, which stomped and snorted, impatient to be gone.

"Be careful, my lord," she whispered as he turned around in the saddle and bowed to her.

With a jingle of harness and the thud of hooves, he rode away into the pale winter dawn as she prayed silently for his safety.

Chapter 10: Wars, Waiting and A Wedding (1095)

The following months dragged by as Angharad waited for news, received news, was flooded with relief and joy, and then waited for news again. The Welsh victories kept coming one after another, and virtually all the lands taken by Montgomery had been won back. The men of Wales were emboldened, and the rebellion hit Brecknock and Gwent hard. A Norman army, which had been trying to restore order in the southeast of Wales, was ambushed and defeated at Gelli Tarfawg in Gwent. The Normans kept returning and trying to build their castles, but they were fought off each time. Great news came of a phenomenal win for the Welsh when the Normans were defeated at Aberllech. The whole of Wales rejoiced. Still, Earl Hugh stayed in Normandy. Still, Gruffydd did not return.

Angharad spent more time visiting her aunt Gwerful. They would work together on embroidering fine linens for her wedding bed, shifts and robes or making tapestries to furnish her walls. She loved these times.

"He will hardly know you when he returns," her aunt said one day. "You have matured so much and are even more beautiful. You have grown from a lovely girl into a beautiful woman."

Angharad blushed. "I think I have grown up," she admitted. "Everything used to frighten me, and I wasn't sure how to behave sometimes, but now I feel calmer and more hopeful."

"You will make a good wife," Gwerful said. She was a kind-hearted lady, frail in body but strong in mind. Her hazel eyes were misty as she spoke.

"Thank you. I will try. I still cannot believe that father has allowed the marriage." Angharad said, taking care not to drop her stitching.

"Who would not want his daughter to be a queen? It will be an honour for the family, and if he wants to please the Normans, maybe a brother of the Queen of Gwynedd would find himself a good Norman match."

Angharad bowed her head in acknowledgement. "It will be hard for Gruffydd initially as the land is still recovering, especially around Anglesey. Our llys will need to be rebuilt, and we must ensure the teulu is well housed and looked after."

"From what I understand, there has been significant plunder by the Welsh troops."

"True," agreed Angharad, "but Gruffydd is generous in sharing the spoils. Still, with a few good harvests and the fisheries restored, trading happening once again, I hope we can live in comfort."

"And have a family."

"Yes, and have a family. I hope they can be brought up in peaceful times."

"Can you imagine how beautiful your children will be?" said her aunt. "He is such a fine-looking man, strong, with nobility in his features and bearing, and you are so tall, with such fair skin, and both of you have big, beautiful eyes. Ah, what I would give to be young again and to have such a man hold me in his arms!"

"Aunt!" reproved Angharad but with a smile.

"Oh, I had my day. Plenty of young men wanted to dance with me but there, that is long gone, and you mustn't forget that life is short; you must enjoy every day as it comes!"

"Believe me, I give thanks every day, but I would be thrilled if I knew that Gruffydd was safe and all this fighting with the Normans was over."

"Yes," said her aunt, "we must be grateful for every day, but there is always something to worry about. At least we have not been as troubled by the plague as they have in Ireland, and the harvests in the last years have been good. I do worry that Earl Hugh may retaliate harshly, but then maybe he won't even come back from Normandy."

Earl Hugh, the dark shadow always present. Earl Hugh, unstoppable, vicious and brutal, whose military prowess exceeded other Normans. Would Gruffydd be able to resist him if his troops invaded Anglesey? There were no huge, towering mountains to hide in on Anglesey unless they were able to return to Snowdonia across the Menai Straits. A cold shiver ran up her spine, and she shuddered.

"Are you alright, my dear?" asked Gwerful, looking at her pale face.

"Yes, Aunt." She replied automatically, though her thoughts were far away.

"Look, what do you think of these sprigs of apple blossom?" asked her aunt, distracting her with the finely embroidered cloth she was working on. She, too, had sensed an icy chill in the room since they had mentioned Earl Hugh.

Owain began spending more time with Angharad, as they had done when she was younger. He was at pains to ensure she understood her future position and responsibilities.

"At first, it may be a small household that you run, but you will need to understand what is traditionally laid down regarding your role and, as that household grows, to be able to run it commensurate with the position you hold."

"Yes, Father."

"Do you understand what that role entails?"

"Running of the household, providing hospitality for guests and the teulu, being a representative of my husband's family?"

"That is quite correct, but for the Welsh, you must also understand the symbolic and ritualistic."

"I am anxious to learn anything to ensure I behave appropriately, Father!"

"As you know, Angharad, hospitality and generosity are among the virtues the Welsh hold most dear and as a queen, you would be responsible for demonstrating this. There will be feasts, especially Christmas, Easter and Whitsun, amongst others, and you must be well prepared. You will be a cupbearer and drink-bearer, which is a symbol of peace. By the giving of mead to the teulu officers, such as your chief groom and chief huntsman, you are bestowing honour. The King will give two hornfuls of mead, and you will give one hornful of mead."

"I understand, Father."

"Equally, with gifts, you must understand that this is bestowing honour and that friendship and kinship is strengthened through it. In a strong teulu there will be twenty-four officers, and you must be aware of what gifts to bestow. Giving your own garments is regarded as an honour. To your chamberlain would go your cape. To your priest would be given your Lent Penance clothes. To your handmaid would go your older clothing, kerchiefs, shoes, bridles, and saddles. To your court justices and bards, you would give trinkets, but to the chief bard would be given by you and your husband a harp and a gold ring. Garments of wool are given by the king, and garments of linen are given by the queen, and these may be finely worked with embroidery and suchlike."

"I will make sure I remember, Father."

"Remember also that you are seen as an equal to your husband with your own seal, coffers and officers. Your main role is to be visible at public gatherings, respectful, humble, and diplomatic and create a peaceful, harmonious environment where your teulu and people thrive. You will be mistress of the household and, therefore, have influence and offer counsel. You also have the power to offer protection from pursuit and prosecution. You understand that this means you have the power to give immunity?"

Angharad nodded and understood immediately what underlay her father's advice and thinking.

"Meanwhile, although you are regarded as equal to your husband, you will be entitled to only a third of the profit from the land. Eight of the twenty-four court officers will report to you, including a steward, a priest, a maid of the chamber and a groom. Your chamberlain will run errands for you between your chamber and the hall and will oversee your coffers. He will have a bed in the garderobe to serve both you and your husband."

Angharad cast her eyes down, now becoming a little embarrassed. Her father saw it and continued.

"Do not forget that you will be the means by which family history and story is passed on to the teulu and family. This is very important. You will have your own bard but he must not disturb the court and should sing only quietly to you. You can inspire him with your goodness, generosity, kindness, charity and family honour."

"Yes, Father," replied the daughter almost daunted by the obligations.

"You must be patient with your husband: he is a man of strong passions, and while he is clearly generous and kind, he can be volatile and impetuous. At times, you will need to guide him, especially when he is but building up his land and people, and the coffers will not be full. Encourage him to let officers of the teulu go on circuit to relieve the monetary burden. If you wish also, you are entitled to go on circuit as well. Remember, good princes make sure they are in touch with all their people and that is a rule for you to follow and keep in mind.'

'There is a lot to think of, Father."

"Always think of the symbolic significance of everything and, in that way, you will not err. I should also remind you of the laws of Hywel the Good regarding marriage. Gruffydd will be expected to pay me an amobr for taking you in marriage. He will pay you a cowyll the morning after the marriage, which you will keep. There will be an agweddi, or common pool of property, of which, if your marriage breaks up after seven years, you will be entitled to half. If your husband is found with another woman, you will be entitled to payment the first and second times but, if you wish, you can divorce him on the third occasion. I would hope that it would not come to this."

Angharad's eyes opened wide. She said nothing yet felt somehow naïve. She knew that many men had concubines, and society found it acceptable but her father and her uncles had never behaved in that way. She knew that she would not find such a thing easy to accept. Once again, she felt so lacking in knowledge of the world outside their manor and how things were done. She had much to learn, she knew.

"Gruffydd has allies overseas, and you must welcome them with open arms and support your husband in every way to keep those vital relationships strong. Everything you do must be to position your husband as a strong leader respected by all."

She nodded.

"Gruffydd is insistent that you be married in church at Bangor but there is no necessity for that for you to be legally married and for you to have the rights to which you are entitled."

"Oh, but I would wish to be married in the house of God."

"Of course; that is also my preference!"

"I thank you for your wise counsel, Father. There is much to consider. I hope that in all I do, I will bring honour to you also."

Owain looked delighted. Angharad left feeling that she had further repaired her relationship with her father. She really started to think about the responsibility ahead of her and what it all meant. Was she able to do all that was required of her? Would she be able to run a huge household well?

Her doubts were not restricted to being able to manage a royal household. That night she caught sight of herself in the highly polished bronze mirror in her bedroom. Was she imagining it, or did she look more womanly? She ran her hands over her now full and shapely breasts and pressed the linen shift against her hips. Would she be womanly enough for Gruffydd, who could have his pick of beauties? Would he still desire her after he had been away for so long? She looked closely at the unmarked skin of her face. She knew she was fortunate indeed as many women her age had the deep tell-tale pockmarks of disease overcome. When she thought of how soft his lips had felt as they brushed against hers, a thrill of excitement coursed through her body. Would he also be feeling that?

At last, word came from Gruffydd that he would be returning, and Angharad could hardly stop herself from running outside every time she heard a rider.

"We will need to make you a little house of your own at the gate so that you can watch all day along with the porter!" joked Owain, who had been in remarkably good humour. Then finally, at dawn one morning, Gruffydd was there, leaping from his horse, throwing his reins to a servant and swooping her up in his arms. She had been the first up and had rushed out when she heard the hooves clattering in the courtyard.

He held her at arm's length and admired her, beaming in appreciation at his radiant, long-legged, slender fiancée, for she was indeed even more beautiful than he had remembered. She was shy but he was tender with her, understanding how this was all so new to her.

"Have you come alone?" she asked him, not seeing any of his party.

"I left them far behind and have given Cadell the fastest gallop he has ever had but he was as eager to fly here as I was!"

The following days were among the happiest she had known. Her father was generous in his festivities; even Gronwy was less sour than usual. Hearing the news, people would arrive to wish the couple well, bringing gifts according to what they could afford.

The night before they were to leave the house to be married at Bangor Cathedral, Owain held a magnificent feast: there was suckling pig, huge platters of beef, pheasant and two swans, their plumage intact, filled with a stuffing of nuts. All present gasped as the swans were carried with great pomp and placed in front of the young couple.

Gruffydd had brought for his bride-to-be a fine mantle lined with fur and a most beautiful, closely fitting red gown laced at the back with wide sleeves brought in at the wrists by delicately embroidered bands heavy with golden thread. For her feet, he had unfathomably managed to bring her embroidered slippers which fitted perfectly.

"How could you know the size of my feet?" she asked, astonished.

"There is not one detail of you that I have seen, my lady, which is not fixed in my memory."

Angharad smiled and said nothing but knew that she, too, had pictured him so often that every line of his face and body was engraved on her mind.

***

The once magnificent Bangor Cathedral was a shadow of its former self, but inside, it retained all the pomp of the Welsh church.

"One day, we shall rebuild this cathedral," whispered Gruffydd, "in honour of God and to give thanks that we have vanquished our foes."

She was delighted that Gruffydd was so committed to restoring the Welsh church, and the 'we' had not gone unnoticed. Only then did it sink in that she was no longer just an irritating sister, a sweet niece and a dutiful daughter but a true partner, someone with authority to change the Kingdom of Gwynedd.

As they stood at the altar of Bangor Cathedral, Angharad looked shyly at her husband, his cloak ornamented with rich embroidery, his tunic of the finest material worked with silver thread, and she felt her heart leap with joy. He held her hands, tiny in his, and squeezed them gently. She gazed into his eyes, feeling once more that certainty that she had dreamt of him long before they had met. His eyes seemed to bore into her soul, and she felt nothing could hurt her while she was with him. As a beautiful gold ring was slipped onto her finger, she realised that after so many months of waiting, she was finally Gruffydd's wife. The excitement she felt was beyond anything she had known before. Her step was light as she walked hand in hand with her husband into the bright noon sun. Her red gown, decorated with garnets, shone and the gold tassels and gold cross swinging from the girdle around her waist reflected the light, as did the pile of thick hair plaited around her head.

It was late afternoon by the time they had travelled the fourteen miles from Bangor to Aberffraw and their llys. Gruffydd had been at pains to quell any expectations as it had suffered much neglect but she was touched when they got inside and saw that her harp was waiting for her along with many of the fine tapestries she had worked on or had been gifted. He observed her sweet face, wide-eyed and delighted, but her surprise was even greater when she saw that among the servants was Bethan. She had been training up secretly under Susannah, who had stayed at her father's home for a while to oversee the servants in Tegeingl.

"Bethan," she exclaimed, "but what about your baby?"

"My lady, he is a little boy now and a good one. He knows how to stay out of mischief and is here with me. Lord Gruffydd insisted."

Angharad swung around to her husband, eyes shining, for she often thought about her little nephew and of the wide-smiling Bethan.

"I still have much to learn," she said, "but I will work hard and not let you down."

Gruffydd walked her around, suggesting changes he would like to make and asking her for her opinion. Having run the manor for so many years, she found that there were many things she could suggest, things that a man would overlook. With pride, he showed her the royal church.

"It was built by St Beuno hundreds of years ago," he said, "when the people here had little interest in Christianity."

"I remember you telling me that when we went hawking," she reminded him.

"You remember that!"

"I do. Anglesey was the centre for the Druids in Roman times, wasn't it?"

"Until the Romans almost destroyed them but still some hold on to those old beliefs."

A feast had been prepared, and that evening was a joyous one with singing and dancing with the members of the teulu. Fresh rushes had been laid on the ground scented with herbs from the woods, and the light of many expensive fragranced wax candles lit the hall. Then in the early hours of the morning, they made their way to her bed chamber. A huge bed was covered in the sheets she herself had helped embroider with soft pillows of duck down and furs to keep them warm and on the top of the bed was a simple gold circlet engraved and jewels inlaid delicately into the design. He held it out to her, watching her amazement.

"Oh, Gruffydd," she gasped, "it is beautiful."

"For my queen," he replied, and, taking her gently in his arms, kissed her slowly and with such passion that she felt herself melting. He slipped out the ivory combs which held her hair in place so that it tumbled thick over her shoulders. He kissed her neck, and she felt his fingers unlacing her gown at the back and moved her shoulders so that it slipped down to the freshly laid reeds on the ground. Her heart was pounding from fear, desire and love. Such moments of intimacy she could never have imagined: his gentleness, the thrill of the expression of his longing for her, the wild headiness of her abandonment of anything other than their fiery coupling. Then afterwards, the joy of lying her head on his chest, listening to his heartbeat and the intense excitement of his wanting her again.

The next months were ones of utter contentment for Angharad except for the times when Gruffydd and his teulu were involved in an uprising in the south or quelling the activity of Normans, who were trying to rebuild their Welsh castles. Each time, he would return with booty, and although she was troubled for his safety when he was away, she felt less anxious about the debts which needed to be paid.

Gwynedd was responding well to the period of stability, and both Angharad and Gruffydd made it a priority to meet as many as possible of those they now ruled; to hear their views and concerns. Where mills needed to be repaired, fishermen needed new boats, and farmers needed ploughs or oxen, Gruffydd was quick to assist, and they loved him for it. Little whitewashed churches sprang up all over the kingdom, and Gruffydd was a kind benefactor. These small steps went a long way to creating unity and loyalty amongst the people of Gwynedd. As the months went on, Gruffydd, unfailingly considerate, also made sure that his teulu were content, and as if he wanted everyone to join in his own happiness, he arranged some very good marriages for those men who were yet single. Angharad was delighted, as this meant that she had a friendship group of women around her.

One night as they lay together, she asked him, "I have often wondered how it is you came to ask for my hand."

He laughed as he brushed a strand of hair away from her face. "The first time I saw you, you were a pretty girl but my head was so full of proving that I could accomplish the beginnings of resistance against the Normans that I didn't see what was in front of me. The second time we met, you had bloomed into the most beautiful creature I had ever seen, and I could talk to you. I had never met a woman with whom I could discuss anything, and your views were your own, not things you had heard or read or been taught. Honestly, I was stunned. I saw how you ran your father's house faultlessly with grace and dignity. I didn't hear you say one bad word about anyone. I realised I wanted to spend my life with you."

"Even then?"

"Even then, you had captured my soul but when Gronwy said you would be marrying Earl Hugh, I thought what a fool I had been and that, of course, a lady such as yourself would want to marry into such wealth. Why would she consider a poor, impoverished noble such as myself?"

Angharad lifted herself to her elbow and looked at her husband with horror. "I never wanted to marry Earl Hugh. It was my father's idea and my greatest dread."

"So Meilyr told me."

"Meilyr?"

"You have a wonderful brother who cares deeply about you, and thanks to him, I understood the situation."

"And you spoke to my father?"

"Who was a tough negotiator."

"Oh?" said Angharad quizzically.

"Not for you to be concerned about, Cariad."

"Then it must have been Meilyr who told you about Bethan."

"It was, and it was fortunate that Gronwy went away to visit his friend Owain ap Cadwgan so that she could come to the manor and learn from Susannah while you spent time with your uncle and aunt."

She shook her head at the detailed planning he had put into place at a time when his world would have been in chaos.

He waited a little while, gently stroking her face and then asked, "And why did you consent to marry me?"

She gave a small laugh and smiled self-consciously. "The first time I saw you, I thought you were handsome but troublesome. I was nervous about what harm you might cause my family. The second time I saw someone different, a softer version of you. Then the news came about Robert of Rhuddlan, and that shocked me so much: the beheading."

"It was my cousin, not I," he said quickly.

"I know that now, but it was suddenly right in front of me, the brutality of it, and it disturbed me. It still makes me unhappy and confused, but when I saw you again, I wanted to be with you so much."

He kissed her gently.

"Tell me about your cousin," she said, noticing his melancholy look.

"He was older than me."

"Was?"

'He died in the plagues in Ireland, raising support for us to fight back. He was truly wild but an incredible fighter. Part Welsh, part Irish, half Viking, he could drink anyone under the table. He and I had the same name. Both our fathers died when we were small, and strong Viking mothers raised both of us: mine gentle and educated, his as wild as

133

he. He was brought up in the Irish court, where he had a sword thrust into his hand as soon as he could talk, and I was brought up quietly here in Wales, where I learnt to read as soon as I could utter a sound. My mother was a pious woman; you would have liked her."

"I wish I could have met her."

"She would have loved you."

"Why did she take you to Ireland?"

"As a child, I was safe. The Welsh don't kill children, but as I became older, as an heir to the throne, I was a threat, an enemy."

"Of your cousin's?"

"No, he was the king of Gwynedd for a short time, but had I been of age, he would have respected my greater right. No, there were always other contenders, and the Normans knew how to encourage Welshman to kill Welshman to keep us busy with our revenge, warring instead of keeping an eye on their intrusion."

She shuddered as she thought of the enemies they had even now. Gruffydd continued, his eyes distant as he remembered.

"When we went to live in Ireland because it was safer for me to be away from those who would curtail my hopes of inheritance, that is when I learnt to fight. Gruffydd was my grandfather, Iago's nephew, and I was named for him. I learnt much from him. He won back Gwynedd from the Normans when I was just a child but they tricked and imprisoned him. He hated them, Cariad; he hated them so much!"

He was lost in thought for a while, stroking her shoulder absently.

"His daughter was Cadwgan ap Bleddyn's first wife, you know. Gwenllian."

"Maybe that's where Owain gets his wild ways from."

"From his father's side too. My goodness, Cadwgan is a character. I could tell you some stories that would make your hair curl!"

"He is a loyal friend to you, Gruffydd."

"He is indeed, and we have vowed to help each other with Gwynedd and Powys. He was worried about my ambitions at the start, whether I would try to take Powys, but I have vowed that I will not take anything of his."

"We have enough to manage here anyway, Gruffydd. When Gruffydd ap Llewelyn was ruler of all Wales and Lord of Gwynedd, he struggled to keep all the princes under control. Better that you have sound alliances with them all and lead them in harmony, taking nothing, having no title outside of Gwynedd but leading in keeping them united. Those who climb too high are toppled here by the Welsh."

"You are quite a philosopher, Cariad, and what you say is quite right. Eight days it takes to travel from the top of the country to the bottom. Four days across. Eight days is too far away to know what is going on at the distant end of a kingdom when there is trouble, and there is always some trouble! As you say, let us be happy with what we have."

Angharad nestled against her husband's warm, reassuring body, feeling cherished as she drifted into sleep, thinking how fortunate she had been that Meilyr had looked after her.

Chapter 11: Earl Hugh of Chester (June 1098)

Busy as they both were, Angharad loved the times when she and Gruffydd would ride out together along the gentle River Ffraw until it joined the often-wild tumultuous sea. Then, across the dunes to the magic of the big curving bay and above shingled coves where seals lolled hidden below ragged-edged cliffs. Unexpected sandy beaches surprised them where seagulls wheeled, and sandpipers ran across the shallows. Behind them the countryside rolled, green and rich, easy on the eye and filled with promise.

Gruffydd was proud of his lands and loved to teach her about the history of the place. He took her to the village of Llanbedrgoch.

"This was a thriving trading village not so long ago," he said, "with things they made here finding their way to France, Scandinavia and over to England. The Vikings came here, married the local Welsh and brought their culture with them. We need to build up little trading villages like this all over Gwynedd."

She loved his passion for learning, building and creating to make a prosperous place rather than just sitting still and depending on tenants to bring wealth.

One very special spot they visited was the church of St Cwyfan, named after an Irish disciple of St Beuno, who built the little wattle and daub church right on the edge of the sea, maybe thinking of his home in Ireland.

"We'll build a stone church here one day," said Gruffydd, "to withstand the wind and weather."

From the church they would gaze across the headland to the snow-capped mountains of Snowdonia, reminding Angharad how her husband had lived there for so many months with his teulu."

They would often walk on the rocky beach at Porth Saint, where light played on the cliffs, revealing pink, white and grey rocks or at Bwa Gwyn, with its amazing rock arch revealing the power of the sea.

One day Gruffydd took his wife to an ancient village called Din Lligwy, on a small hill on the east coast. There, it was possible to see the limestone blocks, which created perfect round dwellings long before Roman times with much of the protecting wall still intact.

"This was a farming community probably, long, long ago," he said as they walked through, trying to work out what would have been homes and thinking that the rectangular buildings would have been storehouses or workshops.

"They would have had a clear view of the whole island from here," she commented, thinking that even then, there would have been enemies of which to be wary.

"Their culture would have been guided by the ancient Druids."

She touched the stones, "So long ago that hands we will never know touched these stones as they went in and out of their homes."

"And maybe one day, long in the future, people will touch our home and say the same thing. Who were those people who lived at this llys, ate and drank, had families and loved?"

She smiled secretly to herself.

Their favourite spot, when they would visit the other side of the island, was Parys Mountain, where the ground shone with myriad colours of gold and copper, rusts and pinks and where, for thousands of years, men had mined the ground for precious metals. Skylarks soared into the air, and choughs and meadow pipits sent their alarm calls as the horses' hooves clattered on the stony ground. Here, one warm evening as they gazed out at the little fishing vessels coming back to shore, she let him know the news that she had been holding in her heart until she was sure. He looked at her with absolute astonishment that she had kept it so quiet. He scooped her up and swung her around.

"Cariad, you carry our child. I didn't believe I could be even happier."

She turned her face to his and beamed at him, delighted to see his utter joy.

He held her close as they watched the sun beginning to dip in the sky, kissing her neck and running his fingers through her hair.

Later, she would treasure memories of those wonderfully special days as they relished their secret and imagined their future family.

***

The news that threatened their harmony, about the return of Earl Hugh and his determination to take back Gwynedd, came unexpectedly from her father via Meilyr. Gruffydd immediately started amassing his troops. Cadwgan brought his men from the south and sent his son, Owain, to Murtagh, King of Dublin, with gifts to garner aid from the Irish-Danish. Young Owain returned, saying that ships of mercenaries were on their way. Feeling they could protect their people on Anglesey, the word got out for those within Gwynedd to flee to the mountains or make their way to Anglesey under protection. The women from the llys were sent under protective escort to Snowdonia, including Bethan and her young child, but Angharad insisted on remaining behind.

"It is important that I be seen to stay here," she said, but at the same time, she encouraged everyone to have escape plans should they be needed.

"The Earl of Shrewsbury is amassing troops as well, and they will join together and then set out to Anglesey, destroying all before them," Meilyr explained.

"Even in Tegeingl?" asked Angharad fearfully.

"Our father has managed to get protection for the east part of Gwynedd but Earl Hugh is like a man possessed. Father is to guide them and be their advisor and while he will do what he can to protect you, it is a difficult situation for him."

"We will fight them; we have the troops," said Gruffydd confidently.

"No, Gruffydd, you don't understand. This is nothing like you have seen before, and if you engage in open battle, you will be slaughtered."

Gruffydd looked at his wife's white face, bravely trying to mask her fear.

"There are caves," he considered out loud, "wooded areas, marshes, places in the mountains we can shelter our people but we also need to make sure we have boats that can help them escape if things get very rough."

Angharad's heart sank, but she knew she must prove her worth and hold herself together.

Her brother's face looked troubled and before he left, he reached down from his horse, held her hand and said, "You can always come home, you know. Just until things have settled down."

"Meilyr, this is my home," she said firmly. "These people trust us and how would it be if I were to run away?"

"You know that Gruffydd would have you safe?"

"I know that my place is at his side."

"Then I pray to God to keep you safe. Earl Hugh has a venom when he is riled that surpasses any evil I have heard of. He thinks nothing of torturing innocents, and he is bloodthirsty and brutal. I now have even more respect for Father as I see what he has been dealing with. Thank God, Angharad, you did not end up his wife!"

"Believe me, I thank God every day for that, and whatever happens to me now, I have had happiness beyond any expectations."

"Gruffydd is a good man, Angharad, but this battle will be on a different scale from anything he has experienced."

She watched her brother until he and his horse were a speck in the distance.

"May God keep you safe also," she whispered.

**

Cenred, the priest at the ancient church of St Tyfrydog at Llandyfrydog, arrived with several other priests to meet with Gruffydd. They offered assistance, and Gruffydd and his teulu sat with them to explain their plans.

The wispy silver-haired priest with his round, permanently smiling face and thick bushy eyebrows looked Gruffydd straight in the eye. "If the Normans do cross, we can harbour our people in our churches, they will not violate holy sanctuary."

"I do not trust them," said Gruffydd, "they have no respect for the Welsh church."

"Even they would not be so unholy," said Cenred. The other priests nodded their agreement.

"I am arranging for many of the women and children to be ferried across to the mainland and protected in the mountains," said Gruffydd, "but if the Normans do succeed in breaking across onto the island, I would ask you and the other priests to send a warning."

"We can ring the bells of the churches to sound an alarm, and we will visit our flock to let them know that if they should hear the bells, they are to take cover."

"There will be boats ready for some to escape, but not all," said Gruffydd. "Some can hide in the mountains and woods, some in the marshes and some along the coast."

"If the Normans come across, you and your family need to escape. There is no value for Anglesey or Gwynedd to lose their king."

"Let it not come to that," Gruffydd said with a thin smile, but Angharad could tell he was uneasy as he watched the grandfatherly priest lead his companions from the llys.

"Come on, Gruffydd," scoffed Cadwgan. What's the matter with you, man? We have the men; this is our land, after all, and we have the advantage."

Angharad knew that Gruffydd was worried.

Within the week, there was news from all parts of Gwynedd that the Norman army of an unprecedented number of soldiers was marching down the old Roman road from Chester, Earl Hugh's wolf head banner flying high. There was no smiling or laughing as this army trudged across the country; there was a hostile determination. Behind the knights, squires, pages and men at arms came all those vital to the success of a military campaign: armourers, smiths, clerks, chaplains, cooks, butchers and bakers. They camped around Earl Hugh's castle at Abergwyngregyn, which had once been a Roman Fort. Earl Hugh had rebuilt since Gruffydd and Cadwgan had destroyed it. The sun blazed down on shining armour and metal sharpened by whetstone; the sight was daunting.

Escorted by many knights, Hugh the Proud of Shrewsbury rode in full armour up and down in front of his troops, making sure they understood that they were to deliver the nearest to hell that the island had ever seen. The rivers of Afon Goch and Afon Anafon were carefully guarded. The Normans now controlled the ancient crossing point to Anglesey at Lafan Sands, and they had guards scouring the Irish Sea watching for fleets from the Isle of Man or Ireland. They had anticipated that the ancient ties with the Irish would bring additional support to Anglesey.

Some of the Welsh who had not moved across to Anglesey hid in the old oak woods, watched by scampering red squirrels, pied flycatchers and wood warblers whose territory they were sharing. They fished for brown trout in the lakes where legends told of Mawon's son:

When I hear the thundering roar, it is the host of Llemenig mab Mawen—Battle-hound of wrath, victorious in battle.

They waited to hear the thunderous roar as Gruffydd and Cadwgan routed the Norman foe. Below them, not lilting Welsh tones but harsh French voices contrived plans for devastation and destruction, the like of which had never been seen before.

Gruffydd and Cadwgan held a war meeting at Aberffraw.

"They can't land their ships or get across without disadvantage," said Gruffydd, "and as long as we have covered all the beaches where they might land and have half of our troops opposite the Menai Straights, we should be able to pick them off as they come across."

"We have the best bowmen for the job," nodded Cadwgan, "but I wish now that we had kept half the force in Snowdonia and marched down behind them to trap them. How do we stop the Irish plundering when it is all over? They are an untrustworthy lot."

"We are paying them well for their efforts. They know that they must not touch or harm anyone other than the foe, and they are welcome to whatever booty they gain from them."

"As are our men."

"Indeed, as are our men."

Angharad, pale and drawn, wrapped anything movable and precious, including her coronet, and arranged to bury it, hoping it was an unnecessary precaution. Gruffydd arranged for most of the coffers to be hidden also. Angharad had ridden out to see the Norman army arrayed across the Menai Strait, and though she knew little of warfare, she had felt a physical jolt at the immensity of the assembly. She berated herself for her lack of faith, but, at that moment, the future seemed to hold scant hope.

Lookouts on the cliffs announced the fleet's arrival from Ireland, and a skiff was sent with messages of where best to land and a summary of the Welsh strategy. Angharad watched in awe as her husband rallied his troops, kept calm and managed the volatile Cadwgan, whose impatience might have led them to some foolhardy mistakes. She rejoiced in the total respect the men had for their young leader, trusting that he would lead them through and willing to give their lives for that.

Yet Angharad felt ill. Her pregnancy was making her feel weak and nauseous, and her anxiety for Anglesey and her husband was extreme. Used to be at his side, she now felt his absence keenly as long days and short nights were taken up on protecting the island.

Then, the promised hell broke loose. Early morning saw rank upon rank of Norman archers and men with swords and lances assembled on the not-so-distant shore. The Earl of Chester started to move his troops onto the island, boat by boat. They were well-disciplined, mailed brutes with hard faces, long iron-headed spears and lethal two-edged swords. The Welsh reassured themselves that this process would take time and that they had the advantage. At first, the skilled Welsh bowman, clad in thick protective leather jerkins, had formed a defensive line keeping them at bay, and those who did come across felt the wrath of Welsh steel. The Welsh saw the Irish mercenaries and signalled them into safe harbour, feeling very confident that these additional troops swelling their numbers would keep the battle short. Ship after ship glided in, and warriors spilt onto Welsh soil, weapons in hand.

Within minutes of the safe arrival of all the troops on land, the Welsh realised their allies had turned traitors as they rushed towards them brandishing axes, spears and swords. Gruffydd and Cadwgan experienced the absolute horror of the very mercenaries who were there to support them, catching their valiant troops unawares, and at the same moment, the Normans surged over to the island, trapping the Welsh. Unbeknownst to them, the Normans had met with the Irish commanders, and they switched allegiance when the Normans offered an outrageously high incentive for them to do so.

Hordes of Normans rushed them and appeared everywhere, with naval support landing on all sides of the island. The Welsh fought bravely, but realising the carnage that would ensue because they were so vastly disadvantaged, Gruffydd and Cadwgan withdrew their troops, shouting for them to flee to all parts of the island.

As Angharad and a small group of servants huddled together in the small church, praying and awaiting news, they heard the bells ring an alarm all over the island, one church following the subsequent church's lead. Angharad clutched the wooden door frame as she told the servants to scatter and find safety elsewhere: no church belonging to their llys would survive a Norman onslaught.

"You must get out of here!" she screamed at the priest, who was valiantly ringing the bells. She continued to pull the rope, but when he realised the uselessness of arguing, he fled.

"No, no," she cried in agony with each pull of the rope, "Dearest God, save him, please save him, please save him."

Some Welsh managed to sail to the mainland, others hid, and some chose sanctuary at the churches.

Cadwgan literally had to drag Gruffydd off the battlefield.

"For Christ's sake, man," he roared at him, "we need to save our skins if we are to save the Welsh! This is no time for heroics! Get on your horse! If we stay here, our men will fight to the death with us. Is that what you want?"

Gruffydd and Cadwgan galloped to Aberffraw with a small group of men. Angharad stumbled out of the church, drained and pale at their frenzied calls.

"Thank God! Thank God!" she cried, seeing Gruffydd bloodied but alive.

"Get on your horse now!" Gruffydd shouted, pointing to the tethered and saddled Seren. Angharad complied wordlessly, seeing the steely angst on Gruffydd's face. They galloped at breakneck speed across pasturelands, into woods and steeply uphill to a cave hidden by a bushy thicket.

Thick clouds had gathered above them, hiding the sun, seemingly mourning with them.

Gruffydd helped his wife down quickly and roughly, then pushed her into the dark opening.

"Cariad, you must stay here until I come for you. Do not venture out or show yourself. Stay far back inside. Our only safe option now is to go to Ireland until we can gather an army to fight for what is ours."

Then, taking her horse with him, he was gone.

Chapter 12: Escape from Anglesey (July 1098)

The day was interminably long as Angharad sheltered in the dim, dank darkness of the cave and wept many tears, which eventually gave way to dry-eyed despair. She cried for the lost hope of peace in Gwynedd; she cried for fear of what was happening right now to all those good people whom they had failed to protect; she cried for the destruction of all that had seemed so good. Most of all, she cried for her inability to do anything about it.

Now and then, she would hear voices and the barking of hounds, which she supposed were the Normans searching the land around for Gruffydd and his henchmen. Each time her heart pounded wildly, she prayed feverishly that he would not be caught, straining her ears for sounds suggesting a capture. Then she started making bargains with God until there was little she could bargain with; waves of misery washed over her. She had no appetite for the little bread tied up in a cloth beside her, and she felt the nausea of her pregnancy keenly. 'Where is he?' she wondered again and again. She knew they were outnumbered now, and Norman reinforcements would flow in from the mainland. Normans, with their coats of mail, shields, and swords, were brutal in thought and deed. Little hope then for any of Gruffydd's supporters who were found or who decided to brave it out.

Where was he? The smoke-filled air made its way into her hiding place, and she knew that the Normans and the mercenaries would be setting fire to homes and buildings, looting and plundering and worse. Outside, the deep rumblings of thunder rolled across the sky as if echoing the earlier battle drums. The filtered light grew dimmer, and she realised the night was rapidly closing in. How much longer must she stay here? An incessant drip, drip, drip from inside the cave made her realise that it was now raining outside and probably quite heavily. She was glad of it to put out the fires that would be burning everywhere. Gruffydd had told her not to go to the exit for fear of being seen, but her urge to do just that was compelling. She was deep in prayer when she heard voices, deep guttural French voices calling close by. She moved deeper into the cave, taking her scant belongings and crouching uncomfortably behind a rock jutting into the cave's heart. Suddenly, light flooded the entrance, and she heard the voices of at least two Normans seemingly inside. The light from the torches they used to scan the interior washed around the dark stone, illuminating every crevice. She felt her heart beating so wildly she was sure they could hear her, and her breathing was loud to her ears but impossible to still. She could hear them moving in further as their heavy boots grated and crunched the gravel in the cave's entrance. She felt around her for anything she might use to protect herself, grasping a hand-sized rock she held at the ready. Detesting violence, though she did, she felt the strongest urge to protect her unborn child against any harm. The feet moved further towards her. A bat whirled into the air above, causing an alarmed yell from one of the soldiers, followed by an oath and a laugh as the light jerked across the cave. Then, a yell and the crashing sound of metal on metal, a scuffle, a cry and another, and she pressed herself into the rock for what seemed to be an eternity, holding her breath while her pulse raced.

"Angharad?" It was Gruffydd's voice, alarmed, urgent, "Angharad?"

She flung herself out from behind the rock and into his arms, releasing hot tears of relief as he embraced her, pressing her to him, kissing the top of her head.

"Thank God! Thank God! We must go, Cariad, there is little time."

A whispered call from Hywel, one of Gruffydd's teulu, urged them to hurry.

"I am so sorry you were here alone for so long. It is treacherous out there with Normans and hounds covering every pathway, and more are on the way. They have taken our llys as their base and are fanning out along the coastline. I have a boat and men hidden in a cove but you do not have to come with us. Hywel will take you back to safety and your father. Your father is with them; he will protect you. Not even Earl Hugh would go so far as to hurt you."

147

She felt sick when she heard that her father must have known what was happening but had not warned them. *Why would he turn against them like this?*

She was adamant. "Where you go, I go at your side, Gruffydd. That is my place. I am not leaving you unless I will endanger you. Besides, they would probably use me as a bargaining tool even if I reached my father, and he would be powerless to stop them."

The depth of his embrace was all that Angharad needed to assure her of how much her words meant to her husband, but now the man of action was planning the next move. She saw him pointing to the ground in the dim light. She gasped as he lifted a fallen torch, the light revealing the bloodied shapes of three Norman soldiers.

"Quickly! You too, Hywel! We must take their clothing. The darkness and the clothes will give us some kind of chance out there. Angharad, put on this man's things; he is the smallest."

He dragged the body of a young man aside, and Angharad gasped. This could be Llywarch or Rhydir, a soldier but barely past boyhood. She felt a wave of abhorrence but steeled herself to do as instructed. She fumbled with the clothing as Gruffydd handed it to her and then retched as she pulled the uniform over her tunic and shawl: the dead man's stench was on the clothing. She retched again but tried to pull herself together, remembering that only a short time earlier, she imagined Gruffydd being dead and herself being captured, raped or worse. Had they indeed caught Gruffydd, his head would be on display outside their llys beneath the wolf head banner of Earl Hugh. She shuddered violently. The mail was heavy for her, but she summoned all her strength. Whatever Gruffydd told her to do, she resolved to do without complaint.

The rain had abated and a strong wind had swept the sky of cloud cover. Now dressed in Norman garb, they made their way through a small thicket, not speaking and moving as quickly as possible. The star and moonlit sky were a blessing and a curse, making their way

148

easier to determine but causing their presence to be more visible to others. The ground was muddy, so Angharad slipped frequently, but Gruffydd guided her along, and she was grateful for the wind that quelled their noise and blew loose vegetation covering their tracks. At one point, Gruffydd directed them to shelter behind bushes as a group of Welshmen hurried passed in front of them. "Quiet, they may be Welsh traitors," whispered Gruffydd.

At last, they reached a steep slope which Angharad recognised from her rides along the coastal path. Gruffydd and Hywel debated the safest route down. The shrill alarm call of a lapwing behind them gave an alert; five Normans were already bearing down upon them. Their torches glided over the faces of the three, but Gruffydd whispered, "Don't open your mouths," and then strode towards them as if nothing were amiss.

Angharad picked up enough of the conversation to understand that his French was good and that he was discussing the weather, that they were starving and just checking the cove below and would be coming in for the night. The others replied in the same vein, remarking that they had been out there for hours, had seen nothing and were tired and thirsty. Only idiots, they claimed, would be out in the middle of the night, and they hoped that there were enough provisions for them. Gruffydd gave gestures of resignation and remarked that they would doubtless be up before dawn to do the same again.

The terrified young woman stood as tall as she could and turned slightly away. From the corner of her eye, she saw one of the soldiers cast his torch over their faces again and look at them intently. She felt an ice-cold fear grip her, and her heart raced. Beside her, she could hear Hywel breathing heavily and saw him tense his fingers around his sword. Gruffydd continued the conversation unhurriedly, and, at last, farewells were said, and they marched on.

Angharad was just allowing herself a deep sigh of relief when one of the men came running back towards them. Her heart sank. Gruffydd automatically felt for his sword as he moved towards the man, placing

149

himself between the soldier, Angharad, and Hywel. Hywel pushed her behind him and took a step forward, but the soldier merely handed Gruffydd his torch, explaining that their party had enough light and Gruffydd's had no light at all. As their faces were illuminated, Angharad turned away again as if starting down into the cove, concerned that her feminine features may give them away. Still, the soldier was more anxious to get back to his party, which was standing a short distance away, and rushed off.

Gruffydd swore an oath under his breath and hissed, "Move slowly; we don't want to seem panicked."

Hywel shook his head in disbelief and let out a low whistle, "My God, how did you pull that off? That was too close!"

"We could have taken them, Hywel, but I didn't want to risk it. I wasn't sure what others were out here and if they would have heard the commotion. Come, we need to get moving, although, with this wind, it will be tough to get out of the bay."

Below them, the white waves foamed angrily as they crashed violently on the jagged rocks protecting the cove. The three half-slid, half-scrambled down the muddy slope, falling, grasping at gorse bushes to stop them from tumbling onto the rocks below but less fearful of that imminent threat than of the return of the soldiers above realising their error. Angharad dug her nails into the sticky earth to grasp hold of something to steady her but found herself falling only to be caught by Gruffydd, steadied and then slipping and sliding again. Below, far below her, were the sounds of stones they had dislodged bouncing on the rocks. She finally gave up trying to stay upright and, protecting her stomach as much as she could, surrendered to the landscape and slid down the cliff side, halted at intervals by the tenacious bushes growing there. Somewhere above, a fox called its rasping cough.

As they reached level ground, Gruffydd, seeing that she was worn out, lifted her and carried her along the sandy beach. There was no sign of a boat or the men he was expecting, so putting her gently against a rock, he told her to wait while they went around the point. They took the lantern, and Angharad watched as the light bobbed about on the rocks and then vanished around the corner. She could see nothing. It had not occurred to her that there would be no boat, and the thought of clawing her way back up the cliff was unthinkable: she felt more trapped than ever. Where would they go without a boat? By daylight, their presence would be obvious to the Normans, freshly resuming their efforts to find them. This little cove, so beautiful when she had ridden across the cliffs above in peaceful times, was a perilous trap for them now.

The wind had become less strong but the waves still crashed onto the beach in front of her and dragged at the sand with ceaseless regularity. She was bitterly cold and sticky with mud, and her hands were clumsy as she tried to remove the chainmail before giving up and lying on the damp sand. She must have fallen asleep because she woke with a start as Gruffydd shook her gently out of a nightmare of Normans, caves, bats and blood.

"This is as calm as it is going to get. The boat is up by the far rocks. We must take this chance to leave before the wind comes up again or the first light draws attention to us. Are you ready to keep going?"

Angharad pulled herself up with palpable effort but her legs buckled. She allowed Gruffydd to carry her across the sand and over the rocks at the bottom of the cliff. She saw the shape of the boat and could make out a few men at the oars.

"We will row straight out until we are deep enough to clear the rocks and then set our sail," Gruffydd instructed, putting his exhausted wife down on a seal skin before pushing the boat out with Hywel.

Never had Angharad felt so wretched as they pulled away from the Welsh coast. Everything ahead of her was unknown. She thought of the destruction of the llys and whether she would ever see her home again. She found herself weeping despairingly.

151

Gruffydd pulled her to him, rubbing her freezing hands in his and promised, "It will be alright. I will make it right."

Angharad felt numb as she looked back once again across the sea. Atop the limestone cliffs, now bathed in the early morning light, a solitary rider silhouetted against the sky, watched the little boat sail further and further away.

Chapter 13: The Irish Court (July 1098)

Angharad could not fathom how she had survived the trip to Dublin. She had been freezing, feeling nauseous and had clung to her husband for warmth and solace. She saw that he had not come out of the battle unscathed and had a deep cut across his arm, and his face was marked and bruised. When she showed her concern, he brushed it off. He was, at times, angry and then saddened, and in fragments, she understood that Cadwgan and some of his trusted men had already set off by skiff for Dublin.

Angharad still did not understand why her father had willingly assisted Earl Hugh against them. Could he not even have sent word of the treachery of the Irish? Did he desire their downfall so much? Why had her father forsaken them? Even her Uncle Uchdryd had been with the Norman troops. Why? He had been Gruffydd's staunch supporter. What had changed? What could have made Uchdryd, who had championed Gruffydd and Cadwgan's cause, switch allegiances? She felt saddened but too exhausted to give energy to it.

As the boat fought the waves and the wind blew cold rain into their faces, she felt herself draining away to a shadow. Hywel made them a makeshift blanket out of sackcloth and brought them water and bread, but neither of them could eat. She was aware of Hywel's watchful concern and the sadness on his face, as he knew there was nothing he could do to alleviate their sorrow.

Their progress was speedy despite the wind howling in the sails and water crashing over the bows with a deluge of foam covering their already drenched bodies. Gruffydd held her tightly, and she was glad of the extra weight of the Norman mail and padded jerkin to hold her down and offer a little more resistance to the cold. The day was bleak, and she could not stop her incessant shivering or the dark memories that haunted her. Above them, seagulls glided in the air currents, and, for her, they were like ghosts swooping by to judge them all.

By the time they finally reached Dublin, it was evening. The boat slid neatly into the harbour, ropes were thrown, and a gangplank bridged the gap between vessel and quay. She was dimly aware of Gruffydd calling out in a language she didn't understand before he helped her from the boat, steadying her weakened body. She staggered, her legs refusing to hold her, so he carried her the rest of the way to a stone enclosure at the top of a hill overlooking the harbour. Quietly without fuss, they were ushered into a fine chamber. She submitted as Gruffydd peeled off her dripping clothing, wrapped her in a clean shift left for her and washed her cuts gently before she fell into the deepest sleep.

The next day, she was hardly aware of what was going on. Gruffydd brought her a little soup and held her to him as she drank it, still exhausted, nauseous and empty. She must have slept most of the day, and by evening, when Gruffydd, looking exhausted himself, came to bed, she felt much better. She propped herself up, trying not to wince and looked at him. He had lost so much after such a struggle, and she held her hand out to him.

"How are you feeling?" he asked tenderly, stroking her bruised face with his hand.

"Much better," she said in a voice that, despite her efforts, betrayed how she really felt.

He rubbed her belly gently, "The little one is strong enough to endure all this."

She tried to smile and asked, "What about you? You have been through so much."

She pulled his arm to her, seeing where the wound had been bandaged, and rubbed her hand over it.

"I let my people down. I put my trust where I should not have. How many of them are now in captivity? How many have lost their lives? And being here, not knowing..." His voice trailed off.

154

"You did your best, Gruffydd, and so many would have been able to escape because of your planning. Do not be angry with yourself."

He shook his head in despair.

"What will we do now?" she asked.

"As yet, I am unsure, but I will not give up."

***

The next day, Gruffydd departed early to ride with Cadwgan and King Murtagh O'Brien. Angharad, still shaken, took the opportunity to rest in the fine bed and admire the tapestries on the walls. She was still in her bed some while later when there was a knock at the door, and Lafracoth O'Brien, Murtagh's beautiful eldest daughter, poked her head around and introduced herself.

"How are you feeling today after all your adventures?" she lilted, smiling a wide, white-toothed smile.

"Better than yesterday but still feeling a little exhausted and sore," Angharad smiled back, conscious of how grubby she must seem with her salt-matted hair in front of the tall, well-shaped woman whose naturally upright carriage made her seem particularly stately.

"I was thinking you won't have any clothes with you other than those you were wearing, and I thought, we being much the same size, you might like to wear something of mine. We can get Siobhan, my maid, to wash and repair yours. What do you say?"

Angharad expressed her gratitude. Within moments, Siobhan appeared with a bundle of new clothes and took away what was left of her journey and sea-ravaged attire. She looked with surprise at the beautiful fine-woven garments and appealed to her newfound friend.

"These are far too beautiful for me to wear. I couldn't possibly impose upon you." She marvelled at the intricacy of the needlework embroidering the linen underdresses and the fine soft wool of the dress. Lafracoth had even included some beautiful silver brooches and amber beads.

Lafracoth laughed, "I have too many to fit into my chests. I have a terrible way of spending my father's money on new cloth and jewellery at the markets, and Siobhan is the finest needlewoman in the whole of Dublin, so please have them if they would fit you and you like them."

"Was it you who arranged for the shift for me and clean clothes for Gruffydd?"

"It was nothing. Cadwgan arrived a few hours before you, and he looked as if he had been hauled out of the ocean in a net, so when we knew you were on the way, it was an easy thing to do. Let me give you a while, and Siobhan here will help you wash and tend to your hair. It is a mane, sure enough, and will take some sorting."

Then, as quickly as she had appeared, Lafracoth was gone. Slowly and gingerly, Angharad and the maid tried to restore some semblance of her beauty now bruised, cut and scratched. It was remarkable that for all that she had gone through, she was strong enough to walk about, and most importantly, the baby growing within her seemed to have survived the exertions.

Siobhan held her hair in her hands and shook her head at the immensity of the task. At first, she thought the hair so matted that she may have to cut it off as a comb would not go through it, but then she began to wash it with a concoction made of elm bark, willow root and nettles and rinse it in goats' milk with mint to make it easier to tease out the tangles. Angharad took a little bread and milk to settle her still delicate stomach and donned the beautiful clothing. By the time Lafracoth returned, she was clean and presentable, even if she still looked battered.

"Well, I see that Gruffydd has married a beauty after all," Lafracoth teased, "I thought he must have lowered his impeccable standards!"

Angharad was taken aback at the familiarity with which Lafracoth spoke of Gruffydd and the easy absence of the formality she was used to in Wales. The young Irish princess' sunny disposition, however, made it impossible to feel any slight, and Angharad began to enjoy Lafracoth's warm camaraderie.

A bustle of activity and shouts caused the ladies to look out of the window into the courtyard.

"Oh, look who is coming to visit," commented Lafracoth

Angharad looked down and saw a small party of men led by a dark fine-clothed noble on a striking grey horse. She looked quizzically at Lafracoth.

"It is Rory O'Kennedy. He is hoping to make an alliance with my father by marrying me," Lafracoth explained openly.

Her thick, dark braided hair swayed as she spun around, rolling her black-lashed, wide-set brown eyes in a half-mocking look.

"Do you like him?"

'I would be sharing my marriage bed with every other half-decent woman in Leinster, that's for sure. Look at him, he loves himself so much that he thinks everyone must love him as much!! Anyway, my father has other ideas for me to cement foreign alliances rather than ones here at home."

Angharad shuddered, thinking about the horror she had felt when her father considered her a suitable wife for Hugh the Fat.

"Listen, it would suit me to slip out into the town for the day and avoid having to entertain him, especially as I know my father will be getting all the news from Gruffydd while they are out riding, so it will be almost dusk before they return. Shall I show you around the town, and we can be gone out of the back before he sees us? We can visit my cousins, and I will introduce you. Do you feel up to it?"

"I think so," Angharad replied cautiously. "I can't sit here feeling sorry for myself."

"That's the way," Lafracoth encouraged her. "We will take it slowly."

Then looking at Angharad's sturdy leather boots, she said, "Those will be perfect. Although it has been dry these last few days, Dublin is filthy underfoot."

The two women, accompanied by a jug-eared, portly man-at-arms, started into the town just below the fortress. The day was a bright one, and Angharad began to feel as eager to explore as her friend was to escape. Ahead of them, a pottery-laden pony stood motionless, legs braced, ears firmly forward, and eyes rolling expressively as a small, weedy man with a preponderance of jaggedly broken black teeth hissed and cursed, his face puckered with irritation. To Angharad's utter surprise, Lafracoth spoke to the man, took the rope holding the pony from his hand, then whispering and patting the pony, managed to coax it down the incline. Angharad had a way with horses herself but would not have considered assisting a merchant in this way. In her upbringing, such a thing would not have been considered ladylike, and yet Lafracoth was not only a lady but a princess, daughter of Murtagh, High King of Ireland.

The town was surprisingly large, and she compared it with Rhuddlan and Chester. What struck her was the liveliness and freedom here so different to those Norman towns where the castles dominated and oversaw everything. The market days were far tamer affairs under Norman watchful eyes than she was seeing here. There were so many people from different cultures, and a proficient linguist, her ear tuned into the different languages and dialects all around. People and animals jostled in the streets: young, ragged boys leading fat piglets on strings, their squeals competing with the general uproar; calves

158

being driven with no regard for stallholders or purchasers; women with chickens in baskets as well as those who had come to peruse and buy the goods on offer.

Lafracoth stopped at a stall where a wizened old man was carving dexterously out of bone. Arrayed before him were pipes, hair pins, combs, toggle fasteners in different designs, spindle whorls, and beautiful buckles and belt ends with intricate patterning.

"What are those?" asked Angharad, pointing to some little objects she didn't recognise.

"Oh, that's for a game they call Brandubh," advised Lafracoth. "Do you know it? Some people call it Hnefatafl."

Angharad shook her head.

"It is a good game. I have it, and we can play later if you like."

Picking up a belt end with some pretty plant designs, Lafracoth asked the trader the price. Then, reaching into her leather pouch, she pulled out some coins. Seeing Angharad's look of surprise, she held out her hand with the coins.

"These are our own minted coins. You can trade with them, and everyone recognises them hereabouts. Otherwise, if you don't have these coins, they will weigh gold or silver."

Tucking her purchase into her pouch, they moved on, bypassing the yelling or cajoling street vendors, avoiding darting shrieking children, skirting around gossiping women and loud, boisterous men until they came to a leather merchant. From the smell permeating the air, Angharad felt a tannery must be nearby. The stall was full of different styles of shoes and boots, which Angharad viewed covetously, having only the boots she had worn since her flight. With no money or silver to trade, she would need to manage with what she had, but she touched the beautifully soft leather shoes, belts, gloves and wonderfully engraved leather sheaths. The craftsman looked up enquiringly from his work with an awl, making tiny holes, which he would later stitch to make up some boots. Angharad shook her head quickly, indicating that she was only looking. The extraordinary difficulty of the position she found herself in without means of buying what she needed weighed heavily upon her and was reinforced here at the market. As they visited salesmen with incredible rolls of magnificent cloth, including the finest silks, and moved on to jewellery craftsmen working in copper, silver and gold, Angharad became increasingly downcast. Not only was she feeling impoverished, but she was also aware that there was nothing like this in Gwynedd or that she knew of in the whole of Wales. How she had fallen, she thought, from Queen of Gwynedd to beholden to others for clothes, food and a place to rest her head.

Not everything at the market was so wonderful, however. The stench, not only from the tannery and the fishmongers, who threw fish into the street to the glee of opportunist seagulls but from all around, was almost more than her sensitive pregnant stomach could bear. The streets were, as Lafracoth had suggested, disgusting with all sorts of household refuse strewn across the pathways, animal droppings adding to the already pungent residues, maggots writhing, flies buzzing, rats scurrying amongst the waste and even hawks swooping to seize what they could. Scavenging, pitifully thin dogs bared their teeth and fought over discarded bones or rotting meat. Angharad needed to lift her tunic high as they wallowed through debris up to her ankles, so she had no way of covering her nose with her hands, and her stomach churned. She tried to turn her attention to the wares of the wood-turners, potters, and coopers who were producing the fine barrels for which Dublin was famed as they picked their way through the filth.

When they turned a corner, a horror awaited them that Angharad was totally unprepared for. A group of women and children roped together shuffled and stumbled in single file, driven along by a hard-faced, impatient man carrying a sturdy whip that he cracked at intervals. Coming to an abrupt halt as he yelled at them to stop, they had arrived at their fenced destination: the Slave Market. The most dejected-looking souls Angharad had ever seen were congregated in front of her, tethered like animals, some in chains and representing every part of the world, it would seem. Many seemed emaciated, including some tiny toddlers who looked at her pleadingly. Most of them had their eyes cast downwards but she was astounded to hear the babble of English and Welsh voices call out to her, desperation in their words. Some of the slaves were Irish and were destined for masters either in other parts of Ireland or overseas, according to Lafracoth. Her eyes scanned many bruises and welts. Some unfortunates with swollen faces had obviously incurred the wrath of their slave master who contained any show of spirit.

"So many of these women are pregnant," she gasped, her face white with shock and distress.

"The traders get them pregnant because they fetch a greater price," replied Lafracoth, as if she was talking about the animals they had seen penned up along the road.

"Some are just children; they are just children!" Angharad's eyes met the soulful gaze of two tiny, ragged children holding hands next to their mother whose large sad eyes gazed mournfully out of a piteously thin face. From her bearing, Angharad could see that this was a woman, who, like herself, had once enjoyed the privileges of birth, and she was filled with abhorrence. Only days ago, this too or worse, if there was indeed worse, might have been her fate. Angharad felt helpless, and she vowed that if ever she did again hold any position of authority, she would not permit such foul trading.

A slave trader leant against a post, watching them with an impassive, rigid face. He lifted his eyebrows to ascertain their interest.

"Come," said Lafracoth, steering her away from the market, "many will go to good homes where they will be well fed compared to some of the poverty-stricken villages that drought and plague have brought to their knees in these last years. Not only here in Ireland, you know.

Come, you look exhausted already. We will stop for some refreshment and rest at my cousin's home."

They walked through small, dark, narrow streets where wattle and daub fences separated each house from its neighbour. Woven wattle pathways were laid down to the entrance to the homes, where most owners had pens for the various animals and birds they kept. Lafracoth led Angharad along the pathway to one home where goats, pigs and chickens shared a large pen and the overhanging thatch from the house's roof provided shelter from both sun and rain. Three ferocious-looking tethered dogs gave warning of their approach but nobody appeared. As they reached the door, they could hear the shrill bickering of small children, the sound of something having been thrown, and then two boys leapt mock fighting out of the door, bowled into their visitors and, looking particularly alarmed, retreated into the house, shouting for their mother.

"My nephews," laughed Lafracoth. "As wicked a pair as you will find in the whole of Dublin!"

She entered the house, beckoning Angharad in and called out to a fair-skinned woman with piercingly blue eyes. The woman immediately left her loom and glided over the reeded floor.

Ragnailt was middle-aged but still of fine figure and beauty. Angharad found out that she had four children, two older and two younger boys. She watched as Ragnailt directed her servants and noted how impeccably everything was kept inside. Across one wall was a huge tapestry of a hunting scene, and she also noticed a lyre and wondered if it was Ragnailt or her husband who played. Soon they were sitting and chatting as they drank herbal tea, which Ragnailt said would aid the repair of her bruises, cuts and grazes.

"Were you in the battle itself?" she asked, laughing lightly to make her guest feel less conspicuous, so Angharad took no offence, beginning to understand the Irish humour.

"You would think so," said Angharad, trying to be more cheerful than she felt. She was asked to regale them with the tale of what happened and her horrendous sea voyage to Ireland. In some ways, the telling of it helped her but she avoided reference to her father or uncle.

"It's a wonder you can even stand," said Lafracoth sympathetically, probably realising for the first time the enormity of what the wan Welsh woman in front of her had endured.

Ragnailt was tight-lipped suddenly. "Those bastard mercenaries, let them rot in hell. Gruffydd has been a good friend to them and is known for his honesty. It will come back on them, you wait. They have cheated on their own and that is as low as you can go." Angharad was surprised both at the extent of her wrath and her familiarity with Gruffydd but said nothing.

"Is Amlaib away?" asked Lafracoth, looking around.

"Yes," said Ragnailt, "he is off with Magnus Barelegs."

Angharad looked quizzical.

"A strange name for a king, is it not? It is said they call him Barelegs because he wears his tunic short like our Irish men."

"Some call him, Barefoot," said Lafracoth.

"Because he rides his horse with no shoes like our Irish men," laughed Ragnailt.

"And some call him, Magnus the Tall," added Lafracoth.

"Even though he is short, he thinks he is mighty, just like our Irish men."

The two women giggled.

"And then there is Magnus the Strife Lover, which suits him best," elaborated Lafracoth.

"Which is also like our Irish men," the two women said in unison, laughing.

"He tries so hard to win land in Ireland; he surely wants to be one of our Irish men!" said Ragnailt.

"I have heard little of King Magnus," admitted Angharad.

"Well, there is a story to be told," said Ragnaillt, grinning at Lafracoth. "He is the King of Norway, and his grandfather was Harald Hardrada, whose ambition was to be King of England, and he almost succeeded. Magnus probably has that same ambition, and Rufus is wary of him, I hear. Magnus has a reputation for being invincible in battle. He has been busy securing the Irish Sea. Not satisfied with fighting the other Scandinavian monarchs, he set off with a fleet of 160 ships and raided Orkney, where he set his eight-year-old son up as earl if you please. Meanwhile, he is negotiating with the Scottish. Now he has eyes on the other Hebridean isles: Uist, Skye, Tiree, Mull and the peninsula of Kintyre. A hundred of his ships were from the public levy, and those have returned to Norway now that he has secured Orkney, so he wanted to add to his fleet from Dublin."

"So, your husband has gone as a mercenary?"

Ragnailt nodded, and an anxious look crossed her face. "Yes, a mercenary. A man who lives by battle skill and luck. He has taken our oldest boy with him this time. I shouldn't worry; I know he will take care of him, but he is still young to be in the thick of battle. I would prefer he was at home where I could see him. Every time they go to sea, I wonder whether I will see them again, my husband, my brothers and now my son, but that is their life and I knew it when I married him."

Angharad felt a jolt, realising that the same could be said of her. Now that she carried their child, she wondered whether she would feel the same as this lady when her son, if so it was, was of age.

"Are your brothers with Magnus on this trip?" asked Lafracoth.

"They leave to join him tonight. Their boat needed repair which couldn't be fixed in time for them to leave with the others."

"I hope they are careful not to cross allegiances with my father," warned Lafracoth. "He will not be pleased if they are fighting for Magnus in Irish lands."

"They are mercenaries but they would not fight their own. Magnus pays well, and you need to have wealth enough to support your family in these times," Ragnailt flared indignantly. Then, remembering their guest, changed the subject, adding, "I will let them know that Gruffydd is here. They will hardly believe that this day his wife was sitting at our hearth!"

Ragnailt registered Angharad's look of surprise.

"Gruffydd lived with us for a while when he was much younger, and I was like an older sister to him. Back then, he hated fighting; my brothers would give him a hard time until, suddenly, he was better than all of them, so proud and determined to do everything well. Despite his reputation, he is a kind man, but you would know that."

'I do," admitted Angharad.

"I remember when my firstborn came,' Ragnaillt shook her head, "and he was such a difficult child. He would be crying all night and with Amlaib on the sea, of course, I was exhausted. It was Gruffydd who would come and take the child in the early hours of the morn and sing it to sleep. I would wake up, and the baby would be content in the cradle, and your man was gone so quietly. You have broken many women's hearts by marrying him, I can tell you!"

After the visit, they traced their way back through the filth. Angharad had committed all she had learnt to memory but was quiet as she wondered if this was where they would now make their lives; if she too would be a woman, like Ragnailt, always fearful her husband would not come home. Everything seemed so uncertain and so unfamiliar.

165

She returned to their chamber and collapsed onto the bed, where Gruffydd found her a short time later.

"So, you have been to visit Ragnailt," Gruffydd said, cradling Angharad's back against him so that he could hold her belly. "I hope the little one is getting enough rest after what you have both been through."

"I feel a lot better," she assured him, "and the little one is growing well. Nothing escapes anyone at this Irish Court."

"Nothing," he agreed, "Were they all there? Did you meet the family?"

"Just her and the two smallest boys. Her husband and oldest son are with Magnus Barelegs, and her brothers go to join them tomorrow," explained Angharad.

"They are sailing with Magnus?" asked Gruffydd, not sure he had heard it correctly.

"Apparently so."

"And her brothers have not left yet?"

"No, they had to finish repairs on their boat."

His face brightened. "Then I will send a messenger with them to Magnus to let him know what has happened. It is possibly too late but it is in his interest for Gwynedd to remain in Welsh hands rather than be Norman held."

"The trading?"

"Indeed. He is creating an empire, and he doesn't want the Normans encroaching on it."

"Ragnailt suggested he wouldn't mind if England was part of that empire as well."

"True, but he needs to bed down all his other acquisitions first."

"And Wales will be safe from him?"

"We have an understanding," he replied, before rushing off down to the port to find Ragnailt's brothers.

Angharad sat and mused, hoping that their understanding with Magnus was bound by sterner principles than their understanding with the Irish mercenaries whose commanders had betrayed them.

***

That night Angharad joined the feasting. She and Gruffydd were put in places of honour, close to Murtagh O'Brien and Lafracoth. Cadwgan sat on the other side of Murtagh and was already drinking heavily. King Murtagh's appearance surprised Angharad as she had expected someone powerfully built and vigorous. Instead, he looked like a sickly and emaciated man with poor skin, cracked lips and rheumy bloodshot eyes that seemed to read people's thoughts. His thin dark hair was pulled back against his skull. On the other side of Cadwgan were the three brothers of his late wife, Gwenllian, who had been the daughter of Gruffydd ap Cynan, the older. Idwal had dark curly hair, was stoutly built and had a roving eye; Iago was more serious and paler, whereas his older brother was swarthy, with straight chestnut hair, and Cadwaladwr had a solemn face but a fine physique. They liked Cadwgan and he them and, even though they were cousins of Gruffydd's and nearer to him in age, she noticed that they did not have the easy rapport with him that they did with their older brother-in-law, Cadwgan.

The table was overflowing with food, including cheeses, oat cakes, bread, vegetables and all kinds of meats, such as goat, wild boar, venison and hedgehogs cooked in clay so that their spines were removed when the clay was removed. The wine was flowing, and although the night was young, many of the nobles were already drunk.

Some staggered outside to vomit and then returned to drink and feast again.

Cadwgan was called upon to provide entertainment, and swaying slightly, he stood and told the tale of Gwyn ap Nudd, the wild huntsman who lived in the underworld and rode his demon horse at night to hunt souls while his white-bodied, red-eared pack of hounds of hell let out blood-curdling howls. Unlike the Welsh court, where people would listen respectfully, she felt awkward that his story was interrupted with bawdy comments and jokes.

When he had finished, Murtagh slapped him on the back.

"When those traitorous bastards get back here, I will let out my own hounds of hell upon them, and they will rue the day they dealt with the Normans. How dare they shame me and violate my good name. Never mind, revenge is powerful!"

"I would be delighted to help you with that," said Cadwgan, "and take their filthy Norman payment as well."

"We can raise a fleet from the Isles," continued Murtagh. "They will wipe the Normans faces in their own shit."

Gruffydd leant over to Angharad and explained that Murtagh's nephew, Diarmuid, had married a Manx princess, and that gave the family overlordship of the Isles. This gave the King the means to extra manpower and large naval fleets. Not only that, but Murtagh knew he had a place where he could easily control assaults on Ulster and his enemy, Domnall O'Loughlin. Angharad said nothing but wondered if this was not in conflict with what she had heard of Magnus Bareleg's plans.

"But are you not thinking of a Norman husband for your daughter?" Cadwgan asked Murtagh.

"And are you not married to a Norman wife yourself?" retorted Murtagh. "That doesn't seem to have stopped your battles with them."

"But may save my neck one day!"

"True, you need to keep your wits about you and make alliances that protect what may happen tomorrow though you could not foresee them yesterday!"

Then turning to Gruffydd, who was looking gloomy, he said, "You know, we have all dealt with betrayal. I was betrayed by my own brother when he sided with Leinster against me; we didn't speak for years."

"God knows what they have done to Anglesey," said Gruffydd bitterly. "They have probably razed our llys, destroyed our churches and plundered the land. It will forever be on my conscience."

"My ancestral home, Kinkora, was destroyed by the O'Loughlins, and I still fury when I think of it but one day, I will destroy the Royal Seat of the Kings of Ailech, stone by stone. Meanwhile, I rebuild Kinkora, better than before. Revenge is the only way, Gruffydd: let your fury burn outwards, not inwards."

"Revenge does not help the dead," snapped Gruffydd, under his breath betraying the extent of his anger and despair.

Angharad felt a cold chill as she thought of everything they had worked hard to create being destroyed and wondered what their future would be and where their young child would grow up. Would it be here in Ireland? She looked around her in agitation and was appalled at what she saw. Some men had women on their knees and were fondling their breasts or kissing them passionately, openly in front of everyone. A fight broke out between two different nobles, and suddenly, swords were being drawn, and the whole of one side of the hall was wrestling and punching while the king roared, and the fighters were pushed into the courtyard outside. Dogs skulked under the tables, snarling and grabbing at food falling to the floor.

169

The Welshwoman had never experienced such disorder and chaos, and yet Lafracoth and her father looked regal and unmoved. Gruffydd said nothing, staring into his drinking horn.

When they retired to their chamber, Gruffydd said little and looked tight-faced.

Outside someone was vomiting and another fight erupting. She heard women giggling and the grunts of someone taking their pleasure in a dark corner.

"What's the matter?" Gruffydd asked sharply as he saw her disgusted face.

She was hurt by the uncharacteristically sharp tone. "This is a wild place, Gruffydd," she explained herself. "There seems to be little respect, no order, and the town is filthy with refuse everywhere and stinking."

Gruffydd said nothing, and although he held her when they got into bed, he seemed cold and distant. She assumed that he was grieving over the betrayal in Anglesey and its aftermath. Dismissing the rising concern she was feeling, she soon fell asleep, exhausted.

Chapter 14: The Ship-building Yard (July 1098)

It was early when Gruffydd shook Angharad gently awake.

"Is there something wrong?" she asked, surprised because he had been so considerate of her sleeping as much as she needed in the last days, seeing how the sea journey to Dublin had exhausted her.

"There is something I want you to see."

She dressed quickly in the grey-blue light heralding the dawn and the last of the light from the waning moon. She followed him quietly out of their room by throwing on her woollen shawl cloak and catching the smell of her sea journey entwined in its fibres. They crossed the hall where servants were lighting the fire for the cauldron. Some of the nobles who had been carousing late the night before were already having regrets as they sat on the edge of the raised platforms holding their heads in their hands or leaning back against the walls with eyes half closed. In Wales, too, it was common to see such sights after a feast but here it was every night that such drinking was to excess. She noted Gruffydd marking her look of disgust.

"Where are you taking me, Gruffydd?" she said as he held her arm firmly and guided her more swiftly than she felt comfortable with.

His answer surprised her. "I want to show you what makes a nation successful. You have shown such disdain for Dublin and the way our hosts live over the last few days."

"No, Gruffydd," she started to protest, appalled that he thought her ungrateful for all the kindness that had been shown her and here she was dressed in Lafracoth's beautiful gifts. He had lifted a hand to silence her, but seeing the colour flood her face and neck softened his tone.

"You have seen little of the world, and what you have seen here has shocked you because it is unfamiliar, but not everything different is bad."

There was a tone of exasperation. She bit her tongue.

They continued their way on the rough path leading to the harbour where the mighty Liffey met the sea east of the town. Standing a little above, she was surprised to see the hive of activity below so early in the morning. The place was alive with workmen, their saws, planes, axes and files singing out in the clear morning air. Along the edge of the river, carts were already hauling tree trunks, and men were securing timber in a massive bath of water penned along the river.

"See there?" Gruffydd pointed to four partly built ships. These will be helping us secure Gwynedd. Three still on the stocks and one in the water ready for the finishes."

Angharad felt the implied sting and nod towards her ingratitude in his words.

"And see there," he continued, pointing to the carts hauling timber, "finest oak for the strength you need for a keel, the spine of the ship, where it takes the pressure when the boat is dragged out of the water onto the beaches or across rocks. That oak would have been picked out from forests miles away years ago and remembered for when it was needed. When shipbuilding on this scale started, there was plenty of oak, but it is slow growing, so now some of the boat is made of other woods," he pointed to various piles, "ash, pine, willow, birch. All carefully chosen years before."

He let out a roar of pleasure as he spotted a tall, flaxen-haired, broad-shouldered man with an air of authority striding purposefully across the shipyard.

"That man down there is Olaf, the shipwright, who not only commands the force of men who build these ships but knows every forest for miles around."

172

Gruffydd took her arm again and moved her gently along the steep path down to the water's edge.

"Olaf," he shouted and ran forward to embrace the shipwright, who turned with a broad grin returning the embrace with a mighty bearhug. They spoke in a language yet unfamiliar to Angharad, pointing and gesturing as they discussed the progress of the ships. As they spoke, Angharad looked around to take in the scene before her. Nearest to her was a blacksmith forging what looked like nails over a roaring fire. Nearby, two men were wielding huge axes to divide a long straight oak trunk in half; she could see from the wood piled up that they would cut the trunk until it was in eighths. Other men worked with planes on shaping the wood, and beyond them, a worker seemed to be preparing huge wooden nails. Others were preparing planking to form the seats on the boats while some were assembling and stuffing oiled wool in between the planks as they were placed overlapping each other. She walked toward a fine boat with a dragon head and watched as a craftsman decorated the neck of the dragon with a gouge and draw knife. It was as fine craftsmanship as she had seen in any court. Four men were hoisting huge linen sails onto the ship and on the side of the quay was a man preparing huge lengths of rope from seal skin.

Angharad marvelled at the craftsmanship. She had seen such incredible activity before only when she had observed Roger of Rhuddlan's castle being constructed. Gruffydd came to join her.

"These are the best shipbuilders in the world, the best craftsmen. The men who sail these boats are the best seafarers, not only warriors but merchants who risk their lives to travel across the world to trade their goods."

Angharad thought of the wonderful goods she had seen at the market the previous day. Beautiful brooches and ornaments crafted from ivory and whalebone, beads of amber and glass, fine cloth and fabric such as silk in stunning colours. Then she thought of the silversmiths weighing their silver on tiny scales and shaping magnificent jewellery

173

pieces. She cast her mind back to the splendid array of food such as honey, salts, wheat and fruit. She thought of the elaborately decorated boxes, leather goods and knives and the rows of workshops where craftsmen made pottery, turned wooden bowls and where the blacksmith toiled at his anvil next to his furnace creating swords, knives, scythes and whatever demand for his metal there was. She felt shame wash over her and turned now to her husband.

"You are right, Gruffydd. When I went through Dublin yesterday, instead of allowing myself to be overwhelmed by the craftsmanship and industry, I saw only the filth, the rats and the maggots. Last night, instead of the comradeship, the humour and the merrymaking, I saw only the drunkenness, the roughness and the excess. It is not my place to judge our host or his city when he has welcomed us, and we have no home."

Gruffydd held her two arms and looked down into her troubled face. "You see it. Now you see it. I know it is hard but I need you to be strong, to be the woman you have always been who sees the best in everything. Cariad, right now, we are adrift, but we do have a home. We must also remember that the people of Gwynedd will be exhausted. They need time to recover their strength. Even if I raised an army now, it would be useless. When we go back, we must find a way to ensure their safety and give them hope."

"I know, Gruffydd, and I am sorry. I was being selfish, only thinking of what we had lost and judging everything here unkindly. I don't want you to be angry or shut me out."

"I am angry but not with you. I am angry because I didn't do well enough. I also put you so high on a pedestal that when you were anything other than perfect in the way you viewed others, I reacted badly to it. Nobody is perfect. Neither of us is perfect; all we can do is strive to do better all the time."

She was amazed at his honesty, and though it hurt her that she had fallen short in his eyes, she was glad he could articulate such feelings to her.

"I know, Gruffydd, I understand."

"Cariad, when my ancestor Olaf Sihtricson came to Dublin, the place was nothing, but he used what he knew best and created one of the foremost trading posts, fought over for its wealth and prestige where art and culture flourished. I want to take the best of what I have seen in this world, here in Dublin, and the best of what I see in the Norman world and harness it to the strengths of the Welsh. We can make Gwynedd united, strong, and prosperous. We can give it heart, pride, and security. We can make our sojourn here a learning to take back home." He spoke passionately, urgently.

"I believe you can do that, Gruffydd, and I will try harder to see beyond the surface, but…."

"But?"

"Gwynedd needs to be a peaceful place. If I have learnt anything from my father, it is that there is always a middle way, and when we return, we must find that middle way. Let negotiation, not war, help us to find that way with our enemies. No more violence, Gruffydd. I do not want our children to be always looking over their shoulders, always fighting. I don't want to live as your uncle did."

He closed his eyes as he thought of his uncle sailing off into the distance with Robert of Rhuddlan's head stuck to the mast.

"Our children will know how to fight, how to defend what is theirs, Angharad, but I promise you I will not endanger lives unnecessarily or encourage them to. Cariad, to achieve what needs to happen, we must knit our dreams together. Where I am hasty and rash, you are considered and cautious. You are respected for your piety; I am respected for my valour. You know how the Normans think, and I know how to work with the Northmen. Together, combining our strengths but recognising our differences, we can create a Gwynedd that our poets celebrate throughout the world."

At that moment, as his arms tightened around her waist and she felt the small stirring of the new life within her, her love for the man to whom she had bound herself swelled, yet Gwynedd seemed so very far away. She didn't ever forget the eloquence of his words; when times grew dark, she would hold them in her heart and cling to them.

The rowdy festivities did not get any less rowdy, and if Angharad had come to Ireland an innocent girl, she certainly had seen much of the seedier side of life within a few days of being there. Keeping her promise to Gruffydd, though, she looked at what she could learn. She quickly understood the value of the friendships she made, particularly with Lafracoth, whom she found intelligent, quick-witted and compassionate.

She loved talking to Lafracoth about Gruffydd's early years in Ireland as a lanky youth.

"He was very, what you might call, 'refined' and for a long time put up with a lot of teasing. When the other boys were chasing girls and drinking at the alehouses, he would spend time at the monastery with the monks learning about religion, history and literature. Then he would be on his way back, and they would pick a fight with him and knock him black and blue, but he would keep getting up and never give in."

"I think there is a lot of that in him still," said Angharad.

"He was very close to his mother. She was a gentle lady but very strong and determined. His mother was beautiful and may have married again many times over, but her heart was broken when she lost the love of her life, Cynan."

"Do you know much of him?" asked Angharad, as Gruffydd rarely spoke of his father.

"He was here in Ireland as well for a while, I think," said Lafracoth, "but I have not heard much of him."

"And his cousin?"

"The older Gruffydd, you mean. Lord, preserve me; he was wild!"

"I have heard him described like that before."

"He knew every woman in Dublin, I swear, and he had children coming out of his ears! He was a drinker and a gambler, and they say he fought like a demon. He was a massive man, but, in the end, it was the plague that finished him." She crossed herself.

"You had the plague badly here?"

"We lost nearly a quarter of our people. Not only the poor. Even Godred, who ruled Dublin, caught the plague, although he died on the Isle of Islay. It started when we had terrible weather five years ago and so many deaths from that. First, the high winds destroyed the crops. Then another bad year the following year began harshly with huge snow coming in the new year, killing people, animals and birds. That meant hardly anything could be sown, and if sowing is delayed, then the crop doesn't get a chance to grow fully, or sometimes it can be because the seedling itself can't withstand the brutal weather we have."

"We have the same concerns in Wales. Sometimes we have heavy rains in autumn, and then the crop is ruined or, if it is too hot and dry, or if the winds are high, the crop suffers, and the people struggle through the winter."

"And if there is no winter fodder, then the animals die."

"It is a hard life," said Angharad, thinking how often the lands around the manor had suffered.

"Yes," said Lafracoth, shaking her head. "If the crops fail, the animals suffer, the farmers suffer, and in their weakened state, pestilence follows. Then, as they say, where there is famine, there is fever, and the plague lasted from August right through to May. The church said it was because of evils committed; there was almsgiving and abstinence for our wrongdoing. It says in Deuteronomy, God will give you prosperity, bless the work of your hand and lands and children and livestock, but you must keep his commandments, and if you don't, you will be cursed." She turned suddenly to Angharad. "Do you believe that?"

Angharad paused. "I often wonder what some poor people who have always been God-fearing have done to deserve the awful lives they have. I try not to question such things."

"I cannot help but question but that does not change the fact that we have famine here still."

Angharad looked shocked.

"You have famine?" She thought of the loaded tables each night and the feasting.

"We do. Here in Dublin, we hardly see it. If you go just outside Dublin or outside of the other Viking settlements like Wexford, Cork, Limerick and Waterford, places where there is trading, you will see there is death and desperation everywhere. Everything outside Dublin and those other ports depends on working the land or the sea. The trading towns have not been so badly hurt, but the farmers have nothing to live on. Some had to sell their sons and daughters into slavery rather than see them starve to death."

Angharad could hardly believe the extent of the famine and then the plague as well.

"The plague decimated the farming community and reached the towns as well. Here in Ireland, if someone is sick, kin is obligated to look after you and nurse you back to health. That's in our custom and written in our laws, but the disease spread among the kin, and there was nobody to tend them according to the laws, so they just died."

"You have laws about tending the sick?" asked Angharad.

"We have laws about everything."

Angharad looked surprised.

"Ah, you think we seem wild and lawless?"

Angharad's blushes confirmed Lafracoth's thoughts.

"We know how to celebrate life! We drink, we eat, we fight, we share what we have, but underneath all that, we have laws, and those laws sew everything together like a tapestry."

"I know so little of Ireland, and I am grateful to you for explaining what I should know by right. I don't know how long we will be here but I have to understand how things work if I am to bring up a family here."

"And if I come to Wales, I hope you will do the same for me. Our laws are based on what is deemed fair. If someone injures someone else, then they are responsible for nursing them back to health rather than expecting the kin to provide for them until they are well, as is normally the case; they must have peace and quiet, no animals, no gaming or rowdy behaviour, no shouting at children, no fighting, the house must be kept clean, and they eat or avoid certain foods. We believe that to recover, you need a still place and the best food to repair your body. It is all in the laws."

"It is so controlled! Even the food? What foods do they say to avoid?"

"It depends on the illness, but anything with sea salt makes you thirsty, horseflesh upsets your stomach, and honey loosens the bowels. Then other times, honey can be a curative. In some cases, the kin must pay for a liaig, a healer, to give the right medical treatment.

179

Kinship is everything: kinship protects you, makes sure you have a means of surviving, helps you find a partner and gives you status. Kin rely absolutely on each other."

"Kinship is the same in Wales as well, although even in families, divisions can break out and brothers can fight brothers for land or status."

"And that is the same here. Look at my father and his brother. It is probably the same all over the world." She pondered and looked out into the countryside. "Would you like to ride outside the city?"

"I would love to," said Angharad eagerly. She was not yet used to the hustle and bustle; Dublin was very hectic. She longed for the quietness of the countryside and fresh air.

The next day, the two women and two armed servants set out on horseback, and Angharad was surprised to find that their horses were Welsh.

"Welsh horses are very well regarded over here," explained Lafracoth.

As they wound through the countryside, they stopped at little farming settlements. Many of them were completely abandoned. Each homestead was enclosed by a circular stone or earth-raised ring, fenced at the top to stop animals straying and against petty thieves. They rode into one abandoned property. Inside was a byre, a pigsty, an old sheepfold and a calf fold.

"This is where they would store their valuables," said Lafracoth, pointing to a souterrain. At one time, this might have been full of food, maybe dairy products or seeds. This was where you hid the women and children from your enemies if you were attacked."

"We have some like these in South Wales but not in North Wales," said Angharad.

It was so sad to see the farms and fields which had been abandoned. Another farm came into view. As they approached, they saw little, skinny children shooing hens and collecting eggs in a basket. A small girl holding a pet lamb in her arms stared at them and then ran away to her siblings scattering squealing piglets as she did so. Another older girl carried her baby brother on her back, and in her hand, she held a pail. Standing together in the yard were three reasonably healthy milk cows, udders full. In the fields behind the farm, a man was herding sheep. A sallow-skinned old woman sat on the doorstep of the dwelling, eyes half closed against the sun, waving a gnarly hand to shoo flies. She stared hard and then nodded respectfully as they passed by.

"How strange that this farm seems to be flourishing whereas others have really suffered," Angharad remarked, wonderingly.

"Maybe they had enough money to supplement their winter stock provisions, and they had kept themselves away from other families infected with the plague. While nobody tends their neighbours' fields, they may take what crop there is for themselves if they have older children to help with bringing it in."

"The farm looks as if it is faring well!"

"When there is no famine or plague, one thing we know about in Ireland is how to breed and take care of stock, cattle, sheep, pigs," explained Lafracoth. "Cattle grazing suits our weather here, and cattle are important to everything. If you have committed a crime, you may have to pay with so many cattle. If you have land, it is measured in how many cows it will hold. Honour prices are based on milk cows. Where you stand in life is by how many cows you have or could buy. Mainly, the cows are for milking; they are not killed for meat. Much of what people eat is from the milk: cheese, curds and milk itself. Pigs are also raised and do well here; pork and bacon or salted pork are what people eat. The sheep are for the wool; the women look after them. If you are wealthy, you might have a horse for light farmyard work, and if you need to go to war, you use that horse."

181

"Where we live in Gwynedd, it is the hill farmers who have the toughest lives. They raise cattle that thrive up in the summer pastures but it is a hard fight against the weather, and the soil is not good for growing hay on the mountain. Heather, gorse and reeds take over any useful land. They must give the cattle ferns and gorse to help the hay last through winter. The farmers live on what they produce and on what they can forage in woods and growing wild. Yet, most hill farmers would not change their isolated, hard lives. They barter for what they need, share their skills with other hill farmers and keep their customs and traditions. The farmers who live in the valleys have an easier life in some ways, but then they are always looking over their shoulders to see if there is a threat of invasion and are always right under the noses of the Normans who take and take and take."

"Where in Gwynedd were you brought up?" asked Lafracoth.

"In the cantref of Tegeingl. My grandfather, Edwin, was given the lordship of Tegeingl by King Gruffydd ap Llewelyn."

"What is a cantref?" asked Lafracoth.

"It is a large area of land. In Gwynedd, there are twenty-two large estates called maenols, or you might call them manors, which have a llys at the centre which runs the estate. Each maenol will bring in regular rent and renders of meat, bread, honey and beer once or twice a year, and that goes to the lord. Every maenol has at least four trefi, which are small settlements. There would be twelve maenols per commote and two commotes in a cantref. Each cantref would be made up of one hundred trefi. In Welsh, 'cant' means a hundred. Traditionally, Gwynedd has thirteen cantrefi ruled by the thirteen noble families of Gwynedd."

"And your father ruled one of these cantrefi?"

"Yes, but it is more complicated because my father has been given the governorship of Gwynedd by the Normans, who see Gwynedd as theirs."

Lafracoth looked incredibly surprised.

"Is that not against Gruffydd, who is King of Gwynedd?"

Angharad sighed. "It is very complicated."

"Well, things do get complicated! My father calls himself High King of Ireland and has claims to the Isles, but Magnus Barefoot also has such claims and pretensions of taking Ireland. Then there was Godred, who was a King of Dublin and the Isles and yet he and my father were here side by side until my father ousted him. Sometimes they fight together against a common foe, and sometimes, they fight each other. Is that not also complicated?"

Angharad loved the way Lafracoth made her feel at ease. She felt that they had so much in common.

They rode on. There were yet many more farms where spiritless impoverished children gazed blankly through red-rimmed eyes at the party riding by. The sight of the children and their emaciated parents was almost more than either woman could bear.

"I would love to take you to Clonmacnoise monastery one time," said Lafracoth to distract from the melancholy that had beset them both. "It is a monastic town right on the River Shannon near a great crossroads which takes you north, south, east and west. It was founded by St Ciaran when he was only thirty years old, many hundreds of years ago. I went there once with my father. Everything is clean and neat, with vegetables, herbs and flowers growing in gardens. There are dwellings and workshops where artisans work with metal, glass and pottery. You would love to see the monks painting and illuminating manuscripts."

Angharad turned to her with interest.

"It is a great centre of learning," said Lafracoth. "Our history is written there in the annals of Tighernach. Over two thousand monks live there. Can you imagine? The place is so beautiful. I remember going through the water marshes and seeing otters playing and all sorts of flowers: cuckoo flower, marsh marigold, meadowsweet. And birds: swans, curlews, plovers. It is the most tranquil place."

"We have wonderful monasteries in Wales as well, but not as big as I think you are describing."

They walked their horses on a little further; Lafracoth looked into the distance.

"You know St Ciaran died of plague himself only a few years after he had built the monastery. What could he have possibly done wrong in God's eyes?"

***

Angharad was resting on the bed when Gruffydd came in and sat beside her.

"You've been out riding," he said.

"Oh, Gruffydd, they have had such a hard time here with famine and plague."

"And war."

"I have learnt so much. Lafracoth is so kind and patient with me."

"She has a big heart, like her father."

She kissed his cheek and then looked up at him. "What will we do, Gruffydd? We cannot stay here forever."

"I have fought alongside Murtagh before, and there are other battles he knows must come. I know how to lead men. I can help him, and he can help me. We will get back to Gwynedd, but we must plan carefully, Cariad."

"If we need to stay here, then I will be at your side, but I fear for you fighting, especially when these are not your battles."

Suddenly there was shouting and yelling out in the courtyard, and she looked at him in alarm.

"What's happening? Are we being attacked?"

Gruffydd stopped still for a moment to listen to the shouting, and then he said, "No, the mercenaries that went to Anglesey are sailing back in."

Angharad watched as he swiftly dressed himself, ready for combat, strapped on his sword and joined the throng of men, led by an angry Murtagh, down to the port. She quickly dressed and followed, standing on the edge of the hill to see what would happen.

A weak easterly breeze blew into the sails as the ships' crews guided their boats from Dublin Bay up the Liffey. As each boat moored at the edge of the port or pulled their ship up onto the sand, Murtagh's men roughly took them captive and led them away.

Angharad did not know why, but she turned away, went back to their chamber and cried.

Chapter 15: The Battle of Anglesey Sound (July 1098)

When Angharad went down into the main hall, she made her way over to Gruffydd, who was deep in conversation with Cadwgan. Seeing her, he leapt up and brought her to sit near them.

"Well, Angharad," said Cadwgan, "our luck may be turning!"

She looked to Gruffydd, who nodded to Cadwgan.

"I had a talk to one of the bastard ship owners, and it is an interesting story. As expected, the Normans tore through Anglesey, causing as much devastation and destruction as they could. They took captives and kept them at their camp. They had promised our mercenary friends that they could have all the young men and women they took captive, but, instead of that, they put aside the lame, old and helpless as part of their payment."

Angharad blanched, the image too vivid in her mind's eye.

"They showed scant respect for the Welsh or even the church. The Earl of Shrewsbury mutilated Cenred, the priest at Llandyfrydog, castrated him, took out one of his eyes, cut out his tongue and used the church as a kennel for his hounds."

Angharad gasped and clutched her throat with horror, remembering the dear old priest with his white hair and wide smile.

"No," she cried vehemently, the blood leaving her face and her heart hammering.

Gruffydd moved to steady her.

"Yes, indeed they did," continued Cadwgan. "The next day, when he collected his hounds, they had gone completely mad. Word went around the soldiers that God's wrath had been incurred. The Norman soldiers were not happy. Then, out of nowhere, comes a fleet of ships, six of them passing Puffin Island from the north. At the helm of the first was King Magnus Barefoot of Norway."

Gruffydd nodded at Angharad.

"As the Norwegian ships approached the shore, Magnus' men began shooting arrows at the assembled military. Hugh of Shrewsbury, who was clad in full armour as he rode in the shallows rallying his troops, was shot in the eye by Magnus himself! He fell into the water and wasn't found until the tide retreated, and there he was in the muddy shallows just a short while after he had mutilated the priest."

Angharad waited as Cadwgan drank deeply from his drinking horn.

"The Normans turned on their heels and left. If you think of it, each of Magnus' ships held one hundred and twenty strong fighting men, and he could call on backup easily. The Normans were not foolish. If they had engaged in battle, it might have meant a greater problem for them than Gwynedd had created, knowing Magnus' ambitions! Also, they had duped the mercenaries, and there was ill feeling there. They rushed back to Chester with Hugh D'Avranches at their head and carrying the body of Shrewsbury. They fled Gwynedd without any further reprisals."

"What does this mean?" asked Angharad in almost a whisper. "Can we return?"

Before she had a chance to get an answer, Murtagh strode into the hall.

"We have collected all the plunder from Anglesey, all the captives, all the ill-gotten gains from your Norman friends, and all will be returned to you to help repair the damage to Anglesey. They will be punished; some physically, some will be exiled, and their boats taken as a forfeit for your use."

Cadwgan and Gruffydd looked astonished.

"This is too generous," Gruffydd began but Murtagh held up a hand.

"These deceitful oafs have endangered my good name, and all I can do is to repair some of the damage that has been done. The bastards were telling me that Magnus Barelegs has been on Man. That's where his ships came from. They offered to go over to protect Man as if I would trust them: their ships are forfeit to you. Magnus may have saved you but he had better not be messing with what is mine. I will consider what to do about him but meanwhile, let's get to the serious business of feasting and enjoying life! Tomorrow we can talk about what we do to get you men back to Gwynedd and how I deal with Magnus Barelegs." Clapping his hands and shouting for entertainment, the hall was soon as lively and rowdy as it had been every other night.

Cadwgan celebrated as if they had won a major victory but Gruffydd was subdued. The confirmation of what had happened after his departure weighed heavily on him, and the treatment of Cenred disgusted him. Angharad tried to console him but she was heavy-hearted herself and found it difficult to find the right words. She also wondered what part her father had played in all of this. Had he stood aside while they violated the priest and rampaged through Anglesey? If so, it was unforgivable.

The next day, the men gathered to discuss the best approach. Murtagh and Cadwgan felt they should raise a force of mercenaries and cross Gwynedd ousting any sign of Norman presence. Gruffydd was firmly against it.

"No more lives," he said. "We must come to some agreement with them. We need to have firm arrangements in place with our allies outside of Gwynedd and use that as leverage."

As they argued and debated, Angharad found solace in Lafracoth's company.

"So, Magnus Barefoot came to your aid," said Lafracoth thoughtfully. "I wonder if word was sent via Ragnailt's brothers. Magnus would have no intention of letting the Normans curtail his trading routes, and Anglesey is critical to them."

"Thank God for him," said Angharad.

"He and my father have a stormy relationship," said Lafracoth. "At the moment, all is well, and my young sister is betrothed to Magnus's son, Sigurd. When Godred was ousted from Dublin back to the islands where he died, Magnus had my father's help to ensure he had sovereignty over the Isle of Man."

Angharad looked surprised.

"It is, as I said before, even enemies can be allies sometimes."

"Cadwgan has married a Norman wife," said Angharad, "and yet he fights bitterly with the Normans."

"My father sends troops to help Gruffydd fight the Normans, yet he thinks of marrying me to Arnulf de Montgomery."

Angharad looked seriously shocked.

"Yes indeed, we would be neighbours, would we not?"

Angharad sat down heavily. "But why?"

"Keep your enemies close, as they say. Arnulf is interested in Irish support to take on the crown. He and his brother do not support William Rufus."

"But is this what you want?"

"Angharad, you know that Ireland is a place where one king fights against another. We barely have peace for a year at a time. If my father does not ally with the Normans, then someone else will. For me, it is not so bad. They are a very wealthy family, and I like my comforts,

189

as you know. If Arnulf and his brother succeed in overthrowing Rufus, who is far from popular, then there would be all kinds of benefits. If the Normans remain in Wales, I will need to learn your native tongue and what better friend to teach me than yourself? If the Welsh succeed with their independence, I speak French very prettily and have always wanted to see Normandy and drink wine in the sun!"

"Lafracoth, you worry so little. I am the opposite; I worry so much."

"My dear, worrying doesn't help anything. Thinking, considering and working out how to make the best of the situation you find yourself in, is the easiest way. You are an intelligent woman; don't waste your time with fruitless thoughts or look back with regrets. Look forward and make everything an opportunity."

They were crossing the courtyard when a group of men came in speaking Welsh.

"Ohhhh," said Lafracoth, turning her head to speak quietly to Angharad, "there is a fine-looking man if ever I have seen one."

Angharad saw at once that it was Owain, Cadwgan's son. Seeing her, he left his companions and advanced towards her.

"Why, Lady Angharad," he smiled smoothly, his head tilted to one side. "I see you keep friends as beautiful as yourself."

Lafracoth's eyes flashed with delight as he dropped into a deep bow.

"Lord Owain," said Angharad noting a touch of malicious amusement in his face, "I didn't expect to see you. This is Princess Lafracoth."

"Delighted to make your acquaintance," he said, looking her up and down.

"Lafracoth's father has kindly been hosting us all, and Lafracoth has kindly been looking after me."

"That sounds wonderful," said Owain with a grin. "I am hoping you can accommodate a few more who bring news from the Welsh shore."

"Most certainly," said Lafracoth a little flirtatiously. She motioned to one of the servants and quickly made arrangements for their new guests.

"You will find your father and Gruffydd in the Hall," said Angharad, although she was desperate to know the news he brought herself.

"I know my way," said Owain. "I was here briefly a few weeks back."

"Well, well," said Lafracoth, "I wonder how I could have missed him. Are all the men in Wales handsome, or only the ones you seem to know?"

Angharad smiled.

"Be careful, Lafracoth. He is …."

"Like his father, no doubt. Don't worry, I can handle myself, and there is no harm in having a bit of fun!"

Lafracoth confused Angharad. She was dignified yet fun-loving and flirtatious, shrewd yet compassionate, generous and intelligent yet carefree in a manner that Angharad knew she could never be. In a way, she envied Lafracoth's ease with life.

A few hours later, Gruffydd found his wife and took her aside.

"I am going down to the port to take a better look at these ships we seem to have inherited," he said. "Will you walk with me?"

She threw on her cloak and heavy boots and fell into step at his side, relishing the time together. They had not had much time alone in a while.

"Owain brings interesting news," he started. "The Normans have ravished Anglesey and had no respect for the people who had taken refuge in the churches. What they did to Cenred was taken as an evil act by their own troops, and from that time, things started to go badly. The weather was against them, there were accidents in their camps, and they started to fear an attack from the mountains. When Magnus arrived, they were concerned about what might happen to them and started to feel threatened and vulnerable in a place where they felt isolated. When Hugh of Shrewsbury was killed, that was the final straw for them."

"It is as you thought," commented Angharad.

"There is more, Cariad. Your father was so disgusted by the atrocities that he refused to stand on the sidelines any longer and returned to Tegeingl. Earl Hugh feared that he and Uchdryd would turn and lead troops against them. Also, he had learnt that we were here and was fearful of further Irish intervention, which could not be bought off as easily as before. He realised that if we had support from Magnus and from Ireland and with uncertainty in Scotland, he might cause events to escalate at a time when Rufus was overstretched, especially with the undercurrent of hostility from some of the barons."

Angharad felt an incredible weight had been lifted from her shoulders as she learnt that her father had not condoned the atrocities.

"Will Father help us?" she asked.

"Ah, that is where things are not quite so easy. We are not certain of which way your father will fall in all of this."

"But Gruffydd," she began.

"Don't worry, Cariad, with all these things, there are many considerations, but I am beginning to think that there may be a way forward for us, especially with the Normans feeling as though they have bitten off more than they can chew."

"They would have been shocked by the Earl of Shrewsbury's death. That would have been a huge blow."

"Yes, apparently his older brother, Robert, has paid Rufus three thousand pounds to inherit his father's English properties, including the Earldom of Shrewsbury, the Rape of Arundel and, with the countship of Ponthieu and the honour of Tickhill, it makes him the wealthiest of all Rufus' magnates in both Normandy and England. Can you imagine the power of the Montgomerys?"

"Did you know that Murtagh is proposing Lafracoth is married to another Montgomery? Arnulf of Montgomery?"

"Murtagh did tell me that. He also told me that all does not sit well with Arnulf and Rufus. It may play out to our advantage."

They reached the wharf where the larger ships were unloading their cargo of pottery, grains, metals, furs, wine, horses and goods from places far beyond Dublin. Carts carrying wool or grain to go back on those ships were heavily loaded and jostling for space. Smaller boats were coming in with their catch of fish while seagulls wheeled and screeched watchful for easy pickings.

"Trade still goes on despite the famine," Angharad noted.

"You should see it when all is well," Gruffydd explained. "Double the number of boats coming in and out but now they have less wool and little grain to send back. Still, there is money changing hands all the time."

He pointed to several ships tied up but with no activity on them at all.

"These will sail with us when we go back," he said. "We will sort out with Cadwgan as by rights some of what these represent should go to cover his costs as well."

She looked at the finely built ships and asked, "How will we use these vessels?"

"We will take mercenaries if we must when we return. We will use them for defence: we will train our Welshmen like the Irish have their

193

sailors, and we will build up good trade for our wool and cattle. I am thinking of investigating mining again. There are so many opportunities."

"If we can live peacefully. I have seen what Ireland looks like outside of Dublin. Famine, plague, war: the three curses."

"Cariad, I don't know what we must do to get to the point of returning but I don't want any more death on my conscience. I will take the way of least resistance, but I will not abandon the fight that has brought Wales so far."

"So will you send Owain back to my father to see if he will help us negotiate peace?"

"I am not sure that Owain has the gravitas nor the subtlety to understand how to negotiate this, and neither Cadwgan nor I should set foot in Wales until we are certain of our safety. I am not being selfish but we are the spearhead of the movement. My cousin Gruffydd spent years in prison in Chester because he 'trusted' the Normans. What's more, right now, they are afeared of us and the strength we have in our allies, so we have an advantage without showing our hand."

"Let me go to my father, Gruffydd. I can bring your message safely; I can claim ignorance as to the exact strength of your alliances, and I, of all people, understand what we need to achieve."

Gruffydd stepped back and looked at his wife with astonishment. Angharad saw a myriad of emotions crossing his face.

"Firstly, I am carrying my father's grandchild. I am a visible representation of the future of his good name allied to the throne of Gwynedd. Secondly, I know how my father thinks and what he wants to achieve. Thirdly, I am no threat to my father, the news he receives will come with time for him to consider his next steps, and he will think he is in control. And fourthly, once we know what we need to negotiate with my father, then we know he is best placed of all to negotiate with the Normans on all our behalf."

Gruffydd looked at her, astounded.

"Cariad," he said softly, shaking his head. "You mean to go back to him as if you were the innocent girl who left home and hide the knowledge and wisdom you have as the woman you have become."

Angharad blushed.

"I am not unaware of my father's ambitions and shortcomings, Gruffydd, although I see his many strengths also. My priority is what is right for Gwynedd. My father is not young, and I know Gronwy, so we need to manage both Tegiengl and the Norman threat."

Gruffydd grinned. "Well, Cariad, it may well be as good a plan as any, except that I will miss you. More than you can ever imagine. Let me discuss it with Cadwgan."

"Believe me, I would be doing my best to make sure we were apart for as little time as possible," she replied. He held her close and marvelled at her wisdom.

Angharad seemed to have suddenly escaped the suffocating feeling of helplessness. She was ready for whatever challenges lay ahead.

Chapter 16: Farewell to Ireland (August 1098)

It took some days for Cadwgan and Gruffydd to agree to what they were willing to accept in terms with Earl Hugh. They both concluded that they were in a strong position because the Normans were uncertain of the strength and support the two Welsh leaders had outside Wales. The abiding fear of Scandinavian forces finding allies in Britain more than willing to help them overthrow the Norman rule had led William the Conqueror to lay waste to much of Northern England. His son had too many foreign and internal issues to need that pressure from Scandinavia or elsewhere. This was good for Wales.

"We need our safety guaranteed to start with," said Cadwgan, raising his bushy eyebrows, opening his eyes wide and giving Gruffydd a stare to make sure that what he suggested was considered a priority.

"Agreed. Then return of the captives," added Gruffydd, thinking of all the good men who had pledged loyalty to their cause and were now incarcerated in Chester.

"We want agreement that the Marcher Lords will not further encroach on Wales and will remove their men from garrisons inside Wales," insisted Cadwgan.

"I think that is too great a request," Gruffydd commented carefully, leaning forward with a concerned expression. "If we are seen to push for too much, they will fear us more and give us less. We should concentrate on Gwynedd and Powys and let the chief men for the rest of Wales come to their own agreements. If we are successful, they will follow our lead."

"And Ceredigion," said Cadwgan thoughtfully, taking a long drink of the French red wine he had been enjoying in Ireland. "Yes, those ten commotes, those lovely rich lands between the Dovey and the Teifi rivers without too many safe harbours for invasion, I want to add them to the power of Powys but, in return, I will keep an eye on Pembroke for us. Damn, that should have been ours, you know. Uchdryd was a fool at Pembroke! Too hasty and gullible!"

"You can have Ceredigion and are most welcome to it if we can get it that easily. I have too much work to do to build up Gwynedd again to take on more. Right now, I owe it to all the people in Gwynedd to make something of the place without worrying about more land and my obligations to the people of those lands. Such expansion for me must come later."

"What are we going to do about Owain ap Edwin? I am happy to use his special 'friendship' with our foes but do not forget that he stabbed us in the back."

"I swore an oath that I would not touch his lands when I married Angharad," replied Gruffydd in his firm, strong voice. "I will honour that but he is calling himself Governor of Gwynedd and that I will not accept."

Cadwgan nodded his big head and made a contemptuous growl.

"And Uchdryd? Since our little disagreements, he has been fuelling his brother's ambitions, I say."

"No, Uchdryd is solid," Gruffydd argued unemotionally, "and my guess is that he was keeping an eye on Owain while seemingly subservient to 'superior' Norman strength. He has a close relationship with his brother and would not harm him, but he sees the world differently. He wants Wales united as much as we do."

"I dare say they were both rewarded well for marching the Normans through Gwynedd," Cadwgan commented.

"I am not so foolish as to imagine otherwise, but would Uchdryd have led men against ours? Did we see his banner in the fighting? No! Uchdryd would have used it as a time for learning about the Norman strength by spotting the weaknesses in fighting and strategy but staying on the sidelines without giving anything away. He would have been fighting with us if it had not been for the rift that opened between you after the siege of Pembroke Castle was abandoned too early. You need to clear the air with him, Cadwgan. He has served you well, and he lost not a man at Pembroke while taking a fortune in booty!"

"Hmph," snorted Cadwgan, looking away and scowling under his bushy eyebrows before changing the subject. "While we are on the subject of trust, can we trust Murtagh? This business with his daughter and Arnulf?"

"We are in his house, accepting his hospitality, and he has turned everything over from the mercenaries to us. Of course, we must trust him, Cadwgan. I do not believe he will let us down. He lives by his word! He has pledged his support to us but he is an opportunist, don't forget. Lafracoth is a wonderful bargaining tool by anyone's standards. Like nobility worldwide, he is negotiating the best advantage possible."

"Ah, the beautiful Lafracoth. What a bargaining tool! There was talk a while back that you two may have progressed Welsh and Irish relations."

Gruffydd's colour deepened, and he bridled. "I married the jewel in the crown, Cadwgan, and every day I count my blessings."

Cadwgan looked at him shrewdly, and a tinge of envy rose in him as he thought of Gruffydd, in the prime of life, impeccably cultured and deeply contented with his wife. A pretty, buxom maid entered the hall and gave Cadwgan a flirtatious sideways look. He grinned, thinking of the previous evening, gave her a mischievous wink and then turned his focus back to matters in hand.

"So, Gruffydd, what about Magnus?"

"I will settle with Magnus. He has big ambitions, but he cannot be everywhere. If he takes over too much land, then he stretches himself too thin. We have a good relationship. The waterways are of more value to him and Norway than anything Gwynedd has to offer, except as a gateway to England. That is a challenge he aspires to, but he will take one step at a time. It is better to have us as allies than enemies if that time comes."

"Those fertile fields in Anglesey could feed the whole of Wales," commented Cadwgan bluntly. "It would be a prize for him."

"Worth nothing to him now. The smoke from the fields would have reached him in Mann! It will take years to restore the place. He is a warrior, not a restorer. We have no immediate issue with Magnus, and it would do him no honour to cross me when I have fought alongside him in the past. Besides, if he had wanted Anglesey, he had it on a platter the day he shot Hugh, Earl of Shrewsbury!"

Cadwgan nodded his agreement. "So, we are going to hope that Owain is willing to negotiate the terms of our cessation of hostilities with Earl Hugh and Montgomery."

"I believe Angharad will be able to persuade him."

"She is young, though, Gruffydd, and not someone I would think of as a ruthless negotiator. Her father is wily; are you certain she will not disclose our weaknesses?"

Gruffydd bristled, but he said evenly, "Don't underestimate her. She is not hot-headed. She is intelligent and will think things through to our advantage. I trust her with my life!"

"There are a few more lives at stake here as well as your own! Keep that in mind!"

"If you have a better suggestion, I am willing to listen," Gruffydd spoke without emotion, but he fumed inwardly, particularly as he had often wondered if Owain ap Cadwgan's cursory negotiations with the mercenaries had led to the catastrophe in Anglesey. Had Owain, in his youthful arrogance, negotiated too far, leaving them open to the Normans' offers? Had his ignorance of how to form meaningful relationships left the mercenaries with a sour taste in their mouth?

"Angharad it is!" said Cadwgan bringing Gruffydd sharply back to the present. "Who will travel with her?"

"I thought we would send Hywel and then perhaps Idwal, Iago and Cadwallon. Being your late wife Gwenllian's brothers, they are kin to us both. They are trustworthy and fierce fighters, and I know they are keen to serve with you in Wales."

Cadwgan thought for a while. "Yes," he decided, "we can trust them, and they will keep her safe on the journey."

Gruffydd pondered the intricate web of trust in life. He and Cadwgan, comrades on the battlefield, had entrusted their lives to each other. Yet, with Cadwgan's Norman alliances and ambition to expand Powys, was it naive to trust him? If trust couldn't be placed in a fellow warrior, could it be found in kin? The Welsh and Irish revered kinship, but was it not a fact that betrayal, even within families, was rampant when power and wealth were at stake?

The thought that the way the Welsh and Irish allocated inheritance among children so that family land was divided and subdivided into smaller and smaller units had been responsible for those rifts had occurred to Gruffydd. The Normans would give the lion's share to the eldest son, yet they had as much backstabbing and dissension as the Welsh. The Welshman concluded that if he started to question inheritance and whether he could trust everyone, he would drive himself mad with suspicions. There was no point dwelling on how bruised he felt by those he had placed faith in. Angharad left no doubts in his mind: she would never betray him. He would stake the life of his firstborn on it.

All their demands were relayed to Angharad with clear instructions on what she could and could not offer. She listened carefully, asked pertinent questions and, to Cadwgan's surprise, suggested all sorts of scenarios which might arise that they had not considered.

"Well," Cadwgan confided in Gruffydd later, "she has a sound head on her. She is Owain's daughter, fair enough, but can she better that old fox?"

***

The young wife was not looking forward to the journey back to Wales but knew that she would be going back on a much larger vessel, along with the captives taken by the mercenaries from Dublin. Something had been on her mind for some time, and she came to Gruffydd in a quiet moment reaching up to kiss him gently on the cheek. He looked at her fondly and wrapped his arms around her, but she put her hand on his chest and looked up at him earnestly.

"Gruffydd, I would ask you something. I do not want to further burden you but it is important to me."

"What is it? Ask Cariad!"

"When we first came to Dublin, there were so many Welsh among the captives at the Slave Market. I have avoided the Slave Market since, but the fate of those there weighs heavily on me. But for the grace of God, we, too, may have found ourselves there. Gruffydd, if we could stretch what we have or what we can borrow, would we be able to buy those Welsh captives who remain there so that we can return them to Wales with me?"

His face fell, and his frustration was evident.

"Cariad, it is not so simple. These people have come from all over Wales, and we do not know if they have any means of surviving even if they can return to their homes."

"But we could take them to Anglesey. You said that you wanted to build up Anglesey, and they can start afresh. At least they would be speaking their own language with a hope of seeing their families again."

"They have nothing. How will they survive? We cannot just take them to a place and abandon them."

"We can find places for them, Gruffydd."

"Oh, Cariad, I know you want the best for everyone, but we are not even back there ourselves yet."

"Then I will go there first, speak to the priests and see what can be done about finding these people places where they can work their keep, to begin with."

"We do not even know whether there are any priests left on Anglesey."

Angharad was determined and would have taken all the slaver's captives if she could, no matter where they came from but she could see some of the difficulties Gruffydd had raised would be challenging enough. Gruffydd gazed out of the window into the distance, mulling the problem over. She loved looking at his broad shoulders and the way they tapered down to his slim waist, where a large gold buckle shone on his leather belt. She let her eyes linger on his strong, handsome face with piercing blue eyes and his thick golden hair glinting from the sunlight that poured into their room. He turned to her, and she could see from the set of his jaw that his decision was made.

"This is what we will do, Cariad. You make a good point about building up Anglesey, and God knows that is no easy task. When we are safe to return to Gwynedd, I will go to the Slave Market to purchase any Welsh men or women who remain there, and they will return with me. Meanwhile, when you arrive in Anglesey, you will already be taking the captives the mercenaries took from Anglesey, who are in the main from Gwynedd. You should go to the priests as you suggest if indeed there are any. See if they can help any of those captives who have had their homes destroyed. Explain that there are more enslaved but who remain here in Dublin. Ask the priests how those additional captives may be able to live. Send word back. I would not bring them over to suffer because of our misguided compassion."

"Thank you! Thank you!" she cried, throwing her arms around his neck and kissing him all over his face.

He shook his head and said, "I hope we can feed ourselves, let alone all these others you want to bring with you. We may be making a big mistake, and there may be resentment from those who are struggling to survive there as it is."

"Don't worry, Gruffydd," she assured him, squeezing his hands with hers and gazing up at him adoringly, "Everyone will be glad of the extra labour in return for their keep. It will work out. This is a small risk compared to some of the huge risks you have taken in the past," she enthused but Gruffydd retained his reservations.

Over the next days, she had much to do to prepare for leaving Ireland and to say goodbye to people who had been kind to her. Saying her goodbyes to Lafracoth was particularly hard, and she saw that her friend's eyes had welled up. They held each other, and Lafracoth said, "I know we shall see each other again. You have become like a sister to me in such a short time, Angharad!"

"And you to me," she replied, drawing her friend close for another embrace. "You have taught me so much. Write to me!"

"I will! I will also make sure that I keep a watchful eye on Gruffydd and be certain that he keeps his strength up for meeting you in Anglesey!" She gave her friend a broad grin. They both knew that when Gruffydd was wrestling with an issue, he would forget completely about eating.

"It will be very strange here without your smiling face," she said, seriously holding her friend's hands and squeezing them tightly in hers, "but I wish you well with everything, and you might find me in Wales soon. Who knows what the future holds?"

"I would like that very much, and Lafracoth, whoever becomes your life partner, I wish you the same happiness as I have found with Gruffydd!"

"That happiness is rare indeed, and I would settle for half," she admitted earnestly. Then, reverting to her light-hearted self, she added mischievously, "If he was handsome enough!"

Harder still was Angharad's goodbye to Gruffydd. Privately she wept but knew she must show no sign of emotion in front of Cadwgan, who would doubt her abilities and think her weak if she gave any indication of distress.

The night before she left, Gruffydd held her tightly, and neither of them slept. Rain pounded relentlessly on the roof and dripped in small waterfalls into the courtyard, seeming to match their low spirits. Gruffydd pulled his wife closer and adjusted a blanket to cover her shoulders, which were cold from the night air.

"I could never have believed I could love anyone as much as I love you," he whispered as he stroked her face tenderly. "When I am with you, my whole life is complete."

"And I love you with all my heart," she whispered back, wrapping her arm more firmly across his chest and squeezing him closer.

"Then I am satisfied because you have the biggest heart of anyone I have ever known but soon I will be sharing that heart and gladly so."

"I will never love you less. Never! No matter how many children we have, no matter what happens in our lives, my love is until eternity."

Even now, so long after they had married, she could scarcely believe that the handsome, charismatic, intelligent and loyal man lying beside her was really her husband. She knew from the way that other women looked at him that they desired him, but he did not seem to notice them. Other women might be reluctant to leave their husband's side, to be apart for who knew how long, but she trusted him completely.

Too soon, the birds' calling their morning song announced the dawn, and the rain dissipated into residual drips. They dressed and walked down to the ship waiting at the quay. Hywel was already there, and the ship's crew bustled around, making sure everything was ready, cargo had been loaded, and provisions had been stowed for the journey.

Gruffydd held his wife close and whispered, "Safe journey, Cariad." Tears welled up in her eyes, but after a final kiss, he helped her up the rampway, turned to say a few final words to Hywel and then took a step back as the ropes were untied, the anchor stones raised.

As the sleek oaken ship pulled away from the quay, she saw Gruffydd standing there, his cloak billowing in the wind, looking suddenly vulnerable. It was as much as Angharad could do not to shout to the crew wielding their oars to stop and turn around. She watched as he became a tiny dot, and she did not see him move. Then reluctantly, she turned away, heavy-hearted and stared blankly at the vast grey waters ahead.

When they reached the open sea, the sail was raised. The oarsmen rested their ash oars, taking a well-earned break. Thankfully, the crossing was a calm one, although slower because of it. Angharad gazed at the beauty of the sparkling cliffs of Howth's Head as the sun suddenly appeared from behind the clouds. She wondered if she would ever visit Dublin or Ireland again. Seagulls wheeled above them, and they had not been far out to sea when Hywel shouted, "Look!" as two dolphins swam alongside them for a while. He pushed back chestnut waves out of his eyes, and his open face lit up with the excitement of a child.

"What are they?" gasped Angharad, who had never seen such creatures before.

"Dolphins," he grinned. "Have you not seen them off Anglesey?"

"I haven't," replied Angharad shaking her head, watching as the curious creatures leapt out of the water beside them.

"There are plenty off Puffin Island but you mainly see them in warm weather. They are considered a lucky omen."

"Well, we need good fortune," said Angharad, looking around at the dejected-looking captives returning to they knew not what, and knowing full well the difficulty of the task she faced.

"If anyone can change things for the better, it is Gruffydd," said Hywel sincerely, looking back to the quickly disappearing Irish coast.

"I believe that as well."

"He has the common touch. He is generous with everyone before himself. He will never ask somebody to do something he wouldn't do himself and he never gives up. He has taken what happened very hard and is determined to right things."

She thought of her husband and how easily he had turned his hands to making the mews at Tegeingl, with no care for whether it was appropriate for his position. He was always immaculately turned out, with everything he wore being of the finest quality, but unlike other men of his standing, he looked after his things well and had relatively few possessions, preferring to gift others than enjoy many luxuries himself. She knew how hard it had been for him to leave Anglesey and flee the Normans last July. It was only a few weeks ago, and yet it seemed like years. He lived with that agony every day, but she had many times heard Cadwgan reminding him that it had been the only rational choice at the time. She hoped Hywel was right.

As if reading her thoughts, Hywel continued. "That day we were betrayed, Gruffydd was still fighting while shouting to the rest of us to retreat. It was like a wall of steel, in front of us and beside us, wave after wave of impenetrable screaming warriors — blood, guts, metal on metal, the grinding and crashing and slashing. Cadwgan practically had to drag him from the fray, but the worst for him was leaving the dead and wounded where they lay. It is so hard seeing bloodied men trying to crawl for safety without being able to help."

Angharad knew Hywel was also reliving it for himself and saw his face pale and stiff with despair. She shivered as she thought of that day. Even now, she could not hear bells ringing without them bringing back awful memories, though she had been spared the carnage that they had seen.

"The loss must have been terrible."

"He was quick-thinking. As soon as he realised what was happening, he positioned us so that groups could divide and scatter using the bowmen to cover those who had been at the front. The Normans and the mercenaries did not get off lightly despite everything, and once the bowmen retreated into the trees, they had the advantage of cover. There is nothing to compare with Welsh bowmen. Sorry, this is soldiers talk!"

"He has not really told me what happened that day, how it was. It would be nice to be a lady cossetted from it all, running the llys and playing the harp or embroidering, but that isn't really who I am now. I have lived through this with you though I didn't wield a sword. I escaped, as you saw, wearing a dead man's garb. Soldier's talk is part of my world now."

He smiled sheepishly, and she saw the compassion in his eyes; such a gentle soldier.

Had she really given enough consideration to the grief her husband must have felt, or had she turned inwards into her own distress and the demands imposed on her body by her pregnancy? She realised how self-absorbed she had been. Never once had Gruffydd sapped her strength by calling on her for emotional support. How physically and emotionally drained he must have been when, in those first days in Ireland, he had spent his time with Murtagh and Cadwgan trying to craft a plan, piece together a strategy. She longed to hold him not from her own neediness but for him, to tell him she understood. She vowed she would try to be more supportive and acknowledge the nightmares he would always have from fleeing the bloody ground strewn with the wounded and those whose lives were lost.

Angharad slept fitfully overnight on the swaying boat, and when she woke in the early dawn, it was Hywel that she was leaning against. She thanked him, rearranged herself and smiled as she saw the magical cliffs of Anglesey before her. They sailed along the coast to the Menai Straits, and it was as they were landing there in the little familiar port that she had a most pleasant surprise.

As they began to unload passengers, a tall, dark-haired figure, easy in the saddle, was spurring his mare down to the beach and leading two horses: her beloved Seren and Gruffydd's black stallion, Cadell.

Meilyr, her faithful and considerate brother, was beaming his wide, generous smile.

Her legs were wobbly, but as she saw Meilyr, she ran towards him. He, seeing her effort, nudged his horse into a trot to shorten the distance.

"Meilyr," she shouted delightedly. "What are you doing here, and how on earth have you managed to bring our horses?"

"Well, you can thank Uchdryd for that," said Meilyr grinning. "The Normans had taken every beast they could find on the island, and Uchdryd recognised these two and claimed them for himself along with a few Norman mounts, which he says will make good breeding stock. Nobody dared to stop him!"

Angharad shook her head and nuzzled up to Seren, stroking the star that gave the horse her Welsh name. She had not thought they would ever see each other again, and while she was sure that such fine horses would not have come to harm, being precious, she was astonished and grateful at the story. Seren responded in a way which made it clear she had not forgotten her old mistress, sniffing as if to remember familiar smells. Angharad turned back to her brother, eyes brighter than they had been since they had left Dublin.

"I cannot believe you are here!"

"We got news from Gruffydd that you were on your way, and I thought you may need help. Gruffydd said you would stay just a day on the island."

"He is worried about how safe it would be and where we would stay. Meilyr, you are always so kind to me," she said softly, "I hope one day I can repay even a few of those kindnesses."

"You are my sister, and you have done plenty for me already!" he said, typically brushing off the efforts he had obviously made to be there.

Angharad squeezed his hand firmly, her eyes misty and then gestured to the lost-looking souls behind her on a sandy slope above the quay.

"All of these people were taken as captives by the mercenaries who betrayed us. I am not sure what homes they have here still, and before we can help them, I need to know what state Anglesey is in now."

Meilyr looked uncomfortable. "From what I have seen, it isn't good, I'm afraid! The wasteful destruction is shocking."

At that moment, a spokesman from the small group of captives hobbled up. He was an old man, toothless and with one eye partially closed, yet he had the steely character and the look of a defiant robin.

"My lady," he said, bowing as best he could. "My name is Iorwedd, and I speak for all these men and women who were taken into captivity. We would like to know what you want to do with us."

Angharad looked at him and was taken aback.

"I don't know how many of you still have homes to go back to or family here who managed to escape the enemy. I don't know yet what we must do to help you but I am going to try to find out if any priests remain, and they will be able to provide some assistance, I am sure. My main concern is that you all have shelter and food."

The old man squinted at her and asked cautiously, "Do you not want us to work for you, then?"

Angharad looked at Meilyr to try to cover her confusion.

He assumed a low whisper, "I think that they believe that as they were taken captive and as you brought them back here, they were to work for you. They are asking if they are intended to be slaves."

"Of course not," she replied immediately. Turning to the old man, she said, "King Gruffydd would wish you to be able to go back to the lives you had, but we are concerned that may not be possible."

The old man looked surprised but very relieved, "God Bless you both. If it is alright with you, my lady, we will find our own way. Do not trouble yourself. Whatever is in front of us is better than it might have been, and we thank you."

He bowed low and shuffled back quickly to the others, who all turned towards them, looking in amazement. Then one by one, they came to thank Angharad before making their way from the quay in various directions.

"Angharad, you do know that some of these people would already have been slaves, and so you have essentially given them their freedom."

Angharad had not actually considered that, but she said decisively, "If they have been well-treated, they will return to their masters, and if not, then they can make a new start perhaps."

"That will not be easy," said Meilyr sagely, watching the captives vanishing into the distance. Then he turned to his sister and said kindly. "If you feel up to it, then we can go to some of the main places on the island so that you have a sense of what is ahead of you."

She could see he was not sure what to say about her swelling belly, but he had clearly noticed.

"Yes, I am carrying your nephew or niece," she acknowledged, smiling at him and confirming his thoughts.

He beamed and then looked concerned. "Should you even be riding a horse?"

"I can ride. It is not a difficult pregnancy, I think. I was very sick at the beginning, but this little one must be strong, and my taking a horse ride will be the least of what the poor little mite has endured in the last weeks. Anyway, I need to understand how things stand here, and I want to see if any priests still remain."

Hywel had joined them, and he and Meilyr greeted each other with real affection. "The boat will wait here until mid-afternoon and then take us on to the Dee estuary. They will go on from there to pick up goods at Chester to take back to Dublin. Cadwgan's nephews will stay with the boat just in case of any trouble."

"There won't be any trouble, Hywel, unless the ship decides to leave without us."

"It is Gruffydd's ship now. A penalty paid by the mercenaries for their disloyalty," Hywel explained.

"We heard that Gruffydd had come into something of a fleet!"

"It came at a costly price!"

"It did indeed, as you will soon see, sadly. Let's go. Will you ride Gruffydd's horse?"

"I thought I recognised this beauty!" exclaimed Hywel swinging himself easily into the saddle. "This is Gruffydd's saddle and bridle as well: I recognise the silver workmanship. I am surprised that they were not taken for booty."

"Yes, it is astonishing and a long story!"

The three set off, making their way to Aberffraw first. The llys there had been used for the Norman nobles during their campaign and was not in such bad repair as Angharad had imagined. Anything of value that had not been hidden and was movable had long since been looted. There was broken pottery and benches; all the animals had gone, but the outhouses and stables were still in good repair. The little church was empty and just a shell, the doors had been wrenched open, and the roof had been burnt. She was sickened by the thought of how it had been destroyed. The place reeked of burnt wood and thatch. There was no sign of their priest. She remembered how proudly Gruffydd had taken her to the llys on their wedding day, the band of welcomers, the happy times they had had there feasting and making plans. She was downhearted but determined to restore what they had lost.

What they saw as she moved from their llys into the surrounding countryside was sobering. Now was the time of year when the island would have boasted granaries full of sun-ripened wheat, oats and barley. The fields of crops which had swayed in the breeze the previous July were now reduced to blackened stubble, and the little farmhouses were left deserted and charred. It reminded Angharad of the aftermath of the famine and plague in Ireland she had seen. First famine and then plague, she remembered Lafracoth telling her; there was the risk of desperate times ahead as the crops were ruined.

They rode down to the church of St Cwyfan, and here, to her amazement, she found a brand-new wattle and daub structure had been erected. They got off their horses to the sound of hammering and went inside to discover the priest and about six other men working on the interior.

"Father Teilo," she called over the hammering. His large head shot up, and recognising her, his initial look of shock turned into a wide beam. He was a stocky, grey-haired but vigorous man and strode over to them with a quick, firm step.

"Lady Angharad! Is it really you? Blessed God has protected you. There was so much confusion. We were not sure if you were safe or taken captive. This is really good news: an answer to prayer. Is the Lord Gruffydd safe?"

"He is, Father Teilo, thank you, and he intends to be back in Anglesey soon. We want to restore, repair and make it a safe and prosperous place."

"Blessed God has answered our prayers!" he enthused, turning to the workman, raising his arms in gratitude and repeating his sentiments.

All the men bowed to her and smiled weakly, but she could see the horror they had endured etched all over their faces. She could only imagine what they had been through. She could see they would need to see change before they would trust Gruffydd as they had done before.

They pulled up two newly made benches. On that peaceful morning, with the sound of the waves lapping gently below them, they sat talking about what had happened since that fateful July. They spoke at length about how Father Cenred had saved many in the community by assisting them to safety. Father Teilo explained how Cenred had paid for those acts of kindness and elaborated on his grisly death. Angharad's face showed her abject revulsion even though she had heard much of it before. She felt sick to her stomach, appalled at the extent of the barbarity.

"He refused to give details of where people were hidden even until the end!" said Father Teilo. "Those tyrants had all the priests they could find rounded up so that we could watch the torture as a means of breaking us. Seeing his courage made us more determined than ever to protect those in our care."

Angharad found it difficult to speak but Meilyr looked solemn and pale as he said what they were all thinking. "Father, this is an abomination against a man of God. Father Cenred's heroism and endurance will not be forgotten."

"Cenred should be made a saint. When the Earl of Shrewsbury was killed, God showed his displeasure; it was a sign sent to everyone. The earl was completely armoured head to foot, yet that arrow found his eye. The others who were complicit will live with guilt on Earth but their filthy acts will find punishment at Hell's Gate. Proverbs tell us not to seek vengeance but to wait for the Lord, and He will save us."

They sat in silence for a few moments before Angharad asked, "Father, what has become of the people from the deserted homes?"

"Many of the women that were sent away have come back. The majority of their menfolk, if they still live, have been taken into captivity. Some men, like these men here, who fought but managed to escape, have been helping to rebuild where they can."

"Were all the farms destroyed?" asked Hywel. Angharad realised that he had family on the island.

"A few farms escaped destruction and looting at the furthest part of the island from here. Your family and the neighbouring families were untouched, as the Normans had not reached them by the time Magnus Barefoot came with his ships. Your family and their neighbours are the reason that others have managed to survive. Some animals were hidden in the woods or mountains, some in caves. The Normans slaughtered many animals still in the fields or on the farms for their feasting and took good breeding stock with them. Others, who left with their herds before the Normans came, are still in the mountains on the mainland. They will not drive their animals back until they know they are safe to return."

"And those who used boats to escape?" asked Angharad, hopefully.

"Those who had boats or access to them were safe, and they come back, a few more each day."

"How do you feed yourselves?" asked Meilyr

"We forage, we fish; a few have animals to provide eggs and milk."

Angharad noticed how thin the young men looked and saw that despite his stocky frame, the priest was much slighter than when she last saw him.

"And the other priests?" she asked.

"Some escaped and hid and have stayed on Anglesey, like me, and some were taken captive."

Angharad began to explain their plans and the captives they wanted to bring from Dublin to him. He was immediately enthusiastic.

"We need people here, my lady, to build things up as before. All the farms will need help to reconstruct what has been damaged, to work the land and look after the animals. There is huge work to be done. If they are hard workers, they will find good homes here, but we need to do this quickly before the winter sets in."

Despite the confirmation of the destruction, Angharad felt an enormous sense of relief after her conversation with Father Teilo. She also knew that she had a huge burden of responsibility on her shoulders, so she needed to move quickly.

They left the little church and continued further, seeing water mills left in ruins, fishing traps broken and scattered, and ploughs left as charred skeletons of their former function. It was soul-destroying.

"I think we should turn back now," said Meilyr, as each mile they travelled further confirmed the enormity of the task ahead and the hardships which had been endured.

Angharad looked over at the glistening cornflower sea under an azure sky so at odds with the horror on land and imagined Gruffydd somewhere on a far shore. She was glad he wasn't seeing the devastation of his homeland. She surveyed the miles of scorched earth where she had once ridden by lush crop-filled fields.

"Nothing can be done for this year's harvest," she lamented but then added determinedly, "however, next year is another year: seeds will grow; sheep will lamb; cows will have calves; horses will have foals, and slowly we will build this island back to be the pride of Gwynedd."

Meilyr looked at his sister and frowned. She had changed from the cautious, meek young girl he was used to protecting, but there was a long way to go before she could accomplish her vision. He thought of his father waiting for them at the manor, every move anticipated, clear in his thinking, finding advantage for his ambitions, and he felt uncomfortable.

Chapter 17: Homecoming (August 1098)

Despite all her confidence in Ireland, Angharad was surprised at how nervous she was about returning to Tegeingl. How easy, she reflected, to fall back into youthful habits and behaviours, old patterns of relationships when you are revisiting your childhood home. In Anglesey and Ireland, Angharad had been able to be a different version of herself because she was not known. Now back with the family she had grown up with, she realised she was in danger of allowing her father to dominate in the way he always had; of letting Gronwy's sour, scornful barbs dictate how confidently she articulated Gruffydd and Cadwgan's requests. She had been welcomed warmly enough by all other than Gronwy, and she was pleased that her pregnancy was received with quiet enthusiasm by her father.

Rhydir proudly introduced her to his new wife, Lleuci, who was as sweet as Rhydir and very shy. She had rosy cheeks and thick dark hair, which despite her efforts, managed to poke itself out of her headdress. Her face was round and dimpled, and she always wore an expression of bashful delight. Lleuci was also pregnant, and the two ladies formed a warm friendship, comparing notes. The addition of Lleuci to the family was a joyous one, and in the time that Angharad was at home, she formed a close bond with her.

The servants were delighted to see the return of Angharad. Susannah, in particular, could not contain her joy. As she brushed Angharad's hair in her chamber that evening, she was bubbling over. Angharad sat on her clothes chest and looked around the room, unchanged since she left there to be married. The first tapestry she had ever made was still hanging on the wall, along with the pegs on which she had hung her cloak and riding clothing. A small table held a wooden box where she had kept her jewellery, hair pins and combs, where underneath, she now put her travelling boots and embroidered slippers. Susannah could not stop beaming.

"Mistress, when we heard you were coming, we were all so happy to learn you were safe. Your father had said he was sure that you had escaped, but to where we were not sure. Uncertain times they were, but now here you are—and to think you went through all that and were pregnant as well!"

She told Angharad all the news. Nothing had changed with the servants except that Iori was to marry a farmer's daughter from the valley. They talked a little of the Normans and how Owain had made sure no damage had been done to the lands around when the Normans rode through. Angharad felt a tinge of resentment creeping in since the destruction with which she had been confronted in Anglesey was still very raw.

"Mistress, you look exhausted!" Susannah commented, looking at Angharad's weary face.

"I am indeed very tired," she replied honestly, "but I want to be up early in the morning and look my best."

She slipped thankfully between the sheets of her childhood bed, resting her head wearily on the goose feather pillow yet feeling very alone without her husband. She wondered if he could also see the bright moon that shone in the dark velvet sky. Outside, she heard the porter stamping his feet across the courtyard and an owl somewhere near the stables. Such familiar late summer evening sounds, but now she longed for the sounds she had grown used to in Anglesey: the rhythmic lapping of the waves on the shore, the nightingale in the wood near the llys, and the creak of the oak trees rubbing their branches against each other in the breeze. Her eyes were soon heavy, and she drifted into sleep.

She woke to the familiar smell of oatcakes baking in the kitchen and the roar of stags in the woods as they asserted their dominance. The deeper the roar, the larger the beast and the more desirable to the does. The rutting season had begun. Stags would be gathering their hinds to make themselves look more impressive. Soon the leaves would be turning colour, and pigs would be gorging on acorns, beech nuts and chestnuts. She felt the march of time keenly and the pressure to accomplish what she needed to quickly. Winter would not be their friend.

Angharad had thought ahead well enough to bring with her the wonderful clothes that Lafracoth had insisted on giving her, and thankfully, she was still able to fit into them despite her advancing pregnancy. Susannah helped her to dress her hair and arrange her robes. When she walked over the freshly spread rushes in the hall the following morning, she raised eyebrows. She looked elegant and unflustered as she gracefully crossed the room Owain, belying the turmoil inside her head. Cadwgans' brothers-in-law and Hywel stood and bowed to her. She acknowledged them with a dignified nod of the head.

The father considered his daughter thoughtfully and saw that his girl had truly become a woman with presence. Angharad's brothers were taking their guests hunting, and everyone was up early to take advantage of the time that stags would flush out does from their hiding place with less caution than normal. It was not long before father and daughter soon found themselves alone while the excited riders and yelping dogs milled around the courtyard as the group readied themselves for the thrill of the hunt.

"So Angharad, Gruffydd sends you as a messenger," said her father genially once the servants had cleared the hall of trenchers of bread and cheese, jugs of ale and used drinking vessels.

"No, Father. I am not merely my husband's messenger. Gruffydd has important negotiations and business in Dublin. I chose to take the opportunity to return home to assess the state of Gwynedd for myself."

Owain was taken aback and asked carefully, "And what are your thoughts?"

She steeled herself, "I am surprised you could not prevent the utter carnage and devastation on Anglesey, Father. I had hoped that with your relationship with Earl Hugh, you might have been able to convince him that a flourishing Anglesey was to everyone's benefit."

She saw blood come into his face with a hot rush and a vein pulse in his neck but he kept his indignation under control. She kept a mentally civilised distance, but inside, her heart was thudding like a child's.

"If it hadn't been for me, Angharad, the whole of Gwynedd might have been destroyed."

"I understood that Magnus Barefoot was the catalyst for the Normans returning to Chester."

His face registered a faint surprise. She had never spoken to her father in such a manner before, but she knew she must make a stand early. She could see that mentioning Magnus Barefoot had unsettled him, and he was calculating how far Gruffydd's collaboration with Magnus had gone. If Magnus had a foothold in Gwynedd, that might well mean the end of Owain's position in Tegeingl. She saw him looking at her fine attire, her regal bearing. Had he expected her to return, tail between her legs begging for help, impoverished and vulnerable? She was impoverished. She was vulnerable but she must conceal these facts from him. She collected her thoughts while she listened to her father's reasoning.

"I had my part to play in the protection of Gwynedd, and it was a crucial one. I am the Governor of Gwynedd."

"And my husband is the King of Gwynedd."

"Displaced King of Gwynedd."

"Father, you underestimate him. He is the rightful king and will return to Gwynedd, but whether this is by might or by peaceful negotiation is the consideration at hand."

Her father greeted her response with silence, and for a moment, she thought she had gone too far; alienated a powerful ally. His eyes had narrowed below bushy grey eyebrows as he mulled her message over in his mind. She chose her next words carefully, drawing on all she had learnt from many years of watching and listening to her father manipulate his audience.

"Father, I am bearing your grandchild, possibly the future king. I chose to come here because I was brought up in a noble family, and I can trace my heritage to the ruling houses of Mercia and the kings of Wales. My husband has the ear and respect of other monarchs despite his young age, and I have seen that the passion within him can achieve greatness. I am representing him here because I am his equal in our marriage, as you taught me. As your daughter, I had hoped for your open heart and mind to see if we can find a way forward from this mess, avoiding further bloodshed."

A myriad of conflicting emotions crossed Owain's face, and at that moment, Gronwy, in the courtyard, chose to disparage one of the servants loudly in front of the assembled guests. Owain winced involuntarily, and Angharad realised with certain clarity that he was thinking about the future of his name and family held in the hands of his boorish eldest son. In comparison, his legacy at the hands of what she hoped he saw as his composed and dignified daughter was presented differently. She was Angharad ferch Owain after all, Queen of Gwynedd. Outside, Gronwy raged again at someone. Then they heard horses leaving the courtyard, the hunters' cries and the baying of the hounds descending into the woods.

Her father's irritation and rising anger were thinly veiled. "What is it that you want from me, Angharad?"

"I want you to negotiate with the Normans on our behalf, Father. I want the restoration of Northern Wales to the Welsh to be because of you."

He looked at her hard, then sat back in his chair and closed his eyes. *'Owain Fradwr, Owain the Traitor, that is what they call me behind my back,'* he mused. He remembered the painful humiliation at the hands of the Normans in Chester. He remembered his utter abhorrence of the treatment of the priest, Cenred; the savagery and brutality towards men of the cloth. He remembered the fanfare and celebration as Owain and Cadwgan rode towards their manor, how even small children ran to touch their feet or stroke their horses and in times ahead, men and women of Gwynedd would tell their children how they were part of the great uprising. Wouldn't it be something to be regarded with that sort of gratitude, that sort of respect? 'Owain Fradwr' rankled.

"I am the most senior nobleman in Gwynedd," he reminded her with a hint of peevishness.

"Father, you are appointed by the Normans, not the Welsh."

"The men of the east of Gwynedd will follow me wherever I lead."

"While the west of Gwynedd lies shattered and abandoned, and you are blamed for it. Anglesey's farmland is burnt black. Father, the farms are destroyed, and the churches are sacked. People of Anglesey have been taken to Chester in chains, and their breeding stock has been killed or stolen. Gruffydd is coming back but he made a promise to you that he will not break. He is a man of his word. Our intention is that you would retain your lands here, and the lands east of the Clywd would remain under your jurisdiction. If we can negotiate peace with the Normans, then all Gwynedd will flourish."

"Strong words, Angharad! I remind you, I am already Governor of all Gwynedd. Yes, appointed by the Normans but, at this moment, who holds more authority in Gwynedd?"

"Yes, Father, you have the Norman-given title but do not underestimate the strength of the support for my husband in Gwynedd or the loyalty of mighty men beyond our shores."

Owain's grey eyes became hooded as he considered her words. The messenger Gruffydd had sent to let them know Angharad was coming had been a wealth of information. He had told Owain how King Murtagh had brutally punished the mercenaries and turned their vessels over to Gruffydd. Then there was no mistake that Magnus Barefoot had intervened when he did. Gruffydd had credibility. Angharad said he was a man of his word, but if the Irish and the Norwegians joined Gruffydd's cause, then things could be very nasty indeed and not end well for Tegeingl. He turned to his daughter again with a set jaw and thin lips.

"So, you suggest I would retain my position here, yet I must acknowledge Gruffydd as king."

"Of course."

"And Cadwgan? What does he want because he always seeks advantage?"

"The restoration of Powys and addition of Ceredigion."

Owain breathed in deeply and reflected on this.

"And that is it?"

"No, Father, those are the main terms which we propose in order that there be peace but there are many other considerations."

Owain's eyebrows shot up, and he opened his mouth to say something, then thought better of it. Angharad gauged this the time to soften her approach.

"There are things which we would not agree to but which the Normans may require," she explained, looking at him with her clear-eyed sincerity. "And there are other things which we would ask for but which they may refuse."

"Is Gruffydd intending to return along with Irish and Norwegian might?" he asked directly.

"Father, what Gruffydd intends depends on what we can accomplish, and I, for one, would prefer to see peace. Lives enough have been lost."

Owain was glad that the others were out hunting and there was no one to witness this conversation. He felt a myriad of emotions, and the ground was shifting underneath him. Together, they discussed the 'demands' as Owain called them, and by the end of the morning, Angharad felt as if her proposals had met with a level of approval with which Owain was willing to work.

Owain was as good as his word, and once everything had been considered, the decision made, he took matters into his hands with the same determination as had served him well for a lifetime. The next day, with the wind blowing in his face and his bones aching, he rode to Chester to meet with Earl Hugh. His sturdy dark brown cob knew the journey well, and as he approached a spot where Owain would always take in the view, the horse came to a customary halt. Owain sighed and nudged him on without lingering. He felt none of his usual satisfaction at the activities in the fields he passed on his journey. Farms were in different stages of preparing their harvest. The farm workers would often share equipment and help each other so that the timing of harvesting, sowing and reaping was always staggered. He noticed six sturdy oxen being harnessed to a plough outside a church: the plough was kept there for safekeeping, and the labourers would work out who needed to use it first. In other fields the wheat crop was being harvested. The rise and fall of the scythes, wielded by women and men alike, bent double in the heat, was back-breaking work. Often it was the women who had the lighter but more awkward work of tying the sheaves.

He passed another farm where the branches of two apple trees were almost touching the ground, weighed down with ripe fruit, and children were carefully picking to store. Behind them, three men were winnowing, separating the grain from the chaff. Even though it was early morning, they had been working since dawn; sweat poured off their faces as they beat the wheat to remove the grain from the stalk. When the wheat heads were put into a sieve and tossed into the air, the welcome wind today would blow the chaff away from the heavier grain, so there was no necessity for someone to waft a sheet to provide a breeze. A farm worker's life was hard enough, and they welcomed every advantage from the weather. Some workers nodded with respect as he passed but more eyed him with suspicion. '*Understandable,*' he thought, but something inside him bristled against their resentment when his life's work had been to keep these very people safe!

He passed a mill where oxen were turning the capstan and a line of carts heavily loaded with wheat. The drivers and helpers were enjoying a rest beneath the canopy of golden-laden branches of an oak tree as they caught up on local news. This was the busiest time for the miller, especially after a good harvest.

Owain felt a twinge of guilt again as he thought of Anglesey. The mills would be silent. The peasants would be wondering how they would get through winter. He turned his face aside as he thought back to the fires, flames leaping across the countryside, the acrid smell, and the ash raining from the heavens for days. Then his mind turned to Angharad's clear accusation: of all his children, she had loved him the most, and now she was disappointed in him. Almost worse than that was the look of satisfaction on Gronwy's face when Owain had returned from Anglesey and told his sons about the carnage and devastation. Thank God he had forbidden his sons to ride with him. Gronwy had been furious at the time, but if things had turned out badly, he needed his sons to save whatever they could and protect those in the manor. He sighed deeply and tried to keep his thoughts to the negotiations he must make.

He was not looking forward to meeting Earl Hugh. He felt weary and sickened as he recalled the man's brutality, and in truth, he was ashamed that he had led the Earl and his troops across Gwynedd. Yet what choices did he have? Could he now make amends and broker

225

peace? When Owain was younger, he would rise to the challenge of pulling off the impossible. He had such faith in his ability to win any debate with anyone but now, what did he feel now? Half a man. His confidence had been rocked, yet he had to do this.

Owain reached Chester and made his way through the bustling but stinking streets. Soldiers were evident everywhere, their mail shining and their eyes suspicious. Local people were going about their daily business. Women were selling cheeses and butter, wild fruits, apples and bread. Men were driving sheep, goats, cows and pigs to the local market. Some were selling fish and eels, and others cockles and crabs or carried baskets of eggs. Children were running beside ox carts carrying barrels of ale or sacks of wheat, barley and oats. Drunken men tumbled out of the tavern, and desperate women watched for an opportunity to earn some coin. Owain noticed that Chester was thriving, and there was constant traffic between the quay and town. Craftsmen of all types were doing a roaring trade, and he had to admit that under Earl Hugh, Chester had become more prosperous than the sleepy town it had been in his youth.

Owain made his way to the stronghold, which was Earl Hugh's fortress when he was in Chester. It was a motte-and-bailey castle with a large wooden tower built from sturdy oak. Two enormous wooden doors, reinforced with thick iron, stood at the heavily guarded entrance. Owain stated his business and was allowed through. Inside, he looked around the courtyard while his horse was taken to be watered. The noise of craftsmen creating piles of weapons made him very uneasy. A team of fletchers were producing arrows whose sharp tips were doubtless intended for human rather than animal targets. Goose feathers were being attached with strong thread so that they would fly swiftly through the air. Another craftsman and his team were turning out spears whose lethal tips would end lives. Metal was being worked into blades over roaring fires. What was Earl Hugh planning? A messenger was dispatched to see if it was convenient for Earl Hugh to meet with Owain. While he waited, Owain questioned some fletchers as to why there was a need for so many arrows.

226

"The Earl says we must be prepared in these dangerous times. It is good business for us," came the response.

In his hall, Hugh waited for Owain, his face grim. This was the first time the proud Norman earl had met with Owain since he, stony-faced, grey and struggling for breath, had commanded his Norman troops to retreat from Anglesey. Hugh remembered vividly how he had almost suffocated in the smoke from the fires billowing back onto their camp, the heat and humidity; the despair of his troops at Shrewsbury's killing of the meddling Cenred had weighed upon him. The death of the Earl of Shrewsbury had hit him hard. Rumours had gone around the troops that this Welsh place was cursed, and he had indeed felt cursed. Hugh had never felt fear at any battle but had felt his body rebelling against him. Clusters of burning red bumps had appeared all over his chest, neck, face and arms, and his bowels ran with foul-smelling liquid over which he had no control. He, who had been given the power to make or break any law save treason and had funded William the Conqueror's invasion of England, had been attacked by an enemy within. At night he would sweat, toss and turn and, in the quiet darkness, have visions of the bewitched stone in the shape of a thigh, which would return to its place in Anglesey no matter where it was taken. As a joke, Hugh had ordered his men to steal the sacred stone from its resting place and bring it to him. He had chained the stone to one of the Norman knights, and where it had touched the knight's leg, the flesh had become putrid. In the morning, the stone had vanished and was found back in its place on the island where it had been for hundreds of years. No man could account for how it arrived there. Hugh knew evil forces had been against him. Even now, at night, he fancied he could hear the howls of Shrewsbury's maddened dogs or shouted curses and echoes from the hills behind Anglesey.

Maybe, Hugh thought, he should have turned back when they fought those Welshmen at the narrow pass at Cevn Ogo. His men had said that the Welsh had ghostly warriors among them from a battle in the same place long before. Eleven hundred dead from both sides were left lying on the ground as they hurried on to Anglesey in stifling heat with the remaining troops sweating in their mail.

No matter how much he prayed and how much money he gave to others to pray for him, nothing gave him peace. Now, his legs were swollen and weeping, and he could hardly shuffle along. He sat in his huge chair, his bulk swelling over the side, and he knew he stank. His little child would gag when he came near his own father.

Owain came to him, as always, respectful but not obsequious. Hugh saw the disgust on his face. He had always felt Owain was easy to deal with. You asked the Welshman to do something, and he did it, but he, too, had shown his true colours in Anglesey. Hugh was angered that Owain, with his calculating eyes, dared judge him. The Welsh were not to be trusted, even educated ones like this one.

Owain cleared his throat and, despite Earl Hugh's obvious anger, explained what he wanted. Hugh was tired and irritable and wanted the Welshman gone. What madness persuaded him to allow an audience? He didn't want to deal with the Welsh anymore. What was the man asking for? The impertinence.

Hugh's energy faded at the endless demands and he turned inwards to the needs of his body. To Hell with it, let them have everything west of the Conwy; he would keep his dues from Owain's territory. Why worry about garrisons at the ends of the earth, keeping them fed, keeping them safe in that God-forsaken place? His men had destroyed anything of value there anyway, so there were no renders worth having.

Owain droned on. There was more: they wanted the captives returned; they wanted their safety assured; they wanted him to speak to Rufus and Shrewsbury. Then suddenly, the Welshman was talking about violating God's rights and of Magnus Barefoot and Irish kings, and his head ached. Where was the strength and ferocity, deep in his belly, which had driven him all his life? How dare this Welshman talk of violating God's rights. What did that even mean? He felt somehow separate from the conversation, as if he was outside his body, observing. The rage that had made him unstoppable had deserted him and just left him sour, empty and incapacitated.

Strangely he thought of Julius Caesar. The moment he tangled with the heathen Britons, everything went wrong for Caesar. His daughter died, his mother died, he was plotted against, he fell sick, and then the final betrayal: his assassination. Had those Welshmen who thought of themselves as Britons also cursed him?

Hugh winced in pain and wanted Owain gone. Feeling nauseous and not in control of his functions, he inexplicably found he had agreed to Owain's requests, dismissed him, and later sent messengers to Rufus and Shrewsbury, both in Normandy. Then he sent for Herve, the Bishop of Bangor.

Owain returned to Angharad. He was unsure what he felt exactly. It had been easier than he thought. Why? With him, Earl Hugh had always been a man of his word, but he thought it wise to get a formal peace treaty signed between all parties. What was it that Hugh knew that he did not? Was he using Gruffydd, Cadwgan and himself to buffer his richer lands in Chester from the Irish or from the ambitious Magnus Barefoot? Was something happening in England that was of more importance to Hugh, which he needed to keep his focus on, leaving the Welsh to fight against each other, as they ultimately would?

In truth, Owain had gained little joy from governing the whole of Gwynedd. He had liked the idea of his elevated position but the cost was high. Out there in Anglesey, it was impossible to protect from invasion, and he didn't want to be worrying every day whether he would be responsible for failing to stop the Norwegians or the Irish or whoever else decided they wanted a piece of it. As for the other lands in the west of Gwynedd, they were either impossibly mountainous or their leaders were a wild, ungovernable lot. This solution, crafted by Gruffydd, suited him, but he must be careful not to show his hand too early, even to his daughter: position and respect had taken a lifetime to achieve and needed to be maintained.

As he reached his llys, the light was fading, and already tiny bats were emerging from the cracks and holes around the building. Blind but better able to find their way than we on our life's journey, he thought, concluding that men made life far too complicated for themselves.

Angharad greeted him eagerly as he dismounted. "We will speak tomorrow when I have my thoughts clear," he said.

He thought: '*I will think about it all a little longer. Let them wait.*' Then he made his way into the hall and dropped wearily into his chair near the fire, which was already cracking and roaring heavy with logs.

Hywel caught Angharad's eye and lifted his brow quizzically. She mouthed that she was not sure, and he threw her a sympathetic look. He was as anxious for them to return to Anglesey as she was. Hywel was a faithful friend, and she was grateful for his good-natured support.

Angharad put aside any impatience and tended to Owain as she always did, making sure he was comfortable after the long journey, bringing him food and drink. He remembered how she was always calm, thoughtful, and sensitive to his moods.

The visit had sapped his energy, and as he sat in his chair in the lively hall with all the young and vigorous blood around him, he felt lost. He listened as they laughed and joked, clapping each other on the shoulder in congratulation for a particular skill shown as they related the triumphs of the hunt. Was it so long ago that he would have relished the retelling of the bringing down of a stag; or the spearing of a charging boar, leaning treacherously near the ground, the horse adjusting to the sudden change in weight, the final moments when the spear found its mark, the dogs frenzied with excitement and the utter exhilaration of a successful hunt?

Outside, the wind had risen and was whistling through the cracks in the building, and every so often, a gust of smoke would puff out of the fireplace. He heard the chirp of a bird, and his eye caught the small shape of a sparrow which had entered the hall and, after perching above them for a few moments, saw a way out on the other side, flying back into the evening.

"Did you see our feathered intruder?" he said, leaning across to Meilyr, who sat closest to him.

"It wasn't interested in staying with us," Meilyr replied ruefully, "we are all too noisy!"

"Hmm. You are right; even a little sparrow longs for peace. It reminds me of the story of King Edwin's advisor, who spoke of life as being like the hurried flight of a sparrow. I must have told you that story before. The bird enters the hall in the height of a storm when all are enjoying a meal and warmth and, for that short while, is sheltered but then vanishes from sight into the dark winter from whence it came. Life is shorter than you think! Always make the most of it!"

Angharad sat sewing quietly but listening to everything, as she always did. She glanced at her father with a gentle look and saw a rare glimpse of his vulnerability. He caught the expression in her eyes and admitted to himself that he had missed her when she went to Anglesey.

"Angharad, will you play for us?" he asked suddenly, thinking of many evenings spent enjoying her sweet voice.

She moved to the new harp, which had replaced the one she had taken and was now buried with other treasured items in Anglesey. Her slender hands ran over it, admiring it. "What would you have me play, Father?"

"A merry tune!"

As her fingers enticed wonderful sounds from the instrument, Owain mused that it was the Queen of Gwynedd who was playing for him and tired as he was, the thought made him smile.

Over the next few weeks, things moved very quickly. News of Magnus Barefoot sweeping the Isles was concerning to the Normans, as they needed to focus on Normandy, not on protecting their Welsh borders. Rufus had realised that peace with the Welsh was a better option than having to deploy precious resources to that unresolved issue. Let Gruffydd ap Cynan defend Anglesey from the likes of King Magnus and Murtagh O Brien and their wild ambitions.

Meanwhile, Robert de Belleme, the new Earl of Shrewsbury, had another reason for accepting peace. Belleme still wanted to oust Rufus from the throne in favour of the king's older brother, Robert and had assurances from other barons that they were of similar minds. At present, they were biding their time, and Shrewsbury had cleverly garnered favour with Rufus in Normandy for his capture of Elias, Count of Maine. The move had diluted Rufus' anxieties about the power of Shrewsbury and his family, the Montgomerys. Behind the scenes, however, Shrewsbury was pleased with the way that his brother Arnulf's relationship with Murtagh O Brien was progressing with the potential marriage to Murtagh's daughter, Lafracoth. How useful it might be to have Murtagh's Welsh allies, Gruffydd ap Cynan and Cadwgan ap Blyddyn, on his side. Short-term loss of land but long-term gain as he pursued his ambitions to undermine Rufus.

So it was that Owain ap Edwin swiftly manoeuvred a peace treaty which served the purposes of all parties. Angharad hoped that she would shortly be reunited with her husband. It was not until the peace treaty was signed that she allowed herself to put anxiety aside and let her imaginings wander to the birth of their child, the sounds of nightingales and lapping water, and strong arms holding her tightly beneath heavy woollen blankets.

Chapter 18: The Road to Anglesey (Autumn 1098)

It was promising to be cold leading up to Christmastide when Gruffydd and Cadwgan came back to Gwynedd on the feast of St Martins. A heavy mist blanketed the valley as Gruffydd, Owain, and Cadwgan sat together at Tegeingl to clear the way for their future now that the peace treaty bore their seals. Gruffydd insisted on Angharad being a party to the discussion, Cadwgan included his son Owain, and Owain invited his brother Uchdryd and asked that Gronwy be included also. Uchdryd and Cadwgan were cool with each other at first. Uchdryd, in his long black leather boots and thick fur cloak draped over his shoulders, looked formidable. Cadwgan wore an expensive otter fur cloak clasped with a heavy silver brooch, and his stance showed he was making sure nobody thought he could be intimidated. Uchdryd had not forgotten his treatment after the siege of Pembroke Castle, and Cadwgan had felt betrayed by Uchdryd and Owain in what he regarded as support for the Normans, which caused the death of so many of their men in Anglesey. Both men bristled with each other, and then, being of similar temperaments, they aired their differences loudly. Everyone felt the awkwardness keenly but both men knew what was at stake. After a short while, common sense prevailed, and they seemed to reach some sort of reconciliation to the relief of all present.

"I speak for all of us when I say that we are more than grateful, Lord Owain, for everything you have achieved in negotiating this peace treaty," said Gruffydd as things settled down. "We have not seen eye to eye on everything in the past but can we agree that going forward, we do not waste our energies on hostilities towards each other to Norman advantage? Too many times Welshman has fought Welshman over land while the Normans have encroached on our territories."

There were murmurs of assent but Gronwy narrowed his dark eyes and looked at Gruffydd from under heavy brows. There would be no easy relationship there, such as Gruffydd had with Meilyr, Rhydir and Llywarch.

Owain looked at his brother, saw the slightest nod of his head and then, turning back to the others, said, "I agree. We would have peace in Gwynedd, and I, for one, have no designs on Powys."

Uchdryd put his hand on his brother's shoulder and added earnestly, "Had we not agreed to take the Normans peacefully across Gwynedd, they would have slaughtered our people and devastated their crops between Chester and Anglesey. You know that. And yes, we were also protecting our lands by our collusion with the Normans; I do not deny it, but we did not aid them in any way that resulted in even one lost Welsh life."

There was an immediate outcry from Cadwgan and his son, and Gruffydd shook his head violently. Uchdryd held up a hand and continued.

"On the contrary, when we made our stand against the abhorrent treatment of the priests and the excessive and destructive razing of Anglesey for no good reason, it was that which convinced them to return to Chester without further reprisal. I say again, we were not responsible for one Welsh life. The Normans would have found their way to Anglesey without us, and the damage would have been worse."

"Uchdryd, if you and Owain had led a force of Welsh men behind them, they would have been trapped and finished," growled Cadwgan belligerently. The newly reached peace between the two men seemed fragile.

Owain interrupted, "If we had stood against them, we would have been massacred at the start, and to whose benefit would that have been? It is easy to take a stance in retrospect and point fingers but we did what we had to do for the safety of Gwynedd."

"And to line your pockets," growled Cadwgan.

Gruffydd raised his hand, "What is done is done. The betrayal of the mercenaries was the fatal blow."

Uchdryd quickly cut in, "And if we had known of it, Gruffydd, we would have sent word somehow to give you a fighting chance even if I had had to swim across the Menai Straits."

"But we did not," said Owain, and he looked straight into Angharad's eyes as if her acknowledgement of the fact would dispel all the rumours that he had led the wolf to his daughter's door.

Angharad gave the slightest of nods but it was enough.

Owain ap Cadwgan noticed and grinned. Gruffydd caught his look, and the younger man quickly averted his gaze to the roaring fire. His mind wandered to the promised delights Gronwy had hinted at for them at the inn later in the day.

It was a long, contentious day but by the end of the discussions, everyone agreed. Owain retained his title of Governor for the lands east of the Conway where there was still a Norman presence but it was understood that, while there would be no change to his lands in Tegeingl, in time, there would be a gentle ousting of the Normans back to the Dee which had long been regarded as the border between Wales and England. They all conceded that the Normans seemed to have little appetite to re-garrison empty castles. This would make it easier to push the Normans back to the borderlands. Gruffydd was to retain his title of King of Gwynedd and retain overall power within Gwynedd. Cadwgan was now to retire his interest in Gwynedd but concentrate his energies on Powys, Ceredigion and the additional lordships Robert de Belleme had granted him in Merionydd, Cyfeiliog and Penllyn.

Cadwgan was clearly enormously pleased with the way everything had worked out and was puffed up with self-satisfaction. In his enthusiasm, in recognition of his reconciliation with Uchdryd, who had served Cadwgan as his war chief for so many years, Uchdryd received parcels of land in Cyfeiliog, Meirionydd and Penllyn. Uchdryd's pride had been restored, and Gruffydd could not help asking himself whether things might have been different had it not been for the rift between Cadwgan and Uchdryd.

Owain, Cadwgan's son, noted that the agreements were between the three men and not their heirs, and he stored this away for the future. He didn't like Gruffydd, who was a good fighter, even a good leader but didn't know how to have a good time. Gronwy liked Gruffydd even less, and Gronwy might be a useful ally in the future.

Gronwy was exasperated that his father had given away too much. He felt that Owain relinquished a title over the whole of Gwynedd that by right should have fallen to him. His bitterness against his sister and her husband rankled. He looked at his father, his hair thin, almost white, and promised himself that one day he would teach Gruffydd ap Cynan who was who in Gwynedd.

Gruffydd was also uneasy with the arrangement with Owain but his word was his word, and he had vowed to himself that as long as Owain lived, he would honour that agreement. He looked at his wife, luminous-eyed, sitting quietly in her fine red woollen robe, absorbing everything, and felt so proud of what she had achieved. Things might have gone horribly wrong for them but she understood the situation, what was at stake and, most importantly, how to appeal to Owain. He needed peace now to rebuild Anglesey and pay off his debts, and she had worked a miracle with her father to buy them that time.

Angharad felt a thrill of pleasure as she saw her wide-chested, straight-backed husband gazing at her. She had seen the respect he received from the older men and was glad of it. Her heart was full of hope for a tranquil future when neighbour could live alongside neighbour without fear. She prayed that his reputation and leadership were strong enough to make that possible.

It was agreed that Angharad would stay on with her father while Gruffydd set about restoring the llys in Aberffraw and ensuring all was safe for their return. Gruffydd asked Hywel if he would be willing to stay also and then bring her home. Hywel was more than happy to do that. He always got on well with the family, and Gruffydd knew that Angharad was very fond of him.

As they retired to their chamber that night, Gruffydd cupped his wife's face in his hands and kissed her gently on the forehead.

"Angharad, you have done well. A few months ago, I scarce believed we would return to Wales, let alone Anglesey and somehow, this impossible thing has happened. You have made it happen."

"I wish I could take all the credit but it is not all of my making. My father stood beside us in the end and somehow managed to keep his relationships intact! We are, in part, recipients of the fortune of circumstance, I think. The things people fear and create monsters of have worked in our favour."

He looked at her quizzically, and she explained, "The Normans have grave concerns that they are stretched too thin with enemies surrounding them. Sending the message to Magnus Barefoot was perfect timing, but who could have known that he would cause such terror among the Normans."

"I heard that he told the crews to use the Normans for target practise and that he and his best archer competed to see who could fell Shrewsbury."

"I abhor the loss of life, as you know, but that act stopped greater loss I feel."

"We owe him, and that is on my mind as well, but there will be a day when all debts are paid."

"Gruffydd, you must drive home your advantage now and be seen as the instrument of peace for Gwynedd."

He tilted his head to one side and looked at her questioningly. It had been a long, tough day but she was already anticipating their future steps. Her bright face shone with the passion of her thoughts.

"The people of Gwynedd are hungry for peace. They have accepted Norman overlordship with my father as governor to that end but they also long for a hero, someone that can instil pride in their Welshness. Take your time when you go back through Gwynedd; make sure that you stop to speak to as many farmers and landowners as possible. Speak to the mill owners, the fishermen, the blacksmiths, the priests and monks and everyone who needs to hear that Gwynedd is going to be safe. Spread the news yourself so that you are seen as the instigator of peace but also so that the message they receive is the correct message. Be a real person to them, someone they can believe in. If they do not know who you are, then why should they support you as their king?"

"Because they know that someone as wise as you would not marry anyone unless they were astounding, magnificent, glorious," he jested, hugging her close to him.

"Are you learning flattery now from your time at the Irish court or is your head just getting big?" she joked back and then looked at him earnestly. "Gruffydd, please, it really is so important that we make this an opportunity to create our own story, which in turn is the story of Gwynedd. We must tell the people what you have done and what you will do; otherwise, the tale will be lost. Only when it is spoken about do people rally. Then we must show them through things they can plainly see around them: fields full of crops, pastures full of animals, churches and buildings, your ships. When I look at you, I see a warrior king in fine clothes on a wonderful horse and think you are wealthy. I do not see that we have debt or cannot afford what other royals have. So, in the same way, we must clothe Gwynedd so that when the people look around, they think it is a paradise because they believe their own eyes while we are being wise about how we spend and on what."

Gruffydd threw back his head and laughed good-humouredly.

"Cariad, I do understand, and I also know that you are a very, very clever woman," he said proudly, kissing the nape of her neck, drawing her slim waist to him. She turned and slid her hands up under his tunic and undershirt, running her fingers through the hairs on his chest, her heart beating faster.

"I have missed you so much," she whispered and pushed him onto the furs covering the bed, allowing him to pull her on top of him.

***

Their time together was short. Gruffydd left at first light, and Hywel joined him for the first part of his journey to Chester to receive the captives from Earl Hugh as was part of the agreement. Hywel would then return to Tegeingl to wait with Angharad until Gruffydd sent word it was safe for her to return. To the surprise of both men, all went without a hitch. They were delighted to be reunited with so many whom they had fought alongside but also saddened to realise the absence of many others. The thankful band could not get out of Chester quickly enough. They were nearly all men, as most of the women on the island had either escaped to the mainland mountains or hidden deep in Anglesey's woods or caves when the Normans had started their march across Gwynedd.

As Angharad had suggested, Gruffydd took his progress back across Gwynedd slowly, making sure he stopped and spoke to as many of the landowners and those who worked for them as possible. Some of the landowners who had had a good harvest spared some seeds for those who had lost so much in Anglesey; some sent a little barley and some oats. Owain had also sent two cartloads of seed as well as some provisions for their llys.

Gruffydd's investment in meeting his subjects in Gwynedd was a good one. They spoke afterwards about how he had shown humility and genuine interest in their concerns, and the women had spoken about how handsome he was — tall, blonde with big intelligent eyes that noticed everything, and so finely dressed. The men were impressed by how fit he was, jumping up and down off his horse with an athletic spring; they talked of his sword and fine stallion. Many children were subsequently given the name Gruffydd at birth. The women especially asked about his fair queen. He told them that she was not only the most beautiful, but the wisest lady in all of Gwynedd, and they would soon be expecting a little one to join them. Such small talk had not come easily to Gruffydd at first, but over the last few years, he had learnt well. He was genuinely interested in what caused pain points and what made life easier. What fascinated him was recognising that there were opportunities for trade and that knowledge of different ways of doing things, when spread across Gwynedd, could bring rewards.

Wales had always been a place where cattle and sheep provided trade of meat, leather, and wool of wonderful quality, and sometimes even the horns could find buyers, but on Anglesey, cereal crops, such as oats, barley and sometimes wheat or rye, flourished with mild weather and rich fertile soils. Welsh horses were sturdy and much prized in Ireland, so Gruffydd thought of creating studs and the opportunities there might be. Mining was also something which had potential, and he thought of the lead in Flint, where the Romans had mined copper and coal. The enthusiastic man's mind was full of how he might drive Gwynedd back to be the powerful place it once was. Gruffydd found himself filled with the kind of eager anticipation he experienced before a battle. Could he do it? Each conversation reinforced his belief that it was possible. He mulled over the discussion he had had with Angharad, and her words 'clothing Gwynedd' came back to him.

Gruffydd ensured there was enough food for the captives as they made their way home. There was much song and storytelling as they travelled. While some had gone on ahead, leaving the security of the group to reach home earlier, those who had stayed with the band travelling at a slower pace became very close indeed. Although they kept vigilant, there were few people along the way at this time of year.

Sometimes a young goatherd or shepherd would be bringing animals down from the pastures and, seeing such a large group, would keep their distance, distrustful. Occasionally they would encounter women bent over with their backs piled high with kindling for the cold months ahead, or as they neared a larger homestead, they would hear axes ringing out in the woods, felling dead branches to be brought to a waiting ox-cart piled high with logs for winter fires.

Every night, the band would find willing hospitality. They would be offered a roof and straw to sleep on, and with provisions Gruffydd had arranged and with what the hosts would gladly share, they would be well provided for. Over and over, they would be asked to recount their stories of battles won and lost, of Earl Hugh's flight from Anglesey, and the stories grew with the telling. As they approached Anglesey, they would speak to men who had fought with them but escaped; there was always something to celebrate.

The wet weather held off for the first few days of their journey, but the high mountains were already blanketed in thick snow gleaming in the moonlight when they stopped to rest. The travellers would gaze at those peaks; their majesty would fill their souls. Great gusts of wind blew icy cold, stinging faces causing the band to huddle together as they plodded along. Then came the rain, soaking them all to the skin and turning their path into a heavy muddy mire. The oxen pulling the carts strained, churning the earth as they went.

The rivers the band passed or crossed were swollen, raging fiercely, pulling at the reeds and small shrubs along their banks until they bowed down into the dark grey torrents. Small waterfalls appeared coursing down from rocky slopes. Damp and cold, they trudged on. When they stopped for the evening, no matter how the thatch leaked or the wind howled through the cracks, they would be revived by a thick vegetable soup or fish stew soaked up by hunks of bread. Spirits would rise as they supped ale and told stories, laughed and joked, knowing they were ever nearer to home.

Early one evening, a few days after they had left Chester, a young man dressed in bardic clothes arrived on a small Welsh pony. He looked frozen to the core but he smiled and nodded his way through to Gruffydd. The King was sitting with some of the men who had fought with him, applying lanolin to his sword to stop it from rusting. The young man introduced himself as Rhoddri.

"I would like to join you, lord," he said simply, smiling winningly to reveal a gap where he had lost a front tooth. He had a long, thin face with a long but wispy beard, intelligent brown eyes that darted and danced, noticing everything, and hair curled around his head like a circlet. He was spotlessly clean despite the weather he had ridden through, and his expression was one of general optimism.

"I understand that you have no bard, and I would be proud to serve you if it would please you, my lord."

Gruffydd smiled warmly at him, sheathing his sword but didn't speak immediately. A bard would not only compose songs and poems to encourage his men but would bring some order to their evenings and feast days. As they travelled, it would also take the burden off him.

"It is true, I have no bard and the death of Gellan, my loyal harpist and chief poet, weighs heavily upon me. I will be honest and tell you that our llys is only part rebuilt, and our way of life will be modest, to begin with. You will have coin and food enough for a simple life."

"For me, that is no problem," the bard returned, barely concealing his delight, "but I would like you to hear my songs before you decide. I knew Gellan; his voice and poetry are legendary. I cannot claim such proficiency, and though many enjoy my music, you may not like my songs or my voice."

"With pleasure, we will hear you," said Gruffydd, smiling broadly and immediately taking to the man's honesty. "Go ahead and show us what you can do!"

Gruffydd called everyone's attention, and they gathered around the fire as Rhoddri sang something he had composed about how Gruffydd had wooed and won the fairest woman in Wales. While the facts of the story left something to be desired, the tale was enchanting and met with sound approval.

Gruffydd slapped him on the back jovially and welcomed him to their band, introducing many of the men around him. Afterwards, Gruffydd fell into a conversation with the bard about where Rhoddri had trained, how he had followed Gruffydd's progress and how he had a wife, Llinos, who was expecting their first child soon.

Gruffydd enjoyed Rhoddri's company, and soon they were discussing the Irish bards. Gruffydd wanted to introduce some of the Irish traditions into his own country's courtly music and verse.

"I would be very pleased to learn new ways of enhancing the craft," said Rhoddri eagerly. "If you like my music and verse, I will be happy to create new works as you see fit."

Gruffydd thought about Angharad again and her insistence on the correct message being sent across Gwynedd and beyond. He was further convinced of the bard's talents that evening when Rhoddri sang of the battle of Aberlleiniog. They sat around the roaring fire, an entranced audience, all of whom spoke highly of this affable, enthusiastic man who had tracked them down.

Over the next days, their journey continued with lively conversation and wit, diluting the hardship of the slog. They were particularly buoyed when they stopped at a large manor soon after the time when the animals were being slaughtered for winter provisions. The manor was owned by Hoedlyw ap Ithel, who had fought alongside Gruffydd. The band found themselves warmly welcomed, feted with pigs on spits and roaring fires. Gruffydd was delighted to spend time with Hoedlyw and his family. Hoedlyw and his wife were both stocky and ruddy-faced, but while she had mischievous eyes and full red lips, he had a fearsome look aggravated by a scar running down his left cheek, and when he did smile, he had only three teeth left. Their hall was large, with abundant hams and sides of bacon hanging from the ceiling to dry and smoke. Hoedlyw was one of those who had been fighting in Anglesey with Gruffydd but had managed to escape.

"There were about twenty of us that managed to get to the other side of the island, and we hid in a cave. We wondered if we would make it through the night because, at high tide, the sea rushed in. We were all flat against the rock with water around our knees. Anyway, somehow, word got to Cenred where we were, and a boat was sent to us. How none of us drowned is beyond me! It was a miracle! We decided to split up when we got back to the mainland, and I made my way home with a couple of my men."

"And everyone here was safe?"

Hoedlyw stirred the fire alive with a long iron poker. "It was deserted but intact. Everyone was up in the high pastures along with the livestock, you see. We made our way up there, and we had men posted to keep watch. We expected that the Norman bastards would destroy the buildings on the way back to Chester, but, no, they were too intent on getting back to the other side of the border!"

"They went straight past?'

"Like curs with their tails between their legs. When we knew it was safe, we came down. I, for one, will be happy if we can see a few years of peace and happier still if I never see another Norman in my life."

"And I am with you on that!" confessed Gruffydd

"You know," he continued shaking his head, "in all the years that Earl Hugh and his bootlickers have been pushing into our lands, they have not bothered to learn one single word of our language, yet I have heard it said that Caesar learnt our ancient tongue as did St Patrick who had Roman parents. The Normans are too ignorant to see the value in any culture other than their own!'

Aeddan had been listening intently. "They say that Rufus cannot read, and neither could his father, The Conqueror. Can you believe that?"

Some of the group seemed incredulous but Hoedlyw nodded, "He speaks true, hard though it is to believe. Only the young son Henry was given an education by the church so he can write, and they say he is interested in speaking to men of learning, but Rufus, smart and brave on the battlefield though he is, fair play, cannot read a word!"

"And they call the Welsh barbarians!" scoffed Gruffydd.

***

The next day, after their feast the night before, the band made good progress. The following day, on what seemed to be the coldest of the year, Gruffydd and his band of followers crossed the Menai Straits, arriving in Anglesey. They knelt on the sandy beach and gave thanks to God for their return as a flurry of snowflakes drifted across the water.

Gruffydd had already sent craftsmen to commence repairs to the llys and church but was amazed when he saw that the place was not only habitable but finer than before. Everyone helped to unload the provisions. Despite the weather, when news got out that Gruffydd and many of his teulu had arrived, there were visitors bringing gifts of eggs, butter, chickens, ducks, nuts, drinking horns, lovingly crafted carvings and embroidered cloth from all over the island. Father Teilo came and blessed them all. The priest had arranged for fresh bedding and a huge stack of wood for the fires. What most touched Gruffydd's heart was a beautifully carved crib brought by Iorwedd, the self-appointed leader of the captives.

'*If she could see this welcome now,*' Gruffydd thought to himself. He just wanted to share it with his wife, his beloved. How long they had been separated and then so briefly and magically back together and now apart again. The last days had been tough but exhilarating. He longed for peace and time to think, but he knew that no matter how tired he was, how drained he felt inside, how much he longed to retreat, he must now play generous host, the leader of this band of believers, the king of his loyal subjects, the repayer of debt. He turned to the congregated group.

"Come take your drinking vessels, and Rhoddri, take your instruments. We will drink and sing the praises of Gwynedd!" he shouted.

"Gwynedd," came the hearty cheer followed by, "King Gruffydd!" and then, bringing a smile to his face, "Queen Angharad!"

Chapter 19: William and Henry (Year to December 1100)

"What a skinny little rabbit who thinks he is a lion," said Gruffydd laughing as he stroked the face of his tiny son and kissed his wife.

Angharad regarded her little newborn. As was the custom, they had rubbed him in salt and roses while he had screamed loud enough to wake the dead. Then his mother had given him honey on her little finger, and he had quietened for a moment before screaming again when she took her finger away. Their baby was fiery-eyed and missing nothing, even though he was just hours old. He seemed to be punching the air with his little fists, and as he let out another fearsome cry, Gruffydd laughed and said, "We will name him Cadwallon."

"Is he your ancestor, my lord?" asked Bethan as she came in with more blankets and sheets for the little one's crib.

"So I am told; far, far back. Cadwallon grew up in Gwynedd but, along with his best friend, King Edwin of Deira, went to Brittany to get the finest education. The two were like brothers but both fierce. Edwin conquered King Elmet's Northumbria before turning on his childhood friend, Cadwallon, here in Gwynedd. Fortunately, Cadwallon escaped to Ireland and then to Brittany, and when he returned, he crushed the Mercians, regained Gwynedd and took Edwin's Northumbria. He ruled from the River Thames to the River Forth. We will name this little one after that mighty warrior who suffered defeat, experienced exile and witnessed treachery but was eventually victorious."

He held the baby up to his face and beamed at him, "Yes, Cadwallon is a good name for you, little fighter."

Angharad smiled. '*Treachery, exile, victory. A familiar story. If it pleased Gruffydd to name him so, then Cadwallon he would be.*'

It had not been the easiest of births with a long labour, but the little one had fought bravely. He was a healthy little baby, though, as Gruffydd said, skinny as a rabbit with no flesh on him at all. His mother was exhausted but happy that, at last, they were a little family. Gruffydd took him out to show off to his teulu, and the mead drinking started immediately.

Angharad mused whether she and her husband would ever be just the two of them, knowing that this life made almost every private moment a public one. She accepted it and was grateful that at least they did have a llys, a teulu and that Anglesey was recovering.

Slowly, very slowly, things were improving on the island and in Gwynedd. Thankfully, the winter had not been too harsh, although 1099, the last year of the century, would be remembered as the wettest in years. On Anglesey, there were wry comments about needing to build arks, and some were worried that the continual rain and the approach of 1100 heralded the end of the world. Roofs were rotting, and the few possessions many owned were either rusting or falling apart from perpetual dampness. Food and clothing succumbed to mould, and it was hard to keep the wood for the fires dry. Fears were real about too much rain spoiling the harvest and the black growth which could ruin rain-drenched crops, yet the sun shone enough for the harvest to be reasonable. Only when January 1100 had passed, cold and bleak without major concern, the worries for the future of humanity dissipated, and the natural rhythm of life restored confidence.

The Welsh enjoyed the peace while Rufus was still struggling with Norman politics as well as the scheming of the Anglo-Normans, who resented the king's greater interest in Normandy than England. Rufus had been engaged in a war against King Philip of France but signed a truce with France in April after encountering significant resistance. Many said he had done so only because he was anxious that he was losing control in both England and Normandy. On hearing this, the Welsh sharpened their weapons, kept vigilant and hoped that Rufus' eyes did not stray back to the west.

Little Cadwallon thrived, and at the end of the year, a little brother was born. Owain was very proud that his new grandson was named after him. Baby Owain was a much calmer baby than his fiery brother, and Gruffydd carried the two around in his arms, bursting with pride. Before the birth of Cadwallon, a message came from Tegeingl that Rhydir and Lleuci had also become parents to another healthy son they called Llywarch. This was happy news indeed, for childbirth was always risky, and Angharad and Gruffydd praised God that things had also gone well for the gentle pair. They hoped that, in time, the cousins would get to know each other and the bonds of kin would remain strong.

It was a hot summer's day when Uchdryd and his wife Nest arrived to visit Gruffydd, Angharad and their young great-nephews. Uchdryd could hardly contain himself.

"Rufus, King of England, is dead!" he announced to the family and members of the teulu before he even dismounted from his horse. There were cries of surprise and some cheering as well.

"How?" asked Gruffydd, beckoning and then putting an arm around Angharad to pull her closer so that she could better hear Uchdryd's words. "Had he been sick? Wait, where are my manners? Come inside and take refreshments. I will call everyone together to hear this."

The party came into the llys with everyone crowded around Uchdryd. Drink and platters of food were brought, and the excitement began. Angharad sat with Cadwallon wriggling on her knee next to Aunt Nest, who cooed and played with baby Owain.

"Well," boomed Uchdryd, settling himself into a big comfortable chair. He loved nothing more than telling a good story. Cadwallon stopped squirming and gazed, round-eyed, at his bear of a great uncle. "Last Thursday night, Rufus' servants woke up to hear him shrieking like a woman from an awful nightmare. He dreamt he had met with Satan, who told him he was looking forward to seeing him the next day. He could not sleep. The next day, August 2nd, Rufus insisted on hunting with a small party, including his brother, Henry Beauclerc, the one who set himself up with Princess Nest, but there's another story. Anyway, they had been out chasing down deer in the New Forest. Brockenhurst, it was. Gilbert de Clare was one of the group, as well as his younger brother Roger and also Walter Tirel, who had married a sister of the de Clares, Adelize."

"I have heard of Tirel; he is well known as an extraordinary bowman," remarked Gruffydd and others in the teulu muttered that they had also heard of him.

"Tirel is a very good shot, and when the armourer presented six arrows to the King, Rufus took four himself and gave two to Tirel saying, 'Good arrows for a good shot'. Well, they had been having a good day. Rufus had been keen to continue, but by now, the sun was very low. Rufus spotted a stag and took aim and shot but only wounded the beast. As the stag ran past him, Rufus apparently shaded his eyes from the sun with his hand; then, just at that moment, Tirel spotted another stag and let fly, but the arrow went straight into Rufus' chest. Rufus said nothing and tried to break off the shaft before dropping like a stone. Tirel ran up to him but found Rufus dead. Fearing for his life, Tirel leapt onto his horse and fled."

There were gasps of horror and tutting all around. Even though he had been an enemy, Rufus loomed large in the imaginations of the little gathering.

"Was Tirel pursued?" asked Gruffydd, leaning forward, imagining the scene.

"Not a bit of it. No one went after him but listen to this. They left Rufus' body right there on the ground, and his own brother, Henry, chased to Winchester, where he took hold of the treasury. That was his first priority. The body was found later by an arrow maker called Eli Parratt, and he and a few others took his body in the back of a cart to Winchester, dripping blood all the way. There, Rufus was entombed the next day. Henry, meanwhile, wasted no time and

250

headed for London, where he got himself crowned before any archbishop could arrive."

"Was it deliberate, do you think?" asked Hywel, his face grave.

"Well, if it wasn't, it was convenient timing," observed Gruffydd.

"Indeed," agreed Uchdryd with relish, 'interesting for lots of reasons."

"Why is that?" asked Hywel respectfully.

Everyone leaned in to listen.

"Well," said Gruffydd, "you think about it. When William the Conqueror died, he left Normandy to his eldest son, Robert Curthose, who became Duke of Normandy, and William Rufus became King of England. Henry Beauclerc just got some money. But Curthose and Rufus wanted to rule both Normandy and England as their father had so that caused endless animosity. Curthose was hopeless with money and desperate to go on crusade, so he put the animosity aside and mortgaged Normandy to Rufus in return for the funds to keep him at the crusades for the last four years."

"Meanwhile," Uchryd took up the tale, "Curthose has been on crusade capturing Jerusalem, he has also been negotiating a marriage to Sybilla of Conversano, daughter of Geoffrey of Brindisi. Her dowry would comfortably repay Rufus the money he borrowed in exchange for land to restore and secure the whole of Normandy for Curthose again. Now, if Curthose marries and Sybilla produces an heir, there is no hope for Henry with the English throne. Should Curthose have had an heir and Rufus died without an heir, not only would Curthose inherit, being the Conqueror's eldest, his heir would also inherit England. Everybody knows how desperate Henry is to become King of England, so it would be convenient to get rid of Rufus and claim the throne before Curthose can get back to Normandy, repay Rufus and try to claim the English throne himself."

"So, you think Henry arranged Rufus' murder?" asked Hywel, shaking his head at the ease with which they were accepting royal fratricide.

"It looks very possible," surmised Gruffydd. "On the other hand, we know how greedy Curthose is and if Rufus is dead, there is no need for repayment to Rufus of the money for which he pawned Normandy. He would little expect his younger brother Henry to step into Rufus' place."

"His death would also be music to the ears of both the Pope and the King of France," added Uchdryd with a wide grin.

"Surely Duke Robert Curthose would not have been behind his brother's death," said Angharad, "his dowry from Sybilla would have been ample to repay his debt. I cannot believe this has been driven by money."

"Greed," said Uchdryd shaking his head. "No amount of money is sufficient. No amount of land is enough. Duke Robert hated both his brothers from the time that they tipped a chamber pot on him and his friends from atop a balcony. The uproar caused the Conqueror to intervene, and the father sided with the younger two, leading Robert to rebel against the lot of them."

"But there was the agreement Curthose made with his brother Rufus, that if one of them dies, the other inherits their lands and wealth." insisted Angharad.

"They did indeed agree to that, and now I wonder how that will play out with Henry and Robert," commented Gruffydd.

"There was no formal line of succession, though, with Rufus having no children," added Uchdryd.

"In truth, Henry is a sworn vassal of Curthose and really has no right to the English throne," Gruffydd speculated.

"But Henry has the treasury and wears the crown. That's most of the battle. He has his supporters." Uchdryd reminded him.

"Wasn't their brother Richard killed in the same forest?" asked Nest.

"That was an accident, my lady," explained Hywel gently. "He rode into a tree and died as a result, but Curthose's bastard, another Richard, was killed there by an accidental arrow last May."

"Maybe it gave some people an idea," said Uchdryd, winking somewhat disrespectfully.

"The church will be happy," commented Gruffydd. "Not many will be crying about Rufus' death here or in England."

"You are right there," agreed Uchdryd solemnly. "Already the word is that it was God's vengeance for his evil life."

The death of William Rufus was the talk of the evening, with many theories as to whether it was truly an accident or was deliberate. Many of the teulu, who were excellent bowmen themselves, found it hard to swallow that Tirel, known to be a superb shot, could have missed so disastrously. Gruffydd commented that it was intriguing that the accident took place so close to Winchester, where the treasury was kept. And very convenient for Henry, whose response to the thought of succession was so immediate.

Angharad retired to her chamber holding the hand of little Cadwallon, a noisy, feisty one now running from place to place, with Nest carrying his little brother Owain, who was just beginning to crawl.

"Those eyes don't miss anything!" commented Nest of Cadwallon, who had clambered onto her and was pulling at an amber brooch pinned to her robe, then, losing interest, jumped down and ran laps of the room on a pretend horse.

"Indeed, they do not," replied Angharad while watching Owain crawling all over the cloth mat she had placed for him on the floor. He would pull and tug at anything he could reach.

"Owain is strong and seems very healthy. He takes after Gruffydd's side more than yours, I think. Look how quickly he has learnt to pull himself along. Then Cadwallon is very young to be running around like this."

"Cadwallon has been early to do everything," said Angharad. "I think he has learnt twice as fast as other babies because he hardly sleeps for fear he will miss something."

Nest laughed and looked seriously at her niece, "You look tired, Angharad, but it is good that you have the family close together. They will grow up tight with each other."

"Rhydir, Meilyr and Llywarch were very close in age; they have a strong bond. Gronwy was older, but there is not so much in common with him and the others."

"Ah, Gronwy was very upset when Rhydir was born. Rhydir was very delicate, and your mother had to spend a lot of time with him. Gronwy had been used to being the centre of attention, and suddenly, he wasn't."

"I must be careful that it doesn't happen with our children. I would like a big family with all of them getting on if God is kind to us. How is little Llywarch? Have you seen him?"

"We were with your father just two weeks ago. The little boy is the spitting image of Rhydir and is very easy. He sleeps well and is full of smiles like his mother. He is a big boy with plenty of padding but not as forward as Cadwallon here. They were all in good spirits because the harvest was one of the best this year, and your brothers and Lleuci look well."

"And Father?"

"He loves his little grandson. He was always good with babies if they didn't cry! Frankly, though, Owain is disappointed with Gronwy, who is still drinking heavily and, as I said, doesn't get on well with your brothers, particularly Meilyr. Gronwy is such a misery."

"It was obvious when I was at home. He hardly spoke two words to me and avoided Gruffydd as much as he could when he was there."

"He is a surly one. He is good at managing anything to do with the estate but your father confided in Uchdryd that the tenants don't like him, and he can be very harsh."

"Father looked older when I was at home. He had a nasty cough, which he couldn't seem to shake. Is it better?"

Nest hesitated and then replied soothingly, "We are all getting older, Angharad. He suffers from his chest. Lleuci makes a fuss of him, which he pretends not to want but loves all the same. You know your father! He still managed to go hunting with Uchdryd and all the boys, well men they are now, I suppose, and they managed to bring in a huge boar, so I think he can't be too bad."

"He seemed to go downhill after that visit to Earl Hugh when he was helping us to get back to Anglesey. I think he was shocked by the state in which he found the Earl, and I am sure he worries about what will happen if Earl Hugh dies. Will someone worse come? Will they have any respect for Father or for any of us? Now with the new king as well, who knows what will be thrown at us."

"Earl Hugh's son is only a youngster, really, and if something happened to his father, I am not sure who would take over, but they couldn't be crueller than Hugh the Fat, that is for sure. How your father managed to keep a good relationship with him, I don't know."

"Nor I," admitted Angharad.

"I think that what happened in Anglesey with the priest shocked your father to the core, and he cannot forget it at all. He doesn't discuss it, but I think the whole thing has affected his health."

"He didn't talk to me of it, really," mused Angharad.

"No, because he felt so uncomfortable about it. It shocked Uchdryd, I know, but he is battle-hardened and not such a deep thinker as your father. He and Uchdryd were in a terribly difficult situation. If they had not been seen to support Earl Hugh, the rest of Gwynedd would have been the worse for it but they did as much as they could to slow them down. Uchdryd told me he had sent rumours around the Norman troops of evil spirits in the hills behind and the curse on those who attacked the island of the ancient Druids. The Normans were like jumpy cats after that."

Despite the gravity of the topic, Angharad smiled, thinking that was exactly the sort of trick her uncle would play.

"Do you remember when we were little, Uncle would tell us about the magical island of Anglesey, the centre of Celtic religion years ago, where the Druids would cast people to their death in wicker effigies as a sacrifice to the gods? I little thought I would end up living here."

"Oh, he would tell you how Tacitus related the ancient final battle between the Romans and the Druids. How many times have I heard him tell that story at how many gatherings? He would have you all mesmerised with tales of how the Druids stood on the shore, inciting the Gods and invoking magical rituals while women dressed like Furies waved burning brands terrifying the Roman soldiers. Then, how even though the Romans overcame them, many Druids escaped and took their magic arts to Ireland or to the mountains."

"We children would all listen, our imaginations racing, too frightened to sleep that night thinking the Druids would come down from the mountains looking for us."

"I do remember. I would chastise him for giving you all nightmares. You know Gruffydd gave Uchdryd an old sword he found in the bog south of Llyn Cerrig Bach, which they both thought went back to the early times of the Druids. Who would have thought they could find such a thing? Uchdryd was very touched."

"I knew. He showed me the sword. He found a torque and some other old weapons there as well. It must have been a place where they gave offerings to their gods. Once, there were sacred oak groves all over the island, but the Romans cut them down and burnt them to stamp out the Druids."

"They do say there are some who have those magical arts still living here. Have you heard of any?"

"Only gossip, but it is a Christian place, and all the people we have met are good Christians. Gruffydd is building up the churches, and I do as much as I can to support them."

Nest took her niece's slim hand into her old, wrinkled one. "Your father brought you up well. He is incredibly proud of you, you know. He told Uchdryd that he was very surprised at how you handled the peace negotiations and the clarity of your thinking."

Angharad blushed. "I am honoured. It was he who taught me to look at a problem from all sides. I have been thinking of asking them all to come at Christmas. We are getting settled here again now, and the weather we have here is so much better sheltered as we are by Snowdonia: warmer and half as much rain than in Tegeingl. Maybe it would do Father good."

"I think he would love being at the Royal Court of Gwynedd," teased Nest, her soft face wrinkling with mirth, "he loves his mead, and Gruffydd's is one of the finest. You know it would help Owain to know you bore him no ill will."

"I bear him no ill will at all," protested Angharad, but, seeing her aunt's face colour, she hastily changed the subject. "Have you heard

257

any news of Princess Nest, Aunty? I know she has married Gerald the Stewart of Pembroke Castle, one of Arnulf de Montgomery's men."

"She had a son by the new king, Henry. That I know. I am wondering how she is feeling about being married to someone so much older than her?"

"Yes, King Henry, it seems strange to call him that; I knew he arranged the marriage for Nest, and their son has gone with her, but we don't hear much news about them."

"She is still quite beautiful, apparently, and extremely intelligent. Very well spoken of by all. She made her way very well in the English court. I am not sure whether she thinks like them now or remembers she is a Welsh princess, but I hope she doesn't forget what happened to her family in Norman hands.'

"It would be impossible to forget, but I suppose she has had to adapt to survive."

"You do sound just like your father. He always says that you must adapt to survive!"

***

Angharad missed her Aunt Nest and boisterous Uncle Uchdryd when they left, but she was grateful for the companionship of the other wives of Gruffydd's teulu, and there was a lot of laughter. Rhoddri's wife, Llinos, had joined them with their little daughter, Nia. Llinos was as lively and enthusiastic as Rhoddri. She was as well-rounded and well-endowed as her husband was skinny and had dancing blue eyes with a hint of mischief in them. Nia was a tiny version of her mother, with thick ringlets of dark hair framing her face. She would watch Cadwallon wherever he went. They would often play together, she not minding when he bowled her over, having enough padding to soften the blows when she fell.

From Normandy, they heard that Robert Curthose had left Palestine after the battle of Ascalon and had indeed married Sybilla of Conversano. The couple had arrived back in Normandy in September, and Sybilla immediately garnered support, being beautiful, intelligent, and virtuous. Angharad wondered if she would have any influence on her husband.

Gruffydd was still worried about debts, yet Anglesey and Gwynedd started to thrive. The inventive king was always trying to bring in new ideas that would help to regenerate wealth for the kingdom, and after a visit to Cadwgan, with whom he remained very close, he returned with a few of Cadwgan's mares and a long-maned stallion with the idea of building up a stud as Cadwgan had.

He, Hywel and Angharad stood in the stable admiring the new acquisitions with the head groom and his helpers.

"They are beautiful," said Angharad appreciating their fine lines, "Cadwgan has a talent for horse breeding."

"Robert de Belleme brought Spanish horses over to improve the existing bloodlines, and Cadwgan bred them with our Welsh horses," Gruffydd enthused. "The Spanish stock stand a lot taller than our horses and are faster. Mind you, our Welsh horses go back before Roman times and are hardy and strong."

"My father used to tell me that the horses would run free and wild in the mountains, so they had hooves and coats to withstand bad conditions and were very sure-footed," said Hywel earnestly.

Gruffydd nodded. "He was right. They were living up in the mountains from as far back as we can tell. Living wild helped them to develop their intelligence. They had to think for themselves."

"Gruffydd, what do you want the horses to do?" asked Angharad. "Are they for going into battle or for everyday farm work or pulling sledges when it snows?"

"Knights will pay a good price for a war horse that is strong enough to take the heavy armour and is fast crossing the battlefield. With the cross of the Spanish and Welsh horses, we should be able to do well. Then we can also breed a more versatile horse that can trot for miles, again with strength but not necessarily the speed: the sort of thing a squire would ride with supplies and armour but strong enough to keep up with the larger horse."

"When I was in Ireland, Lafracoth was telling me that they love the Welsh horses."

"They do, and I will be sending a few over to Murtagh when they are ready. You are right, there is a good opportunity for trade with Ireland, and I do not see why not to other countries like Scotland, for example."

Angharad thought of Ireland and wondered whether she would see Lafracoth again. She had received news that Lafracoth was indeed going to marry Arnulf Montgomery, the brother of Robert de Belleme. She hoped that he would be kind to her. She voiced her concerns to Gruffydd.

"His mother, Countess Mabel, was known for her cruelty, so I do hope Arnulf does not take after her or his brother, Hugh, who killed Father Cenred," she commented anxiously as they walked along the clifftops one sunny afternoon.

"Yes, a cruel family indeed. Mabel poisoned people if she didn't like them, but then she died a horrific death herself, being murdered in her chamber at Chateau de Buresin in revenge for what she had done to her neighbours. I have not heard of specific cruelties from Arnulf, but, like all the Montgomery family, he is greedy," returned Gruffydd. "He sent Gerald, his steward, to ravish the lands of St David's cathedral a few years ago, and Archbishop Anselm admonished him for it. He has scant respect even for the church."

"Lafracoth says he sent Gerald to negotiate the marriage. I still am not sure why Murtagh would be interested in that union."

"Murtagh is a good friend, and I owe so much to him, but he has a weakness: he wants the world to know about Murtagh. The Montgomerys are incredibly wealthy, and such a marriage would give Murtagh great status and influence. He will be thinking about making sure that one of his precious trade routes from South Wales and Bristol to Waterford is secure. He wants to dominate in the Irish Sea as well as Ireland."

"Meanwhile, if Curthose does challenge for the English throne, Arnulf wants Murtagh's military support," Angharad surmised.

"Exactly. Murtagh has powerful allies such as Magnus, which would be useful to Curthose."

"I thought that when King Henry promised fairer treatment to the barons and the church in his Charter of Liberties, there was security for the English throne, and the barons were satisfied."

"The barons are fickle, and Duke Robert has some pull with them."

"And Cadwgan and yourself? You wouldn't get involved in something like that, surely?" she asked uneasily.

"I cannot speak for Cadwgan. He seems pretty thick with Belleme, but I am going to try to avoid any military manoeuvres despite the teulu being keen to hone their skills. I am keeping their minds occupied with increasing their wealth from good marriages and land interest rather than booty."

"But have you heard any more rumblings about Belleme moving against Henry?" she persisted. Not knowing made Angharad worry more.

"A few," he said evasively.

261

Angharad was relieved to hear it, but she knew that Gruffydd and his teulu practised their weaponry every day, long and hard.

The warrior king was an excellent trainer. He asked the men to wear their mail as often as possible so that they were used to the weight. They would also use extra heavy swords made for the purpose of keeping their muscles strong and would ply these against dummies filled with straw either on foot or on horseback. Fighting each other stroke for stroke with wooden swords kept them sharp and nimble, and there was a great sense of competition among them as they exercised their agility and prowess. A barrage of furious blows would be exchanged, men reluctant to give quarter, the air would be resonant with the sounds of the mock combat, and men shouted encouragement. Yet afterwards, there were no hard feelings against the victors, just more determination to better them next time. Gruffydd knew every man's strength and would make clear that each man had some skill that was different to his fellows and explain how to work this to advantage on the battlefield.

Gruffydd hardly ever missed training and was insistent that every man became accomplished with all weapons, including bow, javelin, mace, spear, axe and swords. He made training fun, using lots of games to increase flexibility and encourage quick reactions while reminding the men that it was not always the strongest man that bettered their opponent. Their fine horsemanship was inspirational: they were all able to run fully armed and leap onto their horses, wheeling them around, swerving around obstacles and dismounting at speed.

Angharad would take the boys to watch the manoeuvres but it was the archery that made her gasp. The Welsh were famed for their use of the long bow, which required exceptional strength. Good archers could fire twelve arrows in a minute, and their accuracy was renowned. Gruffydd would have the men compete to hit ever more complicated targets, taking into consideration the wind, the light and the movement of whatever they were trying to hit.

The men looked forward to honing their skills no matter the weather. Gruffydd made sure that they had the finest wool and leather garments to keep them protected and dry. In the evening, they would often talk about famous battles in Wales and beyond. Gruffydd would tell them what he had read about Julius Caesar's Gallic Wars or the exploits of other famous military commanders. How great a part of their lives this was and how much they longed to prove themselves, Angharad was only too painfully aware.

The next months for Angharad were a time of content. Under summer suns, she watched her children thrive, and her llys prosper along with the lands they ruled. Harvest came and went, and then the news came to them of King Henry's marriage to Matilda, daughter of Malcolm III of Scotland, on November 11th, 1100.

"Such a clever marriage," commented Gruffydd.

"To get Scotland on side?" asked Angharad.

"More than that. Matilda's family is part of the West Saxon Royal House. Her great-grandfather was Edmund Ironside, and she comes from the line of Alfred the Great, so marrying her increases his legitimacy on the throne. The barons will like the alliance, and he needs the support of the barons."

"Wasn't she supposed to be a nun?" she asked.

"Ah well, there is some dispute about that. Apparently, she lived in convents, and Archbishop Anselm got together a council to thrash out whether she could marry or not but, in the end, there she is, married and crowned at the same time in Westminster."

Angharad was always surprised at how astute and well-informed Gruffydd was about what was going on both inside and outside of Wales.

The promised Christmas with her family at Aberffraw was a successful one, and although Owain looked older and frailer, it was a very happy time. Rhydir and Lleuci came with little Llywarch, and the three boys were soon inseparable. Meilyr and Llywarch also joined them, but Gronwy stayed behind in Tegeingl, which made things much easier.

Rhoddri, who now had a small band of bards working with him, provided admirable entertainment of music and poetry. Angharad, who had long been reacquainted with the harp she had buried, also kept them enchanted with her singing and playing. Best of all was the dancing which would go on into the early hours of the morning in the hall decked out with holly and mistletoe and to the light of blazing fires. All were welcome at the llys. Gruffydd was a generous host.

"It looks lovely with the holly," Lleuci enthused as extra bunches were brought in from the woods.

"Now do you know why we decorate with holly?" asked Owain; his children smiled, knowing what was coming.

"Because the holly represents the blood of Christ being the berries; the crown of thorns being the prickles and eternal life being evergreen," replied Lleuci, who listened well at church.

"That is true, but did you know that the Druids also decked their halls with Celyn, or holly, which they thought was magical and brought fertility and eternal life? The same with mistletoe which they believed had great magic and healing powers. Mistletoe was the spirit of the great oak trees because it bloomed when the tree was bare."

Lleuci looked disbelieving, and Angharad smiled, "Father is usually right!"

Rhydir held Lleuci tightly. "Dim uchellwydd, dim lwc: no mistletoe, no luck. Plenty of mistletoe always means there will be a good harvest next time. Bring more mistletoe, I say."

"But leave some holly for the poor birds!" laughed Meilyr.

"What plans do you have for Gwynedd?" asked Owain of Gruffydd as they sat drinking mead while his sons and most of the teulu were braving the cold weather to go hunting.

"Now that Anglesey is back in some sort of shape, though a long way to go admittedly, I want to start building a llys of my own on the sites where the Normans had built their castles. They are good spots strategically, and the land around them can be developed into profitable estates to increase revenue. I want to start at Caernarvon."

"Why Caernarvon?" queried Owain.

"Position. Just south of Anglesey, where two little rivers join the Menai Strait between the mountains of Snowdonia with all the hill pastures for cattle and sheep and the island with all the fertile lands for crops. From our llys, we can grow food for the court in the rich soil close by and have our cattle stock in the upland pastures."

"So, it gives you an opportunity to move your teulu around and to be seen by the people in that area."

"Exactly. We have been pretty quiet here in Aberffraw while we built up Anglesey, but it is time to move through Gwynedd and, as you say, be seen and known. Besides, Caernarvon is also perfect for economic growth. Each of the passes through the mountains ends at Caernarvon: Llanberis Pass, Aberglaslyn Pass and the other along the valley of Dwyfarch. Perfect for trade, with the sea in front, secure behind and those fertile lands around. We could make more of a settlement there. Earl Hugh saw the merits of establishing a base there, the Romans saw it before him, and I intend to improve on their groundwork. I see how England and Ireland have built up trading centres, and we can do the same."

"Don't forget, the Welsh are not so much for towns and villages, though. They tend to prefer their isolation. In England, for example, you have towns with regular markets, a village green with an alehouse where everyone meets, the church at the centre of a community of traders: a blacksmith, a farrier, a cloth merchant and so forth. Here in Wales, the blacksmith may be a farmer who has that skill and helps his neighbour in return for their assistance in building a cart or weaving cloth. It is a different way of thinking."

"It is happening in the south under the Normans. What is it you always said to Angharad? Adapt to survive? We need to look around us, consider the best of what our neighbours are doing and do the same."

"Talking of neighbours," added Owain, "Earl Hugh is very sick now. I saw him a month ago; he is a shell of himself. He seems to have lost interest in the world."

"I do not wish to speak ill of anyone, but after all he did here in Anglesey, I wish him a hasty journey to Hell's fires."

"He has turned to religion and made enormous donations to the church."

"Too late. I hope he lives with what happened to Cenred in front of his eyes every time he closes them."

"*As I do*," Owain thought to himself and shuddered. It tormented him to relive that day and wonder if there had been any way he might have prevented what had happened.

Owain's visit ended, and reluctantly, he left his lively grandchildren to make his way back to Tegeingl, happy in the knowledge that his daughter was expecting another child. The stay had restored much of the affectionate relationship between father and daughter. Gruffydd was eager to learn from Owain, while his father-in-law now gave him the respect due to the rightful King of Gwynedd.

Life at the llys resumed its normal patterns. Angharad, like Gruffydd, had projects she was working on to lift the stability of Anglesey. There were regular meetings with those who advised or served her. She found she was able to get more involved in affairs that before had fallen purely to Gruffydd and she was keen to take some of the load from his shoulders.

At Easter, they had an unexpected visit from Cadwgan. Cadwgan would not have visited unless he was hatching some plan, and Angharad was very wary of why he had made the journey. Nevertheless, she welcomed Cadwgan and his men with kind hospitality. The Great Hall was set with trestle tables again, and the tables laden with pottage, salmon and trout, venison, spring lamb, oatcakes, breads, great wheels of cheese, curds, honey pastries and hazelnuts and walnuts. There was ale and wine, and Gruffydd brought out his mead.

They were sitting in the main hall with the teulu when Cadwgan, who had been drinking quite heavily, chose his moment to elaborate on what was going on behind the scenes of the English crown. The teulu listened with great interest.

"Most of the prominent barons are behind Robert, and he has the right to the English throne. He has been encouraged to make a move by Ranulf Flambard, the Bishop of Durham, who is with him in Normandy."

"I thought Ranulf was a favourite of Rufus and Henry had him thrown into the Tower of London," said Gruffydd.

"You are right, but seemingly, his guards got drunk one night in February, and he shinned down a rope to freedom."

"He had help then!" surmised Hywel, who took a keen interest in what was happening outside Gwynedd.

"Of course! Anyway, he has encouraged Robert, who intends to invade England and is gathering an army." Cadwgan announced, looking around the assembled teulu, who were eagerly waiting to hear what this would mean for them. Gruffydd said nothing but watched the reactions of his men. Angharad's heart sank as her eyes roamed from one face to another, seeing their eagerness for action and booty. Cadwgan continued.

"Belleme has assured me that Arnulf's bride-to-be, Lafracoth, our friend, will be coming along from Ireland with warships full of mercenaries ready whenever they need them."

Gruffydd gave a low whistle. "Don't get involved, Cadwgan. This is not your battle. You might lose the lands you have fought so hard to retain."

"If things go as planned, we will be well rewarded. The Montgomerys are wealthy."

"We? You think I should get involved in this?"

"It is a chance for you to put Gwynedd on its feet, once and for all, and to gain a foothold in other parts of Wales. Imagine the booty, man!"

Angharad's hands were clenched, and she felt sick. Gruffydd could see the anticipation on the faces of his teulu, yet he registered the tense expression on his wife's pale face. He spoke carefully.

"If it comes to a fight, I am not afraid, but this is not my fight. Any of my teulu who wish to join you if you decide to put your men into the fray, I give them leave but I will not join you this time, Cadwgan. Rather, I would have you come with me to negotiate with whichever King ends up on the throne. We still have powerful allies that they fear, whether that king is Henry or Robert. They know our fighting men are strong and ready. This is the time to make peaceful negotiations from a position of strength."

Angharad allowed herself to relax a little but remained unsettled.

Cadwgan considered Gruffydd's words. "Let's see what news the next months bring us," he conceded and turned to the teulu, "but you have heard your lord, if I go to battle alongside Belleme, you are welcome to join me."

The smiles on their faces made it clear that they were more than ready to test their skills against a foe. Rhoddri, the bard, picking up on this sentiment, inspired them further with songs about their prowess in battle and how they had overcome the Normans.

Afterwards, when they had retired for the night, Angharad put her arms around Gruffydd and said, "It is so important that there is no more fighting, Gruffydd."

A look of irritation crossed his face. "You heard what I had to say to Cadwgan."

"I did, and I was so proud that you stood up to him."

She felt him tense up and take a deep breath, but he said nothing more.

Chapter 20: Murtagh's Visit (Summer 1101)

It was not long before the sands shifted once again. On July 21st, 1101, Duke Robert crossed the channel with his army, landing in Portsmouth. Henry had expected such a move but had taken his English forces to Pevensey. The king had not been idle and personally educated his men on how to outsmart the Norman cavalry. On hearing that Duke Robert was making his way to London, Henry turned his troops around and made for Alton in Hampshire, where he met his brother. The two forces were at a standstill, and to Henry's credit, rather than risk losing lives, he sat with Robert at the negotiating table. To everyone's amazement, Robert decided to turn back in return for a pension of three thousand marks per annum, the restoration of Bishop Flambard to his see and a guarantee that no action would be taken against his supporters.

This news brought sighs of relief to Angharad and the other wives of the teulu, who were equally unenthusiastic about any unnecessary fighting. Some of the women, newly brides, were not eager to let their husbands put their lives at risk so early in their marriage. They knew they had married warriors but relished the comfort of peace, wanting it to continue as long as possible. Now, they felt, the barons would surely have to accept Henry as their king. This, they knew, meant that Cadwgan's plans would come to nothing, but they also knew this might give Henry more time to turn his focus on Wales. Still, they thought, better to have peace now.

On the heels of Duke Robert's return to Normandy came other news. Earl Hugh of Chester had died on July 27th in St Werburgh's Abbey, four days after he took his monastic vows. His last week had been spent in agony and penance.

Much mead was consumed that night. The whole of Gwynedd celebrated, and although wonderful words were said about the earl at his funeral, few lamented his passing. Angharad felt guilty at the relief she felt at someone's death: relief that he would be causing no more destruction in Gwynedd. Her concern, however, was the same as her father's, as to who would fill the vacuum of the powerful Marcher Lord.

If Angharad had been concerned by the visit of Cadwgan, the visit of Murtagh O Brien on his way to survey his island provinces was more worrying. He arrived with what seemed like half his court, and Angharad, tired and struggling in the throes of another pregnancy, was in a panic that the llys did not have sufficient resources to entertain them. She wanted to make sure their welcome of Murtagh was sufficient to thank him, at least in part, for looking after them so well in Ireland. Thankfully the visit was short-lived. Their stores were limited at this time of the year.

"I have formally proclaimed myself High King of Ireland," Murtagh announced grandly, looking very pleased with himself. "I have the church on my side as I have given them the fortress on the Rock of Cashel."

"A generous and strategically clever gift," commented Gruffydd diplomatically. Turning to his teulu, he explained, "The Rock of Cashel is believed to have been thrown from twenty miles away when St Patrick banished Satan from a cave in the Devil's Bit."

"And it is where St Patrick converted the King of Munster hundreds of years ago," added Murtagh proudly. "It was the seat of all the Kings of Munster, and now I have donated it to the Church."

"It was a magnificent gesture," nodded Gruffydd, acknowledging that despite the strategic advantage it would give him, the overwhelming generosity was typical of this man.

"Thank you. Now, with the church behind me, I am ready to campaign."

Gruffydd seemed uneasy. He glanced at his pregnant wife's strained face, which looked at him with anguish. His teulu were clearly intrigued.

Murtagh continued with passionate intensity, his warrior mind mapping out his plan. "When I get back from the tour of the Isles, I will return with additional men, and I plan a campaign of between four and eight weeks. Quick and decisive. I have agreement from many kingdoms other than Ulster, of course, that they join me. We will march north to the River Erne, then to the Inis Eoin Peninsula, taking care of Ardstraw and Fahan on the way. I intend to take the fort of Grianan an Alleach in Ulster from the Northern Ui Neill."

"Your revenge?"

"Yes, Gruffydd, my revenge. I have waited long enough, and the time is right. Timing is everything. I will carry every stone from their fortress back to Munster and see if they dare to challenge my kingship. Are you with me?"

Gruffydd had known what was coming; he deliberately didn't look at his wife, and his teulu cheered as he replied firmly,

"I am with you, Murtagh."

Angharad got up and excused herself. Inside she felt a deep hurt and a sense of betrayal. Her husband had made the decision without any consultation with her. All Gruffydd's promises about avoiding conflict, and now, after advising Cadwgan to stay out of battles that had not to do with him, he had thrown himself into the fray.

As she checked on her boys, she was grateful that they were both sleeping peacefully despite the commotion in the main hall. Cadwallon was holding on to a little wooden sword that Gruffydd had fashioned for him. In an unusual fit of pique, she snatched it from him. Is this the life Gruffydd was proposing for his children? Aggression and destruction?

Angharad undressed into her shift and lay in bed but she could not sleep. Hour after hour, she listened to the singing and drinking, the bawdy jokes and could hear Gruffydd being the generous host, drinking horn after horn of mead, no doubt. It was the early hours of the morning when Gruffydd lurched into the chamber. She was about to reprimand him when he shocked her to the core.

"Are you ill?" he asked coldly.

"No," she replied, lifting herself onto one elbow.

"Then how dare you disrespect our guests and humiliate me in front of them!" he spat out savagely.

She got out of bed to stand to face him and realised she was shaking.

"How dare you agree to go to Ireland to fight without consulting me!"

"Consulting you?" he raged. "Consulting you? Who do you think you are to have me running behind you at your beck and call like a common cur?"

"I am your wife, your queen."

"Then start acting like one. You swan around offering money and gifts to this one and that, making promises it is hard to keep, telling me that I can't support Cadwgan and humiliating me in front of the teulu who are laughing behind my back that I am not strong enough to stand up to my wife!"

"That is untrue!"

"When do you once think about how it is for me trying to pay off debts, trying to keep a fighting force of men happy and engaged?"

"I just want there to be peace, Gruffydd, as you agreed."

"Peace at any price!" he retorted angrily, his temples pounding, "You would emasculate me in front of my men and allies. Can't you see what you've done to me?"

She gasped, and for a moment, she looked as if he had hit her across the face. She turned away so that he would not see the tears now

273

beginning to trickle down her cheeks. She felt her heart tighten, and her breath came only with difficulty.

"Get out, Gruffydd, you are drunk," she managed to say hotly before she heard the door slam shut and her husband making his way unsteadily to his own chamber.

She flung herself onto the bed. Soon, her pillow was wet with crying, and she could not sleep. Gruffydd's words just echoed and re-echoed in her mind. She felt so many conflicting emotions: anger at the way she had been treated, fear that their relationship was breaking down, frustration that he misinterpreted her intentions, and sadness at how he felt she had diminished him. By morning she had wrestled with her emotions for hours and still vacillated over what she should do or say. A part of her hoped Gruffydd would walk into her chamber and apologise. She listened for his footfall but when she heard him making his way to the hall, her eyes smarted with tears.

Murtagh was leaving that morning. She pulled herself together, dressed well and played the part of gracious hostess asking his forgiveness for retiring so abruptly the evening before. Gruffydd looked on stony-faced.

"You are with child, and I understand that these times can take a toll on a woman's body, especially when you have already had two babes in quick succession." Murtagh grinned knowingly at Gruffydd, and Angharad felt insulted.

She did not show it and smiled as sweetly as she could, but inside, she was thinking, "Am I to be regarded with no more respect than a milk cow?"

It was at that moment that she made her decision. She called Bethan and asked her to pack. They were going to Caernarvon for a few days. Her bags were loaded onto a cart, the children and her courtiers at the ready before noon, and she had prepared what she would say to

Gruffydd. He had ridden to the port to farewell Murtagh and had not returned.

"We are ready, my lady," said Bethan, and she saw the party waiting outside with their horses. There was no sign of Gruffydd.

"Let us go," she said, and they made their way down to the ferry. Murtagh's ships had long since left. She kept turning to look back towards the llys, but there was still no Gruffydd. In her head, she played out how they would be getting on to the ferry, and he would come riding down in anguish. Uncharacteristically, she decided she would be cool and let him know she would be back in a few days. Let him think about what he had said and how he had treated her. They crossed on the ferry but Gruffydd did not appear, and as they made their progress towards Caernarvon, she felt a deeper emptiness. She clung to her two wriggling boys, who were wildly excited about the trip and noticing everything new to them along the well-worn track

Her ladies liked the new llys at Caernarvon and were chattering about staying there, perfectly happy to enjoy the novelty of a change of scene. They laughed and joked, and although she replied as gaily as she would usually have, she felt oddly out of step with them.

'*He will come later today,*' she thought and asked the servants to prepare enough food in case her husband should arrive with his teulu. They didn't come. When darkness fell, she knew she could not expect them until the next day, and she retired early, exhausted but unable to sleep as her mind raced.

The next day rain had set in, so they all stayed indoors. The women did their embroidery, the children wrestled with each other, and Cadwallon had a few tantrums when he couldn't get what he wanted. She had meetings with her advisors about various issues that fell into her domain, but Gruffydd did not come. Exhausted, she fell into bed again, listening to the relentless rain pounding onto the ground outside. Finally, she fell into a fitful sleep where vivid images of bloody battlefields and horses screaming in their death throes coloured her nightmares. The alarm cry of a curlew sounded close, and she bolted upright, searching the cold darkness while her heart pounded. Automatically her arm stretched out for her husband, and then the reality of the last days flooded her thinking. Had they destroyed the love they had so treasured, that had brought two beautiful children into the world? She put her hand to her swollen belly and felt the kick of another child born of love. Her stomach turned as she went over and over what had happened and rethought times when Gruffydd had seemed moody, distant, and irritable. Could he have tired of her?

So it was for five days. On the fifth day, she went to Father Carein in the little church they had built next to their llys. Without going into too many details, she explained what had happened, her voice thick with her grief.

"Do you love your husband?" the burly priest asked bluntly, his small, blue, unsmiling eyes boring into her soul.

"Of course," she responded, taken aback that he should question that.

"Doesn't Corinthians tell us that when we love, we do not take into account a wrong suffered?"

"Yes, Father, that is true but what we had agreed was that there would be no more warring."

"Yet you are warring with your husband? Did you want me to tell you that you are right and he is wrong?"

"No," said Angharad begrudgingly but now feeling ashamed. The priest's thin lips wore an expression of contempt.

"The Bible tells us that it is the wife's duty to submit to her husband, and the bible tells us to forgive and to love. Pray that God will lead you in the right direction and that your husband will forgive you for your actions."

Angharad knew that her behaviour was not commendable and was not sure why she was reacting so defiantly. All her life, she had avoided conflict, and yet now, instead of talking through the issue with her husband rationally, she was prolonging the disagreement. She did indeed pray and reflected that she had acted too hastily. She also realised that the way she had spoken and the resentment she was feeling was eating at her and changing her nature in a way she didn't like herself!

The distraught woman tried to work it through. She was hurt because Gruffydd had stopped treating her as a partner. She still smarted from the way he had accused her of not putting the best interest of Gwynedd above her own desires. She thought back to Cadwgan's visit and Murtagh's visit. Had she allowed her hatred of war and violence to mar the relationship she had with Gruffydd? She closed her eyes as she relived the moment he had accused her of emasculating him. The image was painful. She thought of the years of relentless training he had led with his teulu and their need to prove themselves against a foe. She concluded that she needed to go home to Aberffraw and apologise.

The llys was packed up again hastily, and they returned to Anglesey. Now she could hardly wait to tell Gruffydd how sorry she was, and she imagined their reconciliation. She would throw herself into his arms and apologise, acknowledging that he and he alone should make decisions on military matters. He would take her to her chamber, and they would cement their understanding passionately. She needed his arms around her. She longed for the touch of his lips on hers. In her head, everything was resolved, but as they reached the ferry, she saw that now not only Murtagh's ships had departed but that the Gwynedd fleet had also gone.

A wave of panic engulfed her, and when she reached the port, she rushed over and immediately questioned some of the men working on some fishing boats.

"King Gruffydd and his men have sailed for Ireland," said one looking at her quizzically. "The wind was a fair one, so they took it while they could."

***

The weeks went by, and as Angharad's belly grew ever more swollen, she became more and more conscious of the depth of the rift between her and her husband. No message came from him. Her hurt that he had left without so much as a word wrenched at her soul, and she vacillated between despair and concern to rising resentment, which she tried to quell.

The women of her court would stop talking when she came into the room and stare at her with pity when they thought she did not notice. She did not confide in any of them, keeping her pain inside.

One morning after a long night of little sleep, she lay listening to the familiar sounds of life waking up in the pre-dawn: birds, dogs barking at a passing animal, someone dragging a sack across the ground, horses neighing. Usually, she would cherish these sounds and be ready for whatever challenges the day brought, but she just lay there still and feeling empty. Not even the thought of her two little boys or the baby within her was able to summon any wish to do anything other than to lie in the dark, broken.

Angharad forced herself out of bed and resolved to seek help from the church. The day was dry but cold, and the wind blew in great gusts, pushing billowing clouds across the heavens. Trees and buildings creaked. Wood smoke from dwellings rose in waving ribbons or seeped out of cracks in the walls and roofs, providing hints at life within. It was as bleak as she felt within her heart, and she longed for a resolution when she visited Father Teilo. This time she was more forthcoming about what had happened between her and Gruffydd, knowing the old priest as she did. He listened attentively as she related the events, his old eyes filled with understanding and kindness.

"I think you will not like what I have to say, Lady Angharad," he said solemnly, pursing his lips and shaking his head slightly.

"Please, Father, I seek your advice. I would rather hear the truth of what you are thinking."

Father Teilo sighed deeply, turned his head to one side as he searched her face with compassion and then unusually leant forward, taking her fine hands in his large, gnarled ones.

"My lady, you and King Gruffydd have done so much good in Gwynedd. You have both worked tirelessly and restored order and wealth to a part of Wales that had been devasted. Everyone here knows that."

Angharad gave a small nod.

"Your husband's position is only secure when he satisfies his followers. His teulu depends on him for strong leadership. They are fighting men, trained for conflict since an early age, and he has tried his best to occupy them by giving them land, giving them wives and turning them into farmers in the main."

Angharad looked at him and felt she knew where this was heading.

"They respect and admire you, Queen Angharad, but they must feel that their king is all-powerful. Your views on peace are well known, and King Gruffydd has made it clear that he wants the land to heal. By walking away from your duty to honour a powerful visiting king who was your guest, a guest who was the first to help you in your hour of need, you allowed King Gruffydd's authority to be questioned. By abandoning him, you cemented that humiliation."

"I didn't abandon him; I took myself and my family away from the conflict."

"You left your husband's side, and a queen could be divorced for that."

It was as if he had knocked her to the ground. She blanched and instinctively put a hand on her belly. In all her thoughts, she had not considered that Gruffydd could divorce her.

"What must I do?" she muttered as soon as she had recovered her wits.

"Have you sent word to him?"

"No," she admitted and now felt even more uncomfortable. It was so obvious. That was the first thing she should have done.

"You must send a message to him through the Irish court, making sure that he understands that you realise that you have behaved outside your queenly remit and that in future, you will be at pains to respect his authority and position."

"But, Father, I am his partner."

"Yes, my lady, you are indeed King Gruffydd's partner, his queen, and you have rights according to the laws of Hywel Dda but what you have done is in flagrant disregard of such a partnership."

How quickly her self-doubt was reinforced as she heard these harsh words from someone she utterly respected. She had always regarded herself as a person who had only ever wanted to do what was right and dutiful, yet now, she knew that she had allowed her pride to dictate her behaviour. She felt childish and stupid. All sorts of realisations hit her. She had taken the partnership with her husband for granted and, without even sensing how uncomfortable her husband was becoming, had pushed him to the brink.

She returned to the llys a shattered woman, confused and insecure. After shedding many miserable tears of regret and frustration with herself in private, she crafted a message that she hoped would be enough to hasten Gruffydd's return. Then she waited. They heard news from traders who had come via Dublin that King Murtagh had indeed made his way through to Grianan an Aileach, the royal family

280

seat of the O'Neills, and had destroyed it in retaliation for that clan destroying his family seat at Kinkora. Each man who had fought alongside Murtagh was asked to bring a stone with him back to Munster. Every stone was placed into the parapet of Murtagh's new residence in Limerick. Now Murtagh not only had more control in Ireland but could easily get to the Hebrides and other parts of Scotland.

"Surely Gruffydd will now come back," she thought, as she walked along the cliffs in all weathers, hoping to sight the return of the ships but they did not come. Word came that Magnus Barefoot had plundered Scattery Island at the estuary of the great Shannon River. Angharad imagined Murtagh and Magnus drawn into a headlong collision with her husband and his teulu in the middle. If Gruffydd had been hurt, she would have heard, surely. What could be keeping him away from her and their boys?

As each day passed without any response to her message, she became more and more agitated. She could hardly eat, but each day, she made herself get up for the love for her children. Susannah and Bethan would keep them occupied, knowing their mistress was deeply distressed. They would try to cajole her to eat to keep up her strength, but she would take a few spoonfuls and then leave the bowl largely untouched. The mood was one of rising anxiety as none of the other ladies had heard from their husbands either: when they saw their queen in such a parlous state, their own fears were exacerbated.

Sometimes when Angharad was alone, her thoughts would become even darker. She would cast her mind back to the Irish beauties at Murtagh's court, how they would watch Gruffydd as he strode passed them, and while she could see their desire plainly, he would not notice them. Now, apart from her for so long and feeling resentment towards her, would he succumb to their wiles? Or would it be him seeking out comfort? The thoughts began to haunt her. She recognised how she had humiliated him but had she ruined everything they had built up together, destroyed their family? Had he tried to communicate how trapped he was feeling, and she hadn't listened? She thought of the ambitious young men of his teulu: virile, athletic, hard-drinking, hard-fighting men. Had keeping the peace he had promised her, jeopardised his leadership? The cheers around the room as he agreed to go to Ireland echoed in her head and taunted her with an answer she did not want to acknowledge. She had driven him away.

Chapter 21: Magnus Barefoot (Spring 1102)

The weather turned bleak, and Aberffraw seemed even emptier because of it. She kept up a brave face despite her distress and tried to behave as naturally as usual, but inside, she felt torment. As each day passed, her confidence in the strength of their marital relationship grew weaker.

As the weather grew colder, most of the wives of Gruffydd's teulu went back to their homes to make sure that everything was in order for the winter. The quiet gave the unhappy wife even more time to reflect. Angharad dealt with the various administrative affairs and always made time to spend with her two little boys, who were often accompanied by her little nephew or Rhoddri and Llinos' little daughter, Nia.

"They are all growing so quickly," said Bethan

"So quickly," Angharad agreed and was bending forward to pick up Owain when suddenly her waters broke. She gasped in alarm, for the baby was coming too early.

Bethan was shocked but quickly took charge, "Have you any pains yet, my lady?"

"No," said Angharad, trying to keep the panic out of her voice. "Nothing."

"You must go to bed and pray that the pains start," said Bethan. "I am sure they will come soon now."

Angharad knew that without the pain of pushing the little child into the world, it would not be able to survive for long after the waters had broken. She started to pray with Bethan at her side. Long hours passed with both women tense and frightened. Had she behaved so badly that this was some awful punishment? She was distraught. Bethan rubbed her back and held her hand; she got up and tried moving into different positions to encourage contractions. Bethan brought her hot spiced beer and then some mead. Nothing helped, and time was moving on.

Angharad watched the moon moving across the sky. The baby inside her was still. Finally, in the early hours of the morning, her pains started, and she prayed that they were not too late. The gnawing, debilitating pains were worse than she had experienced in either of her previous pregnancies, but the baby did not seem to move. She started to feel seriously ill: hot, then shivering and nauseous. So many women died in childbirth, she knew, as had her own mother. She felt lost and desperately wanted Gruffydd there beside her. She clenched Bethan's hand with each wave of pain. Somewhere outside, she could hear her baby boys crying, and she tried to lift herself up but couldn't.

"Mammy, mammy!" screamed Cadwallon, and she tried to call back, yet she seemed to be drifting in and out of consciousness. She heard herself groaning and then felt the agonising pain again. She couldn't grasp what was happening around her.

Bethan was wiping her brow with a wet cloth and stroking her head.

"Sshh, my lady, shhh," she soothed.

She clutched Bethan's hand, "Tell Gruffydd I'm sorry," she rasped. "Don't forget. Tell him I am sorry."

"Yes, mistress, shhh, I will tell him you are sorry."

Her entire body shook, and she saw in front of her the open-staring eyes of the Norman soldier on the hard, cold stone of the cave. She tried to call for Gruffydd but he wasn't there, and then she was on a boat with blood dropping from the sky onto her tunic. She looked up and saw Robert of Rhuddlan's head attached to the mast. She tried to scream, but the blood fell into her mouth, foul, stinking, sticky blood.

"Cariad, I'm here, Cariad," she heard Gruffydd's voice, and she looked up again but this time it was Gruffydd's head on the mast.

284

"She's going. She's going!" Bethan was weeping.

"She's not going anywhere." Who was it that was stopping her from going? Where was she going? The world was tumbling around her. She cried out in agony; she was being pulled and stretched, dogs were tearing at her, and she heard her babies crying but couldn't reach them.

"Don't hurt them," she screamed. "Don't let the dogs take them!"

"Shh, shh!"

"I'm sorry, Gruffydd," she whispered as she was floating in an icy cold sea: it was grey, and she could taste the salt on her lips. She was sinking, and it was so dark. She gasped for breath as she twisted and sank. Her legs were being pulled down, and she was passing strange floating bodies of people with wild staring eyes who had died long, long ago. She was too far down to fight her way back up, and there was nothing up there: nothing at all.

She didn't know how long she had been ill, but when Angharad came to, she saw it was dark and quiet. She could hear someone muttering prayers beside her, and she put her hand out to touch the person. Her fingers could feel thick hair like Gruffydd's. The head jerked up.

"Cariad?" It was Gruffydd's voice, and suddenly, he was caressing her face and kissing her. "Cariad, thank God!"

"Gruffydd, is it truly you? Please say it is you," she gasped, her breath thick.

"Cariad, shh, I am here. I am here."

"You've come home. I'm sorry, Gruffydd. Oh, I am so sorry!" The words were so hard to form; her throat and lips were so dry, her tongue thick.

"Shh, Cariad. Here. Don't talk." He lifted a goblet of water to her lips. "Just take a little, not too much."

She drank, and swallowing hurt. Her mind was still muddled, but an urgent thought gripped her.

"My baby?"

"A girl."

"Dead?"

"Very weak but alive. She is very tiny, Cariad, but she is fighting."

"Can I see her?"

"Just rest."

"I have to see her."

"Shhh, shhh, I will fetch her."

He left the room and returned with a tiny bundle wrapped in a blanket. By the light of a torch, the proud father showed Angharad the little one's face and her mop of red hair.

"She's beautiful. I want to hold her," Angharad whispered, with a huge effort, her eyelids heavy as lead.

Gruffydd lifted his wife's blanket and slid the little baby into the bed next to her mother. Angharad smelled the new baby smell of her little girl and pulled her as tightly as she could manage against her before she drifted back to sleep.

When Angharad woke next, it was morning, and Bethan was at her side. She looked down beside her for the baby.

"Oh, my lady, it is a blessed miracle," Bethan said, crossing herself and then seeing Angharad's eyes searching, "The baby is with King Gruffydd."

"Is she, is she….." Angharad stumbled.

"She seems a little stronger. We have a wet nurse. She has taken a little milk."

Angharad fell back onto the pillow. "And Gruffydd really has come home!" she marvelled, unsure if last night was a figment of her imagination.

"He is really here. He was so frightened, so desperate when he saw you. We thought we were losing you. He was like a madman. I have never seen anything like his grief. He sent people all over the island for someone who could help you. The priest brought a healer with him, and she delivered the baby somehow, and then he just clung to the little one. He wouldn't let anyone touch her, and he wouldn't leave your side. The healer brought herbs I hadn't seen before, and they seemed to take down your fever, but it took so long to pass. Your skin was like fire. Now King Gruffydd has sent almost everyone away from the llys so that you can have rest."

Angharad managed a wan smile. "The Irish way."

"He hasn't slept for two nights, just sat beside you and prayed and held the baby and prayed."

Her eyes filled with emotion. There was a creak, and Gruffydd, who looked as exhausted as she felt, put his head around the door. He smiled a small smile as he saw that she was awake, but she saw fear in his eyes. She had never seen that before.

"How do you feel, Cariad?" he asked softly.

"I am feeling better, I think. I should try to nurse the little one," she responded, putting on a brave face.

In a moment, he was back again with the tiny baby, who gazed up at him. Bethan left them, and gingerly, Angharad began to feed her daughter as Gruffydd lay propped up on one elbow on the bed beside her.

"She has a strong suck for such a fragile little thing. She wants to live; I know it."

"She has your spirit!" he said, touching the little baby's hand and then caressing Angharad's hair and face.

"We should name her Gruffydd."

"Unless you want to name her something else, I would like to call her Gwenllian after Cadwgan's late wife. She was a wonderful woman and always kind to me."

"Gwenllian," said Angharad, "little Gwenllian."

They sat in silence for a moment.

"I am so sorry, Gruffydd," she said, "I couldn't go past my hurt when we quarrelled. I forgot my place."

His voice was deep with emotion. "Cariad, I am the one who should be sorry. I was so angry with you and my anger burned inside me until it possessed me but when I came back and thought I was losing you, I didn't know what to do. My life is empty and worthless without you."

Her love for him welled up inside her, and she pulled him to her and kissed him. He rested his head against hers on the pillow.

"Don't leave me again like that, Cariad," he said, holding her hand. She turned to face him and was about to speak when she realised he had fallen asleep, his flaxen hair flopping over his eyes. He looked so peaceful. She gazed down at her little girl, who had now fallen asleep at her breast, a trickle of milk dribbling from her open mouth, and she felt an intense happiness that she had not felt for many months.

***

Angharad was strong, but her recovery from the birth of Gwenllian took longer than she had expected. Gruffydd fussed over her and took charge of what she should eat and how it should be cooked. The healer came every day for the first week and brought her the most foul-smelling herbal mixture she had ever tasted. Gruffydd was incredibly attentive, kind and absolutely mesmerised by his little daughter, who became healthy and strong despite her unpromising beginning. Gradually Angharad also regained her strength with Gruffydd encouraging her to walk with him outside, further and further each day, to take in the fresh air. These were special times, and they spoke of plans to improve Gwynedd, of local matters and most importantly, of their children. They both avoided the topic of Gruffydd's visit to Ireland as neither wanted to revisit something which had been painful for them both.

On a spring day when the first shoots were peeping above the ground, and the sun left its warmth on the courtyard wall, a messenger arrived by boat. Gruffydd came to her and asked if she felt strong enough to host Magnus Barefoot. She agreed that she felt much better and that she would be fascinated to meet the famous king and man who had done so much to restore them to Anglesey.

"Will he be bringing his wife, Margaret," asked Angharad, realising that if he did, the likelihood of his needing to secure Gruffydd's military support was less.

"I don't believe so," he replied. "He is on his way to Ireland." Silently she prayed that Magnus was not visiting to convince Gruffydd to join in one of his campaigns.

Since Magnus' intervention assisted them in securing Anglesey, the Norwegian king had been preoccupied with attaining the Swedish provinces of Dasland and Vastergotland. He believed they should be Norwegian lands, and naturally, Inge Stenkilsson, King of Sweden, disagreed. Magnus had ravished the forest villages in those areas resulting in Inge amassing an enormous army. Magnus ignored pleas from his men to retreat and made it clear that once a campaign was started, you should never withdraw. His words became famous, "Kings are made for honour, not for long life,' which made Angharad shudder. Nevertheless, with a surprise night-time attack, he defeated the Swedish king and conquered Vastergotland, leaving 300 men on the island of Kallandso over winter. What happened next in Angharad's mind was an example of pride coming before a fall. The Norwegians taunted Inge, who was himself a mighty warrior, for taking a long time to come to fight them. As the ice thickened between the island and the mainland, Inge arrived with three thousand men. He made an offer to Magnus for them to return to Norway with their plunder but they refused. Inge crossed the ice and burnt their fort, humiliated the Norwegians by beating them with sticks and sent them home, surrendering their possessions. Magnus was set on revenge but Eric Evergood, King of Denmark, who had already been affected by Magnus' raids, managed to broker a peace between the three Scandinavian kings who agreed to preserve their ancestral borders. By marrying Margaret, Inge's daughter, Magnus acquired lands he had tried to win by force in Dasland. Now Magnus had the time to push into other areas, which was exactly what Angharad feared.

Huge preparations were put in place for Magnus and his retinue. Angharad arranged for an ox to be killed and roasted on an enormous spit in the courtyard. Provisions arrived from all over the island, including fine mead. The kitchen was buzzing with activity as everyone hastened to ensure everything would be perfect. Gruffydd called the bards and entertainers. Tables and benches were set up in the long hall. The best cutlery and tableware were brought out, and all the tapestries, cushions and rugs were beaten outside to remove the dust. Fresh reeds were gathered and laid on the floors with herbs scattered to perfume the air.

A call went up from one of the sentries, and nearly the whole llys stopped what they were doing and hurried to see the approach of the Norwegian fleet. It was impossible not to be impressed at the mighty ships, royal drakkars, golden dragons' heads on prows and sterns, as they drew close to shore. Wind billowed through the rectangular woollen sails speeding the vessels closer and closer. Shields adorned the sides of the ships showing the places where each man would sit when they needed to row. On the leading boat, Magnus stood magnificent in his military attire, his helmet shining in the sun, a ruby red cloak, an enormous shield emblazoned by a mighty lion on a rich red background and a golden belt around his waist which, as they came closer, Angharad saw held a sword of ivory hilt inlaid with gold.

"He isn't going to attack us, is he?" she asked nervously.

Gruffydd laughed, "No, Cariad, this is to impress you and to remind me that he is one of the mightiest of kings."

The shallow draft of the ships' hulls made it easy for them to come right onto a beach and navigate rivers. Magnus jumped off the lead ship as it approached the shore and, removing his helmet, bounded up the beach. He was a fine figure of a man, shorter than Gruffydd by a few inches but built as you might expect a warrior to be. His hair was golden, and he wore a moustache and beard, which made him look older than his years. He and Gruffydd were similar in age.

"Well, Gruffydd, you have been hiding away your beautiful queen," he said, immediately bowing to Angharad, who dropped into a deep curtsey.

"To keep her away from you!" Gruffydd laughed easily.

"Ah, that is wise. I can't help myself falling in love with beautiful women," he joked back, and Angharad saw the twinkle in his large sapphire-coloured eyes.

He came bearing gifts.

Gruffydd was astounded when Magnus called one of his attendants forward, and he held out a snowy white gyrfalcon covered with a soft red leather hood. Gruffydd was overwhelmed.

"This is an absolute beauty." Gruffydd thanked Magnus profusely.

"She has come a long way from lands covered in ice, across perilous seas, but she has courage and resilience. I flew her myself and watched her catching prey three times her weight by flying close to the ground, overtaking her quarry and then bearing down on them. She is strong. Maybe we can fly her tomorrow?"

"With pleasure," Gruffydd returned.

Then, with a flourish, Magnus presented Angharad with a golden box containing a stunning gold pendant set with a turquoise stone and intricately worked gold casing.

Angharad was almost speechless. "Thank you so much! This is too beautiful!" she gasped, her eyes shining with delight at the exquisite craftsmanship.

He also brought gifts for the children. Two finely carved boats with little woollen sails, tiny men and oars inside for the boys and an intricately made spinning top for Gwenllian.

Magnus knelt to the little boys, and his eyes lit up when they were so excited by the boats.

"Would you like to go on one of my ships?" he asked them. Their eyes nearly popped out of their heads. "They are a bit different from your Dada's ships."

"Do you mind?" he checked with Angharad and Gruffydd. "We won't be long," and taking the little boys into his arms, he gave them a tour of his Drakkar.

"What are these for?" asked Cadwallon, pointing to the rows of chests on each side of the ship.

"This is where my men sit when they need to row and look," he said, lifting a lid and showing them where each man could store his armour and personal belongings.

"And these sails," he pointed to where the sails were rolled up, "these take our women all winter to make. They are woven from the wool of sheep."

Magnus patiently answered all their questions before returning them to shore.

"You are very kind," Angharad thanked him genuinely. She had been astonished that a king as proud as Magnus would take such time with her two little boys.

"I love children," he said, "I love seeing how their minds work and the joy they have in things we take for granted."

"You have children yourself?" asked Angharad.

"Eystein, Sigurd and Olaf are the boys, and Ragnild and Tora are the girls."

Later Gruffydd told her that each of the children had a different mother.

It was impossible not to like Magnus. Despite his determination to conquer the world, he was generous, polite and intelligent. His men loved him, and he loved his men. He flirted outrageously with all the women of the llys, but he did not make them feel uncomfortable or unsafe.

That evening there was a lot of laughter and much mead consumed. Gruffydd asked Magnus to tell the story of how he had won the Mull of Kintyre from the King of Scotland. Magnus, who was a great raconteur, beamed at the opportunity.

"This is an old story now and tells much of my youthful impudence! There was a lot of fighting in Scotland, one king with another and King Edgar was worried that he could ill afford to do battle with me. I had my eye on Scotland; at that time, my men and I lived for battle glory! Edgar was cautious and wily and made me an offer. Magnus mimicked the deep voice and accent of the Scottish king, 'Take any island that you can reach with your rudder set west of Scotland in return for peace.' 'That is a generous offer,' said I but I also had a mind to take Kintyre, which was not an island. The next morning, I told my men, 'lift up my boat with the rudder set west and let me sit in it.' They wondered if I was mad. 'Come,' I said, you will carry me across Kintyre and with my rudder set west, I did indeed take that journey in my boat across dry land."

He paused for effect.

"And the Scots watched as my men dragged my boat across the isthmus at Tarbert with me sitting at the helm enjoying the view! Edgar gave me Kintyre!"

Gruffydd threw back his head and roared with laughter, and all the men enjoyed the tale.

"Tell the story of Murtagh and your dirty shoes," cajoled one of his men.

"Ah! This is one of those stories where to my shame, I think I must have drunk too much mead," Magnus admitted, "but it was very good mead. We had been enjoying a feast, and for some stupid reason, I decided, as a joke, to send my dirty shoes to Murtagh and instruct him that if he carried the dirty shoes around on his shoulders on Christmas Day and announced that the King of Norway had allowed his lands to be safe, then he would have no trouble from me! I intended to rile him, I suppose, but Murtagh was smart and treated the messengers finely, sent back gifts and said he would rather eat the shoes than one of his provinces be ruined by me! Clever! Well, now we have a peace treaty and Murtagh's little daughter, Blathmin, is married to my son Sigurd, who is my co-king of the Western lands. Murtagh acknowledges me as King of the Isles, Dublin and Fingal, and I give him support and peace. A happy outcome for all. Meanwhile, I am helping him with some of his internal troubles!"

"Ulster again?" assumed Gruffydd

"Ulster again!"

Angharad tensed up, but before they allowed the conversation to progress, Gruffydd called the bards to perform.

"Are they as good as the Irish bards?" Magnus asked with interest.

"I have brought some Irish bards across, and together with our own, they are enhancing our Welsh tradition, so I believe they are better," said Gruffydd.

Towards the end of the evening, Gruffydd turned to his friend and said, "You write poetry. Will you share some of your work with us?"

After much persuasion, Magnus agreed and, in the most melliferous tones, told a poem he had written for a love of his, Matilda. She, beautiful with her light brown hair, denied him fun and pleasure and stirred up strife, but whose caring comments left him deeply moved.

Gruffydd turned his head to one side and looked enquiringly at Magnus.

"Yes, my Matilda is with Henry of England now. He has made a very skilful match. I thought I had time on my side but time eludes us all!"

"Ah," said Gruffydd feeling for his friend's loss. "Matilda is well-liked in England already. She will make a good queen."

"If Henry lasts," Magnus confided doubtfully. "One of his barons from Lincoln sought me out and has offered me a fortune if I bring my troops to help them if they decide to rebel. The 'reward' is being held in Lincoln for me. It may be an interesting proposition but I would want to be sure we have the power on our side. I wouldn't want to seem less than a victor in the fair Matilda's eyes!"

The bards came to excuse themselves, and Magnus showered them with silver.

"You will be remembered for your generosity and valour, King Magnus!" said the chief bard looking deep into Magnus' eyes.

As they left, Magnus became serious, speaking quietly so that only Gruffydd and Angharad could hear him. "I sometimes wonder about the afterlife. Something strange happened before I left Norway. At dinner one night, there was talk about the legend that my great uncle Olaf the Saint's body would never be marred by death and remain perfect in his shrine. I am not sure why it annoyed me that there was such a belief in this but I ordered the shrine to be opened even though everyone counselled me against it."

Angharad looked shocked and tried to understand what could have made Magnus do such a thing. She listened attentively.

"The tomb was opened at my insistence. There was my great uncle as in life, peaceful and unravished by death. He had beside him the crystal chalice of peace, and I took the chalice as a memory of him before we closed the tomb. That night I had a nightmare, I will never forget; it was so real. Uncle Olaf came to me and told me that I could choose between losing my life and kingdom in thirty days or leaving Norway. I don't fear death at all, you know that but I have chosen to leave Norway for a while. I took the chalice of peace with me, and now I have left it in a monastery in Mann."

"You should not have done that, Magnus!" said Gruffydd, appalled. "I do not fear death either but there are some things which are not for us to know about; they are beyond the realms of reason."

"Well," said Magnus, changing to a deliberately light tone, "if I should die, I will come back and educate you on them!"

The men spent the following day hawking. Angharad was glad of the time to prepare for the day's meals and get the llys in order. When they returned, they were full of praise for the gyrfalcon, which had performed brilliantly, bringing down two hares and a fawn.

Magnus was in fine humour and proposed an archery competition of skill.

Five of Gruffydd's finest bowmen were called, and Magnus chose five of his. Then, taking a bowl of apples, they placed one tentatively perched on the branch of an oak tree. If the apple was missed, then the bowman had to retire; if not, he would have another turn after all his teammates had taken theirs.

Magnus shot first, and his arrow pierced the centre of the apple, knocking it off the branch. Gruffydd went second and did likewise. Then each of their bowmen tried their skill, all hitting their target. They moved further and further back, increasing the challenge, and gradually, each team lost men until only Magnus and Gruffydd remained. Neither failed. The light was now fading.

"Gruffydd," said Magnus, "if you were a better host, you would allow me the victory."

"I am the better host for not deceiving you," he replied candidly.

"Then I think we had both better agree not to fight each other," said Magnus and embraced his competitor warmly.

"You have used so many apples we have enough to make a winter's worth of cider," laughed Angharad, shaking her head.

The night was one of feasting and song, and it was with a heavy heart that Gruffydd said farewell to his friend the following day. They all missed the magnanimous Magnus Barelegs when he left them. They watched the ships disappear into the distance, and Gruffydd let out a deep sigh.

"He is a true friend, Angharad, one of a kind."

"I can see that," she replied, holding her husband's hand and giving it a squeeze. In her heart, however, there was a sadness, a foreboding that it took her some time to shake off.

Chapter 22: Shrewsbury (May 1102)

Only days after Magnus had sailed for Ireland, Gruffydd asked Angharad whether she would like to go to Shrewsbury to meet with King Henry of England at Robert de Belleme's castle. She was fully back to health by then and felt confident enough to say that she would love to.

"He has agreed to meet with Cadwgan and I," explained Gruffydd. "I hope to make a more formal agreement with him."

"But what about Cadwgan?" asked Angharad. "Didn't you say that he is still wanting to oust Henry with Robert de Belleme?"

"Cadwgan is cock-a-hoop about meeting the King of England, and I hope an agreement with Henry will keep him out of trouble."

"*And that he stops asking you to get involved,*" thought Angharad, but she didn't want to open old wounds.

"Will we be safe?"

"Henry can ill afford conflict. We will be safe."

"And I will meet the infamous Robert de Belleme. I am not sure I will be able to look at him without trembling."

"He will be the consummate host but we will do well to be wary of him."

"Will I wear my coronet?" she asked uncertainly.

"Of course, you are a queen after all!"

Angharad was pleased about visiting Shrewsbury as well. She had never been there before and had heard much about it.

It was interesting that King Henry chose the town of Shrewsbury to negotiate with the two most significant Welsh leaders, Angharad thought. Robert had built a mighty fortress there. She felt King Henry was sending a clear message to Robert de Belleme, on whom he was rumoured to be spying, waiting for him to set a foot wrong.

Angharad's expectations of the fourth largest town in England, surrounded by greens fields and woods, were more than satisfied. She felt a great rush of excitement as she saw the town laid out before them. She marvelled at the size of the castle with pennants fluttering from the ramparts: it was vast.

"They knocked down fifty houses to build the castle," said Gruffydd, "and apparently, a further fifty were ruined so that the castle had a good view."

"That would have been awful for the people here," gasped Angharad, disgusted at the wanton destruction.

"At the time, there were only three hundred houses, so you can imagine how they felt!"

The castle was as impressive as it was large! Made of timber with a huge wooden palisade and tower, it stood on an enormous mound overlooking the River Severn. Inside the ramparts was a substantial inner bailey where the Great Hall and other buildings servicing the residents were situated. South and west of the motte was an incredible outer bailey which had been erected over the old Saxon town wall. It straddled the main road that all travellers needed to use to enter or leave the town. Also inside the outer bailey was the beautiful Chapel of St Nicholas.

The town was bustling with people from all walks of life: merchants, monks, soldiers and serfs. You did not need to look far to see that trade was thriving; a plethora of goods were being made and bought: all imaginable carpentry and wooden items, fabrics of all qualities, clothing and ribbons, saddlery, armoury, pottery as well as food items and live animals. Angharad gazed around as they travelled through and thought it more amazing than Dublin.

"There seem to be a lot of leather merchants and tailors," she remarked.

"Shrewsbury has always been a good trading centre for fine Welsh wool and our leather. You will find more glovers and shoemakers here than almost anywhere else. You can smell the tanneries and skinners," said Gruffydd.

There were two bridges in the town, one of which they crossed on the way to the castle. Little boats were all over the river, fishing and casting nets.

People stared at them as they passed through. Gruffydd's clothing and carriage on his fine horse made it clear he was someone of importance, and he was the most handsome of the half dozen young, athletic-looking warriors of his teulu who made up their party. Angharad knew that her bright clothing flattered her, and the two ladies in waiting who accompanied her were young and pretty. She was enjoying the reaction from the people around and smiled as a group of young children ran alongside their horses, calling out and cheering.

As they approached the castle, they were aware of an increased presence of soldiers, all in their mail and well-armed. The king had not yet arrived, but a number of carts bringing food supplies queued along the road outside the castle.

Gruffydd held his head high. They were ushered inside the castle grounds, where everyone seemed to be rushing around in preparation. Huge fires were burning, and spits holding parts of all kinds of beasts were already being turned. Servants rushed forward to help them with their horses, and some senior members of the household welcomed them into the castle, arranging for their belongings to be brought inside and directing them to where they would be sleeping.

The castle was lavishly furnished with tapestries, rugs and ornaments of gold and silver. As they were guided to their chamber, Angharad began to take note of things which she might do in their royal llysoed.

Their chamber was a good size and made very comfortable. A large bed piled high with blankets and pillows was at the centre of the room. Around were chests on top of which were long, brightly coloured cushions so that you could sit on them comfortably. The tapestries on the walls were of hunting and rural scenes. On a small table were some bronze goblets and an ewer of wine. Next to the wine was a platter of fruit. Gruffydd picked up an apple and threw it to his wife: she caught it expertly. He came to join her at the window, looking down into the courtyard below, nuzzling her neck.

"What a place!" he whistled, with his large eyes gazing at the magnificent buildings before surprising his wife by gripping her tiny waist and pulling her onto the bed. "You look so beautiful with your big blue curious eyes taking in everything and your full red delicious lips; I just want to spend all day here in bed with you. Do you know how hard it is for me to ride beside you for hours on end, ignoring the impulse to leave everyone else behind, and ride into a quiet place in the woods with you? You are irresistible."

She closed her eyes, her heart beating fast, excited by his passion and tenderness. She eagerly returned his kisses as he crushed her in his arms.

"But first, we need to get you out of your riding clothes, my queen," he whispered playfully, removing item by item as she did the same for him. He gazed with pleasure at her full breasts, slim body and long legs. Her glossy hair fell like a golden silken mass over her shoulders and down her back. She came to him, touching his arms and chest where more recent scars had joined older ones. She felt the tense flatness of his stomach, the hard strength of his muscles. She heard his breathing, heavy and erratic and then slid her arms around his back, pulling him towards her. Their lovemaking was the slow, indulgent pleasure of two people who knew each other's bodies intimately.

Afterwards, as they lay in each other's arms, content and happy, he said, "To think, you could have lived in castles as fine as this in Normandy and England with wealth beyond your dreams."

"But not be married to you? No! I like nice things, lovely things but I can do without them. All I need is to love and be loved. If we had to live with nothing but I was with you, and you loved me, I would be satisfied."

"What a different woman you are to most others," he said, looking into her large, indelibly blue eyes and pulling her closer.

Something inside her tensed up. '*He has never compared me to other women,*' she thought, '*why now would he say something like that?*' '*Had he been close enough to other women to know how they really thought?*' Then she forced herself to dismiss the nagging doubt in her mind, an irksome suspicion which hung over from their time apart. '*Surely,*' she told herself, '*it was just a turn of phrase he had used.*'

Just at that moment, the heralds' trumpets and drumming hooves announced the arrival of the king. They went to the window to see the pageantry below.

The procession looked glorious. The king was dressed in a sumptuous gold cloak with rich embroidery around the edges and on the collar. When he dismounted, he seemed quite a lot shorter than his knights. Like his brother Rufus, he was barrel-chested and stout, but he had jet-black hair and a moustache.

"So, there you are, Henry," said Gruffydd looking down at the splendour of flashing jewels and rich attire. "Well, Cariad, we had better look our best; we do not want to disappoint the English king."

A bowl and pitcher of scented water had been laid out for them so that they could refresh themselves after their journey. Angharad had packed their clothes with dried violet petals and now shook them out to remove the flowers and lessen the creases. If Gruffydd was nervous, he didn't show it, but her hands were trembling. Though she had met the King of Norway and the High King of Ireland, there was something that made her feel anxious about meeting King Henry.

As they entered the Great Hall, Angharad's eyes did not know where to gaze next. Trestle tables had been set up and covered in crisp linen tablecloths. Upon the tables were goblets rimmed with silver, fine cutlery and silver pitchers of wine. Circling around the hall were men and women more richly dressed than she had ever seen, some dazzling with jewellery, some more plainly but impressively attired.

Angharad was dressed in a turquoise silk gown made with gold trim, fitted to above her hips and pleated in a full skirt cinched at the waist with a delicate golden rope. Pretty embroidered slippers graced her small feet. Her sheer turquoise headdress was secured with her golden coronet. At her neck, she wore the gift from Magnus: the golden necklace with the turquoise stone.

Gruffydd's tunic was of pale gold silk, embroidered richly around the neck and cuffs. A polished belt with a gold buckle encircled his slim waist. His long boots were soft brown Welsh leather. Draped across his broad shoulders, he wore a fur-lined olive-green cloak of silk fastened with a large, intricately engraved gold brooch.

Holding her arm, Gruffydd strode confidently, escorting Angharad towards a tall, grey-haired, elegantly dressed man with an aquiline nose, long, narrow eyes and a steely expression. He stood next to a richly dressed, once beautiful but incredibly thin, middle-aged lady who was clearly his wife.

Seeing Gruffydd, the man abandoned his wife and came towards them with an air of authority. He smiled, but his eyes were icily cold.

"We meet at last, Gruffydd ap Cynan," he spoke matter-of-factly in Norman French. "Folklore speaks much about you. I am pleased we are not facing each other across a battlefield today."

Gruffydd bowed and replied in French, "Earl Robert, I can see from your wonderful hospitality that you intend to kill us with kindness. Thank you for your welcome. May I introduce my wife, Queen Angharad?"

Angharad dropped into a deep curtsey.

Robert turned to Gruffydd. "Your queen is as beautiful as I have heard tell. The Jewel of Wales."

Angharad rose, blushed prettily, and in perfect French, replied, "You flatter me, Earl Robert. I am delighted to be here. I also thank you for your thoughtful hospitality."

Earl Robert raised his eyebrows. "The Jewel of Wales speaks French as well!" he remarked with surprise. "Never underestimate the Welsh! Come, you should meet King Henry, and then I will introduce you to my wife, Agnes. I am sure you two ladies will find something in common to discuss."

Angharad started to feel more nervous. Gruffydd sensed it and squeezed her arm reassuringly.

Henry was magnificently dressed in a red and gold embroidered silk tunic to the knees fastened at the waist with a golden belt. On top, he wore a fitted bliaut of red pleated silk cut wide at the wrists, which was lined with vair: red squirrel fur. The side seams were open so that when he turned, his legs were shown in their silk hose. His dress was completed with soft leather shoes.

As they approached the king, he turned, sharp-eyed and looked Angharad up and down before giving her a lascivious smile. Formalities were completed in French, and then Henry turned to

Gruffydd. "I look forward to sitting down together tomorrow to discuss business, but tonight we get to know each other a little better."

"I look forward to it too," replied Gruffydd, looking Henry straight in the eye.

"How are you enjoying Earl Robert's magnificent castle?" Henry asked Angharad, his eyes travelling over her body.

"It is an incredible place," she replied.

"Yes," he agreed thoughtfully, "it really is. We Normans know how to build something special. Have you visited London?"

"I must confess I have not, but I have heard much of it."

"We have the most magnificent buildings there. Our stone masons are the best in the world."

"So I have heard. There are both magnificent churches and towers, I understand."

"Indeed. They will last a thousand years."

At that moment, Earl Robert brought his wife to meet them. Angharad noticed that he held her arm with more pressure than necessary and pulled her along faster than was easy for her; she almost stumbled as she approached them. She darted an anxious look at her husband and tried to collect herself.

Angharad curtseyed and thanked Agnes sincerely for hosting them. Agnes took her aside while the gentlemen chatted. Angharad saw that her eyes were red, as if she had been crying. She brushed a stray strand of hair back underneath her headdress, and her wide sleeve fell back, showing a red welt around her wrist. She quickly adjusted her sleeve.

"I believe my name Agnes is Nest in Welsh," said Agnes warmly but a little distractedly, her puffy eyes straying back towards her husband.

"It is. Pure is its meaning."

Agnes smiled, and Angharad could see that her lip seemed swollen. "And Angharad, what does that mean?"

Angharad blushed, "Much loved."

"And I can see you are much loved," she said, looking across at Gruffydd. "He almost bursts with pride when he looks at you."

Angharad smiled her thanks.

"Do you have children?" Agnes asked.

"We have three children. Two very lively boys and a little baby girl. This is the first time that I have ever left them. It seems strange. Do you have children also?"

"I have a son, William, but he is in Normandy, in my home town."

"You must miss him."

"Of course, but we travel between England and Normandy often, so it is not so hard."

They spoke a little about Normandy and Shrewsbury, and then Agnes asked her if she was interested in tapestries.

"I see you have some very beautiful ones,"

"Come, I will show you some I made myself," she said. When they were out of earshot of the king, she whispered, "Be very careful. I saw Henry looking at you, and you are very beautiful. He might make it very awkward for you and your husband. Do you understand?"

"I think I understand," Angharad replied cautiously, though her mind was now racing.

"He is very open about his appetites in front of his wife as well, although she is not here today. They are soon expecting a child, so she stays in London."

"Thank you so much for your concern. He has been very polite to me, but I will be aware of what you have said."

Angharad glanced back across the room and saw that Cadwgan had arrived and that Gruffydd was deep in conversation with him and Robert de Belleme. Cadwgan had put on a lot of weight. She remembered Gruffydd saying that he was unhappy with his Norman wife, which resulted in a lot of drinking. He wore a huge bearskin cloak, which made him look enormous, and Robert looked at him with disdain.

Meanwhile, Henry was walking towards Angharad and Agnes. Angharad blushed, which made her look even more alluring.

"You are admiring Countess Agnes' handiwork? She is very talented," said Henry, examining the tapestry in front of him.

"I am most envious of such skill," said Angharad, turning to Agnes, who smiled warmly at the compliment.

"Do you enjoy working with the needle?" asked Henry.

"I confess my preference is to play my harp."

"You play the harp?" said Henry. "King David's instrument. I would like to hear that."

"My skills are doubtless no better than any of the other ladies, but if you wish it, I would be pleased to play."

At that moment, everyone was called to the table as servants brought in huge platters of all kinds of meat, including boar, swan, beef and lamb, then soups, stews, bread and vegetables, puffy golden pastries and freshly caught fish. Henry led Angharad to the table and, to her surprise, found that he sat her next to him.

"As I have no lady of my own this evening, I am borrowing your beautiful wife, Gruffydd," he called to the Welsh king, who was approaching the table by the side of Robert Belleme.

"Of course, sire," said Gruffydd politely. Although Angharad shot him a worried look, he smiled and nodded at her reassuringly.

The meal was magnificent, and almost every luxury imaginable was provided to the guests.

"You are admiring the fine fare," Henry noted.

"I am indeed, and it is more than generous."

"You, too, enjoy entertaining, I hear."

Angharad shot him a look of surprise.

"I hear you feted Magnus Barefoot recently."

Angharad was wary, but before she could say anything, he added, "There is not much I don't get to know about one way or another. Tell me what hunting you have in Gwynedd."

Angharad knew enough about hunting to keep the King's interest, and she found herself relaxing as she spoke to Henry. He was easy to talk to, and she spoke about Normandy and his childhood, and then they got onto the role of the church.

"I understand that the Welsh use the church to further learning."

"The church has always been important in passing on information about our culture as well as religion," explained Angharad carefully. "The lives of the Welsh saints are one of the main ways we inspire our people to adhere to the Christian principles."

"Your Welsh church allows priests to marry!"

"We see no problem with it, but I understand that Archbishop Anselm does have an issue with it.'

He laughed. "Anselm is a stickler for total devotion to the faith. He has very firm ideas on things. He would not return from Normandy until I promised him that my courtiers would cut their hair and cease to look 'effeminate'!"

He sniffed, changing the topic of conversation. "Have you seen the wonderful little chapel here?"

"No, lord, not as yet."

"Then I will take you to see it a little later. You will be interested in some of the craftsmanship there."

"Thank you, lord."

"In Normandy, we consider music one of the seven liberal arts. It is taught in both the cathedral and in the monastic schools."

"I have heard of Fecamp Abbey with the school of singing there and the famous William Volpiano and John of Ravenna."

"You are full of surprises. Yes, you are correct; two Italian men taught us how to sign music so that anybody might read the notes."

They spoke a little of the Welsh bards and the kind of poetry they wrote in their particular form, of the great competition that existed between different poets and of how it was considered an honourable craft. Angharad was impressed with how learned Henry was, and he exuded charm.

"Have you heard any of the poems of the troubadours and trouveres?"

"I have heard a little, lord."

"Have you read any of the work of the Guilhem, seventh count of Poitou and ninth duke of Aquitaine?"

"I have not, lord."

"Ah, then you must acquaint yourself with it. He writes of feudal politics, love and women," he leaned closer; she felt his leg touching hers. "He writes of his sexual achievements. He is a great seducer of women."

Angharad was unsure how to respond but said, "He must cause great scandal."

"People love scandal. They love his frankness and wit, and women fall prey to him wherever he goes." He turned away to survey the table, and she adjusted her robe, which had been pulled down a little off her shoulder when the king had leaned across her.

"Have you tried the swan?"

"I have not, lord."

Henry took his knife and plunged it into a tasty-looking piece of the swan. Then, taking it into his fingers, he held the meat up for her to eat. Angharad was not sure what to do, and not wanting to cause offence, she took it in her lips.

"Good breast," he said and, taking a second chunk on his knife, picked it off and popped it into his mouth while his eyes lingered over her body. She looked around, embarrassed, but nobody seemed to notice other than Hywel, who was seated at a table below them, watching intently.

Henry put a little wine into her goblet from the silver jug on the table and leant closer to her.

"Earl Robert produces this wine on his Normandy estates. What do you think?"

311

"It is very fine, lord," she replied, taking a careful sip.

"Let me fill your goblet," he said, close enough now that she could smell the wine on his breath. As he poured, a few drops fell onto her gown.

"I'm sorry, allow me," he said and, taking his linen napkin, rubbed it sensuously over her breasts and down into her lap. He breathed in deeply, half closing his eyes and whispered into her ear, "You really are quite, quite lovely."

She felt as if the whole hall was watching her as the king mentally undressed her. She looked up. Everyone was engrossed in conversation, and still, only Hywel seemed to notice her distress. What was she to do? She could not leave the table; she had learnt that lesson from Murtagh's visit. She didn't want to give offence as that might jeopardise her husband's negotiations. She was embarrassed but felt she was safe enough at a table surrounded by people if she could just navigate her way to the end of the meal.

"What lovely hands you have," Henry continued, lifting her hand and stroking her long fingers. "I can imagine the music that these hands can make." He took her hand underneath the tablecloth and pressed it against the lower part of his tunic. "Look what you are doing to me," he gasped as she tried to wrench away, but he held her tightly, rubbing her hand firmly against the growing sign of his desire.

"Please, lord," she said, really distressed and trying to pull herself away, her face burning with shame and horror.

"I know you Welsh ladies; you torture a man until he is wild with need," he breathed heavily.

Alarm flashed in her eyes, and she felt like a fawn caught in a trap.

"God save King Henry!" shouted Hywel standing with his goblet high in the air and feigning drunkenness. Time seemed to be suspended for

312

a moment, and then suddenly, everyone was standing up, holding their drink. "God save King Henry!"

Angharad saw her opportunity and tugged away sharply. She stood, masking her distress as best she could, holding her goblet high. Her knees and hands were shaking, but she was cheering with the rest. Gruffydd looked at Hywel with absolute astonishment.

"God save King Gruffydd," Hywel roared, and everyone shouted for King Gruffydd. Gruffydd acknowledged the cheer and shot a look of warning at his friend.

"To the Earl of Shrewsbury," Hywel continued. Gruffydd was completely perplexed, indicating with his hand that Hywel should sit down.

"What the hell is he doing?" Gruffydd asked Cadwgan in Welsh across the back of Robert de Belleme, who was busy accepting the acknowledgements.

"Christ knows!" returned Cadwgan, also in Welsh, "I thought you must have set him up to something. I think he has gone mad!"

Hywel waited until the noise had abated, and then, propelling his voice around the room, he spoke again. "To celebrate this wonderful hospitality and propitious fostering of good relations, I call on Angharad, Queen of Gwynedd to play the harp for us."

"Bring the harp," shouted Robert de Belleme, thinking that such behaviour was somewhat unusual but evidently a Welsh custom.

Angharad got up, threw the most thankful look at Hywel, and, still shaking, made her way to where the harp had been placed. Henry scowled at Hywel, who lifted his goblet again to the king, nodding and smiling.

Angharad was flustered but did not show it. Taking the harp, she thought for a moment and then started playing and singing a portion of the epic poem, The Song of Roland, about the protagonist Roland and the Battle of Roncevaux Pass in the reign of Charlemagne. She selected a part where Charlemagne and his army had fought the Muslims in Spain for several years. The last city that stood was Saragossa, which was held by King Marsile, who took advice from his advisor, Blancandrin, to offer to surrender to Charlemagne. Marsile's messengers went to Charlemagne, offering treasure and promising that Marsile would convert to Christianity if he returned to France. Charlemagne's men were weary, so he agreed to the peace.

The song was well chosen as it hinted at the concord that should exist between the Normans and the Welsh. Angharad surprised everyone with her clear French singing. At the end, the king got up, and everybody else rose from their seats.

Hywel made his way to Angharad's side before anyone else.

"Are you alright, lady?" he asked in a low voice.

"I think so. Would you be willing to stay nearby? Henry is coming towards us again."

"Of course," said Hywel. As Henry approached, he bowed low and assumed his pretence of intoxication.

Henry gave him a cursory nod and gazed at Angharad.

"You sing very sweetly, Queen Angharad."

"I call her my nightingale," said Gruffydd, arriving at her side, oblivious to what was happening.

Henry looked up at Gruffydd, nodded again at Angharad, and, surrounded by his men at arms, removed himself briskly from the hall.

"Hywel, what in Hell's name was that all about?" demanded Gruffydd, "I have never seen such a performance."

Hywel glanced at Angharad's face, and her warning look.

"I am so sorry; I was overcome."

"Overcome? Overcome? Pull yourself together, Man. I suppose you have done no harm, but you can't leap up and down and yell like that in this sort of place. Usually, there is not a peep from you. I don't know what they put in your wine, but go and sleep it off!"

Hywel mumbled his agreement, caught Angharad's eye to make sure she was alright, and left the hall, seeing her barely perceptible nod.

Gruffydd and Angharad thanked the Earl and his wife once again and retired. Angharad had been badly shaken but said nothing to Gruffydd as she could imagine his reaction. She was appalled at Henry's behaviour and felt somehow dirty. She resolved to avoid Henry if she could for the remainder of the visit.

"You played beautifully," said Gruffydd appreciatively. "Very clever choice of song."

"Thank you. I was nervous."

"You did well. You and Henry seemed to have a lot to talk about. Anything interesting?"

Angharad wanted to blurt out what had happened, but she knew the backlash could lead to hostility and even death for Gruffydd. She kept her voice level. "We spoke about poetry and music and the church. He knows Magnus stayed with us, you know."

"That doesn't surprise me. Henry has spies everywhere. He is concerned about Magnus now that Magnus has sorted out his issues in Scandinavia. He is frightened of what he is planning next. Also, Henry is married to Matilda, who well knows from Scotland Magnus' military might. Knowing Henry, he is probably paying off someone in Magnus' warband to keep him informed."

"And Robert de Belleme. You spoke a lot to him."

"He was civil but prying. Taking the measure of Cadwgan and me. He hates Henry, you can tell, and Henry hates him."

"But Henry chooses to meet here."

"Henry is letting him know that for all Belleme's wealth and power, he is not afraid of him."

The serious talks took place the next day, and Angharad was anxious to be away from the castle. She encouraged a couple of her ladies to explore Shrewsbury with her, keeping well away from any unwanted chance encounters.

"Do you mind if we take Hywel with us?" she asked Gruffydd as he pulled on an intricately embroidered fine new woollen tunic.

"Certainly, he doesn't need to be involved in the talks this morning, and after last night, I would say the fresh air would do him good! I have never seen Hywel unable to hold his drink, and of all people to jump up like that; I didn't know what had taken hold of him."

The three ladies, accompanied by Hywel, whose athletic good looks drew much comment from the women of Shrewsbury, made their way into the town. As she had noted, there were many leather traders. They stopped to watch a cobbler making turnshoes. The shaft and sole were stitched together inside out so that the seams were protected inside the shoe when they were turned to their right side. Angharad felt some soft leather and bought herself a pair of fine deerskin boots. Moving along, she saw fine gloves being made and bought a pair for Gruffydd. Turning to Hywel, she surprised him.

"Please choose a pair. The smallest thank you for helping me yesterday evening."

Hywel looked embarrassed. "You do not need to give me a gift, my lady. I am happy to serve you."

Angharad moved away from the other ladies looking at a stall selling fabrics and said, "You are always so gentle and humble. What you did for me at dinner yesterday evening would have almost killed you to do with everybody looking at you."

He grinned sheepishly. "I must admit I would rather have faced the Irish hoards than do what I did, but I would do it a hundred times again."

She gave him a soft smile and convinced him to choose a nice pair of kid gloves. She asked the glove maker to wrap them for him.

"Thank you, my lady," he said in a voice thick with emotion.

They continued their discovery of the fascinating town, and Angharad tried to store in her memory things which might work well in Gwynedd. She was enchanted by Shrewsbury Abbey, which was Benedictine. Inside were stunning sculptures of religious figures such as her beloved St Winifred, St Beuno and John the Baptist.

An elderly monk explained that Roger, Earl of Shrewsbury, had died at the Abbey after he became a monk at the end of his life. Angharad's mind cast back to Hugh the Fat, atoning for his sins by becoming a monk when he knew he would die within days. How unfair it would be for such malevolent people to reach heaven by becoming a monk, she mused and yet didn't the bible say all sins would be forgiven if you repented?

Loaded up with things they had bought, they returned to the castle, where Angharad had a pleasant surprise. As they walked into the central courtyard, she heard her name being called, and there was Lafracoth. The two women fell into each other's arms.

"I so hoped you would be here," Lafracoth said, "and since my sister-in-law told me that you were, I have been searching for you all over the castle."

"Here I am. But I forget myself. Congratulations! You are now a married woman." Angharad beamed.

"I am. My days of freedom are gone."

The two women took themselves off to Lafracoth's chamber and talked and talked.

Lafracoth was well-informed on what had happened in Angharad's life since they last met.

"I hear you have the sweetest baby girl and the liveliest two sons in Christendom," she said, chuckling lightly.

"They will find trouble wherever it is. Just before we left, they almost drowned themselves, racing two wooden ships Magnus Barefoot gave them. We must watch them all the time. They climb trees, though they are so small, they find their way under horses' hooves, and if they are not trying to kill themselves, they are trying to kill each other. Baby Gwenllian looks as if she will be feisty as well."

Lafracoth smiled, picturing the mayhem. "It sounds familiar, like a typical Irish upbringing to me," she said. "So was Magnus staying with you?"

"He was. He wasn't a bit like I'd imagined."

"Why do you say that?"

"Well, you can tell he is a fierce warrior and very proud, too impulsive, I suppose, but he is generous, kind-hearted, funny, and seems to have a sensitive side."

"Did you find him handsome?"

"Who would not find him handsome? He knows how to dress to turn heads. He and Gruffydd were like two children competing against each other: hawking, hunting and shooting their bows and arrows. I didn't know Gruffydd could be so competitive."

"You didn't think Gruffydd was competitive?" scoffed Lafracoth lightly.

"Not so overtly, no."

Angharad saw Lafracoth was going to say something but then stopped herself. "Did Queen Margaret come as well?"

"No, she stayed in Norway. Magnus had come from Mann."

"Why was he there?" asked Lafracoth. "I would have thought he would be busy making babies with Margaret so that he would have legitimate heirs."

Even though Lafracoth was a dear friend and despite Angharad not knowing if Magnus had a motive for the visit, she was cautious. How easy it was for political fears to lead to someone's downfall, and knowing that Lafracoth was straddling the Irish and Norman worlds, she knew she must weigh her words carefully before speaking.

"I think he was just interested to see how Gwynedd had recovered after the invasion. Mann is very close, and he was on his way to your father."

"I heard he has been building on Mann, wood from Galway."

"He seems to like the place. He says it is very beautiful."

"My little sister is Magnus' son's wife now. They are both very young, but it is a match that keeps the peace. Magnus and my father either love each other or hate each other. There is nothing in between."

The conversation turned to Arnulf.

"I do not love him, but I knew that love was unlikely. He keeps to himself; I keep to myself unless we are entertaining or being entertained when he needs to trot me out like a prize mare. He buys me beautiful things, or at least does not stop me from buying them

319

myself. We have plenty of lands to keep me interested, and I am looking forward to discovering the pleasures of Normandy, and at night," she paused, "some nights, I have the burden of being his wife."

"I wish you could have found love," sympathised Angharad, feeling for her beautiful, vivacious friend.

"I have found love," she volunteered, looking down, "but he is taken."

It was as if something had hit Angharad across the face. Surely, Lafracoth could not mean Gruffydd. She looked at her elegant, mesmerising friend. Lafracoth had known Gruffydd long before Angharad had. They had a deep friendship, but had it been stronger since Gruffydd had been in Ireland? She pulled herself together sharply. What she was thinking was ridiculous.

At that moment, there was a knock at the door. Lafracoth swept to open it, and an attractive lady stood at the other side. She smiled, showing perfect white teeth and full lips. Her eyes were sage green, large and liquid, and were quickly assessing the chamber and who was in it.

"Come in, Nest, come in," Lafracoth greeted her. "Do you know Queen Angharad?"

Angharad was stunned as she watched Nest glide gracefully into the room, "Is it Princess Nest?"

"I go by Lady Nest, now, lady. I remember you well when we were both children."

"As I you."

"Lady Nest is married to Gerald of Windsor, who is the constable of Pembroke Castle," Lafracoth added.

Angharad knew, of course, that the man Nest had married was ruling over Nest's father's lands on behalf of Arnulf.

"It was Gerald who came to Ireland to arrange my marriage to Arnulf," Lafracoth continued.

Nest smiled warmly, disguising any uneasiness she may have felt toward the woman who was married into the very family that had destroyed her own.

"Like you, Angharad, Nest and her husband have been building."

Nest was quite humble. "As part of my dowry, I brought the manor of Carew, and we are building a modest Norman-style castle there."

"They have already built a stone keep," Lafracoth encouraged Nest. Despite her earlier suspicious thoughts, Angharad loved her friend for the way she made Nest the centre of importance despite being of higher rank.

"At the moment, the rest is of timber," Nest explained.

"It is in a beautiful position, I believe," said Angharad

"It is on the top of a limestone bluff which overlooks the Carew inlet, and some mornings when the mist lies across the water, it seems almost magical."

"And you have Cilgerran as well," Lafracoth prompted her.

"I am very fortunate. It is a timber castle above a gorge looking down on the River Teifi. I could spend days watching the river meander past, the way the light shines on the water, the birds flying across at sunrise, the glow of sunset."

Angharad's admiration for this lady grew. Nest took what joy she could in a world which promised her little, and she adapted to her fate, quelling any resentment she might harbour.

Later, when Nest had gone back to her rooms to dress for the evening meal, Angharad commented how hard it must have been for her since her father had been killed.

"She is one of those genuinely lovely people," replied Lafracoth. "I have not heard her speak a bad word against anyone; she is loving and accepting, and even though she is so clever, she does not use that cleverness at the expense of others. They say Henry was besotted by her but was talked out of marrying her. That would have hurt."

As they talked more, Angharad realised that Nest was an extremely intelligent lady, and she reflected on how hard her life must have been. She knew that Nest had been taken as a lover by King Henry, and after yesterday evening, Angharad wondered what choice Nest had had in the matter. Had she been seduced by the charismatic Henry but found that her status was not sufficient to be the wife of a king of England? Highborn enough to bring legitimacy to Norman rule in Deheubarth but not highborn enough to retain her title.

The women spent a wonderful afternoon together, and that night at dinner, it was Nest who sat at the king's side. She did not look uncomfortable, and her husband, Gerald, did not seem at all concerned. Angharad saw that Gerald was a lot older than Nest but then so was Arnulf, a lot older than Lafracoth, who now sat beside her. She noticed how easily Lafracoth spoke to Gruffydd, joking light-heartedly, how Gruffydd's face lit up and how he threw back his head laughing at things she said. Lafracoth was dazzling, her eyes sparkling with mirth, leaning towards Gruffydd in some private joke, holding his arm with familiarity, and he so easy in her company. A small shadow of suspicion crossed her mind again, which she tried to put aside.

"Lafracoth looked very beautiful tonight," she said to Gruffydd when they got back to their chamber.

"Yes, she was shining!" He was thoughtful, "Such a waste for such an intelligent, beautiful woman to be married to Arnulf. He has no personality and only thinks about money and land."

"I've missed her," said Angharad.

"Yes, I have been thinking about her a lot," said Gruffydd absently.

Angharad felt a chill creeping up inside her.

"She is a good friend," she said in a small voice, "and she looked after you well when you were in Ireland?"

"Of course. Irish hospitality is legendary!"

Her stomach dropped like a stone, but she knew she could not prod further, so she deflected the conversation to what had happened with Gruffydd and Henry. Gruffydd was delighted with the formal agreements with Henry.

"Cariad, he has agreed to acknowledge that I am King of Gwynedd and has confirmed that he will withdraw any Norman presence in Llyn, Eifionydd, Ardudwy and Arllechwedd. I think, with Earl Hugh gone, he doesn't want to have the responsibility of fighting over lands he can't control. He says he wants peace with the Welsh. And Belleme seems to be on good terms with Cadwgan. Cadwgan has all the lands in Powys and Ceredigion but as vassalage to Belleme. Belleme is powerful, and while on the one hand, Henry seems at pains to please him outwardly, and he Henry, you can tell there is distrust there."

"It is interesting that Arnulf has come to Shrewsbury as well."

"Yes, when Henry leaves tomorrow, we will also leave. Cadwgan and the Montgomerys are 'talking', and I do not want to be drawn into anything when we have just negotiated a formal peace."

"You think they are still plotting behind Henry's back?"

"I do."

Long after Gruffydd was asleep that night, Angharad lay awake agonising as she lay nestled in Gruffydd's arms. What did it matter, she tried to rationalise, if Gruffydd and Lafracoth had been more than friends? Yes, it was betrayal, but now Lafracloth was another man's wife. She knew that Gruffydd loved her and, if he had strayed, had she not driven him to it and should forgive him. Yet she would never break their marriage vows. As if Gruffydd read her thoughts, he pulled her closer to him in his sleep.

The following morning, they left Shrewsbury. To break the journey, they decided to take a detour through Tegeingl and sent word to Owain that they were coming.

Angharad was longing to return to the children but when she saw her father's appearance, she asked Gruffydd if she might stay longer.

"He looks frail, Gruffydd," she explained.

"Ah, he will live until he is one hundred; he just looks a bit older." Gruffydd made light of her concern, but he, too, had seen a huge change in Owain and agreed to the delay in her return.

Gruffydd generously revealed to Owain all the details of the visit to Henry. They spoke at length about everything that had happened in Shrewsbury. He showed genuine respect for the older man and asked his advice on several matters, which pleased Angharad.

Angharad's brothers were keen to know all the details of the famous Montgomery stud.

"I hear he has Arabian mares," said Rhydir.

"A lot of those who are returning from the crusades have brought Arabian bloodstock with them, and Belleme has jumped on the opportunity to bring some over."

"They would be expensive," said Llywarch, his eyes lighting up.

"Oh yes," agreed Gruffydd. "The Spanish ones were expensive enough, and they have Arab in them but these purebred are way beyond that."

"I understand that monks are responsible for a lot of the horse breeding in Spain," said Meilyr.

"The Arabs keep an oral tradition of the pedigree of their Barb and Arabian horses," explained Gruffydd. "But in Europe, because monks are literate, they are the ones who keep the records, and so some of the nobles have got the monks interested in horse breeding as well. The Carthusian monks in Spain kept all the records for the Spanish Jennet."

"What is a Spanish Jennet?" asked Llywarch

"Don't you know anything?" scoffed Gronwy rolling his eyes, his chin tilting arrogantly. "Don't show your ignorance."

"It is one with Iberian or Barb extraction," explained Gruffydd, "and it has plenty of stamina. The Barb was raised in the deserts of North Africa, so you can imagine how hardy they had to be. The Jennet has a smooth ambling gait and a docile but very elegant carriage. It is a colourful horse often heavily patterned and highly prized by the European nobility."

"So, you saw the stud?" persisted Llywarch.

"I did! Cadwgan and I went out there to have a look. The horses are better housed than most people are, and everything was spotless."

"I wager it was heavily guarded," said Rhydir.

"Oh yes, indeed. There is no way anyone would be getting one of those horses."

In private, Owain asked Gruffydd if he would assist in a special task.

"Gladly," he replied.

"I would like Gronwy to marry a daughter of Hoedlyw ap Ithel. Her name is Genilles, and she is a sensible but beautiful girl who will tame him somewhat, I feel. The family are in Abergele."

325

"I know them. Hoedlyw fought alongside me, and in fact, we stopped there when I was on my way back from here to Anglesey with the people the Normans took captive." Gruffydd responded warmly, "They are a very good family, and the lady you mention is a pious lady, capable and shrewd but also very attractive."

They discussed the negotiations, and Gruffydd arranged to spend time with the family again on his return to Anglesey. When Gruffydd left, he presented Owain with an illuminated book that he had bought from the Abbey in Shrewsbury and had carried carefully on the journey. The cover was jewelled and finely worked. It was the story of Saint Beuno. Owain was absolutely delighted. He had a few books, and this beautiful addition to his collection would be the most treasured.

"Look at this!" Owain exclaimed ecstatically, holding up the book for all to see.

"Without Father, Gruffydd ap Cynan would be a nobody," Gronwy turned aside to Rhydir and spoke in a sour, lowered voice. "He didn't ask Father to join in the negotiations, and a book is a cheap price for the position Gruffydd is in now."

Always proud yet protective of his father, Gronwy's comments stung, but Rhydir did not want to be drawn into Gronwy's divisive resentment.

"Gronwy, Father can handle himself. He knew Gruffydd was going, Gruffydd sent word, and if he had wanted to be included, he would have told him."

Gronwy watched Gruffydd with a face twisted by malice. Then he looked at his father, coughing and struggling to talk. He didn't feel pity; what he felt was impatience.

The next day, leaving Hywel and the ladies behind to accompany Angharad on her journey, Gruffydd set off with the rest of his party and took time to meet as many people as possible in Gwynedd.

The family had a happy few days and Hywel, who was well known to them by now, fitted in well. In the evenings, they would gather around as they did when they were growing up with lots of music on the harp, pibcorn and crwth. Lleuci was an accomplished singer. Little Llywarch was engaging and delightful, providing a wonderful antidote to everyone's growing concerns about Owain's persistent cough.

One night, Meilyr watched as his sister played the harp and sang. The room was lit by candles and a roaring fire. Angharad looked beautiful. From where he sat, he could see that everyone was transfixed by the music but Hywel's honest face had a most soulful expression. When the music stopped, Hywel was still staring at her, oblivious to the chatter around him.

The next day, Meilyr managed to get Hywel alone as they went to the mews. He was direct.

"You are in love with my sister, aren't you?"

Hywel shot him a startled look, and then, seeing that there was no hostility, he replied, "I would die for her in a moment."

"She doesn't know?"

"She is so full of Gruffydd, she doesn't see anything else."

"And that is as it should be."

Hywel sighed, his hazel eyes pooled with sadness, "It is how it should be. I would not betray Gruffydd, you understand. Twice he has saved my life in battle. I cannot forget that he is my king, and a finer man never walked the earth. I will never do anything to hurt them. It would break her heart."

Chapter 23: Montgomery (1102)

"What were you thinking, Uchdryd?" said Gruffydd as they sat beside the crackling fire in Aberffraw.

Angharad played with little Gwenllian on her lap and listened without saying anything. She was pregnant yet again and nervous after the last time. She didn't want Uchdryd stirring up trouble.

"You know what it is like to keep a teulu engaged," said Uchdryd. "They live for the spoils. Cadwgan and I have been doing nothing recently to keep them happy."

"That is not what I heard."

"A few small skirmishes here and there but nothing of consequence. Arnulf paid us well, and you know it could have turned out that we were on the winning side."

"So, on Arnulf's say so, you struck Staffordshire and ravaged it."

"Great rewards there, I tell you, livestock and captives."

"And then you hid the Montgomery share in the mountains in Powys?"

"We did."

"And you didn't think it was likely to generate recourse."

"Look, there was one point there where the barons had the might of the Irish, the Welsh and Belleme's own forces as well as a lot of wealth, and it looked very promising for Belleme. Then Henry summoned him to court. His spies had trumped up forty-five different charges against Belleme, including building Bridgenorth castle without royal permission. Arnulf was called as well but didn't come. Belleme might have worked his way out of it, but instead, he asked to leave to consult with his vassals privately and escaped the royal court on a horse. It was downhill from there!"

"Belleme knew that he would not get out of the charges. He was just stalling to prepare for war when he made that escape."

"I think he could have manoeuvred," said Uchdryd. "Anyway, Henry raised a feudal host and besieged Belleme's castle at Arundel for three months, and after that, Belleme seemed to lose his way."

"Yes, and from what I understand," pursued Gruffydd, "Henry sent to his brother to stand firm in their agreement regarding traitors. So Curthose besieged Belleme's castle at Vignat as well but that failed because Curtose can't see anything through!"

"Henry was unstoppable. He besieged Bridgenorth and built a siege castle nearby to allow catapults to easily fire into the castle. Meanwhile, he sent Bishop Blout of Lincoln to besiege Tickhill. The Earl of Shrewsbury was by now holed up in Shrewsbury Castle. Henry had raised an army the like of which had never been seen before, and by the time he got to Shrewsbury, the Earl was wetting himself. He walked out personally to hand the keys to Shrewsbury to the king. He and his brothers, Arnulf and Roger Poitevin, were told they must be exiled immediately. All their lands were forfeit to the crown."

Angharad thought of her lovely friend Lafracoth and how this would affect her. What a disastrous marriage it had turned out to be.

"But what I don't understand is how Iorweth ap Bleddyn turned against Cadwgan in all of this," said Gruffydd.

"Belleme made a fundamental mistake. William Pantulf was a former vassal of the Montgomerys, and when Henry was besieging Belleme's castles, Pantulf offered his services to Belleme, who rebuffed him. Can you believe the arrogance and stupidity at such a time? Pantulf was offended and went straight to Henry, offering the support of

Belleme's Welsh allies. Next thing, Henry promised Iorwerth all sorts of gifts, and he started to attack Belleme's lands."

"I heard he was promised Ceredigion, Powys and half of Dyfed, all of which were then held by Cadwgan and Maredudd."

"He was, and of course, his warband attacked the areas 'held' by Belleme and took all the booty from Staffordshire. That meant extra pressure on Belleme. He couldn't use those resources and had no backup from Wales."

"Henry, of course, was also exploiting strife between the brothers to diminish the power of Powys very conveniently."

"Well, there is that. Things seemed to settle down, and Iorwerth shared his gains with his brothers. Everything seemed to be alright for a few months."

"Until Iorwedd captured Maredudd and handed him over to Henry! What on earth was he thinking? I always thought those three brothers had a sensible relationship. They had always got on well and respected each other but it seems greed crept in again. The Welsh curse where land and inheritance are concerned!"

"I think Henry must have put pressure on Iorwedd and threatened the peace," said Gruffydd. "I can't understand otherwise what the point of it was."

"It still doesn't make sense. If he wanted to be King of Powys, why the big reconciliation and sharing of the lands after Belleme's exile?"

Gruffydd frowned. "Guilt? Fear of Cadwgan's star rising?"

"Maybe, but Cadwgan was wary of Henry and unwilling to challenge Iorwedd, which we could have done easily. Then Henry lured Iorwedd to his court with promises of further gifts and had him arrested and imprisoned."

Angharad's mind went back to Shrewsbury and how easily they might all have been held captive by Henry.

"That leaves Cadwgan in charge of all Powys. Be careful, Uchdryd, Henry is an intelligent strategist. Now he only has one brother to pick off, not three."

"Where do you stand, Gruffydd?" asked Uchdryd.

Angharad looked up sharply. She had been here before, and the outcome had not been good.

Gruffydd looked at Angharad, but she quickly looked down, not wanting to reveal her concern. "I love Cadwgan like a brother. We have fought together, spent long nights drinking and strategising together, and dreamed together about how to make a perfect world, but I need to show the people of Gwynedd that they can safely plant with the expectation of harvest. I advise Cadwgan to keep sweet with Henry and not to inflame his Norman ire unless he touches our lands."

"If Henry attacks Powys, then what?"

"If Henry attacks Cadwgan without due cause, I protect Cadwgan, but I do not want to risk what I have worked so hard for here only to end up devasted once again. But I don't think Henry will fight where he can use other ways. Look what he has done in Normandy. He has married his illegitimate daughters, Juliane to Eustace of Breteuil and Matilda to Rotrou Count of Perche. That way, he is securing the Norman border. He gives land in England to entice Norman lords to his side. He is clever. Robert Duke of Normandy needs to keep his eyes open."

"Murtagh would support Cadwgan, you know," said Uchdryd, trying to get a firmer agreement from Gruffydd.

"Murtagh is up to his eyeballs as it is. He tried to campaign against the Cenel Chonaill, but the Dublin fleet was reduced to nothing. Then he tried allying himself with Magnus Barefoot to fight against Ulster, he gave up his control of the Isles, he recognised Norwegian control over Dublin and Fingal, and, despite all he had given up, Magnus and he lost one battle after the next. Now, Murtagh and Magnus are licking their wounds together through the Dublin winter along with Lafracoth and Arnulf, and there's another grand plan gone wrong. Murtagh is lying low. Tell Cadwgan to steer clear of trouble."

Uchdryd looked grim and admitted reluctantly. "It was a mistake to support the Montgomerys. They were very persuasive, and old Belleme knew what he was doing when we took over Staffordshire."

"Yes, but Henry has won a low-cost victory. He besieged and besieged and besieged."

Uchdryd grinned. "I enjoyed our part in it, though; we had rich pickings for the men!"

It was nice to see Uchdryd despite the tension his relationship with Cadwgan brought. He always brought news from Tegeingl. Meilyr was going to marry the daughter of a prominent family from Powys, and Lleuci was pregnant again. Gronwy seemed happy about his pending marriage to Genilles.

"And my father?" asked Angharad.

"He is not so well, Angharad. He struggles with his cough and cannot go hunting or out into the cold." He stretched out his hand and covered hers, "He talks about you all the time. He misses you."

"And I miss him. Sometimes, when the children do something special, I want to tell him. Or when Gruffydd tells me about something that has happened in England or Wales, I want to ask him what he thinks. Perhaps he can come and stay with us when the weather is warmer."

Uchdryd patted her hand and sighed. "Yes, maybe when the weather is warmer."

When Uchdryd had returned to Cadwgan, Gruffydd seemed restless.

"What is it?" Angharad asked him one day as they watched the two boys running around with their little wooden swords. "You seem so preoccupied!"

"I don't know. I feel unsettled. Relationships with people never stand still. You can be so close to someone, know them so well, know their thoughts, and suddenly, life moves on, takes you far away, and something is lost. Sometimes I think about Ireland."

Angharad's heart skipped a beat, and she felt like she was navigating precarious ground.

"You miss the Irish court?"

"Yes, I suppose I do. Murtagh has been like a father to me. I have deep friendships there that go back to my youth."

"But you are happy here?" she asked carefully, her heart beating faster.

"Of course. This is my home, my birthright. I just miss some of the people over there sometimes. You know how the Irish are, how they grip your soul: you felt it when you formed such a close friendship with Lafracoth. Perhaps you should offer that she visit you here to escape Arnulf for a while."

It felt as if a stone had dropped in Angharad's stomach. Her world was reeling, but somehow, she kept her composure. She remembered how Gruffydd had described Lafracoth as 'shining' when they had been at Shrewsbury, and though she loved her friend, the comment had pinched at her heart. She knew it was an unworthy thought, but she did not want Lafracoth's shining beauty gracing their llys and capturing her husband's attention.

At that moment, Cadwallon hit Owain around the head with his sword. Owain, with a great cry of pain, rushed at him and knocked him over. Gruffydd strode over and picked them up, one in each arm.

"You understand; you do not hurt each other; otherwise, I will take those weapons from you."

There were cries of protest from both boys. Gruffydd took them both and put them on a fat branch of an oak tree. "Now, that is where you will stay until you promise not to hurt each other."

They both promised.

"Do you want to hear the story of the red and white dragon?" he asked.

"Yes!" They shouted with glee.

"Once upon a time, a Welsh leader called Gwetheryn ruled Wales and what is now England. He was forever fighting to keep people from stealing his lands, so he got help from two men from another country called Hors and Hengist. Over they came, and with their help, he managed to safeguard his lands.'

"What happened then?" asked Cadwallon eagerly.

"Be patient. As a thank you, Gwetheryn gave them some marshy lands in England. They invited all their friends and family, but they needed more land, so they devised a plan to invite three hundred Welsh leaders to a huge banquet. Suddenly, their hosts shouted, "Get your knives!" Caught unawares, all the Welsh leaders were killed except for Gwetheryn. They forced Gwetheryn to agree that they could keep all of Southern England. Gwetheryn moved to the mountains, where he built a strong castle. The next day, it collapsed after his castle was complete, so he asked his craftsmen to build it again."

"I don't like this part of the story, Dada!" said Owain.

"It gets better. The next day, the castle was demolished again. So, he fetched a wise man who said there was an evil spirit destroying the castle and that they must find a boy without a father and spill his blood over the ground. Gwetheryn gave a reward of a bag of gold to anyone who could find such a boy. Finally, a small boy was found, but before they could sacrifice him, the boy told them that in that mountain, there was a cave and, in the cave, there was a lake, and in the lake, there were two dragons: one white and one red. Every night, they would fight so the earth would move and destroy the castle. Gwetheryn's workmen dug a hole in the mountain and found the cave. The next time the dragons fought, the loser had a way to escape, and the white dragon flew away, leaving the red dragon sleeping peacefully."

"Who is the red dragon, Dada?" asked Owain.

"You know," protested Cadwallon. "The red is the Welsh, and the white is the English."

"And is our red dragon sleeping?" said Owain.

"Our red dragon is very peaceful," said Gruffydd

"But he keeps one eye open for the white dragon," clarified Cadwallon.

"That he does! Now get down and play."

"I am the red dragon," shouted Cadwallon

"No, I am the red dragon," shouted Owain, waving his little sword.

Angharad smiled as she looked at her little family, but there was a sadness inside her. Was it Lafracoth that Gruffydd was missing? Was Gruffydd Lafracoth's love that had been taken?

"I hope you mean that the red dragon is sleeping," she said gently, holding on to Gruffydd's arm.

He plucked Gwenllian from her arms, "This red dragon needs all the sleep he can get, and our little girl has a deafening cry!"

He nuzzled his face into the baby's chest so that she dissolved into giggles. "You mustn't disturb, Dada! I must keep an eye on the English!"

Chapter 24: Change (August 1103)

"How different things are along the borders from when we first met," remarked Angharad one day in August as she and Gruffydd discussed news from afar.

They sat together on one of the courtyard benches sheltered from the wind and enjoyed a sunny position at that time of day.

"Yes indeed. No powerful barons pushing into Wales. No Hugh of Chester. Shrewsbury and Hereford are in the king's hands. Robert Fitz Hamon of Gloucester concentrated on Normandy. It is peaceful, but we must not be complacent."

"No, I know that. I was just thinking. I can't believe it was only last year that we were in Shrewsbury and now, how fortunes have turned with Belleme and Agnes in exile."

"True. I knew there was a story I meant to tell you. It is rumoured that the earl has imprisoned his wife, Agnes, in Belleme castle."

"Why?"

"That is not clear, but I don't think he had much love for her."

"I suspect he may have been unkind to her," said Angharad, remembering the nervous Agnes and the deep marks on her wrist.

"Well, he is known for his brutality, as was his mother, Countess Mabel. Yes, cruelty seems to run in the family. Stories have come out that Belleme would prefer to torture his prisoners than to ransom them. He did some horrific things, such as impaling men and women on hooks. He starved three hundred prisoners one year over Lent and even gouged out the eyes of his little godchild with his own nails after they argued."

Angharad felt her stomach turning. She thought again about Lafracoth and wondered how things were with Arnulf. Despite her suspicions,

337

which she constantly tried to quell, she cared deeply about her friend. Gruffydd tilted his head to one side as he saw his wife's reaction and squeezed her hand.

"The family is despicable," he continued. "What examples of Norman brotherly love: there is Curthose, who had promised to support his brother against traitors and has been 'given' the Montgomery family castle of Almenêches by Arnulf."

"He betrayed his brother's trust?"

"Both men are untrustworthy. Belleme, to get Almenêches back, burned the nearby nunnery where his sister was the abbess."

"To have so much wealth, so much power and to use it for wanton destruction and ill-intent towards your own family," said Angharad, shaking her head. "It is beyond belief."

There was a whoop of joy from the stables, and their two boys came running out laughing and chased by Hywel.

"Gruffydd, you must find him a good wife. He would be such a wonderful father. Look at him with the children and how they adore him."

"He has no interest. I have tried to get him introduced to so many different women, all attractive and from good homes, but he always finds some reason to put it off."

"Do you think he prefers ….." started Angharad.

"No, no, not at all. He says he would find it hard to fight if he had the responsibility of a family. You know how serious he is about everything."

"Is it hard fighting when you have a family?" asked Angharad thoughtfully.

"Before you have a wife and a family, you can go into battle knowing it doesn't matter if you live or die. You have a thirst for the fight. When you have a family, doubts creep into your mind. Who will look after them if something happens to you? You think you might not get to see your children grow up. Without a father, they might follow the wrong path in life. It is hard."

"I didn't realise you felt like that."

"I'm not afraid, don't think that, but when Hywel told me his reasons for avoiding marriage, I understood."

Angharad watched Hywel walking toward her with the two children, his face shining from chasing the boys, and she smiled back.

"You are so lovely with the boys," she said. "Thank you!"

"Uncle Hywel, can we play more, please?" asked Cadwallon.

"Not now," said Angharad briskly. "Uncle Hywel will sit here with Dada, and I will get them both a nice drink. If you come with me, we will see if there is some honey cake in the kitchen."

"And an apple?" asked Owain hopefully.

"We will see."

She fussed with the children for a while and then, abandoning them to Bethan, returned to the men with one of the serving girls carrying drinks and small, tasty savouries. She stopped in her tracks. A man was standing next to Gruffydd, who had his head in his hands. Hywel jumped up as he saw her approaching.

"I'm afraid it is bad news," he warned her in a low voice.

She blanched, and he held out an arm to steady her.

"Magnus Barefoot has been killed."

She sat heavily on a bench, gripped by a paralysed silence as she watched her husband dismiss the messenger who had brought the news and walk away from the llys courtyard to the little chapel.

"What happened?" she asked finally.

"Murtagh had launched a campaign against the O'Lochlainns, and he had been defeated at the battle of Mag Coba," answered Hywel. "Magnus had decided to return to Norway, and it was agreed that Murtagh would send provisions. For one reason or another, the provisions were delayed, so Magnus decided to find his own. On St Bartholomew's Day, he landed his army in swampy land near the River Quoile, intending to take some cattle. As Magnus landed on the shore around noon, a huge army of Irishmen came out of thick undergrowth, shooting arrows and throwing spears. Magnus ordered Eyvinder, one of his chiefs, to sound the trumpet and gather around the royal standard, closing ranks and overlapping their shields until they got to dry land. There was a fort there, and Magnus instructed another chief, Thorgrim, to take his men across the rampart and set up archers on the hill to protect his party until they could join him. They did as he asked, but when they got to the hill, they covered their backs with their shields and made for the ships."

'Betrayal,' whispered Angharad.

Hywel nodded. "Magnus yelled after them that they were cowards and that he had better have sent his son Sigurd. Just at that moment, a spear pierced his thigh. He pulled it out and fought on. His men screamed at him to save himself, but he shouted back, 'Better a courageous king than an old king!'"

Angharad's eyes filled with tears as she imagined the valiant, vibrant Magnus fighting on fiercely.

"Without the archers to cover them, they were outnumbered. Magnus received another spear in his other leg, but he fought on until an Irishman came at him with an axe and delivered a savage blow to his neck. He was buried near the church of St Patrick, and his sword was sent back to Norway."

"Why? Why did it happen?" asked Angharad tearfully. "Was he betrayed?"

"Maybe Thorgrim was paid off by someone to betray Magnus. More Irishmen died than Norwegians, so Magnus could have defeated them if they had followed his instructions. He had not won much booty while fighting with Murtagh, so maybe his warband felt resentment that they were ill-rewarded. It is hard to tell. Sigurd has left his young bride and returned to Norway."

"Magnus was so young," said Angharad dismally. "He loved life and his children so much."

Hywel held her back gently, as you would a distressed child. "He was a great warrior," he said. "He lived for the fight. He was a mighty Viking."

When Angharad had composed herself, she followed her husband into the church, and they prayed for Magnus together.

"His children are so young," she said, thinking how hard it would be without Magnus in their lives.

"Something is not right about it," said Gruffydd, still wrestling with his grief. "How is it that such a large fighting force was at the ready when he came onto land?"

"Hywel suspects Thorgrim," suggested Angharad softly.

"Somebody was behind it. I hope to God it was not Murtagh. I can't believe it, but why were the supplies so late? Murtagh does everything with precision, and if he had said that supplies were coming at such and such time, they would have come."

"Do you think that is why Sigurd left without his bride? That he suspects Murtagh is complicit?"

"Possibly." Gruffydd leaned forward and frowned thoughtfully. "Murtagh may have worried about a further challenge from Magnus, but, my God, they have just spent the winter together. No, I don't want to believe it of him."

"Could it be King Henry seeing an opportunity to rid himself of a potential enemy? You said you wouldn't put it past Henry to pay off someone in Magnus' warband."

"And if he found out about Magnus' treasure trove in Lincoln, it would make him even more uneasy."

"So young and yet so many enemies!"

"Too young, true, but he has lived enough for many lives. He would have died without regret."

"He will leave behind some broken hearts," said Angharad gently with a wan smile.

"Lafracoth's most of all. She will be distraught?"

"Lafracoth?"

"Did she not tell you? He was the love of her life. She worshipped him."

"Lafracoth?" she said again, incredulously.

"Yes, she told me that part of the reason she had agreed to marry Arnulf was that Magnus had married Margaret of Sweden. I think she had hoped for a long time that they might make a match. That would have been a perfect partnership if a fiery one!"

Angharad was lost for words. She had not considered that her friend was romantically attracted to Magnus. While she felt so sad for the grief her husband was suffering from Magnus' death and for her friend's unrequited love, she felt guilty for the enormous surge of relief swirling through her. It would seem the tie between Gruffydd and Lafracoth had been nothing more than friendship.

As they walked away from the church together, hands linked tightly, she looked at the oak tree where Magnus and Gruffydd had shot arrows into apple targets. Below was a little toy boat Owain had been playing with. Tears came into her eyes. How fragile life was.

Days passed, summer-ripened crops filled the barns, the harvest was bountiful, and Angharad's baby grew inside her. She had learnt to take nothing for granted. Magnus' death was another lesson on that. It was a very hard lesson to learn. She was worried about the birth after her difficulties having Gwenllian, and after much deliberation, she finally asked Father Teilo for directions to the healer.

On a day when Gruffydd was listening to disputes on the other side of the island, Angharad rode through the woods alone, not wanting anyone to know of her concerns. The little oak grove was where Father Teilo had described it to be, and she followed a well-used track to a small hut in a clearing. As if waiting for her, the healer so instrumental to Angharad's recovery from Gwenllian's birth stood at the door. The lady was small, with long dark hair thickly braided and sharp-eyed, with a soft, unlined face belying her years.

"Lady Queen," she curtseyed low, inviting her guest into the little hut. It was one room only filled with all sorts of dried flowers, herbs, barks and stones. Despite the darkness, the glow of a fire made it seem comfortable. The healer invited her to sit.

"You need not concern yourself," the healer said without prompting. "Your child will be healthy and strong."

"How did you know I would be asking that?" asked Angharad.

"I can see things others cannot, but common sense tells me that when a pregnant lady visits me, and she had a difficult birth previously, this would play on her mind."

"You can see into the future?" asked Angharad.

"I can," she replied matter-of-factly.

Angharad was so tempted to ask, so very much wanting to know what lay ahead for her, but she resisted, as foretelling seemed to fly in the face of Christ's teachings.

"Will you help me when my time comes?" she asked instead.

"I will, my lady. Let me collect some herbs so that you can make a herbal drink to help you through your pregnancy."

As the healer collected what she needed into a small cloth bag, Angharad asked her how she had learnt about herbs and cures.

"My family had lived in Anglesey long before the Romans came. The Druids' knowledge has been passed down through generation after generation."

Angharad bit her lip, and the healer smiled at the little gesture.

"You do not need to worry. We only use what nature provides to help healing and do good as the Druids taught."

"But the Druids were known for…."

"For animal sacrifice, for human sacrifice? Long ago, that might have been true, but it was common in many societies. Isn't the bible full of animal sacrifice? Was not Jesus Christ a human sacrifice? The Druids were people of great learning. They were drawn from the families of the nobility and trained for twenty years until they had committed enough to memory to be considered a Druid. They knew about the movements of the stars, understood and revered nature, held the histories of our peoples inside their heads, had good laws, helped trade, encouraged art, poetry, and music to flourish, and knew of medicine. Yes, they could predict much of what was to come."

Angharad felt uncomfortable having the conversation, as if she was somehow betraying her faith, yet she was mesmerised by how well the woman spoke. She had a kind of authority which was extraordinary for one who lived so simply.

"I had thought that the Romans had destroyed all the Druids," Angharad ventured.

"Not every Druid. Romans wanted to stamp out the belief that when we die, we are born again in another body. This made our warriors utterly fearless in battle, a threat that the Romans."

"And the teaching has survived for over a thousand years since then?"

"Hasn't Christianity survived for over a thousand years as well?"

Angharad's eyes widened as she realised the significance of the woman's words.

"You are a Christian, though?"

"I do not quarrel with Christianity," the woman replied, unruffled.

The healer passed the bag to Angharad, who reached into a little leather purse and pulled out some silver coins, which she pressed into the woman's hand. As she did so, the healer seemed to flinch, closing her eyes as if absorbing a spasm of pain. Her pallor was suddenly grey, and she looked older.

"Are you alright?" Angharad asked, holding the woman's arm.

The woman seemed to shrink back from her, then composed herself and, letting out a small breath, assured Angharad that it was nothing. After Angharad left, the healer sat heavily on a chair and let out a small groan.

'*What a life is ahead of her. What a blessing some things are best unknown,*' she muttered to herself.

As Angharad rode back through the grove of oaks to the llys, she reminisced. She could scarcely believe how much had happened since a flaxen-haired stranger had come to her father's house and thrown her whole life into the air. She thought of Magnus, Iorwedd, Maredudd and the unsuppressible Uchdryd all juggling the dice with the mighty Henry of England.

As she emerged from the leafy canopy, Angharad stopped her horse briefly to watch the skylarks soaring up into the blue, cloudless sky. What an unexpected life she had been dealt, she mused. She had encountered nightmarish horror, stupefying fear, deepest sorrow and yet, amongst it all, happiness beyond her wildest fantasy. Here she was with her three beautiful children, her new babe inside and the husband she loved more than life itself.

In the distance, her llys stood out, light shining on the haven for Angharad and her family. She wondered what would happen within those walls as her children grew. She smiled and then shivered involuntarily, drawing back from her imaginings.

Angharad nudged Seren on, ready now to be surrounded again by those she loved most. Who knew what the future might hold for them as greed and lust for power threw fortune's dice high into the air? But for now, right now, these were precious peaceful times. Her lips moved in a silent prayer of thanks while, behind her, the first golden leaves from the oak trees swirled down to meet the dust her horse's hooves had stirred up: an ending and a beginning in the circle of life.

Historical Notes

This book is a work of fiction but draws on some real characters whose stories are dimly hinted at by the few documents that survive from the time. Most of the events are real, but I have interpreted them in a way that makes sense to me. I have sometimes changed the dates of minor events to better allow for the flow of the story. I hope the below elaborates on my thinking in putting together the existing fragments of history and explains some of the unfamiliar terms used.

Welsh names

In Wales, a son or daughter was given a first name and then further identified as being the child of their father, so Gruffydd ap Cynan is Gruffydd, son of Cynan, and Angharad Ferch Owain is Angharad, daughter of Owain. The Welsh word for a son is 'mab', but it becomes 'ab' or 'ap'. To keep it simple, although the convention is to use 'ap' before consonants and 'ab' before vowels, I have used 'ap', meaning 'son of' throughout the book. Similarly, although the word for daughter is usually 'ferch' in modern Welsh, 'verch' was used in the Middle Ages. I have used 'ferch' to mean 'daughter of'. I have anglicised some names to make it easier for those who are not Welsh-speaking or because there are many with the same name, and I want to make the story easier to follow.

Gruffydd ap Cynan.

After his death, a book about his life was put together in Latin: Historia Gruffydd vab Kenan. This history intended to establish the right of Gruffydd's heirs to the royal throne, and it was a marketing exercise setting out the character of Gruffydd as Arthuresque. After doing some research, I felt that Darrell Wolcott presents a very compelling argument in his essay 'History of Gruffudd ap Cynan- A New Perspective' in which he suggests that the history tells the life of two men, both called Gruffydd ap Cynan. One is the nephew of Iago, and one is the grandson. I have chosen to make the grandson the hero of my story.

Ednowain Bendew

Ednowain Bendew was a real character, but there was confusion about when he lived. I have chosen to make Owain ap Edwin's wife his sister. Darrell Wolcott has written an interesting article called 'The Ednowain Bendew 11 of Medieval Pedigrees', which suggests that there may have been an Ednowain Bendew contemporary with Owain ap Edwin.

Owain ap Edwin

Owain ap Edwin was also known as Owain Fradwr or Owain the Traitor. His relationship with the Normans was unusually good, and it seems strange that he decided to marry his daughter to Gruffydd ap Cynan unless he wanted to have a foot in both camps. This is the view that I have taken in the story.

Uchdryd ap Edwin.

Owain ap Edwin's brother, leader of Cadwgan ap Bleddyn's warband. There is confusion over why Uchdryd seemingly changed sides from Cadwgan's to Owain ap Edwin's and the Normans. I have suggested a reason, although there is no written evidence supporting that reason.

Marriage date of Angharad ferch Owain and Gruffydd ap Cynan.

There is some confusion over the date of this couple's marriage. Some theories suggest that Gruffydd's return from Ireland to retain Anglesey was linked with the marriage of Owain ap Edwin's daughter in 1098. I have taken the view that their marriage was likely in 1095, allowing for more time for the birth of their children in line with what happened in their lives subsequently.

Meeting with King Henry of England.

The Historia tells us that Gruffydd met with King Henry at his court. I have made the meeting at Shrewsbury to explore other characters' lives relevant to the story.

Cantref/ Cantrefi

The division of land in Wales in the Middle Ages was based on a cantref comprising several commotes. At the time of Gruffydd ap Cynan, Anglesey comprised three cantrefi (the plural of cantref). These were Aberffraw, where the king's llys was; Cemais and Rhosyr. Cant means one hundred, and Tref means a town, but originally, a cantref might be made up of one hundred settlements, some as small as a couple of houses. Each cantref would have its own court.

Llys

A llys is a royal court where judiciary matters would also be settled.

http://ardal-wales.co.uk/english/local-history/royal-courts/

Teulu

Kings of Wales would have an armed retinue called the teulu. Powerful relationships were formed between the king and his teulu. The king was responsible for looking after them; the greater his teulu, the better his reputation. The teulu would, in return, fight to the death for their king against an enemy.

Cariad

A Welsh term of endearment equivalent to 'My Love.'

Normans

At this time in history, the Normans were often referred to as the French, but I have chosen to call them the Normans.

The Welsh

The Welsh rulers were united with a common culture and language and saw themselves as the Britons. Since a movement to unite Wales and Welshmen was happening at this time, I often have my characters refer to themselves and their countrymen as Welsh.

The Laws Hywel the Good

The Welsh laws were codified by Hywel the Good in the mid-10th century. They were very different from the Norman laws. They included laws on capital punishment, which was rare as the Welsh preferred the system of compensation to families, inheritance and laws for women. The Laws for women stated that on marriage, an **amobr** or fee was to be paid to the woman's lord. On the morning after the marriage, a fee was payable to the woman by her husband for taking her virginity, which was called a **cowyll**. During the marriage, the **dower** was a common pool of property which was due to the woman if they separated before seven years. After seven years, the woman was entitled to half the common pool. Another Welsh law different to the Norman laws was that when a landowner died, his land was to be divided between his sons equally. This even included illegitimate sons if their father had acknowledged them.

Anglesey

I have chosen to call the island of Anglesey by the name it was known to Vikings and Normans. The Welsh would refer to the island of Anglesey as Ynys Mon.

From the Author

If you enjoyed this book, please consider leaving a review on Amazon or Goodreads. I would greatly appreciate it.

Arianwen Nunn

Other Books by Arianwen Nunn in the Welsh Warrior series

The Welsh Warrior's Inheritance (Book Two in the series)

Bards Sing of Love and War (Book Three in the series)

Children's Books by Arianwen Nunn

The Welsh Warrior's Wonder

Where Dragons Still Roar.